His gaze lif ... **nce**
meeting him, he ...
He looked hot. Very, very hot.

"You're playing with fire," he said as his thumb caressed the inside of her arm.

She should've called a stop to things right then and there. It no longer mattered that he found out about her embarrassing infatuation with his handcuffs. What mattered was doing something really stupid. Something that would no doubt come back to haunt her like every other stupid mistake. Unfortunately, any logical thinking had been completely consumed with naughty fantasies.

"Maybe I like playing with fire," she said as she met his heated gaze head on.

There was only a second pause before he spoke. "Then get ready to get burned."

"Katie Lane writes books that are hotter than Texas in July, and every reader always prays that they will keep on coming."

"I really enjoyed reading *Trouble in Texas*... The small town feeling with its grudges, history, and eccentric residents was a blast. I spent a lot of my time giggling and wondering what the henhouse ladies were going to do next... Lane has made me very curious about the previous three books, and I want to know what happens next in this series."

CATCH ME A COWBOY

"4½ stars! A heartwarming return to Bramble, Texas, with many familiar faces. This is an emotional story that will bring the reader to laughter as well as tears and spark a desire to see more of the characters, both new and old, who live here."

"An absolute hoot!... *Catch Me a Cowboy* is home to a plethora of wacky characters who make this a fun story... A winner!"

"Perfect for a lazy summer afternoon."

MAKE MINE A BAD BOY

"A delightful continuation of *Going Cowboy Crazy*. There's plenty of humor to entertain the reader, and the people of the town will seem like old friends by the end of this entertaining story."

"If you're looking for a romance true to its Texas setting, this is the one for you. I simply couldn't put it down."

—TheSeasonforRomance.com

"I absolutely loved Colt! I mean, who doesn't like a bad boy? Katie Lane is truly a breath of fresh air. Her stories are unique and wonderfully written...Lane, you have me hooked."   —LushBookReviews.blogspot.com

GOING COWBOY CRAZY

"Romance, heated exchanges, and misunderstandings, combined with the secondary characters (the whole town of Bramble), who are hilarious...This is the perfect summer read. Katie Lane has a winner on her hands; she is now my new favorite author!"

—TheRomanceReadersConnection.com

"Romance, steamy love scenes, humor, witty conversation with a twang...I'm looking forward to reading other books written by Katie Lane."   —BookLoons.com

"I enjoyed this book quite a bit. It really reminded me of an early Rachel Gibson...or early Susan Elizabeth Phillips. Faith became a sassy, intriguing heroine...The chemistry between these two ratchets up to white-hot in no time."   —TheSeasonforRomance.com

A Match Made in Texas

Also by Katie Lane

Deep in the Heart of Texas series

Going Cowboy Crazy
Make Mine A Bad Boy
Small Town Christmas (anthology)
Catch Me A Cowboy
Trouble in Texas
Flirting with Texas

Other Novels

Hunk for the Holidays

A Match Made in Texas

KATIE LANE

FOREVER

NEW YORK   BOSTON

Copyright © 2014 by Cathleen Smith
Excerpt from *The Last Cowboy in Texas* copyright © 2014 by Cathleen Smith

Forever
Hachette Book Group
237 Park Avenue, New York, NY 10017

www.hachettebookgroup.com

www.twitter.com/foreverromance

Printed in the United States of America

OPM

First edition: March 2014
10 9 8 7 6 5 4 3 2 1

Forever is an imprint of Grand Central Publishing.
The Forever name and logo are trademarks of Hachette Book Group, Inc.

The publisher is not responsible for websites (or their content) that are not owned by the publisher.

The Hachette Speakers Bureau provides a wide range of authors for speaking events. To find out more, go to www.hachettespeakersbureau.com or call (866) 376-6591.

To Gabby and Sienna,
my most precious princesses —

Acknowledgments

A special thanks goes to Randy Rogers, not only for helping me out with the law enforcement aspect of this book
but also for being the kind of police officer who went
above and beyond. I will miss seeing your squad car as
you patrolled the neighborhood on Halloween, making sure all little ghosts and goblins were safe :o) Happy
retirement, dear friend!

Chapter One

ELVIS WAS ALIVE AND WELL.

Alive and well, and annoying the heck out of Brianne Cates.

It wasn't his red silk scarf fluttering over the shoulder of his rhinestone western suit that annoyed her. Or the hand with its chunky gold and diamond rings draped over the side mirror. Or the sky-high black hair that defied the stiff west Texas wind. No, it was the fact that the man was going thirty miles an hour in a sixty-mile-an-hour zone, and he wasn't willing to let Brianne pass.

Most folks who knew Bri said she had the patience of a saint, no doubt because she'd survived a childhood with four arrogant and rowdy brothers. But the truth was that Bri didn't have patience as much as the ability to hide her impatience beneath a calm façade and innocent smile.

After spending the last thirty minutes playing a cat-and-mouse game with the big ol' cherry red Cadillac, Bri wasn't calm. And she sure wasn't smiling. Gritting her teeth, she pushed down on the accelerator for what seemed like the hundredth time and eased into the other lane. But just as she caught a glimpse of one long rectangular sideburn, the Cadillac shot forward, forcing her to let up on the gas and pull back in her lane or end up wallpapered against the grille of an oncoming semi.

She wanted to blast the horn and flip the bird to the King. But if she had learned anything in the last few weeks, it was that everybody and their brother carried cell phones and one defiant act could go viral within hours.

Which explained what Bri was doing on the two-lane highway in the middle of west Texas. This was her punishment for one little act of defiance. Or maybe not a little one as much as a huge one. And while she was being honest, it hadn't been her first act of defiance.

It was just the first act her family had found out about. They had been devastated when they'd discovered that their "sweet little Bri" wasn't as sweet as they thought. And if there was something that Bri couldn't endure, it was disappointing her family. Nor could she endure staying behind Elvis for one second longer. As soon as the oncoming lane was clear, she moved over and floored it.

If she had been in the massive SUV her brother Brant had insisted she drive for safety, she might've been able to pass the Caddie. But she wasn't. She had borrowed her Granny Lou's car in an attempt to ditch her ex-boyfriend, who had been stalking her for the past few months.

Both the boyfriend and the car had been bad choices.

The speedometer inched forward at a snail's pace, giving the Caddie plenty of time to pull away. But Bri refused to give up. With pedal to the metal, she continued to accelerate down the wrong side of the highway.

It took a while for her to draw abreast of the Cadillac. And Elvis seemed as surprised as Bri that a Smart Car could hit ninety. He shot her a shocked look before his lip cocked up in a smile-sneer. He said something, but with her windows rolled up and the radio on, she couldn't hear what it was. Probably "thank yew, thank yew very much for putting up with my crap for so long."

She sent the man one of her most innocent smiles... while her foot remained smashed down on the accelerator. She probably would've continued driving next to him all the way to her turnoff if she hadn't glanced up to see the car headed straight for her.

Bri slowed down with every intention of pulling back behind the Cadillac. Except Elvis wasn't quite done screwing with her. He slowed down as well, blocking her from getting back into the right lane and forcing her to play chicken with the oncoming car. And not just any car, but a black-and-white with a row of flashing lights on top. Fortunately, it veered off to the shoulder of the road before they had a head-on collision. Unfortunately, there wasn't much shoulder to the road.

In her side mirror, Bri watched in horror as the sheriff's car sideswiped a couple of fence posts before coming to a dust-spitting stop. It didn't stay stopped for long. In a spray of gravel and sagebrush, the patrol car whipped around and, with lights flashing and siren blaring, came hauling butt after them.

Or not them exactly.

Elvis quickly slowed and pulled over. Bri was the only one who kept going. And she wasn't sure why. Part of it was that she wasn't willing to cause her family any more embarrassment by getting a traffic ticket. The bigger part was the same thing that had gotten her in trouble in the first place. The screwed-up thing inside of her that

seemed to feed on pure adrenaline and danger. And there
was no doubt that being chased by the law was adrenaline
pumping and dangerous. It didn't help that about then a
Miranda Lambert song came on the radio, and Miranda
could make any good girl go bad.

Bri's heart kicked into overdrive as the Smart Car
inched back up to ninety. Of course, the roller skate–size
vehicle was no match for the black-and-white cruiser—
even if the cruiser had a crumpled hood and dragging
front bumper. Within seconds, it pulled up behind her.

She glanced in her rearview mirror.

The man sitting behind the wheel looked like a typi-
cal Texas law officer. A tan Stetson was pulled low on
a pair of mirrored aviator sunglasses. The scowl on his
face reminded Bri of her brothers' whenever she brought
home a new boyfriend. Maybe that was why she kept
going. She'd had to deal with arrogant men all her life.
She didn't have to deal with this man. At least, she didn't
if she didn't stop. She might not be able to outrun him, but
at forty miles to the gallon she could outlast him.

Unfortunately, he turned out to be the type of man
who didn't care to follow. Whipping into the other lane,
he pulled up next to her and motioned for her to pull over
with one rather annoying jab of his finger. Most people
driving a go-cart of a car that was already vibrating from
the excessive speed would've accepted defeat and pulled
over. But most people didn't have controlling, dominating
brothers like Bri's. So instead of following his hand signal, she chose to ignore him.

Up ahead, a line of traffic had slowed for the flashing lights and siren, leaving the law officer no choice but
to speed up and pull in front of her. It turned out to be

a smart move. With the slow traffic on one side and a barbed wire fence on the other, he boxed Bri in, slowing down and forcing her to do the same. When they were finally stopped, he flung open the door and got out.

She expected to see a big-bellied country boy. Instead, a lean cowboy unfolded before her eyes. A lean cowboy with broad shoulders and a wide chest that tapered down to a waist with not one ounce of fat on it. He wore a taupe sheriff's shirt that desperately needed a hot iron and faded jeans that had been washed so many times they hugged his lean, muscular legs like preschoolers to their mamas. A black belt hung on slim hips. While most law enforcement officers had a wide array of gadgets attached to their belts, this man appeared to have only two: a radio and a gun.

He unhooked the safety on the holster of the gun as he strode toward her like a predator zeroing in on his kill. Some women might feel intimidated by such raw masculinity. To Bri, he was just another arrogant man she had to deal with—something she had become somewhat of an expert at. Latching on to the first idea that popped into her head, she threw open the door and jumped out.

"Oh, thank God you showed up!" She hurried toward him, prepared to do some major lying, when she tripped over a crack in the asphalt and ended up plastered against the man's chest. She now understood how a bug felt when it hit a windshield. The man was an unmoving oak tree of hard muscles. Instead of catching her, he just stood there in the middle of the highway with his boots spread wide and his hands at his side.

Even in heels, Bri had to tip her head wa-a-a-y back to meet her reflection in the twin mirrors of his sunglasses.

She didn't exactly look like a scared woman. Her Granny Lou's straw gardening hat, also part of Bri's getaway disguise, sagged in loopty-loops around eyes that sparkled with excitement.

She lowered her gaze to the star on the pocket of his shirt and tried to work up a few tears. "It was the most terrifying experience of my life." She sniffed. "One second, I was going a mere fifty-six miles an hour, and the next, I was careening out of control." She smoothed out a wrinkle in his shirt. "It was horrible, I tell you. Simply horrible."

"It sounds like it." His deep voice rumbled from his chest, the drawl thick enough to slice. Then, before she could do more than blink, she found herself facedown on the back of his squad car with her legs spread and her hands behind her back. "You have the right to remain silent—"

"Wait a minute!" She tried to wiggle free. "Didn't you hear what I was trying to tell you? My car is defective. It must have the same thing wrong with it as those recalled cars had—it accelerated without warning. Which is why I was in the other lane. It was either that or crash right into the back of the car in front of me."

He ignored her. "You have the right to an attorney. If you can't afford an attorney, one will be supplied at no cost."

With her cheek pressed against the trunk of the squad car, Bri felt cold metal slip around her wrist. Most women would be terrified. And Bri was scared. Unfortunately, fear was usually followed with a burst of adrenaline and crazy thoughts. This time was no different.

Was she actually getting arrested? Would she have to pose for a mug shot? Get fingerprinted? He stepped closer, the front of his thighs brushing the backs of hers, and another kind of excitement coursed through her veins—this one settling more in her panties than her stomach. The unexpected feeling snapped her out of the adrenaline-drugged haze.

What was she thinking? This wasn't some thrill-seeking adventure. She was going to jail. And she couldn't go to jail. If the picture being spread around the Internet wouldn't tarnish her family's name, a stint in a west Texas jail certainly would. He grabbed her other wrist, and she quickly backpedaled.

"Okay! I was lying. There's nothing wrong with my car besides a really sluggish engine. I was in the other lane because Elvis wouldn't let me pass. If anyone is responsible for what happened, it's him."

Warm fingers paused at her pulse point. "Elvis?"

"Well, not Elvis, exactly. Just a man who looks like him. Didn't you see him? He was the lunatic in the red convertible Cadillac."

His fingers tightened. "I must've been so busy trying to avoid a head-on collision that I missed Elvis. Was he singing 'Love Me Tender'? That's one of my favorites. Or maybe the one about the hound dog. Now there's an oldie but goodie."

"I'm not kidding. This man was being a complete jerk. He would go thirty until I wanted to pass, and then he would pick up speed."

"Maybe he was just having car problems. A faulty accelerator." He started to cuff her other wrist but stopped suddenly. She didn't understand why until a stiff breeze blew over her, carrying with it the faint sound of music. The music grew louder. And since they had just been talking about the man, it only took Bri a second to recognize the song.

It wasn't "Love Me Tender." Or "Hound Dog."

It was much more annoying.

"...rock, everybody, let's rock. Everybody in the whole cell block was dancin' to the jailhouse rock..."

Just that quickly, Bri was released. She straightened in time to see the Cadillac pull around them with stereo blasting. She couldn't see Elvis's eyes behind the gold-rimmed sunglasses, but she didn't need to. His smirk and two-fingered salute said it all.

Every bad word her brothers had taught her pushed at the back of Bri's throat. But a lifetime of restraint had her using one of her nephew's favorite words instead.

"Poopyhead!" As soon as the word was out, she cringed. She turned to find the officer watching her. Clearing her throat, she tried to regain some kind of decorum. "Pardon me, but he really deserved that."

The mirrored lens remained trained on her for only a second before they returned to the highway. The Cadillac disappeared on the horizon, the bright October sun reflecting off the chrome bumper and license plate that Bri would never forget.

King 1.

"Well, I'll be damned."

The officer's words had her glancing over to see one corner of his mouth cocked up in a crooked smile. Relieved that he was no longer scowling, she relaxed.

"I know what you mean. If I hadn't seen it with my own two eyes, I never would've believed it." She held up her hand and jangled the handcuffs that were still attached to her wrist. "I think you owe me an apology."

The smile faded as he turned to her. "And what exactly would I be apologizing for? Your reckless driving? Your blatant disregard for the law? Or how about almost getting both of us killed?"

Since he had some very valid points, she nodded. "Okay, so I'm the one who should be apologizing. But as I explained earlier, I was trying to pass a lunatic who was speeding up and then slowing down just to tick me off. I had to go fast to get by him. But you're right, I should've pulled over and explained things instead of ignoring you." She held out her hand with the cuff. "Now can you take these—"

Bri was cut off by a hissing sound. They both turned to find steam pouring out from under the hood of the officer's car. There was a sputter, and then the engine died. She glanced back in time to see his jaw tighten.

"Of course, I'll pay for that," she said.

"You're damned right you will." He pointed a finger at her. "I'll need to see your driver's license and registration."

"You're not going to give me a ticket, are you? Not when it wasn't my fault."

"And just whose fault is it? You were the one on the wrong side of the highway, not Elvis." He unhooked the radio from his belt and pushed the button on the side. "You there, Cora Lee?"

"I know that it was my fault," Bri continued, "but surely we can get this worked out without a bunch of legal red tape."

His hat dipped as he gave her the once-over. "Really? And just what are we talking about?"

She cleared her throat, surprised at how just a look from the man could make her feel all warm and trembly. "You can give me your address, and I'll pay you in full for any damages to your car. You can just tell your boss that you had a little accident with a cow."

He studied her for a long, uncomfortable moment until a loud female voice caused Bri to jump.

"What's up, Sheriff?"

Sheriff?

Every muscle in Bri's body tensed as he lifted the black receiver up to his mouth. "I need you to call Ralph and have him drive out to mile marker one oh nine. I need a tow." He hesitated. "And get the jail ready. I'm bringing in a prisoner."

While Bri was digesting the information that he was planning on taking her to jail, the woman continued.

"Will do. And could you do me a favor? Please get yourself hitched before I gain a good hundred pounds. Today Ronda Sue brought in homemade sticky buns. That makes the fifth baked goods this week that some desperate woman has brought in to bribe you to the altar. And just how do you expect me to stay on those paltry Weight Watcher meals with that kind of temptation around? Besides, if you got married you wouldn't have to look for another housekeeper now that Loretta up and quit due to your surly personality."

Bri watched his brow knot above the bridge of his sunglasses. "Who wouldn't be surly after what she did to my laundry?"

A burst of laughter came out of the receiver. "Just the thought of gruff Sheriff Dusty Hicks in pink undies tickles my funny bone. You got a license or plate number that you want me to run on that prisoner?"

The question seemed to make the sheriff even surlier. "I'll have to get back to you on that." He released the side button and hooked the radio back on to his belt before taking Bri's arm and escorting her to the Smart Car.

She stumbled along next to him, her hat flopping and her brain working overtime, trying to figure a way out of this mess. She couldn't go to jail. Not when Brant was already trying to cover up her last mistake. When they reached the still idling Smart Car, he released her.

"License and registration."

With no other choice, she leaned in and grabbed her purse. She dug around in the huge satchel, but before she found the smooth leather of her Prada wallet, her fingers brushed hard, cold aluminum.

As with all her bad decisions, Bri didn't know exactly how it happened. One second, she was standing next to the sheriff with her hand in her purse, and the next, she was spraying him in the face with the pepper spray her brother Billy had given her as a stocking stuffer. She only planned to give the sheriff a short squirt. Just enough to momentarily incapacitate him. But it took a full five-second spray to get his hands off her throat.

Once he released her and bent over coughing, she hopped into the minicar and floored it. She zipped around the sheriff's car, barely missing an oncoming tractor before she pulled back in the right lane. With her heart racing a marathon, she watched in the rearview mirror until the flashing lights disappeared from sight.

Her smile came out of nowhere.

Brianne Cates was on the lam.

Chapter Two

IT WAS A PATHETIC LITTLE TOWN. The main street couldn't have been more than a block long. The gas station had only two pumps. The grocery store was the size of a convenience store. And the thing they called a diner was a hideous collision of pink train caboose and ramshackle shed. Still, the diner appeared to be a crowd gatherer. And Reverend Josiah Jessup had never passed up a crowd.

He pulled his Cadillac into the dirt lot of the diner and parked in the handicap space right in front. Not wanting to have another close call with the law, he reached into the glove box and pulled out his bogus handicap permit and hooked it on the rearview mirror. He took a moment to check his hair, smoothing back one stray strand that had come loose when he'd been teaching that young woman a lesson in patience.

Josiah smiled. Only noon, and he had already used his power for good.

After tucking his silk scarf into the lapels of his jacket, he climbed out of the Cadillac and headed toward the door. For a weekday, the diner looked to be full.

Through the glass, he could see that all the booths and tables were taken, and only a few bar stools at the counter were empty. Clearing his throat, he stepped inside. A bell jingled on the door, and conversation ceased as all eyes turned to him.

Having been the center of attention to millions of people, a few country bumpkins didn't faze him. He held out his arms and spoke in a commanding voice that was loud enough to be heard halfway to heaven.

"The Lord has truly blessed His humble servant on this fine autumn day. After a long and wary journey, He has directed me to this oasis of friendly faces and succulent aromas."

The folks of the diner looked at one another before staring back at him in confusion. Although it didn't take long for someone to speak up.

"Are you one of them Elvis impersonators from Sin City?" The woman sitting at the counter swiveled around on the stool, displaying a tower of teased hair and a wealth of cleavage. She pointed a sharp-looking orange fingernail at him. "My cousin went there a few years back and said it was just like seein' the King himself. Could you sing that song about the wise men? I just love that song. I ruin my mascara every time I hear it."

Josiah pulled his gaze from the plump temptation of her breasts and smiled. "I'm afraid that I'm not much of a singer, but I'd be happy to tell you the story of three wise men who followed a star."

The woman looked thoroughly disappointed.

"Well, I'll be." A middle-aged waitress moved out from behind the counter. "You're that Reverend Josiah Jessup who had that television show."

The word *had* annoyed Josiah much more than he let on. "A woman of knowledge, I see." He walked farther into the diner, stopping to shake hands with people as he went. "But I have left my television ministry behind to travel the country and meet my brethren face to face— and heart to heart."

The waitress's gaze pinned Josiah with a mean look. "Or swindle folks into givin' you their lifesavin's so you can build a big ol' mansion in Caribou."

Josiah wasn't surprised by the accusation. It was the reason he was here in this Podunk town. The media had had a field day with the story on his misuse of donations, and this was the price he had to pay if he wanted to return to his million-dollar television ministry: mingling with the common folk.

He pulled on his mask of repentant sinner. "You are absolutely correct, Miss..."

"Dean," she said with narrowed eyes. "Rachel Dean."

"Nice to meet you, Miss Dean. And I completely agree with you. I never should've built a house in Malibu for senior citizens without first consulting the kind people who generously gave."

Rachel Dean's eyes squinted even more until he could hardly see them. "You built that house for old folks?"

"There are two lovely, elderly ladies living there as we speak." Josiah tried not to grit his teeth at the thought of his demented grandmother and great aunt enjoying his spa and media room while he was stuck in Texas. Especially when the two old coots didn't seem to know the difference between his grand mansion and the tacky retirement home he'd jerked them out of when the scandal hit.

"Well, that shore doesn't sound like a misappropriation

of funds to me." A big-bellied man with an impressive handlebar mustache got up from his bar stool and held out a hand. "Harley Sutter. I'm the mayor of this fine town."

Josiah smiled brightly. He had always believed in starting at the top and working his way down. He had learned early on that if you could knock down the kingpin, the others would follow.

He hurried over and shook the mayor's hand. "It's a pleasure to meet you, sir. I must tell you that I was quite impressed with what I learned from your town's website. In this time of economic hardship, Bramble seems to be thriving. Which can only be the direct result of strong leadership."

Before the mayor could even absorb Josiah's praise, the hussy with the delicious cleavage spoke up. "Oh, Harley ain't responsible for the website or the jobs. Hope Lomax is the one who makes sure Bramble stays put. Her and them Cates brothers who run Dalton Oil. Harley just organizes the parades."

The mayor nodded. "I do love a parade."

Josiah stared at the imbecile for only a second before he regrouped. "And what would this country be without parades, I ask? There is nothing like good, wholesome family entertainment to bring folks together." He waited for the mumbles of agreement before he continued brownnosing the mayor. "Besides, great leaders shouldn't be expected to deal with the little details of running a government. Their job is to see the entire picture and find the right man—or woman—for the job. And it looks as if you, Mayor Sutter, have done just that."

The mayor scratched his head. "Well, I guess that's one way to look at it."

"Of course it is." He thumped the mayor on the back. "Why, with your leadership skills, I don't doubt for a second that the political leaders of your party will be beating down your door come the next gubernatorial election."

The mayor's eyes brightened as he took the bait. "Are you tellin' me that I could be the next governor of Texas?"

"That's exactly what I'm telling you." Josiah eased back a little so as not to prematurely jerk the hook from the man's mouth. "Of course, you'll need to prepare for such an endeavor. Gubernatorial races are demanding and cutthroat." He gave the mayor a once-over. "You'll be spending a lot of time in front of a camera, so you might want to think about losing a few pounds. And you'll need to come up with a slogan. Something snappy that catches people's attention."

The old man at the end of the counter, who Josiah had thought was sleeping under his straw cowboy hat, snorted before he got up and shuffled to the door. "I've had about enough of these shenanigans."

Josiah waited for the door to close behind the old coot before he continued. "Let the naysayers spend the rest of their lives trying to dissipate people's dreams with the vile venom of their negativity." He looked around the diner at all the confused faces. "But I'm here to tell you that God has a grand plan for each and every one of you. And all it takes to open His abundant gift is a little faith." He looked over at the waitress. "Let's take you, for instance, Miss Dean. What is a beautiful, intelligent woman like you doing working as a waitress? Do you really want to spend the rest of your days in a dinky little diner serving food? Or do you want to open the grand gift that God has for you and enjoy it to the fullest?"

Her beady eyes brightened. "And just where do I find this gift?"

He leaned in closer and tapped her temple. "Right here. The gift is waiting right in here. All you have to do is dream it. Do you want to be a ballet dancer? A painter? Or discover the cure for cancer? Anything you want to do, you can do. It's all within your grasp." He pointed to the hussy with the fine breasts. "What is your dream, sister?"

Her eyes filled with tears. "To have me another weddin'."

After being married three times, the last to a she-devil who exposed his misspending, it was a struggle for Josiah to remain positive. "Weddings are the beautiful union of two halves into a whole. But sometimes we let our own desires choose a half that is completely wrong for us. I tell you, sister, it is time to release your fleshly desires and look to the heavens for your rightful mate." He glanced around at the crowd. "Can I get an amen!"

There was only a brief pause before the diner rang out with the type of affirmation that had always been music to Josiah's ears.

"Amen!"

An hour later, Josiah was back in his Cadillac and cruising down Main Street. The diner sermon had been one of his best. He had used every trick he'd learned growing up with his revival preacher daddy and a few that he'd picked up during the years spent as a used car salesman. The idiots of Bramble, Texas, never knew what hit them and were now under his spell. Of course, he wasn't sure how he'd use them. But over the years, he'd learned to build bridges rather than burn them. The townsfolk would come in handy sooner or later.

Even if only to boost his television audience.

Once he had a television audience to boost. Which was exactly what he was doing in Bramble.

He turned down the residential street and glanced at each address until he found the one he was looking for. It was a neat little clapboard with a cluster of bright flowers growing along the porch. He was halfway up the front pathway before he realized that the flowers were plastic.

Although the artificial flowers didn't surprise him as much as the man lying in the middle of them.

Josiah glanced up at the sky. He didn't actually believe in God, but lately he'd started to wonder if someone up there didn't have it out for him. First, Catherine told the fraud story to the newspapers, and now he had found a dead man in a plastic flowerbed. Only a fool would think it was a mere coincidence.

And Josiah was no fool.

The curtains in the front window fluttered, and before he could make a run for it, the door flew open and a scary-looking woman in an ugly purple hat came racing out in a housecoat and slippers.

"Reverend Jessup?" She clutched her hands to her chest and stared at him in stunned awe, the grapes on her hat quivering with her contained excitement. "My prayers have been answered."

"Never doubt it." He moved up a step and held out a hand. "You must be Wilma Tate." Instead of shaking it, she genuflected and placed a moist kiss on the back of his hand. He smiled and subtly wiped it off on his pants as he nodded at the man in the flowerbed. "I think we need to call an ambulance—or perhaps the sheriff."

The woman looked down at the man, who had his face

planted in the dirt and an armful of plastic daffodils, and scowled. "No need to call the sheriff. That's just my good-for-nothing husband, Elmer."

Josiah waited for more of an explanation, and when it didn't come, he asked, "Is he all right?"

Mrs. Tate shook her head. "The man has been under the spell of that devil alcohol ever since we got married. And nothin' I do or say will keep him from it." She looked over at Josiah and got excited all over again. "Is that why you're here? Did you get my twenty dollars and prayer letter and decide to come pray for him in person?" She climbed down on the step next to him and grabbed his arm. "I knew you weren't a swindler. I knew the money I sent you went for prayers."

Josiah patted her hand. "That's exactly why I'm here. Together we can pull your husband from the jaws of inebriated destruction." He reached into his jacket and pulled out the folded piece of pink stationery. "But first, I'd like to talk with you about this other letter that you sent me."

She took the paper from his hand and unfolded it. Lifting the glasses that hung on a chain around her neck, she held them up and only had to glance at the letter before she nodded. "It's shockin', ain't it? That kind of sin right here in the fine state of Texas."

"I'm sure you're mistaken, Mrs. Tate. Their website shows a legitimate bed-and-breakfast."

She leaned closer. "That's exactly what they want you to think. But I know better."

A flicker of excitement sparked to life inside of Josiah. And for the first time in more than a year, he felt as if his luck was about to change.

"So you're saying that the bed-and-breakfast is only a front for a . . ."

"Whorehouse." Mrs. Tate finished his sentence with a superior tone in her voice that would do any churchgoer proud. "That's exactly what I'm saying, Reverend Jessup. And you've gotten here just in time to snuff out the pure wickedness of Miss Hattie's Henhouse."

His wife's vehement words roused Elmer, and he sat up. His thinning hair was mussed, his eyes red, and one cheek had the imprint of a daisy. He weaved a little before he echoed his wife.

"Wicked Mis-sh Hattie's Henhouse."

Josiah smiled.

Amen.

Chapter Three

"Welcome to the Henhouse!"

The woman who popped out from behind the lilac bush was so scary looking that, for a second, Bri thought about jumping back in the car and locking the doors. But before she could even close her fingers around the door handle, the woman hurried over and shoved her out of the way with her massive, tattooed body.

"Don't you worry about the luggage, that's what ol' Olive Washburn is here for." She moved around to the back, her big work boots thumping against the brick driveway. "Although I can't figure out how you fit anything into this speck of a car."

"You're the new bellman—person?" Bri watched as the woman lifted the hatch, displaying the tattoo on the underside of her muscular arm. While the others were too convoluted to distinguish, this one appeared to be of a naked cowboy wielding a six-shooter. But before Bri could lean closer to get a good look at his impressive gun, the woman lowered her arm.

"Yep," Olive said as she started pulling out suitcases.

"And van driver, toilet fixer, and anything else Miss Minnie needs me to do." She took out the last bag. "Well, I'll be an armadillo's uncle. You sure managed to get a lot in this teeny back end. Are these your initials?" She tapped one of the gold Louis Vuitton emblems with a finger that had a thick line of grease under the nail. "I knew a Louise Varner once. You wouldn't be related, would you?"

"No." Bri reached out for the bag, then jerked her hand back when the handcuffs swung into view.

Olive's eyes narrowed for only a second. "It's probably a good thing you ain't related to Louise. She was in the stir with me for killin' her old man. And mean drunk or not, I figure he didn't deserve rat poison Spam hash." She man-handled the suitcases until she had all five hooked over her shoulders or held in her hands. Then, as if she was carrying no more than a clutch purse, she started for the porch.

Bri glanced out at the highway, then back at her car.

"Do you think I could park my car in the barn?" she called after the woman. "It's my grandmother's, and I don't want anything to happen to it."

Without turning around, the woman yelled back. "Seein' as how it ain't bigger than a minute, it shouldn't be a problem."

Bri released the breath she'd been holding ever since spraying the sheriff with mace. She didn't know how she had gotten to the Henhouse without being pulled over. The sheriff might not have gotten her license plate number, but in west Texas, a Smart Car stood out like a fly in the salad of beat-up trucks and American-make SUVs. Of course, hiding the car wasn't going to keep her from getting arrested. Not when her description had probably been broadcast from one side of the state to the other.

And if that was the case, then why wasn't she more terrified? Instead, her fear was muted beneath a healthy dose of giddy excitement. Obviously, she belonged in a mental ward. There was something very wrong with a woman who enjoyed being scared out of her wits.

"Hey!" Olive's gruff voice caused Bri to jump. "You think you could hold the door?"

Bri didn't want to hold the door. She wanted to hide her car. But seeing as how the woman was lugging her suitcases, she couldn't very well say no. She hurried up the front steps, then froze when she saw the blob of matted fur in the middle of the porch.

"Dad-blame it, Jiggers!" Olive scowled. "Instead of sleepin' all the time and gettin' in people's way, you need to be out in that barn workin' for your Meow Mix. You're still on probation after you peed in Miss Hattie's bed."

A cat that was the size of a small lynx got to its feet and stretched before it sent Bri a hostile look and released a low growl.

"Don't mind Jiggers," Olive said. "He's had a bad disposition ever since Starlet ran over his tail." Bri finally noticed the crooked tail that hung like the letter L from the cat's behind.

Bri carefully stepped around the cat and opened the door. "So Starlet still lives here? I thought Brant said she was moving to Nashville to pursue her singing career."

"She is, but not for a few weeks. The poor girl is scared witless about livin' in a big city, and I can't say as I blame her. Once, in Nashville, I got tossed in the pokey for just stealin' a six-pack of Diet Coke." She shook her head as she stepped into the foyer. "An unfriendly lot, them Nashville folks." Since Bri didn't know how to reply to that, she kept silent as she followed her inside.

Miss Hattie's might look like a pretty farmhouse on the outside, but on the inside, it was decorated as richly as any five-star hotel—a nineteenth-century hotel. An antique chandelier hung from the ceiling, hundreds of crystals dripping from the delicate bronze frame. A thick Oriental rug ran the length of the entryway, the deep red plushness cushioning Bri's feet as she walked toward the elevator that was located behind the massive staircase.

Bri had only been to Miss Hattie's twice since her brothers had purchased it. Even though it had been turned into a respectable bed-and-breakfast, Bri's mama was leery of having her only daughter stay in the same rooms that prostitutes had "entertained" in. Mary Anne Cates was convinced that her baby girl was a virgin. And she wanted to keep Bri that way.

As did the rest of the Cates family.

Never one to disappoint, Bri kept her sex life to herself. Until now.

Now her sexual exploits were on the Internet for all to see. And what was really annoying was that she was being blamed for something she hadn't even done. Of course, what she *had* done would make her family even more upset. Which is why she chose to keep her mouth shut and allow Brant to exile her to Miss Hattie's.

And after assaulting an officer of the law with mace, she might have to spend the rest of her life in west Texas, surrounded by nothing but mesquite and a bunch of old women who referred to themselves as hens.

As if Bri's thoughts had conjured them up, three women appeared in the doorway of the kitchen. There was Baby, who, despite the thick glasses, looked like an older version of Marilyn Monroe with her short platinum hair and pouty-red lips. She wore a fifties-style, off-the-shoulder blouse, black slim-fitting pants, and a pair of bright red vintage high heels that Bri instantly coveted. Unfortunately, bright red stilettos didn't belong in a demure young lady's wardrobe.

Sunshine stood next to Baby, a good foot taller and a good decade ahead in fashion. She wore clogs, bell-bottom jeans, and a crocheted sweater that looked like they were straight from Woodstock. And since Sunshine had lived during the sixties and done her fair share of partying, it was possible.

The leader of the hens and the proprietor of Miss Hattie's sat in a wheelchair in front of the other two women. Minnie didn't have a decade as far as fashion went. She wore a black satin negligee that hung on her frail body like an expensive trash bag. She looked thinner. More than likely due to the chemo she'd gone through in the last year. Chemo would also explain the huge Dolly Parton–style wig. Except Bri knew that Minnie had always been partial to wigs.

The tower of curls bounced as she zipped her wheelchair toward Bri.

"Well, it's about time you got here, Brianne Cates." Minnie pulled within inches of the toes of Bri's beige pumps. "Now we can finally have a little peace and quiet without your brothers callin' every hour on the hour to see if you got here safely." She squinted her eyes. "Did you shrink? You look even tinier than last time I saw you."

Bri smiled politely. "No, ma'am."

Minnie studied her for a moment before shaking her

head. "I don't know how you ended up so short when your brothers are as tall as hickory trees."

Bri didn't understand that, either. All the boys in her family had taken after their father and mother while Bri had acquired the short genes and big butt of her Granny Lou.

"I guess I'm just luck—" Her words cut off when Olive dropped the luggage by the elevator and, in two strides, had Bri lifted up in a bone-crushing hug.

"This little bit of a woman is Brianne Cates?" Olive jiggled her like a colicky baby. "Well, why the hell didn't somebody say so? Any sister of them good-lookin' Cates boys is a sister of mine."

"Put her down, Olive," Minnie said. "Let's try not to kill her before she has a chance to settle in. Speaking of which…" She waited for Olive to release Bri before she continued. "I'm afraid all the upstairs rooms are rented out for the next few days. So you'll have to room with Starlet—which I think will work out nicely since you two are around the same age."

"Or she could bunk with me out in the tack room." Olive grinned, revealing a set of teeth with more than a few missing.

"Thank you so much, Ms. Washburn," Bri quickly said, "but Starlet's room will be just fine."

"Just Olive." She picked up the luggage and started down the hallway next to the elevator. "And it's probably for the best. If Sunshine sneaks Jiggers too many chocolate chip cookies, that cat can get to fartin' worse than my granddaddy after a couple bowls of Texas chili." A laugh escaped Bri's mouth, and Olive flashed her a grin. "But I guess you're used to that growin' up with four brothers."

"Actually, being the only girl, I've always had a room to myself."

Olive shot her a confused look. "Well, that must've been lonely."

Bri was taken aback by the words. Everyone had always thought she was so lucky to get a room of her own in a family so large. And Bri did feel lucky. But there were also times when she had felt, if not lonely, then segregated. Especially at night when her brothers' laughter and roughhousing would ring down the hallway.

"Starlet's with her mean ol' pi-anna teacher right now," Olive said as she stepped into a bedroom painted a pretty spring green and filled with beautiful antiques. "But I'm sure she'll be tickled pink to see you. And maybe if she has a few friends her own age, she wouldn't be spendin' all her time writin' letters to her mama." After dropping the luggage, she moved over to the dresser. When she turned back around, she had a hairpin in her hand.

"Here." She held out a hand. "Let's get rid of those handcuffs."

Bri hesitated for only a second before she held out her hand. It didn't take long for Olive to jimmy the lock. With a wink, she handed them to Bri.

"It's a little trick I picked up." Her smile faded. "You in trouble with the law, Little Missy?" While Bri tried to come up with a good lie about the handcuffs, Olive continued. "Whelp, I'm a livin' testament that you can't run from your mistakes, but you can sure hide out for a little while." She held out her hand. "Give me your keys, and I'll take care of your car."

It had been so long since Bri had trusted anyone with the truth that she almost felt like crying. "Thank you,

Olive," she whispered as she laid the keys in Olive's calloused palm.

Once Olive had clomped out of the room, Bri moved over to the window to make sure that Granny Lou's car got safely in the barn. As she stood there, her gaze swept over Miss Hattie's prize lilac garden. In the spring and early summer, the bushes were covered with purple blooms. Now the blooms were all gone, and the leaves were a faded autumn green. As were the leaves of the big cottonwood trees. In fact, the only splashes of vivid color in the garden were the dots of red that rested against the two headstones in one far corner.

To those who didn't know the story, the graves would seem out of place in such a serene setting. But one of the headstones belonged to Bri's great-grandfather, William Cates. The other belonged to Miss Hattie, the notorious madam who started the Henhouse.

From what her brothers Billy and Brant had pieced together, William had met and fallen in love with the beautiful madam on his way back from a business trip to Bramble. After going home to his family in Lubbock, William discovered that he couldn't live without Miss Hattie. So he broke it off with his wife and returned to the Henhouse. Angered by her husband's betrayal, Bri's great-grandmother followed him and shot him down in cold blood. William died in Miss Hattie's arms.

While most people thought the story romantic and tragic, Bri thought it was foolish. Foolish for William to fall in love with a prostitute. Foolish for him to leave his wife and son. And foolish for her great-grandmother to waste her time following him when she had an inheritance that would financially take care of her and her son for the rest of their lives.

Which was why Bri had no intentions of ever getting married. She had money. She could adopt kids. And she'd had more than her fair share of men. This was proven minutes later when her cell phone rang. She grabbed it from her purse and looked at the number before answering.

"Hi, Brant."

"So you got there." The words were as straightforward and dry as her oldest brother. He didn't wait for her reply before he continued. "I don't think you'll need to stay long. Just long enough for things to quiet down. I can't remove the picture from the Internet, but I sure as hell can call in some favors and keep the story from hitting the newspapers and television. For now, you need to lie low. Stay away from the guests as much as possible."

"No fraternizing with the guests," she repeated.

"And I wouldn't be letting your friends know where you are," he continued. "Or do any social networking."

"No friends or social networking."

"And I don't want you learning any dances from Minnie—"

The phone beeped with an incoming call, and Bri glanced at the number.

"Can you hold on, Brant?" she said. "It's Billy." She clicked over to the other line. "Hey, Billy."

"Hey, yourself. Did you get to Miss Hattie's okay?"

"Safe and sound."

"Good. Shirlene and I are getting ready to board the cruise ship, but I wanted to check in with you first." There was a long pause, and Bri could just picture Billy running a hand through his hair. "Look, Bri, Shirlene doesn't think I should push you. But if the sonofa... if he forced you, I'm going to break every bone in his—"

"No," Bri cut in. "Jared didn't do anything." It was a half lie. Jared hadn't forced her to go to Mexico. Or cliff jump. He *had* posted the half-naked picture of her on the Internet. And he *was* stalking her.

Bri flopped down on the bed.

Men.

"It doesn't make sense," Billy said. "An innocent young lady just doesn't decide to do something like that out of a clear blue sky."

Bri could've argued that she wasn't that innocent, but instead she kept her mouth shut. Partly because she knew Billy was too hardheaded to believe her and partly because she couldn't stand to corrupt the saintly picture he held of her. She might think that men were a bunch of Neanderthals, but she adored her family of cavemen.

"Listen, Billy," she said, "Brant's on the other line so I'll let you get on with your vacation. Have fun, and kiss Shirlene and kids for me. Did you want me to check on Jesse while you're gone? I would imagine that he's pretty upset about missing the trip."

"Not as upset as Shirlene. Personally, I think the kid failed his last test on purpose just so he wouldn't have to go on the Disney cruise. So there's no need to worry about him. He's staying at his friend's, and I have the entire town keeping an eye out." He paused. "Listen, Shirlene's waving so I better go. Love you, Bri."

"Love you, too." She clicked back to Brant. "Sorry. What were you saying?"

"I just want you to keep to yourself until Elizabeth and I can get there," Brant said. "We would be there sooner but Minnie said the Henhouse was full. And I refuse to sleep out in the barn with that ex-con Minnie hired to drive—"

The phone beeped again. Glancing at the number, Bri made her excuses.

"I'll call you later, Brant. Beau's calling." She pressed the button. "Hi, Beau."

"Hey, Bri." Beau's congenial voice came through the receiver. "Are the hens taking good care of you? I'm sorry I wasn't there to welcome you, but Jenna got a bee in her bonnet about building a girls' school in Africa. And since we didn't take a honeymoon, I figure it wouldn't hurt to let her have her way."

A wall of guilt washed over Bri. "I'm so sorry I didn't make the wedding, Beau. I guess you figured out that I wasn't sick."

There was a pause. "I guess I can't point any fingers since I missed my fair share of family functions in the last two years. But I'll be truthful with you, Brianne; you've got us all a little worried. What's going on—?"

Beep.

Bri jumped on the excuse to cut their conversation short. "I've got to go, Beau," she said. "I'll call you later." Hoping this was the last interruption, she pushed the button and Beckett's teasing voice came through the receiver.

"Hey, Willie." He used the nickname he'd called her since birth. "You take any more naked pictures?"

She laughed, relieved that this brother was much less suffocating than the other three. "Stop being a smart butt."

Beckett paused. "So what happened?"

Bri leaned back on the bed and released her breath. "Bad decision making. Similar to the time you hacked into Billy's e-mail and sent all those love letters to his ex-girlfriends. Fortunately, only I know about that.

Everyone seems to know about my little mishap. Talk about a big black eye on the family name. I rank right up there with Great-Grandpa Cates and his love for a prostitute."

Beckett laughed. "Stop being so dramatic, Willie. It's not that bad. So you decided to have sex on the beach—"

"I was not having sex."

"So why was your top off?"

For a moment, she considered telling Beckett the truth. But before she could, Baby's breathy voice echoed down the hallway.

"Minnie! Minnie! You aren't going to believe who's at the door."

Fear tiptoed up Bri's spine as visions of mirrored sunglasses flashed through her mind. "I'll call you back, Beck." She hung up and jumped from the bed, glancing around for an exit. She had just decided on an escape route out the window when Baby continued.

"It's the King. The King has come to Miss Hattie's!"

Chapter Four

DUSTY HICKS BARELY WAITED FOR RALPH to pull up in front of his office before he opened the door and jumped down from the tow truck.

"You sure you don't want to go to the doctor's for your allergies, Sheriff?" Ralph asked. "I've never seen a nose or eyes so red in all my born days."

A wall of anger welled up inside of Dusty, and he gritted his teeth. "It's nothing that a little Claritin won't take care of. Thanks for coming out to get me, Ralph. Give my best to the missus."

"Will do, Sheriff. And I'll try to get your car back to you by next week."

"No hurry. The county still hasn't auctioned off my old squad car, and I figure it will do for the time being." He glanced back at the battered car hooked to Ralph's tow truck. With an oath, he slammed the truck door and turned to his office.

It was a pathetic, old building with sagging walls and cracked and peeling stucco. After the jail roof leaked so badly during the last rainstorm, Dusty had petitioned the town for money to build a new jail and sheriff's office, but Culver, Texas, was one of the towns hardest hit by the recession. Not only was there no money for improvement, there was talk about moving his headquarters to Austin.

Dusty wasn't moving to Austin. Or any big city, for that matter. There was only one reason he'd live in urban craziness, and that reason had been taken away from him.

He tipped his hat at a woman walking by pushing a baby stroller before he pulled open the glass door. A blast of cool air hit him in the face, and he was relieved that the air conditioner wasn't on the fritz again. For October, it was hotter than blue blazes.

"Good Lord in heaven, Dusty," Cora Lee, his receptionist, greeted him before the door had even finished closing. "What happened to you?"

He could've lied like he had to Ralph, but he trusted Cora Lee to keep things confidential. "I got pepper sprayed."

The creak of vinyl cushions had Dusty turning to the small waiting room.

His bad day suddenly got much worse.

A grinning cowboy stood in front of the couch, his hat in one hand and a partially eaten sticky bun in the other.

"Did you have to use your gun, Sheriff? Or just the Taser?" Kenny Gene finished off the sticky bun in one bite and talked around the lump of bread. "Sheriff Winslow has a gun, but everyone knows it ain't loaded after that accident with Buford Tyler's prize heifer. But I bet you're a much better shot. I bet you could hit a plug nickel from a hun-nerd yards."

Dusty closed his eyes for a brief second. When he opened them, Kenny Gene was still there. Although he had moved over to the bulletin board that was filled with wanted posters.

"I've been lookin' at these here pho-tos of criminals, and I think if you had yourself a dep-u-tee you could catch some of these crooks. Like this Mexican Cartel feller that escaped a couple weeks ago." He touched the wanted poster of Alejandro Perea. A poster Dusty had studied a lot in the last few weeks.

Alejandro had been the leader of a New York City drug ring that was tied to the Mexican Cartel. Dusty's friend Jenna Jay Scroggs had been living in New York City at the time, and when a backpack of drug money had gone missing, Alejandro had assumed that Jenna was responsible for taking it. He showed up at the Henhouse, along with his posse of thugs, and would've no doubt murdered Jenna, Beauregard Cates, and the hens if Olive Washburn hadn't intervened. Alejandro and his men had been arrested. And that would've been the end of the story if Alejandro hadn't escaped during a jail transfer. The feds believed that he had headed straight for Mexico. Dusty wasn't so sure.

If eyes were the windows to the soul, then Alejandro didn't have one. The eyes that stared back from the poster were black holes of emptiness. Dusty had seen the look before while working in Houston. Criminals with eyes like Alejandro's were the most dangerous, simply because they didn't give a shit about life—theirs or anyone else's. Criminals with eyes like that weren't concerned about being free as much as they were concerned with getting revenge.

"I figure with a good dep-u-tee we could have this feller behind bars in no time," Kenny continued. "Or this feller." He went to tap another picture, but his sticky fingers stuck to Alejandro's poster, ripping it from the tack. He shook his hand a couple of times, but the poster refused to come off. Which led to a crazy, hokey-pokey dance that had Cora Lee giggling.

After the day he'd had, Dusty didn't find it amusing. Without saying a word, he turned and walked straight into the bathroom. Once he'd placed his hat on the hook, he lathered his hands with bacterial soap and washed his face. He was lucky he'd had his sunglasses on. Very little pepper spray had gotten into his eyes. Although the skin beneath his eyes stung like hell. Or maybe what stung the most was his pride.

Bested by a teeny bit of a girl. Or not a girl so much as a woman. She might've been petite, but the breasts that she smashed up against his chest were 100 percent woman. Just the thought of her full softness in the cashmere sweater brought a zing of desire. Which would explain why she'd gotten the best of him. His preoccupation with her nice breasts and curvy ass had caused him to lower his guard and left him wide open to her deceit. And what really pissed him off was that it wasn't the first time a classy-dressed woman with a sweet smile had bested him.

Obviously, he was a slow learner.

The cold water made him feel better. And after rinsing and drying his face, he stepped from the bathroom ready to take on Kenny Gene. But Kenny was nowhere in sight. Just Cora Lee holding a much-needed cup of coffee.

"I sent him for lunch," she said as she handed him the cup. "You looked like you could use a few minutes of peace and quiet."

"Thanks," Dusty said. "Will the man ever give up?"

"It doesn't look like it. He's been here every day for the last two months. Ever since Sheriff Winslow stopped letting him help out in Bramble." She walked around her desk and sat down on the yoga ball she used as a chair. "Of course, I can't blame Sheriff Winslow. Kenny is a little like my second cousin on my mama's side—a few marbles short of a bag. But he has a good heart." She looked up at Dusty. "And it really wouldn't hurt to let him be your deputy."

"Not a chance. I don't have time to babysit Kenny Gene. Not with everything else on my plate. Did you find me a new housekeeper yet?"

"I'm afraid not. Women in the town aren't willing to put up with your ornery nature for anything less than a wedding ring."

"Then I guess I'll just have to clean house and do laundry myself." He blew on the coffee.

"And from the looks of that wrinkled shirt, I'd say you were doing a fine job of it." Cora twisted around on the huge white ball and pulled open a drawer in the filing cabinet. "Since you came in alone, I figure the pepper sprayer got away. Did you send out an APB? Or did you want me to?"

Dusty's shoulders tightened. "I took care of it."

It was a lie. He hadn't sent out an APB, and he didn't plan to. Not only because he was embarrassed about being bested by a woman but also because he didn't want just anyone bringing her in. He wanted to keep that pleasure for himself. He hadn't gotten her license plate number, but how many Smart Cars could there be with Texas plates? And the woman was definitely from Texas—east Texas. Her thick country twang was a dead giveaway.

Dusty took a sip of coffee. As always, it was strong, black, and perfect. He really should get Cora Lee a good Christmas present this year.

"Could you pull up all the Smart Cars registered in Texas?" he asked.

Cora's gaze lifted, and a smile seeped across her wide mouth. "The guy who got the best of you drove a Smart Car?"

"He didn't get the best of me," he said. "He just took me by surprise, is all." Cora turned away, but her shaking shoulders were a dead giveaway. Okay, so maybe he wouldn't splurge on a nice gift. "Did I get any messages while I was out?"

Her shoulders stopped shaking, and when she turned, her smile was much more sympathetic. "You sure you want to deal with that right now?"

He paused with the cup halfway to his mouth. "Heather?"

Cora Lee nodded. "She wants you to call her back."

The tension in Dusty's shoulders tightened into two hard knots.

"See if you can get me that list of Smart Cars," he said as he headed back to his office.

Once inside, he changed into a clean but wrinkled shirt before sitting down behind his desk and turning on his cell phone. He hated most technology, but cell phones were the worst invention since flavored coffee. The only thing they were good for was causing accidents and making people rude. He didn't know how many accidents took place because of texting or how many times he'd lifted a hand in greeting only to be ignored by the person in favor of the phone glued to their ear.

Heather, on the other hand, slept with her cell phone. He didn't even hear a ring before she picked up.

"I want you to stop calling Emma," she snapped. "She gets very emotional after she talks with you, and her therapist says it could be the reason that she isn't sleeping all through the night."

Dusty probably should've listened to Cora Lee and put off the phone call. He was in no mood to deal with his ex-wife. His next words proved it.

"Fuck the therapist."

Heather gasped. "You know how I feel about foul language, Dustin. And the therapist is only trying to help our daughter through this difficult time."

"Your so-called therapist is another one of your hired 'experts' who screwed me over in court and gave you full custody. So I don't give a shit if you like my language or not."

"She was only doing what's best for Emma."

He leaned up and ran a hand through his hair. "What's best for Emmie is getting to spend time with her father."

"Not when her father has a bad temper and a tendency for brutality."

Right about then, Heather was right. Dusty wanted to jump up and ram his fist through the wall. But that was exactly what she wanted. She had manipulated a display of temper out of him in court and gotten full custody of their only daughter, but he'd be damned if she'd continue to manipulate him. No matter how hard it was, he sat back in his chair and tried to remain calm.

"I won't stop calling or showing up for my visitations," he stated. "I don't care if your fancy lawyers get a restraining order. I won't have Emmie thinking that I deserted her."

There was a long, exasperated sigh. "Fine. But don't call her at bedtime. You can call her in the morning when she has all day to forget about the lies you tell her."

Dusty's hand tightened on the phone. "I've never lied to Emmie. Or you for that matter."

"Ha! What would you call promising to love and honor? You never loved me a day in your life, Dustin Hicks. You just seduced me to get your hands on my daddy's money."

Dusty could've argued the point, but what was the use? Heather's father had brainwashed her, and nothing Dusty could say would change that. He had given up fighting for his marriage, but he would never give up fighting for his daughter.

"So it's still morning," he said. "Put Emmie on."

There was a long pause followed by the sound of heels clicking against marble flooring. "Emma James! Your daddy's on the phone."

A shriek echoed through the receiver, filling his heart with joy and, at the same time, making it feel as empty as a crushed aluminum can.

"Hey, Pa!" Emmie yelled so loudly that Dusty had to pull the phone away from his ear.

He grinned at the name Em had started calling him after watching an episode of *Andy Griffith* on some pay channel. "Well, hey, yourself, Nugget."

"Did you catched any crim-aminals today?"

"Nope. What have you been doing?"

"I gots to make pea-nutty butty cookies with Elsa." She lowered her voice, her words muffled against the mouthpiece. "And I don't like pea-nutty butty cookies."

Dusty laughed. "I know that. You threw up all over me the last time I gave you one."

"When was that, Pa? I don't me-member."

It took a strong will to keep the raw emotion from his voice. "It was the last time I came to visit. When we went to the Houston zoo."

"Oh! I've been there with Grampy. I like the flame-minkos the best. Did you know that they can standed on one leg, Pa? Just like this. Can you see me, Pa? I'm a pink flame-minko." There was a loud thump, followed by Emmie's cries.

"Emmie!" Dusty sat up in the chair. "Baby, are you okay? What happened? Where's your mother?" But Emmie didn't answer. She just continued to cry until her mother got back on the line.

"Now do you see what I'm talking about? Can't you just leave well enough alone?" The line disconnected, and Dusty was left cradling his cell phone, wishing with all his heart that it was his daughter instead.

But it didn't take long for his pain to be transformed into anger. He pulled the phone from his ear and scrolled through his contacts until he found the number he wanted.

Like Heather, his friend Ryker picked up immediately.

"Hey, Dusty. What's up?"

Dusty released the breath that he'd been holding. "I was wondering if you've found anything out."

"I'm sorry, man, but the last time I followed her, all she did was go talk to her accountant. Are you sure there's a guy?"

Dusty wasn't sure of anything. He was simply grasping at straws. Anything to prove that Heather wasn't the saintly mother her lawyers had made her out to be. Anything to get his Emmie back.

His shoulders drooped. "Just let me know if you

discover something. I'll send you another check as soon as I can."

"I hate to take your money, man," Ryker said, "especially when that bitch and her rich daddy gave you such a bum deal. But business has been kinda slow—"

"It's no problem." Dusty cut him off. "We all have to eat." Between hiring better lawyers and a private detective, Dusty was a little worried about eating himself. His savings was dwindling fast. Maybe it was a good thing his housekeeper quit. That was just that much more money to go for getting back Emma.

"I'll call you if I find out anything," Ryker said.

"Thanks, man." Dusty hung up the phone just as Cora Lee tapped on the door and walked in.

"I pulled up a list of all the Smart Cars. There's more than you would think." She set the list down on top of the desk, and Dusty was shocked by the size of the spreadsheet. Obviously, Texans weren't as attached to gas-guzzling, American-made cars as he'd thought. There was no way in hell he would be able to figure out who the woman was. No way to punish her or get the money he needed to reimburse the town for the damage done to his squad car.

It was just another dark cloud in an already miserable day.

When Cora Lee continued to stand there, he glanced up. "Is there something else?"

She sent him a weak smile. "I just got a call from Miss Hattie's Henhouse. It seems that Miss Minnie has just shot Elvis."

Chapter Five

BRI STARED IN HORROR AT THE MAN stretched out on Miss Hattie's front porch. She had fantasized about Elvis getting his just deserts for his part in her becoming a fugitive, but she hadn't once considered murder.

"Whelp"—Olive stood over the man—"if Elvis wasn't dead before, it looks like he's dead now." She glanced back at Minnie, who was still holding the smoking gun. "You want me to bury him under the lilac bushes or under that old chicken coop behind the barn?"

Minnie didn't seem to be the least bit rattled that she had just shot a man in cold blood. She placed the derringer back in the side pocket of her wheelchair before pulling out a Dum-Dum sucker, carefully unwrapping it, and popping it between her wrinkled lips. After a few seconds, she finally spoke.

"He's not dead. Not unless he died of a heart attack. The bullet I shot was a good two inches above his head." She pulled out the lollipop and pointed it at Sunshine. "Check his pulse."

Sunshine immediately squatted down and took the

man's wrist. After only a few seconds, she smiled an airy smile. "He only fainted."

"Serves him right," Minnie huffed, "comin' here stickin' his nose into hen business and tryin' to sweet-talk me into givin' him information. I've been sweet-talked by the best, and he's not even close." She glanced around. "Where's Baby? Olive, go tell her to bring a bucket of cold water so we can get this slick-talkin' riffraff out of here."

Once Olive was gone, Bri stepped closer. He didn't look so much like Elvis now. His big sunglasses had slipped off his bulbous nose, and his toupee rested behind his balding head like roadkill. Still, his presence made Bri nervous. Two chance meetings in only a few hours seemed like too much of a coincidence.

"Did anyone get his name?" she asked.

"He said it was Reverend Josiah Jessup," Sunshine said. "Does that mean he's a preacher, Min?"

"I would say so. It would explain the holier-than-thou attitude and stream of BS," Minnie said. "What it doesn't explain is what he's doin' out here."

The reverend groaned, and his eyes fluttered open. They zeroed in on Bri with an intensity as piercing as Minnie's before a bucketful of water hit him in the face.

"That should wake him up." Olive tipped the last of the water out of the bucket.

Sputtering, the reverend sat straight up, his soaked toupee still partially attached to the back of his scalp. Suddenly, he wasn't so bent on sweet-talking.

"Why, you daughter of Satan!" he yelled as he came to his feet. "How dare you try to douse the light of the Lord with your waters from hell. I was told that there was wickedness going on out here, and now that I have seen it with my own two eyes, I will not rest until I have crushed it beneath my heel of righteous—"

The click of a gun being cocked cut him off midsentence. Everyone turned to Minnie, who this time was pointing the gun straight at the reverend's heart. "You want to see what heaven looks like, Rev? Because I'm about one second away from showin' you."

The man had enough sense to know when to shut up. Casting a narrow-eyed look at the women, he stumbled down the porch steps, trailing water behind him. He didn't speak again until he was pulling away in his cherry-red Cadillac.

"You haven't heard the last of Josiah Jessup!" he yelled. "Miss Hattie's day of reckoning is at hand."

A bullet hit the side mirror, sending glass flying and the reverend hot-tailing it out of the driveway in a spray of gravel.

Not knowing exactly how many bullets Minnie had left in the gun, Bri reached over and took it from her hand. "I think we've had enough excitement for one day, Miss Minnie—at least, I have."

"Darn yammin' fool," Minnie grumbled. "And what ticks me off more than anything is his disgraceful use of the King's image. For that alone, he should be pushing up daisies."

Baby came hurrying out the door that Olive had left open.

"Is he dead?" she asked in her breathy voice.

"And just where the heck have you been?" Minnie asked.

Baby's face turned a bright red, and she fidgeted for just a moment before she answered. "I had cookies in the oven."

Minnie's eyes narrowed, but she didn't call the woman out on the obvious lie. "Could you please bring a few into the library, along with some hot tea? I think I need a little refreshment after that sermon. Why don't you join me, Bri?"

Somehow Bri didn't think it was a request. "I'd love to," she said as she followed the woman inside.

The library was cozy. Books lined the shelves, and an overstuffed leather couch sat in front of a stone fireplace. It was still too warm to start a fire, but numerous candles flickered from the mantel. Jiggers had staked out his territory on the Oriental rug in front of the fireplace, and when Bri sat down on the couch, he lifted his head and growled.

"Oh, stop being ornery." Minnie tapped on her leg, and the cat popped up as if on a string and walked over so Minnie could scratch its big, matted head. After the cat was purring loudly, Minnie looked over at Bri.

"You and I have never had much of a chance to chat, have we? Not with your overprotective brothers keeping a close eye on you. I'm surprised they aren't here with you now."

Bri smoothed out the crease in her pants. "Billy's on a Disney cruise with Shirlene and their two younger kids. And Beau is in Africa with Jenna. But I'm sure Brant and Elizabeth will be here shortly."

Minnie studied her for a long, uncomfortable moment before she pulled the sucker from her mouth and tossed it at the trash can by the desk. It hit dead center.

"I'm not one to butt into other people's business," she said. "But I do have to wonder why a young, single woman would want to spend a vacation out in the middle of nowhere. Especially when most young women fresh out of college want to hang out in big cities and party their asses off."

That was a pretty good description of what women Bri's age wanted to do. Her sorority sisters had been the definition of Girls Gone Wild. And Bri might've joined in with their partying if she hadn't been so worried about shattering the proper-Southern-girl image her family had bestowed on her at birth. Instead, she chose to sow her wild oats in other ways: Skydiving. Heli-skiing. Cliff jumping. Running from the law.

Obviously, she should've gone for the partying.

"I guess I'm not much of a partier," she said.

Minnie snorted. "You sound just like my granddaughter, Elizabeth, before she got married to that rascally brother of yours."

Bri had heard the rumors about Elizabeth. Supposedly, at one time, she had been a rather prudish librarian. But Bri only knew her as the kindhearted woman who had brought Brant out of his depression after he'd lost his first wife and their son.

"I take that as a compliment," she said.

"It wasn't meant as one." Minnie stopped petting Jiggers. "Until Brant and us hens got ahold of her, Lizzie didn't have a clue how to let loose and have fun and would've spent the rest of her born days as a lonely old maid." She sat back in the chair and studied Bri with those intense eyes. "So why did your brothers exile you here?"

Bri could've lied, but what was the use? Her brothers loved Miss Minnie, and sooner or later, they'd bring her into their confidence.

"Someone posted a compromising picture of me on the Internet, and Brant thought it would be best if I hung out here until the media attention died down."

"Compromising as in naked?"

Bri's jaw tightened. "Partially."

Minnie laughed. Not a tiny chuckle, but a boisterous bellow that rang off the high ceiling and caused Jiggers to jump up and head for the door, his L-shaped tail swinging.

"No, I guess you're not like Elizabeth," Minnie hooted. "Here your brothers are thinkin' you're this sweet innocent that needs to be shielded from the evils of Miss Hattie's and the hens, and you're off gettin' naked pictures taken."

Something ugly rose up in Bri. She had been taunted by Elvis. Bullied by a sheriff. And now this old woman was making fun of her. Enough was enough. Her calm façade crumbled as she jumped to her feet.

"I am sweet!" She waved her hand around, not even aware that she still held the gun. "One mistake doesn't change the fact that I'm a loving daughter, an excellent hostess, a proficient flutist, and a really good scrap booker!"

Minnie stopped laughing as suddenly as she had started. "You're right. One mistake doesn't change who you are, Brianne Cates. So why are you letting Brant bully you into hiding out here?"

"He didn't bully me."

"I don't know what you'd call the list of dos and don'ts he gave you on the phone."

Bri's eyes widened. "You listened in on our conversation?"

"Overheard. And I make it my business to know what's going on in the Henhouse. Especially with my hens."

"I am not a hen!"

"That might've been true before." Minnie smiled. "But after assessing the situation, I've decided that you are now. If anyone needs a little 'hen power,' it's you,

Brianne Cates. And the first thing we need to do is get you away from all those controlling males in your family and give you some space to find yourself. Although I don't see how that's going to happen if Brant is coming out here." She tapped the arm of her wheelchair with one nail. "Still, there must be some way we can stall—"

There was a click followed by a deep voice that made Bri's blood run cold.

"Drop the weapon."

Bri whirled around, but she only got a flash of mirrored lens before she was tackled to the ground and the gun pulled from her hand. Once again, she found herself facedown. This time, Sheriff Hicks straddled her from behind, his muscular thighs pinning her to the carpet.

"Let me go," she fumed.

"Not a chance in hell." He pulled her hands behind her and clicked cuffs around her wrists. And damned if the hot tingle didn't return.

"I've never minded a little roughhousing," Minnie finally spoke up. "But only when both parties are consenting. And Brianne doesn't look real happy, Sheriff Hicks. So I think you better let her up. Especially since the gun she was waving around wasn't even loaded."

"It doesn't matter." Sheriff Hicks pulled Bri to her feet as if she didn't weigh more than a ragdoll. "This woman's a fugitive from the law, and I plan to take her in."

"No kiddin'? Brianne, you continue to surprise me." Minnie's lips curved up in a smile, but it faded when she looked back at Dusty. "So I guess you have a warrant, Sheriff."

Sheriff Hicks kept a tight grip on Bri's arm. "Are you saying I need one, Miz Minnie?"

Minnie wheeled over to the desk. "Why don't you sit down, Sheriff, so we can talk about this? Fugitive or not, I doubt that Brianne can go anywhere trussed up like Sunday dinner."

Sheriff Hicks hesitated for only a second before pulling Bri along with him to the two chairs in front of the desk. He pushed her down into one, while he remained standing, arms crossed and mirrored sunglasses aimed at Minnie.

"This woman ran me off the road while driving recklessly down the wrong side of the highway," he said. "She then resisted arrest—not once, but twice. Then I get a report of a man being shot, and I arrive here to find her wielding a gun. Now if that's not enough to toss her butt in jail, I don't know what is."

Minnie's eyebrows disappeared beneath the fringe of blond curls. "Well, that certainly seems like enough to me." She pulled out a sucker from her side pocket. "Dum-Dum?" Sheriff Hicks shook his head, and instead of unwrapping the sucker for herself, she rolled the stick between her fingers. "So how long do you plan on keepin' our little Brianne?"

"Just until the judge can sentence her and she reimburses the town for the damage to my vehicle."

Minnie snorted. "Seein' as how Judge Seeley would rather hunt or fish than do his job, that could take a while."

The sheriff's shoulders tightened beneath the wrinkled material of his uniform. "I have nothing but time, Miz Minnie."

Minnie relaxed back in her wheelchair, her sharp eyes moving to Bri and then to the sheriff. "You still living out at that ranch all by yourself, Sheriff?"

The sheriff seemed to be as confused by the quick subject change as Bri. He shifted his weight and answered hesitantly. "That's the way I like it."

"Of course it is." Minnie smiled brightly. "What man doesn't love peaceful solitude?" She stopped twirling the sucker and looked at Bri. "Or what woman, for that matter." Her eyes narrowed in thought for only a second before she nodded. "I've decided to let you take Brianne."

Up until that point, Bri had kept her mouth shut, assuming that if the head hen could handle her brothers, she could handle one annoying sheriff. Obviously, Bri had been wrong. She struggled to her feet, which wasn't easy with her hands cuffed behind her back.

"You can't let him take me! I can't go to jail. Think about what this will do to my family—your family."

Minnie nodded. "Family is important. But sometimes a woman needs to put herself first."

Before Bri could figure out how being thrown in jail was putting yourself first, the sheriff pulled her toward the door. Suddenly, all thoughts about keeping her identity a secret fled.

"I'm Brianne Cates," she said. "My brothers own C-Corp, and when they hear about this—"

Sheriff Hicks came to a satisfying halt. "You're a sister to the Cates brothers?"

Bri straightened her shoulders and sent him a haughty look. "Baby sister."

A look came over the sheriff's face—annoyance mixed with a whole lot of hate.

"Then I'm sure you'll have plenty of money to post bail."

Chapter Six

JOSIAH DID NOT BELIEVE in forgiving and forgetting. He did believe in an eye for an eye. It was the golden rule that he'd lived by his entire life. When those high school boys had taken his Halloween candy, he'd retaliated by slitting their tires and keying their car doors. When his father had overreacted and spanked Josiah for stealing the action figure from the drugstore, he'd laced his daddy's bottle of Jack Daniel's with pure rubbing alcohol that had sent him to the hospital for a week. And when his last wife had revealed his misappropriation of funds, he'd paid a very unsavory character to dish out punishment. Although a little physical intimidation wasn't even close to the hell his ex had put him through.

And now he had another score to settle.

How dare the flamboyant hussy in the wheelchair ignore his congenial efforts at friendship and call him a blustering windbag. He was a man of God. A man of God who refused to be spoken down to by a two-bit hooker who should be spending her last days on earth repenting instead of enjoying her life in a mansion twice the size of his.

It was wrong.

And Josiah would not rest until he had corrected the error.

He pulled his cell phone from his jacket pocket and dialed through his contacts until he found the number he was looking for. As he waited for the television producer to answer, he steered the Cadillac with his knees and tried to repair his toupee in the rearview mirror. It was impossible. The expensive hairpiece was beyond repair. Just something else to hold against the whores at Miss Hattie's.

Instead of a friendly hello, the phone was answered with exasperation.

"I told you, Reverend, I can't get you another time slot," Mike Fowler said. "Your ratings dropped lower than that Cadillac you like to tool around in, and I'm still dealing with lawsuits. And speaking of lawsuits, if you don't stop hassling me, I'm going to slap a restraining—"

"I would never dream of hassling you, my son." He gave up on trying to fix the toupee and hooked a hand over the steering wheel. "Not when I've finally realized that you are absolutely one hundred and ten percent correct. My television show had run its course. Like Carol Burnett, Lawrence Welk, and soap operas, evangelistic television is going the way of the dinosaurs. People today want to watch something more than Bible preaching and choir singing."

"You got that right," Mike said. "They want shows with plenty of action and—"

"Scandal?" Josiah finished for him.

"I was going to say realism, but scandal is definitely in the top ten. I'm sorry, Reverend. It looks like you'll be forced to do most of your preaching from the pulpit. Now I need to—"

"What if I could promise you scandal and realism?"

There was a long pause. "What are we talking about here? Because if this has anything to do with coming clean about the money you used for that house in Malibu, I suggest you keep your mouth shut. Not only for your sake, but for the network's."

Josiah pushed back a strand of his toupee that kept flapping in his face. "I have nothing to come clean about, Mike. I built that house as a home for the elderly who would otherwise be tossed out on the streets. I thought everyone knew that."

Mike snorted. "Yeah right. So what are you talking about?"

"I'm talking about a television show like no one has ever seen before. One that would give people the action, scandal, and realism they crave and, at the same time, the righteousness that they need."

There was a pause before Mike spoke. "Go on."

"I would still preach the word, but I'd be preaching to the people who really needed it—the deprived, retched souls who had lost their way in the bowels of wickedness."

"Are you saying you want to take the cameras on location?"

Josiah could hear the excitement in Mike's voice, and he smiled. "That's exactly what I'm saying. Every week, I'd go to another den of iniquity and bring a ray of light to their otherwise dark world."

"And just what dens are we talking about?"

"You name it. Crack houses, strip clubs . . . whorehouses."

Mike laughed. "You know of a lot of those, do you?"

Josiah bristled. "Are you making fun of me?"

"Actually, no. I think you could be onto something here. Of course, I'll need to run it by the higher-ups. But before I do, we need a teaser—thirty minutes of film should do. Do you have any ideas on where you want to start your crusade against evil?"

Josiah smiled. "The infamous Miss Hattie's Henhouse."

"I thought that place had closed down."

"An obvious lie to keep the wickedness going." He glanced in his rearview mirror, surprised to see the flashing red lights. He looked down at the speedometer, but since he was going under the speed limit, he figured the officer was after someone else and pulled over out of the way. "But I'll need to do some more investigation and get back to you."

"I'll look forward to it," Mike said.

The producer's about-face had Josiah smiling even broader. The smile died when the sheriff's car pulled up behind him. Not because he was worried about getting a ticket but because the sight brought back the memory of the woman who had been pulled over earlier. The same woman who had witnessed his humiliation at the Henhouse.

He'd recognized her as soon as she'd stepped out of the door of Miss Hattie's. Not her face as much as her shapely hips that had been so nicely displayed when the sheriff had her bent over the trunk of his car. And Josiah rarely forgot a nice ass. Which was another thing that pissed him off. He might've succeeded in getting a little piece of it if the crippled hag hadn't pulled out the gun. And who knew, maybe he still would. There was something very familiar about the woman's face. He had seen her before, and not just today.

The sound of crunching gravel beneath boots brought him out of his thoughts and back to the present. He glanced in his side mirror, half expecting to see the sheriff who had arrested the woman. Instead, it was a much older man.

"I'm sorry, Sheriff," Josiah said before the man had even reached him. "Was I speeding? Or is this about me talking on my cell?"

The sheriff hooked his thumbs in his loaded-down utility belt. "I wish it was one of those." His eyes narrowed. "Nope, this has to do with my wife."

Josiah's smile froze as he mentally stumbled over the list of married women he'd screwed in the last year. It took a while. Married women seemed to love having sex with preachers as much as a dog loved chasing his tail. Up until this point, Josiah had suffered no bad effects from his little trysts.

But he figured that was about to change.

He looked down at the gun handle the sheriff toyed with and held up his hands. "I'm sure I can explain without things getting violent. Your wife probably misunderstood something I said . . . or did."

The man looked confused before he followed Josiah's gaze down to the gun on his hip. "Oh, you're one of them city slickers that are a little fidgety around guns." He rested his hand on the handle. "No need to worry. You're not in trouble. The reason I stopped you is because my wife, Myra, never has let Wilma Tate get one up on her. And if I let you leave Texas without her gettin' to meet a celebrity, I'll be eatin' TV dinners for the rest of my born days."

At the news, Josiah relaxed. "Well, of course, I would love to meet the wife of such an esteemed officer of the law. I have always been appreciative of all our crime fighters in uniform—but especially sheriffs. To me, a sheriff is a heroic Wyatt Earp ridding our country of vile criminals with his blazing fast six-shooter."

The sheriff squinted. "Blazin' fast? I don't know if I'd go that far."

Josiah continued to lay the bullshit on thick. "Humility. I'd expect nothing less from a true hero. Although, someday, I hope to get a demonstration of your skill. But for now, lead the way, Sheriff." He popped the Cadillac into drive. "Your good wife awaits."

The confused look remained on the sheriff's face as he turned and headed back to his squad car. In the side mirror, Josiah watched as he stopped and tried to do a quick draw. The gun had no more than cleared the leather when it slipped from the sheriff's hand and bounced out into the street.

Josiah smiled.

Just like taking candy from a baby.

Chapter Seven

BRIANNE CATES.

Dusty glanced in the rearview mirror at the woman in the backseat and wanted to cuss a blue streak. It was just his luck to have arrested the only daughter of the most influential family in the state of Texas. This morning, he'd been worried about his headquarters moving to a bigger city. Now he was more worried about keeping his job.

Which didn't explain why he hadn't released the woman once he'd found out who she was. That would've been the smart thing to do. But Dusty had never made exceptions to the law, and he wasn't about to start now. Especially for some snooty, rich socialite who reminded him way too much of his ex-wife.

Heather threw her name around as well. Of course, her real estate mogul father didn't come close to having the power that the Cates brothers did. And maybe that was why Dusty hadn't backed down and released Brianne. He was damned sick and tired of getting pushed around by money—and beautiful women.

There was no doubt that Brianne Cates was beautiful.

He had been only too aware of her great body both times he'd handcuffed her, but he had no idea how creamy her skin was or how perfect her features were until now. The sunshine that shone through the side glass of the back window highlighted a high forehead, straight nose, and full lips. Even in profile, it was hard to pull his gaze away.

"It's not too late to change your mind, you know." She glanced up and caught him watching her in the rear-view mirror. She smiled. Not a full smile, but just enough to show off dimpled cheeks. "I won't say a word to my brothers if you return me to Miss Hattie's."

"I'm sure you wouldn't," he said drily as he returned his gaze to the highway. "But that's not going to happen."

"So you're one of those people who live by the rules," she said. "And believe it or not, so do I. I'm not sure what happened today. I guess I just sort of lost it."

"Well, be sure to tell that to the judge when you see him."

"You do realize that I probably won't see the judge. My brothers will take care of the situation long before it gets to that point. In fact, I wouldn't be surprised to find them waiting for us when we get to the jail."

Dusty wouldn't be surprised, either. Not when the Cates boys had a helicopter and a jet at their disposal. He should just accept defeat and return her to Miss Hattie's, but he couldn't seem to do that. This spoiled, arrogant woman had completely disregarded the law, and he wanted her punished for it. Even if she only had to spend an hour behind bars, she was going to damn well do it.

The Cates brothers weren't waiting for Dusty when he pulled in the parking space marked "Sheriff Hicks." He glanced back at Brianne hoping to finally see a little fear, but, instead, she looked almost as relieved as he was. Her shoulders sagged as a smile curved her lips.

Confused by her reaction, it took him a while to get out and open the back door. Unlike Heather, Brianne was a little bit of a thing. She didn't even come up to his chin. Which is probably why he felt so guilty when she cringed in pain as he helped her out of the car. Regardless of how much she deserved to be uncomfortable, he took off the handcuffs as soon as they stepped through the back door.

Taking her arm, he escorted her past his office and straight to Cora Lee's desk. Cora was bent over the filing cabinet, her butt bouncing up and down on the yoga ball to a country tune that blasted from the radio.

"Five-one-five-oh," she sang in an off-key voice, "somebody call the po-po. I'm going crazy—" She glanced up and stopped in midsentence. Her gaze drifted over Brianne from the top of her glossy black hair to the tips of her expensive heels. A wide smile spread over her face. "Well, it's about damned time." She bounced to her feet and held out a hand. "Cora Lee Simmons."

Bri took her hand and smiled. It was twice as genuine as the smile she'd given Dusty. And he didn't know why that pissed him off.

"Brianne Cates. It's a pleasure to meet you, Ms. Simmons."

Before the farce could continue, Dusty butted in. "Could you get all the paperwork filled out for Miz Brianne Cates, please, Cora. She'll be staying with us until her family can arrange for bail."

Cora's eyes widened, and her smile drooped. "She's the one who shot Elvis? That's too bad. I was hoping that you were Dusty's new gal. He certainly needs one. A little

TLC would make his disposition better and my life a helluva lot easier—so why did you shoot Elvis?"

Since Dusty wasn't about to let Cora Lee take over his interrogation—or continue to impart personal information—he took Brianne's arm. "Come on, Miz Cates, I'll show you to your room."

She hesitated for only a second before allowing him to escort her down the long corridor to the door at the end. Dusty took the ring of keys off the hook and unlocked the door. The room with the three jail cells was dimly lit and stifling. Once the door locked behind him, he flipped on the light and took off his sunglasses.

Instead of waiting for him to direct her into a cell, she chose the middle one.

The only one with a small window.

He followed her in, not realizing how tiny the cell was until she turned around and looked at him with eyes the same color as his favorite chambray shirt.

"You expect me to use that." She pointed at the toilet in the corner.

"It's a jail, Miz Cates, not the Hyatt." He walked over to the window and opened it, checking to make sure the bars hadn't fallen out of the crumbling stucco and also allowing the cool breeze to alleviate some of the heat. "Did you shoot Elvis?"

She laughed, and he turned to find her sitting on the small cot. "Believe me, there was a point when I wanted to." She smoothed a hand over the wool blanket that had been tightly tucked around the paper-thin mattress. Her fingers were long and slim, her nails as neat and manicured as the rest of her. "But no," she continued as her hand lifted to toy with the diamond solitaire that hung around her neck. A diamond no doubt worth at least a month of Dusty's salary. "I didn't shoot Elvis. And neither did anyone else. Minnie just fired a warning shot to scare him off."

Dusty wasn't surprised. The ornery old woman was always shooting at some unwary man who happened to stop by Miss Hattie's without invitation.

"Who is he?" he asked.

She shrugged. "Some traveling evangelist." She dropped the diamond, and it swayed against the top swells of her breasts as she sat up. "Look, you've proven your point. I was wrong to run you off the road and mace you. But it looks like you'll live. So why don't you quit playing this little game of bad cop and let me go before my brothers get here and make both our lives hell."

Dusty studied the diamond before he turned and walked out of the cell. "Somehow I don't think your life has ever been hell. And as for my life"—he slammed the bars—"it already is."

When he got back to the reception area, Cora was pulling one of her Weight Watcher meals out of the microwave.

"Have you lost your mind, Dusty Hicks?" Cora juggled the hot plastic container over to her desk. "It just dawned on me who that little gal is. She's Brianne Cates—*the* Brianne Cates. And there's no tellin' what her family will do once they find out you tossed her in jail. I don't care if she did shoot Elvis."

"She didn't shoot Elvis," Dusty said. "She maced an officer of the law. And I'm not letting her go until Judge Seeley sets bail, regardless of how pissed off the Cates brothers get."

"Oh, they'll be pissed off, all right," she said. "Everything I've read about the Cates family leads me to believe that they're very family oriented. And her brothers aren't the type of men who will sit back and let their little sister rot in jail." She picked up a white Sonic bag and handed it to him. "Kenny brought by lunch and told me to tell you that he'll be back after he finishes his patrol route."

Dusty jerked the bag from her hand. "He doesn't have a damned patrol route! And I don't care about the Cates brothers. Breaking the law is breaking the law." He whirled and headed back to his office, slamming the door behind him.

Once there, he paced back and forth in front of his desk. When he realized that he'd once again let his temper get the best of him, he stopped pacing and forced himself to sit down in his chair. But instead of eating his cheeseburger, he pulled the stress ball out of his desk drawer and called Judge Seeley. It came as no surprise that the judge was out of his office. Quail season was in full swing. Which meant that Minnie was right. It could be a while before the judge posted bail.

Uttering a curse, Dusty grabbed the paper sack off his desk and headed out of his office. On the way down the corridor, he stopped and bought a Diet Coke from the soda machine.

He unlocked the door to the jail to find Brianne escaping. Or not escaping as much as stuck. Obviously, the crumbling stucco hadn't been strong enough, and she had managed to get the bars off and her upper body through the tiny window. Fortunately, her hips were too wide to fit through. She wiggled and squirmed as her bare toes pressed against the wall just above the bed she'd pulled beneath the window.

Dusty watched for a few moments, his gaze pinned on the curves of her butt, which pushed out so temptingly. As much as he hated to admit it, she had one nice ass. Beneath the soft material of her pants, her cheeks curved out in lush fullness. And Dusty couldn't help wondering what it would feel like to curl his fingers around those hips and still her wiggles with a hard thrust.

The train of his thoughts caused desire to ooze slow and thick through his veins straight to the bulge beneath his fly. His reaction drained all the humor out of the situation and had him walking over to unlock the cell. He pushed open the bars, and at the creak of the hinges, she stilled.

"Is someone there?" She tried to pull her head back in, but she really did appear to be stuck.

Dusty walked over and set the bag and soft drink on the end of the bed. "Problems?"

She hesitated for only a second before she answered. "No, no problems. I was just getting a breath of fresh air."

A smile crept over Dusty's mouth. "Really? And how's the weather?"

"A little windy." She remained teetering in the window, her toes a good foot from the mattress. Since her fingernails were painted a pastel color, he was surprised to find her toenails painted an electric blue with...he leaned closer...little white lightning bolts on the big toes.

"Do you think you could help me out here?"

Her words had him jumping guiltily as if he'd been looking at something more than just her bare toes. Of course, he had no business examining anything on the woman—nice butt or weirdly painted toes. She was his prisoner, and he needed to remember that.

"My sweater appears to be stuck on the latch," she said.

He stepped closer to the bed and rested a knee on the mattress. "Lean to the side a little," he ordered. When she complied, he reached up and tried to unhook her sweater. Unfortunately, her struggles had thoroughly entangled the yarn in the metal frame and no amount of tugging would free it.

"Could you hurry up? I can't hold myself up anymore." She slipped down a few inches from the window, sliding her sweater up her rib cage. Her stomach was flat and trim...and inches away from his mouth. A mouth that suddenly felt as dry and desolate as the Sahara. If he tipped his head just a little, he could press his lips to the pretty little freckle right under the gathered material of her sweater.

Dusty pulled back. *Damn*. Obviously, his self-inflicted abstinence had finally caught up with him. One peek of skin and he'd almost lost it. Unfortunately, one peek wasn't all he was going to get.

"To hell with it!" Bri said, right before she raised her arms and completely slipped out of the sweater, leaving it hanging from the window. Dusty barely registered the hot pink bra and miles of soft skin before Brianne tumbled into his arms.

He told himself to put her down and step away, but his hands wouldn't cooperate. He held her trim waist in a death grip, her feet dangling and her curvy butt flush against his zipper. And keeping your willpower with a fully dressed woman you weren't touching was much easier than keeping it with a half-naked woman you were.

Slowly, she glanced over her shoulder. He expected her

wide blue eyes to be filled with snooty disdain. Instead, they were filled with something that looked like the same rampant desire that swirled around inside of him. Still, he might've been able to let her go if she hadn't slipped a hand around his neck and offered up those pump lips.

Months of abstinence turned to dust as Dusty closed his eyes and melted into the kiss. For such an innocent-looking woman, she had a wicked way with a kiss. Their lips had barely touched before her tongue came into play, giving his bottom teeth a sexy little flick before coaxing his tongue into a hot tango that turned his cock as hard as the concrete beneath his boots.

While one of her hands caressed the hair at the nape of his neck, the other took his hand and drew it up to her satin-covered breast. He gently squeezed, and a groan escaped his mouth. How long had it been since he cradled a woman's breast? Kneaded the resilient flesh? Strummed the hard peak? So long that he couldn't seem to get enough. Once he had thoroughly inspected one breast, he moved on to the next. But as his hand swept over her cleavage, his fingertips brushed against the cold hardness of the diamond solitaire. That was all it took to take the starch right out of his lust.

He dropped his hands and stepped back. She wobbled a little before slowly turning to look at him. Her hot blue, desire-drugged eyes almost had him reaching for her again. To keep himself from it, he stepped out of the cell and slammed the bars closed. Still, it took a few moments before he could speak.

"I'll have the judge here as soon as I can. Even if I have to track him down on a hunt myself."

The words seemed to clear the desire from Brianne's

eyes. Although the humor that replaced it bothered him even more. She adjusted her bra, displaying her plump cleavage to a mouthwatering effect, and smiled sweetly.

"Take your time, Sheriff. Jail isn't quite as bad as I thought."

Chapter Eight

"Now that's a real interestin' story, Ms. Cates." Judge Seeley leaned back in the chair behind Sheriff Hicks's desk and rested his hands over his camouflaged hunting vest. "I especially liked the part about Elvis. I've always been a big Elvis fan, myself, even after he gained weight and started dressing like Liberace."

Bri sent the man a dimpled smile. "So is my mama. She's been to Graceland at least ten times—six on the King's birthday—and has every Elvis souvenir known to man. Although my daddy put his foot down on the velvet painting."

A derisive snort had her turning to the man who leaned in the doorway with arms crossed and scowl deep. If Bri had thought Sheriff Hicks had been ill tempered before their kiss, it was nothing compared to after. And his anger was baffling. Men usually didn't hold grudges for kisses. Especially men who desired you. And there was little doubt in her mind that Sheriff Hicks desired her. She had felt the rock-solid proof of that desire when she'd fallen into his arms.

Yet here he was, studying her as if the entire episode in the jail cell had been all her fault. True, she had been the aggressor, something that was completely out of character for her, but he hadn't put up much of a fight.

"I take it that you're not an Elvis fan, Sheriff," she said.

"Oh, I love Elvis, Miz Cates," he said. "I just don't have time for a bunch of chitchat about a man who's been dead for going on forty years—and neither does the judge." Without his sunglasses, his eyes drilled right through her. From this distance, they looked the color of Brant's favorite brandy. But after being up close and personal, she knew the dark pupils were surrounded by a subtle splash of dark green.

"Speak for yourself, Dusty," Judge Seeley said. "There's nothin' wrong with a little chitchat. Especially when Brianne's almost like family." He reached for the stress ball that sat on the sheriff's desk. He examined it for only a moment before putting it back. "I met her daddy when he first started his farmin' equipment business. And I've talked with her brother Brant at more than a few political fund-raisers."

"Now that I think of it, I remember my brother mentioning you," Bri gushed. "I can't believe we haven't had you out to the house for some of my mama's Shoofly pie. It's the best in seven counties—"

"She maced an officer of the law." Sheriff Hicks cut her off, his words hissing through his clenched teeth.

Judge Seeley held up a hand. "And we certainly can't ignore that." Before Bri could panic, he sent her a wink. "Nor can we let a pretty little thing rot in jail—one night was bad enough."

Surprisingly, the night in jail hadn't been bad at all.

Cora Lee had seen to that. The gregarious woman had brought her a comforter and pillow, a dinner of Kentucky Fried Chicken, and a laptop with numerous DVDs. The sheriff hadn't shown his face until that morning when the judge had arrived.

The judge lifted his white eyebrows. "Especially when it sounds like she might've been the victim of an overzealous sheriff."

Sheriff Hicks pushed away from the doorjamb. "She was driving down the wrong side of the highway!"

"Because of Elvis," Judge Seeley said. "Haven't you been listenin' to a word this young woman has said?"

Bri sent the judge her wide-eyed innocent look. "Some folks are just better listeners than others."

"This is such bull—"

The judge pounded twice on the desk with his fist. "I'll warn you to watch your mouth, Dusty, or I'll have to charge you with contempt."

Sheriff Hicks stepped closer to the desk. "Contempt? This is my office, not a courtroom."

"As a district judge, any place I'm presiding is a courtroom. And I'll thank you to remember that." He sat back and steepled his fingers beneath his stubbly chin, his gaze pinning the sheriff. "You okay, son? Is the stress of the job gettin' to you? You seem a little hot around the collar for a mere pepper sprayin'."

A laugh slipped out of Bri's mouth before she could stop it. She coughed to try to cover it, but it was obvious that the sheriff knew better.

"Just set bail," he growled.

The judge sat up and cleared his throat. "Now I don't think there's any need for that. In fact, since Ms. Cates has pleaded guilty to all charges and offered to pay for any damages, I don't see why we can't settle this without bringing bail or a jury into it."

Bri smiled. "That sounds perfectly acceptable to me, Judge. And please...call me Brianne." She shot a glance over at the sheriff. "After all, we're almost like family."

Sheriff Hicks leaned his knuckles on the desk and glared at the judge. "So you're just going to let her go scot-free."

"Of course not. People need to take responsibility for their actions." He looked back at Bri and winked. "What would you think of a little community service?"

The sheriff emitted a growl as Bri smiled brightly. "I think that would be just fine and dandy. I've always believed in giving back to the community. And I was wondering, Judge Seeley, if we might keep this little episode as confidential as possible. You know how things like this can get blown out of proportion with the press." She paused for just a second. "And it might be best if we didn't mention it to my family, either."

Since her brothers hadn't shown up, that could mean only one thing: Minnie hadn't told them. If that was the case, Bri certainly wasn't about to.

"Why, of course, Brianne. No need for anyone to catch wind of this." He glanced over at the sheriff, who now looked more than hot under the collar. He looked like he was about to explode. His hands were clenched in fists, and the veins in his neck protruded. "You can keep a secret, can't you, Sheriff?"

The sheriff didn't answer. He just stood there maddogging the judge, who seemed to be completely unaware of the anger directed at him. The judge got to his feet and headed for the door.

"All we need now is to draw up the paperwork. And rather than take Cora Lee from her exercise ball, I'll just…" His voice faded as he pulled the door closed behind him.

Being stuck in the same room with a surly sheriff was not Bri's idea of a good time. She got up with every intention of following the judge when Hicks stepped in front of the door and blocked her way.

"You're not getting away with it. I don't care what the judge says."

If Bri had learned anything from her brothers, it was "show no fear." So she tipped up her head and sent him a superior look. "Oh, but I think I have gotten away with it."

A muscle twitched at the right corner of his mouth. Figuring that it was probably best to put some space between them, she turned on her heel and strolled around the desk in the pretense of studying the books on the shelves. But that wasn't the only reason she moved away. There was something about being close to the man that took all the oxygen out of the air. Which was exactly how she had ended up kissing him in the jail cell. One minute, she'd lost her balance, and the next, she was in his arms, experiencing the same feeling she got the first time she went skydiving—all breathless and filled with heart-stopping adrenaline.

Even across the room from him, she was having trouble breathing. And keeping her eyes off the handcuffs that dangled from his belt. In an attempt to get some kind of control over her crazy emotions, she turned her back to him.

"You're a very angry man, aren't you?" she said.

"Only when the scales of justice tip the wrong way."

She studied the framed Texas Tech diploma on the

shelf, somewhat surprised that he had graduated from college. "Let's be honest, we aren't talking about a major crime here. All I did was wound your pride. You're just upset because you got bested by a girl, and now you want to get even."

There was a moment's hesitation before he spoke. "Probably."

The truthful answer had her glancing over her shoulder. He didn't look angry anymore. His fists had relaxed, and his neck held only the bump of his Adam's apple and some stubble that he'd missed with his razor.

"So what is it going to take to make you forgive and forget?" she asked, turning back to the shelves.

"You doing more than just handing out canned goods at the local food bank."

"How about if I pick up trash on the highway or clean out porta-potties? Will that soothe your ego enough?" A cluster of photos on the second shelf caught her attention. One was of a chubby, bald-headed baby cocooned in the crook of a man's muscled arm. Another of a cute blond toddler. The last was of the same little girl at about three.

Bri had no more than picked up the picture to examine it when the sheriff walked over and pulled it from her hand.

"This isn't just about my ego," he said. "It's about justice. Things should be fair for all people. Not just the ones who have money."

"Ahh," she said. "So that's it. You have a thing against wealthy people."

His gaze moved down to the photo. "I have a thing against people who think they're above the rules. Spoiled people who don't care about anyone but themselves and their own selfish wants and desires." When his gaze lifted, it was cold and chilling. "And I won't forget or forgive, Miz Cates. You can count on it."

Just then the door opened, and Judge Seeley walked in with Cora Lee close behind him.

"So have we called a truce?" he asked as Cora set a stack of papers on the desk. She gave Bri an almost sympathetic smile before scurrying back out. Before Bri could give much thought to what that smile meant, the sheriff answered the judge's question.

"Not hardly."

Judge Seeley frowned. "Now that's too bad. A little friendliness would make things a lot easier." He held out a pen to Bri. "Just sign on all the lines that Cora highlighted."

Bri didn't waste any time taking the pen. If she hurried, she might still have a chance to make sure Minnie didn't contact her brothers. Without one glance at the documents, she signed each highlighted line, then handed the pen back to the judge.

He took it and released his breath. "So that's that."

Bri held out her hand. "Thank you, Judge Seeley. And I hope you will stop by Dogwood real soon and say hi to the family. But for now, would it be too much to ask for a ride out to Miss Hattie's?" When the judge looked a little surprised, she quickly amended. "Of course, if you're worried about your reputation—"

"Not at all," the judge said. "Minnie and I go way back. It's just that I thought that you understood the conditions of your release. You can't go back to Miss Hattie's until you start your community service."

Her eyes widened. "Today?"

He glanced down at his watch. "Seein' as it's still early, I think it's an ideal time."

Since the judge had already been so lenient, there was nothing for Bri to do but nod. "Of course. I'll just call Miss Minnie and let her know I'll be home a little later."

"No need for that." The judge grabbed his bright orange cap that was hooked on the back of the chair. "I already talked with Miss Minnie, and she knows that for the next two weeks you won't be gettin' home until late."

Two weeks?

Bri's mouth dropped open, and she stood there staring at the judge for what felt like a good five minutes before she could find her voice. "Exactly what will I be doing for two entire weeks?"

The judge pulled on his cap, the side flaps dangling down over his ears. "You'll have to ask the sheriff that since your community service is becoming his new housekeeper."

"What?" the sheriff and Bri both said in unison.

The judge only smiled at their shock. "It's a great idea, isn't it? Seein' as how the sheriff was the one who suffered, it seems only fair that he should be the one who benefits from your community service. Of course, I didn't come up with it entirely on my own. Miss Minnie was the one who called my cell and got me here. The one who, after finding out about Dusty losing his housekeeper, suggested the perfect solution."

"Minnie did this?" Bri's voice had become shrill and unfamiliar.

The judge chuckled and shook his head. "That woman has always had a good head on her shoulders."

"A crazy head!" The words slipped out of Bri's mouth

as her anger started to build. "And you're even crazier if you think that I'm going to work for that man." She jabbed a finger at the sheriff. "This is America, and you can't force a woman into servitude."

The smile left the judge's face, replaced with confusion. "But I thought you agreed with the terms." He nodded down at the signed papers. "And it's not servitude as much as community service. A community can't have a stressed-out sheriff. And anyone can see that Dusty's anger is due to the stress he's been under since his housekeeper up and quit on him. A man can't have pressure at work and pressure at home. A man needs a clean house and a warm meal to replenish his mind and body."

"So you're giving Miz Cates to me?"

The deep voice of the sheriff cut in, and Bri glanced over at him. His sullen anger was gone. Now he looked smug, like a cat that was holding a mouse in his mouth just waiting to swallow.

"As if!" Her eyes narrowed on him before she turned back to the judge. "You'll have to find him another housekeeper. I'll even be happy to pay her time and a half—no doubt she'll earn it working for such an angry man."

The judge gave her a stern, fatherly look. "Now, Brianne, I'm sure your folks would agree that you owe more than just money to the sheriff. And a little light housekeepin' for two weeks isn't gonna hurt you." He picked up the papers. "But if you'd rather go through the system, I can set bail and call your brothers so they can get their lawyers—"

"Fine!" she snapped. "I'll work for the sheriff."

Judge Seeley's shoulders relaxed. "Now, that's my girl. I'll just go get Cora to make copies of these."

Once the door had clicked closed behind him, Bri turned to Sheriff Hicks, who was now leaning on the desk.

"I assume by that smug look on your face that this will appease your desire for revenge, Sheriff," she said.

"Nope." He folded his arms over his chest. "But it's a start."

Chapter Nine

BRI WASN'T SURPRISED THAT Sheriff Hicks didn't live within the city limits of Culver. Most people from small towns didn't live in the actual town. Bri's parents' farm was seventeen miles from Dogwood. And Brant and Elizabeth's hundred-acre spread a good twenty.

What did surprise Bri was the size and condition of the house that the sheriff pulled up to. It was no more than an adobe shack with a sun-bleached door and a front window with a huge crack angling down the center.

"You don't need a housekeeper. You need a bulldozer." It was the first time she'd spoken since climbing into his squad car, and as soon as the words were out, she felt a twinge of remorse. No matter the circumstances, her mama had raised her to be polite and kind, not rude and heartless. She started to apology when he spoke.

"Now, why would I need a bulldozer when I have me a slave?" He turned those mirrored glasses on her for a brief second before opening the door and getting out.

Bri watched as he rounded the hood of the car. He was almost to the front door before it dawned on her that he had no intention of opening her door. His breach of manners should've annoyed her; instead, it was liberating. Why did she have to be nice and mannerly to a man who had obviously been raised in a barn?

With something that felt an awful lot like relief, Bri climbed out and followed him inside. She stepped over the threshold to find him pushing back the heavy drapes that hung over the window.

The front room was small and had a kiva-style fireplace on one side and a tiny kitchen on the other. There was very little furniture. A worn recliner and wooden rocker sat in front of the fireplace, and a small table and mismatched chairs separated the living room from the kitchen. The walls could've used a good coat of paint and some pictures, but the floor looked like it had recently been tiled. The red Saltillo tiles shone in the little bit of sunshine that was strong enough to filter through the dirty glass of the window.

"You can start with the windows," the sheriff said as he walked into the kitchen. He opened a cabinet beneath the sink and pulled out a bottle of Windex and a roll of paper towels.

Bri really wanted to use the standard "I don't do windows," but she bit back the words. It was only two weeks and much better than the alternative.

She started toward him to take the cleaning items and tripped over the crumpled edge of a throw rug, landing hard against the sheriff's chest. It was becoming a regular occurrence. A rather nice occurrence.

He dropped the Windex and his hands closed around her waist like two bands of very warm steel as her cheek bumped against the star on his chest. She caught a quick whiff of laundry detergent and spicy soap before she was set back on her feet.

"You're sure a clumsy little thing," he said.

She glanced up to find mirrored lenses looking back at her from beneath the brim of his tan hat, and she had to wonder how he could see in the dimly lit room. Maybe he was like a bat and had some kind of internal tracking beam. A tracking beam that not only located prey but drew prey to him.

Bri felt drawn. Drawn to the muscular curves of his body and the seductive slant of his mouth. Gliding her hands up his chest, she rose to her toes and tipped her head to the side. But before she could get a taste of those unsmiling lips, his radio crackled and Cora Lee's voice rang out.

"We've got problems, Dusty."

It took a moment for the sheriff to step back and unclip the radio from his belt. He lifted it to his mouth, the same mouth Bri still wanted to kiss, and pushed the button on the side. "What's up?"

"It seems that the sheriff of Haskins County has just shot himself in the foot."

"Sam Winslow?" The sheriff moved over to the refrigerator and pulled out a bottle of water. But instead of drinking it, he pushed up his hat and rubbed the cold bottle over his forehead. "Some kids must be playing a trick on you, Cora. We both know that Sam doesn't carry a loaded gun."

The radio crackled again as Cora answered. "I would've thought the same thing if it hadn't been Doc Mathers who called me. They were loading Sheriff Winslow into the ambulance as we spoke."

The sheriff placed the bottle on the counter. "Well, damn. What hospital are they taking him to?"

"The one in Odessa, but I think you should wait on the hospital visit until you've checked out things in Bramble. According to Doc Mathers, the entire town has gone crazy." Cora Lee paused. "Or crazier than usual."

The sheriff released his breath in an exasperated sigh. "I'll check it out." He started to hook the radio back on his belt when Cora spoke again.

"Did you drop Bri off at your house? You aren't working her too hard, are you, Dusty? I mean, she isn't exactly used to that kind of work—or probably any kind of work, for that matter. But she's sure a sweet little thing. It just about broke my heart leaving her in that jail cell last night with only grumpy ol' you for company—"

"I'll talk with you later, Cora," the sheriff said, cutting her off. Before Cora could utter another word, he turned down the volume and headed for the door, issuing orders as he went. "Once you finish with the windows, you can clean the bathroom. The cleaning supplies are under the sink—"

"You stayed at the jail with me last night?" Bri asked.

He stopped and slowly turned. "We don't usually leave our prisoners alone. Especially ones who try to escape out the windows."

"I didn't fit."

"I noticed."

She stared into the mirrored lenses. "So why didn't you let me know you were there?"

He stared down at the floor for a moment. "I think it's best, Miz Cates, if we stay as far away from each other as possible."

"And how do you figure we do that when I'm going to be working for you for the next two weeks?"

"Very easily. You arrive after I go to work and leave before I get home. I'll have a list of things I want done waiting for you every morning." He turned and reached for the door handle.

"Wait!" She grabbed his sleeve. "You can't just leave me clear out here without a car or a phone. What if you get delayed?"

He took the cell phone out of his front pocket and handed it to her. "I'll be back to take you to Miss Hattie's after I check on things in Bramble."

Before Bri could argue, the door squeaked closed behind him. She thought about calling Miss Hattie's and balling Minnie out for getting her into this predicament, but then decided to wait until her temper cooled. With nothing else to do, she pocketed the phone and picked up the Windex and the roll of paper towels. Although within thirty minutes, she realized that Cora Lee was right. She didn't know squat about housekeeping.

The front window looked almost as bad as before she'd started. Once she got one streak rubbed out, another would appear. She had just finished working on a streak by the huge crack when the cell phone vibrated in her pocket.

Since it was Dusty's, she probably should've ignored it. But what if it was an emergency? Something that needed to be handled right away? Without another thought, she pulled it from her pocket and answered. There was a long pause before a child's voice came on.

"Oops, I think I gots the wrong number. I'm lookin' for my pa."

"Does your pa have a name?"

"Dustin James Hicks," the little girl said as if reciting something wonderful. "But everyone calls him Dusty. Except for my mommy, who calls him Dustin. I just calls him Pa. Who are you?"

It took a moment for Bri to digest the information that the mean sheriff was a "pa" to a cute-sounding little girl. No doubt, the same little girl who had been in the photographs in his office. Bri glanced around the house, looking for any evidence that a child had been there. Or a wife. Of course, the sheriff couldn't be married. Not when half of Culver's female population was bringing him baked goods in hopes of a marriage proposal.

"I'm your pa's housekeeper." Bri moved into the hallway and glanced in the first room. It was obvious that this was Dusty's room. His wrinkled sheriff shirts spilled out of a clothes hamper. And an identical pair of cowboy boots to the ones he wore sat just inside the open closet.

"Like Cinderella?" the little girl asked.

Bri laughed as she moved on to the next room. "Sorta."

"Does you have yellow hair and a tiara?"

"Black hair and no tiara."

"Like Snow White at the dwarfs' house," the little girl stated.

Bri glanced in the small bathroom with the tiny sink and mirror. "Yeah, pretty much. So you're Dusty's daughter?"

"Uh-huh. Emma James Hicks. Emma for my grandma who dieded and James for my pa's between name. But I don't really like James 'cause it's a boy's name. You gots a between name?"

The child had an infectious personality that had Bri smiling.

"Yes," she said. "And it's a boy's name just like yours.

Brianne William Cates. And William is a lot worse than James. Especially when you have a brother who likes to call you Willie."

Emma giggled. "Willie is a silly name. But I like Brianne. It sounds like a princess name."

"Thank you. I've always loved the name Emma."

"Pa calls me Emmie," she continued. "And Nugget because I looked like a little tiny nugget when I was in my mommy's belly."

"Do you live with your mother?"

"Uh-huh, but soon I get to come see my pa."

Bri opened the last door in the hallway. This room had no furniture in it and looked to be in the early stages of remodeling. A plastic tarp covered the tile floor, and paint cans, brushes, and rolls of wallpaper sat just inside the door. In the center of the room, some kind of a workbench had been set up with chisels, sandpaper, an electric saw, and a drill. But Bri didn't pay attention to the tools as much as the tall wooden structure that sat in the middle. Since the wood was unfinished, it took her a moment to figure out what she was looking at. The front had tall towers and parapets and the back was open with three shelves that would be perfect for dolls to play in.

"It's a castle." Bri didn't realize that she had said the words until Emma chimed in.

"My pa's house?" she said in an excited voice. "My pa lives in a castle? 'Cause I knew he would. And when he gets my room all ready for me, I gets to come and visit him at his castle. And we gets to stay up late and watch *Beauty and the Beast* and eat—"

"Emma James!" A woman's voice came through the receiver. "Where are you?"

"Gots to go, Brianne," Emma whispered. "But take good care of Pa's castle."

The phone went dead.

Slowly, Bri took the cell phone from her ear, but her gaze remained on the partially finished dollhouse. It was obvious that a lot of time and effort had gone into building it. The wood was smooth from multiple sandings, and all the screw heads had been covered with wood putty.

Bri's own father had built her a dollhouse and surprised her with it one Christmas, but Bri hadn't even thought of all the time and love that had gone into the house until now. And if her daddy had been there, she would've given him a big hug and kiss to show her gratitude.

Thinking about her daddy had a good dose of guilt settling in Bri's stomach. She hadn't thought of the sheriff as a father. She'd just thought of him as another arrogant male she was forced to deal with. Now she realized that he might be arrogant, but he was only doing his job. She was the one at fault. The one who ran him off the road, pepper-sprayed him, and acted like a spoiled child who wasn't willing to take responsibility for her actions.

Glancing once more at the castle, she turned and walked out of the room, closing the door behind her. In the living room, she picked up the window cleaner. She couldn't make up for what she'd done, but she could certainly do a little housekeeping.

Not for the arrogant sheriff, but for the pa who was building a castle for his little princess.

Chapter Ten

NOTHING LOOKED OUT OF THE ORDINARY when Dusty pulled into Bramble. All the shops that lined Main Street were open for business, and folks seemed to be going about their weekday routine as usual. He thought about stopping by Doc Mathers's but decided the best place to find out what was going on in the town was at Josephine's Diner.

Besides, after spending the night at his office, he could use a cup of Josephine's strong coffee. He hadn't slept a wink the night before. Not because the couch in the reception area was uncomfortable—it had been comfortable enough the other nights he'd slept at the jail so he could keep an eye on a prisoner. No, his sleepless night had more to do with the prisoner.

Brianne Cates not only screwed with his mind, she screwed with his body. Ever since meeting her, he'd been in a constant state of arousal. And the kiss in the jail cell had only added to his horniness. Throughout the night, his mind conjured up all kinds of scenarios about what would've happened if he hadn't stopped kissing her. And when he finally did doze off, his dreams were filled with prisoner and prison guard fantasies that had Dusty waking with a hard-on that could jack up a semi.

Hell, his desire hadn't even dwindled when the judge arrived to issue his ridiculous verdict. Of course, just the thought of Bri being his slave was a turn-on. Which was why he had no business going along with the judge. Even if he didn't see Bri during the day, the thought of her being in his house—touching the sheets he slept on and the clothes he wore—was enough to make him crazy. So the sooner he released her from her community service the better. And he intended to do just that as soon as he dealt with whatever was going on in Bramble.

Dusty was only a few feet from the front door of Josephine's when he realized something was very wrong. People weren't sitting in the booths or at the tables gossiping over their morning coffee. Instead, they were all crowded around the counter. When he pulled open the door, a wall of angry grumbling welled out, and he had to raise his voice to be heard over the din.

"Hey, now. What's going on here?"

The grumbling stopped, and everyone turned. Having spent his fair share of time in Bramble, Dusty recognized a number of faces. It was Rye Pickett who answered him. Rye was a gentle giant who never had a bad word to say about anyone. Although now he had more than a few.

He held up his cup. "Is it too much for a man to ask for a hot cup of coffee, Sheriff? This is as cold as the water in Sutter Springs in late February."

"If you think your coffee is cold, you should try my eggs," Darla said. Darla was a sweet, middle-aged woman who was always working on one craft or the other. Today was the exception. Her fingers moved like she was knitting, but there were no needles or yarn in sight. "As cold as my eggs were," she continued, "you'd think that Josephine was keepin' her hens in the deep freeze."

"At least you got coffee and eggs," Rossie Owens chimed in. Rossie owned Bootlegger's Bar and had given Dusty a free beer on more than one occasion. "I've been here over an hour and haven't even been waited on."

That started the grumbling again.

"Now, folks," Dusty said, "I'm sure Rachel Dean will be more than happy to take care of your concerns without you getting all riled up."

"Of course she would," Rye said, "if she was here. But that's the problem, Sheriff. Rachel Dean quit yesterday, leavin' us at the mercy of her." He jabbed a thumb over his shoulder.

The crowd parted to reveal a woman Dusty never would've placed behind a diner counter. To his knowledge, Cindy Lynn had never worked a day in her life. As Bramble's resident snob and president of the Ladies' Club, she preferred to gossip, plan parties, and flirt with anyone who wore pants. Now, here she stood with her normally curled and teased bleach-blond hair shooting in all directions and her thickly mascaraed eyes leaking down her cheeks.

"I don't care what the reverend says," she sobbed. "I'll try to stop gossipin', but servitude is for the birds!" She jerked off her stained apron and tossed it to the counter before racing past Dusty and out the door.

Everyone started speaking at once, not about why Cindy Lynn was working at Josephine's, but about the poor service and cold food. Dusty listened to their complaints for a few moments before he held up a hand.

"Would someone please tell me why Rachel Dean quit?"

The crowd quieted as Darla answered the question. "So she could discover the cure for cancer."

Thinking that he was so distracted by her hands knitting with no needles that he hadn't heard her correctly, Dusty leaned closer. "Excuse me?"

"She quit so she could discover the cure for cancer." Rye Pickett set his coffee cup down on the counter none-too-gently. The thick stuff inside barely even rippled. "And I've got to tell you, after drinkin' this sludge, I might just need it."

The crowd started to get riled again, but Dusty jumped in before they could get out of hand. "So you're telling me that Rachel Dean thinks she can cure cancer? Where did she come up with that crazy idea?"

Everyone spoke at once, but this time they said the exact same thing.

"Reverend Josiah Jessup."

It only took a moment for things to fall into place. Dusty's muscles tightened in his neck.

"Is this the same reverend who looks like Elvis and drives a big red Cadillac?"

Rye nodded. "That's the one. I ain't never been much of a religious man myself, but Reverend Jessup has changed all that. The man is like one of them one-eight-hundred fortunetellers—except he don't charge you five dollars per minute. The saintly man gives all his fortunes for free." He hooked his thumbs into the tool belt strapped around his waist. "He took one look at me and told me I was in the wrong bid-ness. Said I had carpenter hands just like Jesus and needed to build things."

He lifted the most pathetic-looking birdhouse Dusty had ever seen off the stool next to him and set it on the counter. "So I quit my job at Dalton Oil and started buildin'. I figured I needed to start small before I moved on to a big project. I worked straight through the night and, after only fourteen hours, ended up with this beaut." He tapped the very peak of the birdhouse, and with a creak and a clatter, it folded like a house of cards. Rye stared at the pile of wood in confusion. "I guess I needed to use more Elmer's."

"Try hot glue," Darla said as she knitted with the imaginary needles and yarn. "It works like a charm." Her expression turned sad. "In fact, you can just have my glue gun and cases of glue since I won't be needin' them now that the reverend has made me see how frivolous my craft hobbies were."

Dusty's shoulders tightened even more. He had always thought that Darla's creations were a little over the top. Especially the "Guns and Roses" float she had made one year for the homecoming parade. But the woman reminded Dusty of his mama, who also liked to knit, and the thought of some evangelistic minister showing up and talking her out of doing something she got so much pleasure out of really pissed him off.

Not to mention the fact that Rye was now out of a job.

Or that Dusty really could've used a cup of Rachel Dean's coffee.

"Where is this reverend?" he asked.

"I'm not sure where he is right now," Darla said. "He was stayin' with Sheriff Winslow and Myra until Sam shot off his pinkie toe and they had to head to the hospital."

Without another word, Dusty turned for the door as Rye yelled out.

"But ain't you gonna do something about my coffee?"

"Sorry, Rye," he called back over his shoulder. "I'm a sheriff, not a restaurant manager."

Dusty was almost to his squad car when he made the mistake of glancing down the street. He stopped dead in his tracks, and his jaw dropped. Doc Mathers had been right. The entire town of Bramble had gone stark-raving crazy. And the cherry on the top of that craziness was heading straight toward him.

"Hold up there, Sheriff!" Mayor Sutter called as he pedaled toward Dusty.

At least, Dusty thought it was Mayor Sutter. The voice and handlebar mustache were the same. What was different was the clothing. Instead of western wear and cowboy boots, the mayor wore tight biker shorts that revealed a pair of skinny, white-as-death legs and a black nylon shirt with a vibrant orange stripe.

"I'm glad I caught you," the mayor said as he rolled to a stop. With his biking shoes clipped to the pedals, the bike started to topple like Rye's birdhouse. Fortunately, Dusty caught it before the mayor hit the ground. While Dusty held on to the bike, Harley worked to get his feet free. When he finally succeeded, he took back the handlebars and stood on his tiptoes, his big belly protruding out like a nine-month-pregnant woman's.

And that wasn't the only thing protruding out of the tight nylon. Dusty cringed and looked away.

"Thank you, son," Harley said. "This exercise stuff is going to take some getting used to, but no one becomes the next governor of Texas by sitting on their butt." Before Dusty could get over the governor thing, the mayor continued. "So I guess you heard about Sam Winslow."

"Exactly what happened?"

"I'm not real sure. Sam was already drugged up by the time I reached the doc's office, and Myra was too upset to get much out of."

"I'm sure it's upsetting for your husband to get shot."

The mayor shook his head. "Sam will be fine. I think she was more upset about the accident moving the ladies' luncheon from her house to Wilma Tate's. The reverend is the guest speaker. And let me tell you somethin', that man can sure talk. If the ladies' club didn't have a strict rule about no men, I'd head on over to Wilma's myself." He glanced down at the bike, and his mustache drooped. "'Course, I'm a little too busy to hang out at a luncheon. I need to shed a few pounds before the campaign pictures. And figure out a snappy slogan. What do you think of 'Listen to Your Mutter, Vote for Harley Sutter'?"

Dusty couldn't bring himself to reply to that question. "I'm assuming that the Reverend Jessup is the one behind your desire to become the next governor of Texas."

Harley nodded. "I have to admit that I hadn't even thought about it until the reverend brought it up. I had planned on retiring and letting Hope Lomax take over. But the reverend made me realize that a man can't just give up his political duties and spend his days fishin'. He has a responsibility to the people. And if I can help the folks of Texas, I'm more than willin' to jump into the race."

Dusty could only imagine what would happen to the state of Texas if Harley Sutter became governor. Damned good parades and total chaos. Of course, the mayor would never get that far. And Dusty wasn't about to let the man suffer that kind of embarrassment.

"So was this Reverend Jessup there when Sam was shot?" he asked.

"I would imagine so. He was at Sam and Myra's when it happened. And speakin' of Sam, that's why I stopped you." He adjusted the strap on his bike helmet. "I wanted to talk with you about helpin' out while Sam is laid up. The doc said it would be at least a month."

"I don't have a problem helping out until Sam can get back on his feet," Dusty said. "So when is this luncheon at Wilma's?"

"This afternoon." Harley reached out and thumped him on the back. "I knew I could count on you, son. And it won't be like you'll have it all on your shoulders. I swore in a deputy just this morning."

As if on cue, a siren blasted and a patrol car came barreling down the street with lights flashing. Dusty had only a moment to close his eyes in exasperation before the car swung into the parking lot of the diner.

The siren had barely cut off before Kenny's head poked out the open window. "Lookee at me, Sheriff. I got me a si-reen and everything!"

Chapter Eleven

BY THE TIME BRI FINISHED CLEANING Dusty's house, she needed a shower in a bad way. As she stripped off her clothes and stepped into the tiny stall, she couldn't help feeling a deep sense of accomplishment. A feeling she hadn't felt since college.

While the rest of her family worked—her parents still ran the farm equipment business in Dogwood; Brant, Billy, and Beckett worked at C-Corp; and Beau had the Henhouse and Jenna's new nonprofit organization—Bri didn't have anything to do.

She would like to blame her sedentary lifestyle on her overprotective family who seemed happiest when she was doing nothing more than planning a party or getting her nails done, but the truth was she was still looking for her true calling. Thinking she would work at C-Corp, she had decided to major in business. After failing statistics, she dropped that major and went into architecture. When those classes bored her, she moved on to web design. Then interior design. Then engineering. Six majors later, she finally graduated with a degree in university studies. Which qualified her to do absolutely nothing.

But today, she hadn't done nothing. She'd done something. And she had a clean house to prove it.

The hot water felt wonderful, and she stood for a good five minutes under the showerhead. It was the perfect height for her, but she had to wonder how the sheriff managed it. He would have to scrunch clear down to get his head wet. The thought had her smiling. The smile faded when her imagination took a curve and she found herself knee-deep in a shower fantasy. She visualized the sheriff completely naked, imagining a body as tanned and muscled as the forearms displayed by his cuffed shirts. Once she had a good picture in her mind, she added her soapy hands skating over his hard flesh. Molding to the knots of his biceps. Sliding over the subtle ripples of his stomach. Cupping the smooth, hard muscles of his butt.

It was really too bad that the hot water ran out so quickly—the cold spray dousing the fantasy and her desire. Or maybe it was a good thing. She had no business fantasizing about Sheriff Hicks. Especially when he wasn't the type of man who could have a little fun without setting down a lot of rules and regulations. And Bri wasn't about to get into another serious relationship.

Especially when she hadn't gotten rid of her last boyfriend.

Bri still felt badly about Jared. She'd had no idea that he had fallen in love with her. She thought he viewed their relationship the same way she did: two friends who enjoyed thrill-seeking adventures. Her guilt about not making her feelings clear from the beginning was probably why she hadn't put her foot down as far as the stalking went. And why she had played dumb about how the picture had ended up on the Internet. That, and if her brothers ever talked with Jared, they'd find out about her death-defying acts. Which would piss them off twice as much as any naked picture.

Quickly finishing her shower, Bri turned off the water and reached for a towel. It was thin, thread-worn, and so small that, once tucked around her, it barely reached the tops of her thighs. She wrapped another around her wet hair turban-style before she left the steamy bathroom and headed into the sheriff's room to see if she could find a shirt that would work with her pants.

The room looked much cleaner. She had changed the sheets and made the bed. Organized his three pairs of shoes in the closet: dress, running, and boots. And cleaned the windows and mopped the tile floor. The only thing she hadn't touched was the top of the six-drawer dresser, mostly because it was covered with clutter: Chapstick, a pack of Dentyne gum, an extra sheriff's badge, a photograph of Emma in a silver frame, nail chippers... and a pair of shiny handcuffs.

They were identical to the cuffs he'd used on her. And just the sight of them had a tingle of excitement coursing through Bri's body, prompting her to reach out and pick them up.

The metal was cold, but it quickly heated in her palm. Her gaze drifted over to the bed as another fantasy took form in her mind. A fantasy that included her and a very naked sheriff, who was forcing her to do all kinds of naughty, naughty—

"What the hell are you doing?"

Bri's heart jumped to her throat as she whirled around to the doorway. Just that quickly the fantasy was erased by the reality of a fully clothed sheriff with a very grumpy scowl. His mirrored sunglasses pinned her like a fly on a glob of honey.

She hid the cuffs behind her back. "Umm...I was just straightening up."

His head dipped as he gave her the once-over. "In nothing but a towel?"

She tried to control her blush. "I thought you wouldn't mind if I showered."

He stepped closer, and without her heels, she felt like a naughty schoolgirl addressing the principal, which caused another fantasy to pop into her head. She blinked it away.

"Well, you're wrong," he said as he pulled off his sunglasses and tucked them in the open collar of his shirt. "I do mind. You're supposed to be cleaning, not enjoying my shower. Or messing with my things."

"Now why would I want to mess with your thing—things?" She pointed at the chest of drawers in an attempt to get his steely gaze off her. "I was just straightening your dresser. So is that your daughter? She's a real cutie. How old is she? Three? Four? My nephew Bobby is just a little over two and getting into every—" She glanced back and realized that his eyes hadn't wavered from her.

"What's behind your back?"

She sent him her most innocent, wide-eyed look. "Behind my back? Why, nothing." She laughed. "You're certainly paranoid, Sheriff. Now if you'll excuse me, I need to go get dressed so you can take me back to Miss Hattie's." She tried to step around him, but he caught her arm. The towel inched lower, and with one arm being held and the other hiding the handcuffs, there wasn't one damned thing she could do about it.

His gaze dropped to the exposed swells of her breasts. His hand tightened on her arm, and when he spoke, his voice sounded thin and airless.

"You're lying."

With that intense gaze locked on her, she felt a little airless herself. The man was standing way too close. So close that she could smell his spicy scent. So close she could feel his all-consuming heat. Suddenly, she couldn't seem to keep the stream of raunchy fantasies out of her brain. They converged in a tangle of hot, naked flesh and hard, unrelenting need.

Her nipples hardened against the thin terry towel. What little air she had froze in her lungs as she watched the sheriff's chest rise and fall. Once. Twice. Three times. His gaze lifted, and for the first time since meeting him, he didn't look pissed. He looked hot. Very, very hot.

"You're playing with fire," he said as his thumb caressed the inside of her arm.

She should've called a stop to things right then and there. It no longer mattered that he found out about her embarrassing infatuation with his handcuffs. What mattered was doing something really stupid. Something that would no doubt come back to haunt her like every other stupid mistake. Unfortunately, any logical thinking had been completely consumed with naughty fantasies.

"Maybe I like playing with fire," she said as she met his heated gaze head on.

There was only a second's pause before he spoke. "Then get ready to get burned."

In one fluid motion, he dropped her arm and pulled her up to meet his waiting mouth. The quick movement had both the towel on her head and the one on her body dropping to the floor. And there was something about being naked in a fully clothed man's arms that seemed so wrong...and at the same time, so right.

The kiss he gave her was much more demanding than the one in the jail cell. There he had allowed her to have control, but now he took charge, his lips scorching and his tongue unrelenting. His hands settled on her bare butt cheeks, and he lifted her closer to the hard press of his belt buckle and the ridge beneath his fly. She tried to accommodate their difference in height by standing on her tiptoes. When that wasn't enough, she stepped right up on the toes of his boots and wrapped a leg around his hips.

He groaned into her mouth and picked her up, carrying her over to the bed. He pulled away from the kiss with a nip of bottom lip before lowering her to the mattress. Since her experience with men was limited, she should've felt shy as his gaze devoured her from wet head to blue toenails. But she didn't. Her attention was too focused on the chest he revealed as he unsnapped his shirt. It was as tanned and muscular as his forearms and dusted with a sprinkling of golden hair.

His sunglasses clattered to the floor, but he didn't seem to notice as he slipped the shirt off and reached for his belt.

Bri's imagination hadn't even come close to the perfect male specimen who stood before her. With hips tilted forward and biceps flexed as he uncinched his buckle, he looked like one of the half-naked models her sorority sisters had used as their screen savers.

Leaving his jeans on, he knelt in front of her and separated her knees. Then with his hot gaze pinned on her, he leaned down and kissed the quivery spot between her legs.

Bri had had oral sex with only two men. Both experiences

had been disappointing because their technique had left
something to be desired. Dusty's technique left nothing to
be desired. Probably because he didn't just use his tongue.
He used his lips and mouth, sipping and tasting until he
found the exact spot that rocked her world. Once he located
it, he took complete control of her body. With each stroke
of his tongue, he brought her closer and closer to the zenith
of a mountain. To the top speed of a race car. To the perfect
elevation of the sky. And just when she thought she couldn't
take the excitement and anticipation for one second longer,
he sent her free-falling right over the edge.

And suddenly every other thrill-seeking thing she'd
ever done in life paled in comparison to this spectacular,
amazing, mind-blowing release. When she finally floated
back down to earth, she opened her eyes to discover him
watching her.

"So you want me to use those?" he asked.

Not sure what he was talking about, she made a guess.
"A condom? Yes, please."

A crooked smile teased one corner of his mouth. "Such
pretty manners, but I wasn't talking about a condom." He
stood and flipped open the top button of his jeans. "I was
talking about the handcuffs."

The oral sex hadn't caused her to blush, but that did.
Her face burned as she glanced over at the handcuffs she
still held in her hand. "Oh. Umm...maybe later."

His teasing smile died a sudden death. "There's not
going to be a later. You're going back to Miss Hattie's. As
far as I'm concerned, your community service is over—"
He hesitated. "Wait a minute, that's what this is all about,
isn't it? You thought a little sex with the lonely sheriff
would be enough to cancel out your community service."

It was hard to concentrate on what he was saying when her gaze was stuck on the bulge of pink cotton that pushed open his zipper. With her throat too dry to answer, he came to his own conclusions.

"Dammit to hell!" He zipped up his zipper with a zing and reached for his shirt. "You'd think I'd learn, but I'm like a shit-eating dog. I just keep coming back for more."

Bri blinked. "Excuse me?" She sat up. "If you're the dog, just what does that make me?"

"Figure it out!" He turned and headed out the door.

"You jerk." She grabbed the sheet, wrapped it around her, and followed after him. "I am not...poop. And I'm certainly not trying to get out of my community service by having sex with you."

Once he reached the living room, he swung back around. "Then what were you doing?" He waved a hand. "I come home to find a naked woman in my bedroom, drooling over my handcuffs."

"I was not drooling over your handcuffs." She lifted her hand to shake a fist at him before she realized that she still held the handcuffs. He shot her one of those guy looks that said "yeah, right." Which had her throwing the handcuffs straight at his head. He ducked just in the nick of time and now looked more pissed off than smug.

"Don't push it, Miz Cates."

Bri could've continued the argument, but she learned early on that the best way to win a fight with a man was to make sure you had the last word. Lifting the trailing sheet, she turned as if on a fashion-show catwalk. When she reached the bathroom, she flashed an innocent smile over her bare shoulder.

"But I like pushing you, Sheriff Hicks."

Chapter Twelve

Dusty had a crick in his neck.

A throbbing in his temples.

And a pain in his ass.

He glanced over at the woman who sat in the seat next to him. A woman who was looking out the side window of the cruiser as if she was on a Sunday drive. Her dark hair was pulled back in a ponytail. One blue-toenailed foot was propped up on his dashboard. And her arm stuck out the open window like a kid playing airplane.

"Have you ever been in a high-speed car chase?" Brianne glanced over at him.

It was hard to think with those blue eyes pinned on him. They were direct and disconcerting. Or maybe what was disconcerting were the images the pretty blue eyes evoked. Images of Brianne stretched out on his bed wearing nothing but a tiny skull-and-crossbones tattoo right below her hip bone. The tattoo had surprised him. She hadn't seemed like the type for a tattoo. Of course, her preoccupation with handcuffs should've warned him that there was a wild woman lurking just beneath the polished surface. The type of woman he had no business being with.

He looked away.

"There's not much call for high-speed car chases in Culver County," he said. "Although isn't a high-speed chase what got you here in the first place?"

She made a sound that was part snort and part exasperated huff. Exactly like Emmie made when he didn't know all the Disney princesses' names. "That wasn't high-speed. I wasn't going more than ninety. And what got me here is an arrogant lawman who can't seem to make up his mind—first you want a housekeeper, and then you don't." She pulled her arm in and reached for a knob on the dashboard. "Can we turn on the lights and siren?"

"No." He smacked her hand away. "And I want a housekeeper. Just not one who smears up my windows to hell and back, uses all my hot water, and likes handcuffs a little too much."

He wasn't sure why he brought up her preoccupation with his handcuffs. It was a topic best left alone. Especially when he glanced over to find her watching him with a heavy-lidded, dazed look—like she was thinking of all the things she wanted to do with his handcuffs.

To prove this, Brianne tipped her head to the side, a strand of black hair covering one eye, and said, "You can't tell me that you haven't used them for something other than law enforcement."

It took a good three swallows to get enough moisture back in his mouth so he could speak. "What I have and haven't used my handcuffs for is none of your business, Miz Cates." He looked back at the highway. It didn't help.

He could still see those inquisitive, sexy eyes in the clear blue of the Texas sky.

"Don't you think we're past Miz Cates and Sheriff Hicks?" she said.

Oh, they were past it all right. And he was still kicking himself over the fact.

"I think it's best if we keep things professional, Miz Cates," he said. "Which is exactly why I decided to release you from your community service and escort you back to Miss Hattie's. And admit it. You were never going to fulfill your end of the bargain anyway. You might've cleaned my house today, but you would've come up with a way to get out of it tomorrow—no doubt by calling your brothers."

Her arm went back out the window, and she held her palm up and fought with the wind for a few seconds before speaking. "I'd just as soon that my brothers didn't find out about this."

Dusty had to admit that he was relieved. He wasn't one to back down from a fight, but he sure wasn't one to instigate them, either. And he figured arresting their little sister and almost having sex with her was plenty of instigation. Damn, what had he been thinking? If Brianne wanted to, she could easily put together a lawsuit that would get him fired, or worse, end any chances of getting back Emmie. And wasn't that the reason for his abstinence? He wasn't about to give Heather any more ammunition. Well, she'd have plenty of ammunition if Brianne decided to pay him back for arresting her. Fortunately, it appeared that she worried about disappointing her brothers more than she enjoyed getting back at him.

She pulled her arm in and slumped down in the seat.

"They would be terribly disappointed if they found out about my reckless driving and..."

"Seduction of strangers?" The words just popped out. But once they were there, Dusty wasn't about to take them back. Just in case she decided to cause trouble, he wanted to make it perfectly clear who had provoked it. Unfortunately, she had a pretty good case for just the opposite.

"I know you think I planned what happened in the bedroom," she said. "But you're mistaken. How would I know when you were coming home? And even if I was waiting for you, why wouldn't I be waiting for you in something a little more seductive? I mean, how sexy is a woman in turban-wrapped wet hair and a threadbare towel?"

Very sexy. So damned sexy that it filled his mind almost as much as her being completely naked. There was just something about the way the tucked-in towel had weighed against her full breasts and peeked open just below the juncture of her thighs that was twice as sexy as the lingerie Heather had spent a fortune on. But Brianne was right. It didn't make any sense. And if she hadn't planned it, then he owed her an apology. Except he had never been good at apologizing.

"Look," he said as he pulled into the circular drive of Miss Hattie's. "I'm sorry if I misunderstood—"

"Crap!" She dove down to the floor.

"What the hell?" Applying the brakes, he looked around for some kind of justification for her actions. But there didn't appear to be anything amiss. The only thing different about the Henhouse was the silver BMW parked right in front.

He glanced down at Brianne huddled on the floor and waited for an explanation. He should've known it would be a crazy one.

"I lost a contact," she said. "In fact, I think I left it at your house. So if we could just go back and look, I would really appreciate it."

Dusty placed the car in park and turned off the engine before he took off his hat and ran a hand through his hair. "Try again."

The next lie only took a second. "I'm against women selling themselves for money. And even though the hens are retired, I don't want to promote that kind of backward thinking so I'd appreciate it if you took me to a hotel—any hotel."

He stared at the Texas license plate on the BMW. "Since the only thing different about Miss Hattie's is this car right here, I would say that it's the reason behind your floor dive and why you don't want to stay at the Henhouse anymore. Or not the car, as much as the person who's driving it. And since I can't see one of your brothers in a little BMW sports car, I'm going to have to make a guess and say it's an ex-boyfriend that you're not in any hurry to see."

He glanced down, and for once she wasn't giving him the sweet, innocent look that always seemed to precede a lie.

"Fine detective work, Sheriff," she said. "You hit the nail on the head. Although he wasn't really a boyfriend as much as a friend. At least, that's what I thought we were. Jared seemed to think otherwise and isn't willing to let things go."

"So he's stalking you?" When she nodded, Dusty was surprised at how annoyed he felt. "So why don't you just get a restraining order? I'm sure your family has lawyers that can take care of that."

Her eyes flickered. "True . . . but Jared really isn't a bad guy, and I hate to punish him for liking me a little too much. Besides, I'm sure he just needs some time to forget me—out of sight, out of mind kind of thing."

"Well, then you'll have to hide in the barn." Dusty reached for the door handle. "I've got business in Bramble that I need to take care of, and I can't be hauling you all over the countryside." The door was only partially open when she placed a hand on his leg. A pale, manicured hand that was way too close to his man parts for comfort. When she spoke, her voice was soft and pleading.

"I know you don't want me to stay with you, Dusty." There was something about the way she said his name that caused his stomach to do a crazy little flip. "But please don't let him find out that I'm here. Couldn't you just take me to a hotel or something? Any place but here?"

Dusty didn't completely believe her story. Not the part about a man falling head-over-heels in love with her and stalking her—that he had no problem believing. But there was something she wasn't telling him. Brianne Cates didn't seem like the type of woman who feared much. In fact, in the short time he'd known her, he got the feeling that she thrived on danger. So why was she obviously so desperate to leave?

A noise caused him to look up. Baby stepped out the front door and clicked her way across the front porch in her red high heels. She stopped at the top of the steps and stared in confusion at the BMW before her gaze tracked over to the sheriff's car.

Dusty got out and slammed the door. "Hi, Miz Baby." Holding his hat in his hand, he nodded at the car. "New guests?"

"Well, hello, Sheriff," Baby said in her breathy voice

before looking back at the car. "Actually, I don't know who this belongs to. All the guests park over there." She pointed to the dirt lot that held only a couple of cars. "And most of them have gone sightseeing today." She shrugged. "Oh, well, maybe Sunshine or Olive checked someone in that I don't know about. So how is Brianne doing?" She waggled a red-nailed finger at him. "I must tell you, Sheriff, that I was very upset when you took her away in cuffs. That is no way to treat a lady."

"You're right, ma'am." He rolled the brim of the hat in his hands. "But I think we've got things all figured out now."

"Well, I hope so." She smiled. "I always knew you were a good man. So where is Brianne?" She glanced back at his cruiser. "I thought you were bringing her home."

"I plan on it, Miz Baby," he said as he placed his hat back on. "But for now, I just wanted to make sure everything was okay here and Minnie hadn't pulled any more shooting stunts." He paused. "She was the one who scared off the reverend, wasn't she?"

Baby nodded. "I called because I was worried that we were going to have another episode like when Brant showed up and she—" She giggled nervously and backed toward the house. "You be sure and take care of our Bri, Sheriff. For now, I better get on in and help Starlet and Sunshine clean the rooms." With a click of heels, she disappeared back inside.

Once she was gone, he got in the car and drove around the BMW, mentally committing the license plate number to memory before he headed back down the road.

"Thank you."

The soft whisper had him glancing down at Brianne.

He didn't know why he hadn't given her away. Maybe because he understood what it felt like to have a relationship end badly. Or maybe he just had a soft spot for women in trouble. Still, he wasn't about to give in completely to those pretty blue eyes.

"You owe me."

A smile tipped the corners of her mouth. "It would seem that way. Are we back to me cleaning house?"

He returned his gaze to the long stretch of dirt road. "No, but I'm sure I'll think of something."

Chapter Thirteen

BRI DIDN'T REALLY WANT TO GO TO BRAMBLE. If word got back to her brothers that she wasn't at the Henhouse, there would be hell to pay. Still, it wasn't like she had much choice. Not with Jared snooping around. She just hoped that Minnie would send him packing like she had the reverend.

"What in the world is that?" she asked as Dusty drove past what appeared to be a bright pink train caboose without the train.

"That would be Josephine's Diner." He glanced over at her, pinning her with his mirrored lenses. "You mean you've never been to the diner?"

"I haven't visited a lot. Beau and Jenna Jay just finished building a house here. And Billy, Shirlene, and the kids usually come to Dogwood."

"What about their weddings?" His head tipped, and she could feel his eyes narrowing behind the sunglasses. "Come to think of it, I don't remember seeing you at Beau and Jenna Jay's."

She swallowed. "I caught the flu."

"And Brant's?"

"College exams."

"Billy's?"

"I was in New York with one of my friends, and my plane got delayed in bad weather."

He pulled into a parking space in front of the pharmacy, cut the engine, and turned to her. It was very disconcerting how looking at your own reflection could get you to tell the truth—probably because it was hard to lie to yourself. All Dusty had to do was stare at her, and the truth came spilling out of her mouth like an errant kid caught by her daddy.

"Fine! I lied, okay?" she said. "I lied about it all. I didn't go to Billy's because I didn't want him marrying a gold digger whose great-granddaddy had supposedly killed mine. I didn't find out until later that Shirlene is anything but a gold digger, and it was my own great-grandmother who shot her husband. Of course, by then it was too late. I'd already discovered how wonderful it was to miss my brothers' weddings."

Guilt had her looking away from Dusty and over to the old cowboy who sat snoozing on a bench in front of the pharmacy. "With my family's attention on the bride and groom, it wasn't on me. So for an entire weekend, I was free to go and do whatever I wanted without my brothers and parents interrogating me. Or making me feel guilty." She released her breath and slumped down in the seat. "Which makes me the most selfish person ever."

There was a long stretch of silence, and when Bri finally glanced over she found Dusty staring out the windshield. Since he didn't think highly of her in the first place, she expected him to call her out on her selfishness. Instead, he surprised her.

"I can understand that," he said. "I've always enjoyed peace and solitude."

While Bri was telling the truth, she probably should've mentioned that she hadn't really been enjoying peace and solitude as much as thrills and danger. But she figured that it was best to keep that information to herself. Especially when she and the sheriff had finally started communicating.

"So you have a big family, too?" she asked.

"No, just a sister. She lives in Corpus Christi with her husband and two kids. My parents moved there last year after my daddy retired." He took off his hat and smoothed a hand through his hair. "Talk about selfish. I haven't gone to see them once since they moved."

"College exams or the flu?" she teased.

He didn't crack a smile. "Personal problems." He hopped out and within seconds was opening Bri's door.

"I think I'll just wait for you in the car," she said.

Dusty rested an arm on the door. "Your brothers don't know about your stalker boyfriend, do they?"

Damn, the man was too smart for his own good.

"No," she said. "And believe me, you don't want them to know. Your jail isn't big enough for four angry Cates brothers."

Dusty shook his head in a way that said she was the most pain-in-the-butt woman he'd ever met, before he reached for the baseball cap on the dashboard. "Fine. I'll meet you back here in a couple hours and take you to Miss Hattie's." He tugged the hat down on her head, then pulled the cell phone she'd returned earlier out of his pocket and handed it back to her. "I'm sure you can hide your identity for that long."

She smiled up at him. "I think I might've misjudged you, Sheriff Hicks. You might have a heart after all."

"Doubtful, Miz Cates." He waited for her to get out before he walked around to his side of the car. Before he opened the door, he issued a warning. "Try to stay out of trouble."

"Trouble?" She sent him an innocent look as she stepped up to the sidewalk. "Now what would make you think that I would get in trouble?"

Even with his sunglasses on, she knew he rolled his eyes. She laughed as she watched him climb back into the squad car. With a simple tip of his hat, he backed out and took off down the street. Once he was gone, she didn't hesitate to call the Henhouse. Fortunately, Baby answered and, after only a few questions about when Bri would be back, gave the phone to Olive.

"Hi, Olive," Bri said, trying to keep her voice from betraying her anxiety. "So I was just wondering if anyone showed up today looking for me."

"If you're talkin' about the snooty dude in the fancy sports car, then the answer would be yes," Olive said. "He's talkin' to Miss Minnie as we speak."

Bri gave up her ruse. "Damn. She didn't tell him that I'm staying there, did she?"

"Minnie don't relay info to strangers. So who is this guy, Little Missy? And what does he want with you?"

"He's my ex-boyfriend," Bri said. "I broke up with him, and he hasn't gotten the message."

"You mean he won't take no for an answer?" Olive emitted a noise that sounded like Jigger's growl. "Whelp, we can't have that, now, can we? You don't worry about a thing, Little Missy. Ol' Olive will take care of this no-account." The phone clicked.

"Olive?" Bri glanced down at the cell phone, but the call had ended. She was about to call Olive back and warn her not to do anything illegal, when she glanced up and saw her nephew strutting down the street toward her. Billy was right. Jesse didn't look upset at all about missing the Disney cruise. His walk was jaunty and his smile bright as he waved to a group of teenagers who stood in front of the Dairy Treat. Obviously, sailing with Mickey wasn't that big of a deal to a high school kid. What was a big deal was Jesse telling his parents that he'd run into his aunt Bri in Bramble.

Bri tugged down her cap and started in the opposite direction. As she glanced back to see Jesse crossing the street to the Dairy Treat, she ran smack dab into someone coming out of the pharmacy.

"Pardon me," she said to the woman. A woman in lacquered-on jeans, a rhinestone western belt, and a hot pink t-shirt with the words *Gone Country* stretched over her large breasts.

Bri figured it was more like *Gone Crazy* when a sheriff's car drove past with a man Bri didn't recognize behind the wheel and the woman started sobbing like a sinner on Judgment Day.

"I ain't never gonna get married," she wailed as she crumpled into a heap in front of the pharmacy window.

Bri looked around for help, but no one seemed to be at all concerned by the weeping woman. People walked by without a backward glance, while the old cowboy on the bench continued to sleep. Since there was nothing else to do, Bri knelt down next to her.

"Are you all right?" she asked. "Can I call someone for you? Maybe a friend or a family member?"

"Nooo," the woman sobbed. "There's no one who can help—no one at all." She wailed for a few more minutes before she took a pink bandanna out of her back pocket and blew her nose with a loud honk. Once her nose was clear, she staggered to her feet. "Not unless they can make Kenny Gene my right half." Another sob broke loose. And not wanting to go back to the wailing, Bri tried to calm her.

"It's going to be okay," she said as she patted the woman's back. "It sounds like your boyfriend broke up with you, but there are other men out there who I'm sure will be your right half."

The woman stopped crying and stared at her as if she'd lost her mind. "Kenny broke up with me? Why would he do somethin' like that? The man ain't dumb. He knows a good catch when he sees one." She swiped at her swollen eyes before stuffing the hankie back in her pocket. "No, I broke up with him because he wasn't the right half to my whole. Something that was just recently pointed out to me. If he had been the right half, we would already be married." Her eyes narrowed. "And he would've been a lot more upset when I broke it off with him. Instead, he shrugged and said it was probably for the best seein' as how he had deputy duties to take care of."

"Well, if that's how he feels," Bri said, "you're probably better off without him."

"You're right," she sniffed before sending Bri a weak smile. "I'm Twyla, by the way."

Not wanting people to make the connection between her and her brothers, Bri offered up Beckett's nickname. "Willie."

"I bet you're married, Willie, ain't you?"

Bri shook her head. "No."

"Engaged?"

"No."

"Gay?"

Bri blinked. "Umm, no."

Twyla gave her the once-over. "Must be the name and the hair. But don't you worry, honey." She hooked her arm through Bri's and tugged her down the street. "Twyla will fix you right up. Makeovers are my specialty."

By the time they reached Twyla's house, Bri had learned the woman's life story. It seemed that Twyla's pre-occupation with weddings was more of an addiction. She had been married three times already and wouldn't rest until she'd made it four.

"I don't know what it is," Twyla said. "I guess there's just weddin' bells in my blood. This way, honey." She led her along a side path to a set of stairs that led down to a lower level door. On the door was a sign: CENSATIONAL CREATIONS BY TWYLA.

Bri pondered the misspelling and what the creations were until she stepped through the door. The basement had been converted into a beauty salon. Not a full-service salon like Bri went to in Austin. This salon had only one sink, one domed hair dryer, and one cutting station. Still, as she looked at all the hair products and appliances, she couldn't help feeling like a kid in a candy store.

Growing up, Bri had loved fixing hair. She had started with her dolls and worked up to her mother and brothers. Her mother dyed her hair a different color every week so it was more convenient to let Bri do it than go into town. And her brothers didn't like being guinea pigs for Old Man Johnson's scissor-happy hands. So starting in middle school, Bri had set aside time for dye jobs, trims, and the occasional buzzed football number. She had actually gotten pretty good at it.

Of course, it was just a silly hobby. There was no way that the youngest daughter of the Cates dynasty could become a beautician.

"You sit right down, sweetie," Twyla said as she closed the door behind her. "I happen to be runnin' a special this week on haircuts, and your hair could sure use some help. Especially if you want to attract a man."

Bri glanced at the cat clock on the wall and shrugged. "I guess I could use a trim—" The words were barely out before Twyla had her in the chair, cap off, and a cape snapped around her neck.

"You want a Faith Hill? Or a Reba? Personally, I think the Reba would look real cute with those big ol' eyes of yours." She had just picked up the pair of cutting shears, when the phone rang. "I'll be right back, honey." She hurried to the phone that hung on the wall, and Bri couldn't help listening in. Especially when Twyla's voice filled with sadness.

"You need to stop callin' me, Kenny Gene…no, I'm not makin' you potpies for supper. That's not how a breakup works…because the reverend said we ain't"—a tiny sob escaped—"soul mates." She hung up the phone and, before Bri could offer any comfort, raced up the stairs.

Bri started to follow her and then decided that Twyla could probably use a few minutes alone to collect herself. Besides, Bri couldn't wait to play beauty shop.

She tried out the sprayer on the shampoo bowl, looked through all the drawers at the cutting station, and had just started to curl a blond wig in Velcro rolls when a big-bellied man in biking shorts came in through the screened door.

"Hey, Twyla." He took off his biking helmet and hung it on the hat rack. "I hate to bother you without an appointment, but the reverend thinks I'll up my chances of becomin' the governor by a good twenty-seven percent if I cut off—" He turned, and his handlebar mustache twitched. "Well, beg pardon. I thought you were Twyla." He held out his hand. "Mayor Harley Sutter. You must be Twyla's cousin. She mentioned that you were comin' to visit. And I'd say you couldn't have picked a better time." He shook his head. "Poor thing has been a little out of sorts since she broke up with our new deputy."

His biking shoes clicked on the floor as he walked over and picked up the plastic cape from the back of the chair and placed it around his shoulders. "I was thinkin' about a George W. look, but then I thought it might be better to go for something that's a little more widely appreciated." He sat down in the chair and combed his fingers through his thinning hair. "Do you think with a little dye and some teasin' you could make it look like the King's?"

"I don't really—"

"No," the mayor said, "you're probably right. I don't want to seem like a follower. Of course, the reverend wasn't worried so much about the hair as he was about the mustache." He reverently touched the curled, waxed tips. "And I guess if it's all for the future of Texas..."

Chapter Fourteen

DUSTY HAD HOPED to arrive at the Tates' house after the luncheon, but when he stepped up on the porch, it sounded like the party was in full swing. If a party is what you could call it. The voice that drifted out the open window sounded more like a tent revival.

"...and I say onto you, Sisters of the Lord," a deep voice boomed, "it is up to you to keep your husbands on the straight and narrow."

A chorus of "amen" followed.

"Up to you to lead them down the path of righteousness."

"Amen, Reverend!"

"Up to you to find the strength to douse their carnal needs beneath the purity of your holiness—"

Having heard enough, Dusty pressed the doorbell. There was a mumble of female voices before Wilma Tate, who looked like she'd just experienced an hour of great sex, answered the door. Her cheeks were flushed, her eyes were twinkling, and her lipstick was smudged.

"I'm sorry, Sheriff," she said, "but I don't have time for socializin'. Reverend Jessup is almost done with his sermon, and I promised him that I'd play 'Bringin' in the Sheep' on my organ."

Dusty took off his hat. "You mean 'Bringing in the Sheaves'?"

Her eyes scrunched. "Sheaves? Well, that doesn't make any sense. What in the world is a sheave and why would you want to bring it in if you don't know what it is?"

Dusty could feel a headache coming on. Something that happened a lot when dealing with the people of Bramble. "I'm not here to socialize, Miz Tate. I'm here on business."

Her eyes got even scrunchier. "It's Elmer, isn't it? He's drunk again and in jail." She shook her head, causing the fake bird on her hat to dip like it was pecking her forehead. "I swear I've had it with that man. He was supposed to stay here so the reverend could lay hands on him—"

"No, it's not Elmer. I'm here to talk with Reverend Jessup."

"Why?"

"That's between me and the reverend."

"Oh, I get it," she said. "Sheriff Winslow sent you to bust up the luncheon because Myra's all upset because it moved to my house. But I'm not about to let you do it." She crossed her arms over her chest and glared at Dusty. "You march right back to the sheriff and tell him—"

"What seems to be the problem?" The Elvis impersonator appeared behind Wilma, looking much like he did when he drove past in his Cadillac. Except on closer examination, he didn't look like Elvis as much as a used car salesman in a really bad Halloween costume.

"Reverend Jessup?" Dusty asked.

"That would be me." The man gave him a practiced

smile. "And you're the sheriff that apprehended the criminal that was driving down the wrong side of the road."

"What criminal?" Wilma said. "You ran into a criminal in Bramble, Reverend Jessup?" She glanced back at Dusty, causing the bird on her hat to bob. "Well, I can't say that I'm surprised. We have all kinds of hooligans livin' here."

"Could I have a word with you in private, Reverend?" Dusty asked, although it wasn't really a question.

"Of course." He moved around Wilma, giving her a quick pat on the shoulder. "I won't be but a moment, Sister Tate. Why don't you entertain the crowd with your lovely organ playing?"

She gave the reverend a starstruck look before her eyes narrowed on Dusty. "You better watch your p's and q's, Sheriff. Reverend Jessup is a man of God, which means you're dealin' with somethin' much bigger than the law." She whirled around and disappeared into the house.

The reverend chuckled as he closed the door. "I do love a crusader for the Lord. Now what can I do for you, Sheriff? If this has something to do with that crazy driver, I can assure you that I don't even know the woman." His eyes grew thoughtful. "Although she does look familiar."

"And I'm sure you had nothing to do with her being on the wrong side of the road, either." Dusty pinned him with a hard stare.

The reverend's smile didn't even waver. "So is that why you're here? She claimed I was responsible for her reckless driving?"

Dusty shook his head. "Actually, I heard you were there when Sheriff Winslow was shot. I figured you could shed some light on the incident."

"I wish I could help you out, but I wasn't in the same room with the sheriff when the injury occurred."

"But you had something to do with the bullet being in the gun."

"Now why would you think that?"

"Possibly because every strange thing that's happening in Bramble has your name attached to it."

"And what kind of strange things are we talking about, Sheriff?"

Dusty knew when he was being taken down the path, but he decided to play along. "Rachel Dean quitting. Mayor Sutter deciding to run for governor. And Sam having bullets in his gun."

The reverend smiled. "Funny, but those things don't sound crazy to me at all. Waitresses quit all the time, mayors jump into gubernatorial races, and where I come from, sheriffs are supposed to carry loaded guns." He cocked his head. "Are you telling me that yours isn't loaded, either?"

A blast of organ music came out the window that sounded nothing like "Bringing in the Sheaves." It sounded more like Emmie beating on her toy piano. The reverend cringed, but Dusty stayed focus.

"I hope you never have to find out, Reverend." He put his hat back on. "Now I don't mind a little friendly preachin', but when it starts to cause problems for a bunch of kindhearted folks who wouldn't hurt a soul, then that's a different story." He paused. "I think you've worn out your welcome in Bramble."

Reverend Jessup's smiled wilted. "Are you kicking me out of town?"

"Nope. Just making a friendly suggestion."

"And if I don't choose to take it?"

Dusty shrugged. "Of course, that's totally up to you." He pulled his citation pad out of his pocket and started filling it out. "King One, right?" Before the reverend could answer, he tore off the citation and handed it to him. He nodded out at the Cadillac parked in front. "I believe if we measured, you parked within fifteen feet of that fire hydrant. That's a hundred-dollar fine."

Reverend Jessup stared down at the ticket for only a second. "Why, you—"

"Careful, Reverend." Dusty cut him off. "I'd hate to have to show you the inside of my jail. Of course, if you continue to cause trouble, that's exactly where you'll end up."

"You're messing with the wrong person," Reverend Jessup hissed. "I am a powerful man who won't have any problem calling in favors to get your badge."

Dusty tipped his hat. "Well, you just do what you have to do, Reverend . . . and I'll do the same." He headed down the porch steps, and when he reached his car and glanced back, the reverend was still standing on the porch watching him with a look that was anything but Christian.

"Reverend, my ass," Dusty said as he got into his car. Once he made a U-turn and was heading back toward town, he radioed in to Cora Lee and asked her to pull up whatever she could find on Reverend Jessup. He had just ended their conversation, when Kenny came zipping up behind him with flashing lights and blaring siren. Dusty heaved a sigh and pulled over in front of Sutter's Pharmacy.

"Hey, brother in arms!" Kenny greeted him as soon as Dusty opened his door. "I thought you should know that

I'm workin' overtime to clean up Bramble." He hitched up his belt, which was loaded down with every piece of law enforcement equipment known to man—and a few that had nothing to do with law enforcement. Like the Scooby-Doo flashlight. "I've already handed out fifty-two tickets and had to pull out my gun at least ten times."

Holy shit.

Dusty's head began to throb in earnest. He took a deep breath before speaking. "I thought Mayor Sutter and I both told you not to be using your gun?"

Kenny's eyes skittered away. "Well, I didn't exactly use it. I just pulled it out."

"And accidentally shot dead Jimmy Jenkin's front tire," Moses Tate said from his spot on the bench.

Dusty barely glanced at the old man before he held out his hand to Kenny. "Hand it over."

"But it was an accident," Kenny whined. "And Jimmy Jenkin's tire was almost bald to begin with." When Dusty's hand remained, Kenny's shoulders slumped. "Fine! But I'm keepin' the Taser." He pulled out his gun and slapped it in Dusty's palm.

"This isn't a game, Kenny." Dusty tucked the gun in the back of his belt. "And if you can't figure that out, I'll have the mayor hire someone who takes the responsibilities of this job seriously. You're not tasering anyone, and before you write out another ticket, I want you checking with me. Got it?"

Kenny nodded. "Yeah. I got it. But if I can't hand out tickets and practice with my gun, what else is there to do?"

An idea popped into Dusty's head. One that was pretty damned good if he did say so himself.

"Have you heard about the new reverend in town?"

Kenny rolled his eyes. "That's all I've heard about. He's the main reason that Twyla broke up with me. It seems the reverend convinced her that I ain't the right half to her hole. Now, I ain't spent a lot of time in church, but I don't think a man of God should be talkin' to a woman about her hole. Do you, Sheriff?"

Dusty chewed on his lip to keep from laughing. "No, I sure don't. And that's exactly why I'd like you to keep an eye on the man. It seems to me that he's up to no good."

"You want me to stake him out? Because I'm good at stakin' people out." He glanced behind him. "Ain't I, Moses? I staked out Beau Cates and found out that the Cates boys wanted to close down Dalton Oil and ruin Bramble. So I could get the dirt on this reverend, too."

"I believe you can." Dusty smiled. *Or drive the reverend so crazy that he leaves town.* "The man is over at Wilma Tate's as we speak."

"I'll get on it, Sheriff." He hustled back to his car, all the gadgets he had attached to his belt jangling. But before he climbed in, Dusty issued one last order.

"No lights or sirens."

Kenny shot him a sullen look. "Hell, I don't get to have any fun."

Dusty watched as Kenny got into the squad car and zipped off, barely missing the bumper of Dusty's car. It was probably a big mistake turning Kenny loose on the reverend, but it wasn't the first mistake Dusty had made that day. And it didn't look like it was going to be the last.

"You haven't seen a woman in a baseball cap, have you, Moses?" He addressed the question to the beat-up straw cowboy hat tipped over the old man's face.

"The one you dropped off?"

"That would be the one."

"Well, I couldn't tell you where she is now, but she headed off with Twyla about an hour ago."

"Thanks." Dusty turned back to his car but stopped halfway to the door when Moses spoke.

"It does make you wonder." The old man pushed up his hat, revealing blue eyes that were faded but still piercing.

"Wonder what?" Dusty asked.

Moses took his time pulling out the Solo cup and spitting into it. "Just what Sheriff Hicks is doin' with the Cates's little sister." When Dusty didn't say anything, Moses put the cup back and tipped his hat over his face. "It does make you wonder."

Dusty wondered about the same thing. What was he doing with Brianne Cates? If he knew what was good for him, he'd hop right back into his car and get the hell out of Dodge. Unfortunately, about then, an image of Brianne buck-naked floated through his mind like the clouds floating through the west Texas sky. Perfectly formed breasts with luscious, raspberry nipples the size of silver dollars. A smooth, firm stomach with the sweet slit of a belly button. A skimpy line of dark hair covering a tempting pink cove of heat—

Damn, he needed to get a grip. What the hell was the matter with him? Of course, he knew the answer to that question. He was horny. And he had every right to be horny. It had been months since he'd been with a woman. Six to be exact. Six long months since the Widow Murphy had moved to Arkansas to be with some guy she met on Match.com.

Not that Dusty could blame her. He hadn't exactly

treated her like a girlfriend. He'd treated her more like an acquaintance he occasionally had sex with. It had worked out quite nicely for him. Cheryl was pretty, discreet, and available. But, obviously, it hadn't worked out so well for Cheryl.

Now Dusty found himself in desperate need of a woman. Just not a dark-haired beauty with a pirate tattoo.

Which didn't explain why, several minutes later, he was pulling up in front of Twyla's house. Or why he felt a sudden surge of joy when he walked up the pathway and heard Brianne's laughter floating out the screen door.

Dusty peeked in and froze as he soaked in the curve of her hips and the sway of her thick, black hair. She glanced behind her, and a smile lit her face. A smile that caused his heart to seize up as if clenched in her small fist.

"Hey! Come on in. I'll just be a few minutes more." Her smile was so dazzling that it took him a moment to realize what she was doing. She stood behind a salon chair, blow-drying someone's hair. Dusty glanced in the mirror.

Rachel Dean?

"Well, hey there, Sheriff Hicks," Rachel said as soon as Brianne turned off the hair dryer. "Have you already met Twyla's cousin, Willie?"

Dusty pulled open the screen door and stepped into the salon. "Willie?" Brianne sent him one of her wide-eyed innocent looks as Rachel Dean continued.

"Yep, seems she stopped by to help Twyla out. And I must say that she's been a real lifesaver to me after my little accident."

"What accident are we talking about?" Dusty asked.

Before Rachel could say anything, Brianne jumped in.

"It seems that Rachel is attempting to discover the cure for cancer." As if she'd been doing it all her life, she sectioned off a piece of Rachel's salt-and-pepper hair and wound it around a curling iron.

Rachel tipped her head slightly to look at Dusty. "It makes perfect sense considerin' my great-grandma was the most sought-after healer in these parts. Of course, I can't just start with the Big C. I have to work my way up." Her mouth tipped down in a frown. "I thought I had the right measurements for Granny Burke's dandruff remedy, but obviously I did something wrong. Glad I tried a little on my eyebrows before the hair on my head."

"Me too." Brianne shot Dusty a warning look before lifting Rachel's bangs to reveal her forehead.

A forehead with no eyebrows.

Chapter Fifteen

"SOMETHING HAS TO BE DONE," Bri said as she walked down the pathway to Dusty's car. "Next time, Rachel Dean could come up with a concoction that really does some damage. And did you see the pathetic state Twyla is in? The woman is heartbroken."

"With the loud wailing coming from upstairs," Dusty said, "it was hard not to notice."

"I'm just glad that Rachel is going to stay the night with her." She went to reach for the car door handle at the same time as Dusty, and their hands brushed. The jolt that went through her was very similar to the one she'd gotten when she topped out at one-forty in the stock car.

She glanced back at Dusty. With twilight setting in, he'd removed his aviators. His eyes held the last traces of sunlight, along with an emotion that made Bri's tummy all light and airy. She took a step closer. Dusty took a step back.

"I should get you back to Miss Hattie's. I'm sure your boyfriend is gone by now."

"Ex-boyfriend. And I'm not ready to go back to Miss

Hattie's." She moved within inches of his wrinkled shirt. "I'm hungry."

"I know." He took another step back. "But I can't feed what you're hungering for, Miz Cates."

"And what is that?"

"Something I can't give you. Or any woman, right now."

It was the worst possible thing he could've said. Bri had never been able to ignore a challenge.

Tipping back her head, she gave him the pleading look that had always worked on her brothers. "Not even a cheeseburger with everything on it? Besides, we need to figure out what to do about Reverend Jessup."

"We don't need to figure out anything." He left her to open her door and walked around to his side.

"Of course we do," she said once they were both in the car. "We can't just let the man manipulate people's lives like he's doing. You should've seen the tears in Rachel's eyes when she was talking about working at Josephine's Diner. Obviously, she loves waitressing and has no business dabbling in medicine."

She clicked her seat belt. "And poor Mayor Sutter. The reverend has the man believing that he can be the next governor of Texas if he'll just shave off his mustache. I swear the mayor almost passed out when I pulled out the razor."

Dusty glanced over at her. "You didn't..."

"No. I talked him out of it, but I don't know for how long if something isn't done."

"There's not much to do." He pulled away from the curb. "The man hasn't broken any laws."

"But he's playing with people's lives—and their livelihoods. Certainly, there's something you can do to stop him."

"I have him under surveillance, but unless he screws up—something I think he's too smart to do—there's not a thing I can do about his manipulations." He glanced over at her. "And just why are you so concerned about the folks of Bramble? You haven't even known them for more than a few hours."

It was a good question. One Bri didn't have an answer for.

She looked out the window as they drove down Main Street. The stores and businesses were all closing up for the night. One by one, Closed signs were flipped into place and lights clicked off. Even put to rest for the night, the town gave off a warm, comfortable feel.

"I don't know," she said. "Some of it probably has to do with it reminding me of Dogwood. But most of it has to do with the people. There's just something about them…"

"That makes you want to cuddle them," Dusty finished for her.

She laughed. "Exactly. Although I wouldn't expect that sentiment from a big, bad sheriff."

Dusty glanced over at her. "I'm not all that big and bad. If I was, I'd take you straight back to the Henhouse."

"So where are you takin' me, Sheriff?"

His gaze returned to the highway. "Don't look so smug. All you're getting is a cheeseburger."

The truck stop was right off the highway. It had a huge lot for the eighteen-wheelers to park and plenty of diesel gas pumps. But the restaurant was nothing more than a hole-in-the-wall that was only big enough for a few booths and a long counter surrounded by cracked vinyl bar stools. Still, the place was packed. When Dusty and Bri stepped in the door, there were only two stools empty. One on either side of the counter.

But Bri quickly learned that there were perks to being in the company of a sheriff. Upon seeing Dusty, the red-headed waitress stopped pouring coffee and started kissing his behind. Within minutes, she had everyone at the counter move down so the new arrivals could sit together.

"Well, I haven't seen you in a while, Sheriff." The waitress leaned over the counter in front of Dusty, displaying a large amount of cleavage and an overbite that could eat corn through a picket fence. Bri might've felt a little jealous if Dusty hadn't grabbed the menu and studied it as if the woman wasn't even there.

"Been busy," he mumbled.

The waitress turned her attention to Bri, and the look she gave her wasn't exactly friendly. "You the sheriff's baby sister? What high school you go to, honey?"

Bri smiled innocently. "Why, aren't you sweet? But I graduated high school years ago. Of course, probably not as many years ago as you."

While the waitress studied her smile and tried to figure out if she'd just been insulted, Dusty closed the menu. "I'll take the meat loaf, Sue. And my baby sister here will have a cheeseburger with everything on it and a strawberry shake with extra whip cream."

Bri rested her chin in her hand and batted her eyelashes at him. "Aww, thanks, Big Bro. I just love extra whipped cream. Especially the kind that comes straight out of a can so you can squirt it just about anywhere you want to."

The waitress gave them both a weird look before she walked away.

Dusty sent Bri a warning. "For a woman who's so hungry, you are really pushing it. If you don't behave, I'll send you to bed without supper."

"Whose bed?"

He shook his head before he took off his hat and set it on the counter. The hat had smashed down the sides of his hair, and Bri longed to reach out and fluff it back into shape. He had great hair. Thick. Blond. And silky soft to the touch. For a second, she wondered what the hair on the rest of his body would look like...or feel like. Her gaze dropped to the open vee of his shirt and the tiny strands of gold that peeked out.

Heat settled deep inside her and radiated out in wave upon wave of desire. Bri had been attracted to men, but never like this. Never with an intensity that bordered on obsession. And the fact that he fought so hard against their attraction made him all the more irresistible.

"Little sister?" The waitress set a glass and the metal shake container down on the counter with a clank, interrupting Bri's eye feasting. "Yeah, right."

The comment seemed to put Dusty in a bad mood, not that he was ever in a good mood, and he spent the rest of their meal grunting one-word replies as Bri tried to hold up the conversation. Finally, she gave up and concentrated on her cheeseburger, which turned out to be greasy and divine. She had just dipped her last French fry in ketchup when a man stepped in the door.

She didn't know why he caught her attention. He was dressed like most of the other truck drivers. Jeans, flannel shirt, and a ball cap with a tattered, stained bill. Maybe it was the long, greasy hair pulled back in a ponytail. Or the dark penetrating eyes that locked with hers—

Dusty's hand settled on the back of her neck. Since he'd been trying so hard to ignore her, the touch took her completely by surprise. As did the feel of his lips on her ear as he buried his face into her hair. She choked on her fry. His grip tightened, and he pulled her closer.

"If I tell you to hit the floor," he whispered in her ear, "you hit the floor. You understand?"

Her heart seized up, and she nodded. She glanced down to see Dusty unhooking the safety on his holster. His mouth was still next to her ear, his breathing much less accelerated than her own. The only way she could read his tension was the tightening of his fingers on the back of her neck as the man walked past them.

"Sheriff, can I get you any dessert?" The waitress walked up. "Or are you takin' your baby sister home for that?"

Dusty released Bri and swiveled his head to watch the man disappear inside the bathroom before he spoke. "I want you to get back in the kitchen with the rest of the staff, Sue." When she didn't move, he got to his feet and added, "now." That was all it took to get the waitress scurrying back into the kitchen, herding the busboy in front of her.

"You wait for me in the car." He tossed Bri the keys before he cautiously moved toward the bathroom, clearing the customers out as he went.

Bri followed the grumbling group of truck drivers into the parking lot and tried to figure out the emotions that swirled inside her. For a woman who thrived on danger, Bri wasn't enjoying the situation. She was scared. Not for herself, but for Dusty. Which was crazy. Certainly, a lone criminal would be no match for an armed sheriff.

She had to reassess her thinking when she rounded the corner and came face-to-face with the lone criminal. And in the dark, he looked twice as scary. Especially when he carried a gun and flashed a wicked smile that caused his black-as-sin eyes to glitter in the fluorescent light coming from the gas station.

He lifted the barrel of his gun and placed it next to Brianne's temple. So firmly that she could feel her pulse throb against the cold metal.

"One squeak, Little Mouse, and your life ends here." The words rushed over her face in a nauseating wave of tobacco- and coffee-tainted breath.

A car pulled up behind her, the tires crunching on the gravel and the headlights illuminating the man in all his scariness. In the next second, she found herself facedown on the ground with the gun pressed into the base of her skull. Something on the ground cut into her head, but she barely noticed with the adrenaline pumping through her veins. So much that it bypassed the kick of excitement and went straight to mind-numbing, breath-stealing terror. Especially when she heard the click of a hammer being pulled back.

"You lift your head from this ground for one second," he hissed, "and your brains will be splattered from here to Mexico City."

Long after the gun had been removed from her head, Brianne remained on the ground with her heart pounding and her face pressed against the sharp bits of gravel. In fact, she stayed that way until the car had backed up and pulled away. Only then did she lift her head and slowly climb to her wobbly legs. She was still standing there when Dusty came running around the corner with gun drawn. After checking out the back of the restaurant, he returned.

"The bastard climbed out of the bathroom window. He must've heard Sue call me sheriff." He came over and took the keys that she still clutched in her hand, his gaze darting around the dark shadows. "Did you see anything? Anything out of the ordinary?"

With as badly as her knees were shaking, she was surprised that she sounded so calm. "He left in a car. I didn't see what kind it was, but someone else was driving."

Dusty wasted no time jumping into his squad car. By the time Bri got her legs to work and climbed in, he already had the engine started, lights on, and was talking to someone on the radio.

"...call the feds and see if they want us to set up some road blocks. Although by the time those dickheads get their act together, he'll be halfway to Mexico—or worse, the Henhouse." He flipped on the siren and backed out in a swirl of gravel. "I'm headed out that way now."

Feeling as if the entire experience was a dream, Bri just sat there staring out the windshield as Dusty turned onto the highway and accelerated. While her adrenaline eased down to a more manageable state, he stayed on the radio talking to first one person and then the other. The conversation with the FBI agent seemed to take the longest and frustrate him the most.

"...no, I didn't get a positive ID. But it was Alejandro. I'd stake my reputation on it."

"But would you stake thousands of dollars of the taxpayers' money on it, Sheriff Hicks?" A male voice came through the speakers. "Because that's what it will cost if we have to set up road blocks and close highways. And unless you have a positive ID, we're not going to waste our time. Especially when there is no reason for Alejandro to still be in Texas. Our informants told us he was in Mexico City just yesterday."

Dusty hesitated before he released his breath. "Fine, next time I'll take a fuckin' picture." He clicked off the radio and turned off the siren.

"This Alejandro," Bri said. "Is this the same man that almost killed Jenna Jay and Beau? The drug lord from New York City?"

"The same." Even in the darkness, she could tell that his hands tightened on the steering wheel. "He escaped during a prison transfer a couple weeks ago."

"A couple weeks seems like plenty of time to make it back to Mexico. Why would you think that he'd want to come back here?"

Dusty took the turnoff to Miss Hattie's. "Call it a gut feeling. Men like Alejandro don't forgive and forget. And since Jenna and Beau were responsible for his capture..."

As numb as she was, a lightbulb went on in Bri's head. "So that's why Beau was so willing to take Jenna to Africa when she's five months pregnant."

"Beau and I thought it was for the best. Just until we could make sure that Alejandro wasn't coming back for them. Of course, Jenna doesn't know about it." He shook his head. "The woman would take on the entire Mexican Cartel if Beau would let her."

It was the truth. Jenna Jay was one of the toughest women Bri had ever met. Much tougher than Bri, who suddenly felt a little light-headed as Dusty switched off the lights and coasted into the circular driveway of Miss Hattie's.

"You think he's here?" she asked.

"It's doubtful that he'd be stupid enough to come here after what happened at the truck stop." He put the car into park and turned off the engine. "Let's just hope he didn't show up here first."

"Oh, my God, the hens." She reached for the door handle, but he stopped her, his grip on her arm as tight as it had been in the restaurant.

"I want you to wait here."

Before she could argue, he was out of the car and stealthily climbing the porch steps with gun drawn.

She waited until he'd disappeared inside before she got out and followed him. She stepped into the foyer to discover Dusty standing in the doorway of the dining room, his gun pointing up at the ceiling and his stance tense as his gaze swept over the room. A room filled with guests who all thought he was part of some kind of dinner show.

"Oh, look, Harold, it's the county sheriff come to Miss Hattie's to discover who murdered William Cates," a middle-aged woman said. She turned in her chair to get a better view, and her gaze locked on Bri. "Although I'm not sure what the young lady has to do with the story. Or why she's covered in blood."

As if in slow motion, Bri glanced down and stared in confusion at the sweater that had once been a pure ivory but was now spotted with deep red. The last thing she heard before all colors blurred and turned to black was the desperate edge of Dusty's voice as he finally used her given name.

"Brianne!"

Chapter Sixteen

BRI COULDN'T SLEEP. It didn't have to do with the cut on her head, although it still throbbed from the antiseptic Sunshine had used. Or the heat of the October night. Or Minnie's snoring, which drifted down the hallway. It had to do with the excitement that still coursed through her veins. Excitement that only grew as the night's events played over and over in her head.

She'd been accosted by a leader of the Mexican Cartel. Had sliced her head on a piece of broken glass while having a gun rammed into her head. And had driven a good hundred miles an hour with siren blaring and lights flashing.

And now she was expected to go to sleep.

Not likely.

Even after the hot toddy Minnie had forced her to drink, Bri felt all jumpy and jittery. Like she could run the New York Marathon. Or hike the Rockies' highest peak. Or free-fall out of a plane at thirteen thousand feet.

She certainly couldn't just lie there.

Whipping back the covers, she slid her feet to the floor. Once she was standing, she had to admit she felt a little woozy. But she figured it had more to do with the hot toddy than the head injury. Minnie had a heavy hand when mixing drinks. Fortunately, the feeling left as quickly as it came. Since Starlet had yet to come to bed, Bri didn't have to worry about waking her up when she dug through her suitcases for a t-shirt, shorts, and running shoes. She figured that a quick walk around the lilac garden should ease some of her anxiety.

But on the way past the library, Starlet's voice stopped Bri in her tracks.

"What do you mean you can't get me the money? You promised it would only be a loan—that you would pay every cent back. Well, I need it back now. It's a matter of life and death."

There was a desperate edge to Starlet's voice that worried Bri. Of course, Starlet had always seemed a bit emotional and dramatic. That night had been a perfect example. While the other hens had been extremely concerned about Bri, Starlet had been almost hysterical. Especially after hearing that Alejandro was responsible. Although Bri couldn't blame her. She was no doubt traumatized by what happened the night Alejandro and his thugs came to the Henhouse.

Her next words proved it. She went from sounding desperate to sounding like a crazed lunatic.

"You will get me that money! Do you hear me? You'll get me that money, or so help me—hello? Hello!" There was a long pause before something hit the door.

Bri should've left well enough alone and continued out to the garden. Unfortunately, she had never been able to leave well enough alone. She tapped on the door before pushing it open and peeking her head in.

Starlet sat behind Minnie's desk in a Tinkerbell night-shirt. Aside from being a little overweight, Starlet was one of the most beautiful women Bri had ever seen. Her thick hair was a rich brown with natural red highlights that complemented her clear complexion and golden brown eyes. Eyes that widened when they landed on Bri.

"Is everything okay?" Bri asked.

Starlet's face flushed red. "Umm, yeah. I was just"—her eyes landed on the laptop on the desk—"shopping online." She cleared her throat. "I'm sorry I woke you—I get kind of loud when I...shop online."

"It can be annoying." Bri tried not to look down at the busted phone receiver on the floor. "I hate it when you find the perfect dress and it's out of stock."

"So annoying." Starlet tried to smile, but it was a weak effort. Especially when her eyes filled with tears. "I'm so sorry about what happened, Bri."

Bri didn't hesitate to step into the room. "It's not your fault, Starlet. I was just in the wrong place at the wrong time. And you shouldn't be worried that Alejandro is coming back here. The FBI seems to think that he's in Mexico. Which means that the guy I saw was just some criminal passing through."

"But Sheriff Hicks doesn't believe that," she said.

Dusty didn't believe it. He was now more convinced than ever that the man at the truck stop had been Ale-jandro. While Sunshine had been patching up Bri, he had been on his radio yelling at the federal agent. Of course, first he had yelled at Bri for not telling him she was injured. If she didn't know better, she would've thought that his display of temper had been a result of fear and concern for her.

Unfortunately, she did know better.

"I'm sure the sheriff would've stuck around if he was worried about Alejandro," she said.

Starlet glanced at the window. "But he did stick around. He's been sitting outside all night."

Bri couldn't help rushing over to the window and looking out. Sure enough, Dusty's patrol car was parked in the circular drive. And in the porch light, Bri could just make out the shadowy form of a cowboy hat and broad shoulders. For some strange reason, her heart did a little jig. Not that Dusty was there for her. He was just doing his job. Still, she couldn't help smiling as she turned away from the window.

"Is he your boyfriend?" Starlet asked.

"No. Just a friend." Her gaze drifted down to the busted phone on the floor. "Is that who you were talking to, Starlet? A boyfriend?"

Starlet's face turned the same color as the burgundy curtains. "You heard?" she squeaked.

"It was kind of hard not to. You were talking pretty loudly. Do you need money, Starlet? Because if you do, I could talk with Brant—"

"No!" Starlet came up from the chair. "Please don't talk to Brant. He's already done so much for me. He's paying for my apartment in Nashville and my demo CD. Plus, he set up the interview with that music producer. I couldn't ask him to do any more."

Bri held up a hand. "Okay. I promise I won't say a word. You just sounded so upset, I got worried."

"It's nothing to worry about," Starlet said. "I can handle it."

Bri could've called her out on the lie, especially with

the broken phone on the floor, but if anyone understood the need to keep secrets, it was Bri.

"Fine, just don't let him bully you," she said.

It was only when she was standing outside the library door that Bri realized she had no business giving Starlet advice when she had been letting Jared bully her for the last three months. Of course, Starlet's boyfriend probably didn't have naked pictures of her.

As soon as she left the library, Bri headed to the front door. She could've lied to herself and continued to pretend like she just needed a breath of fresh air. But in reality, what she wanted now was a breath of spicy soap and manly sheriff.

Unfortunately, when she got to the porch, his car was gone. She glanced back at the library window and could clearly see Starlet sitting at Minnie's desk trying to put the phone back together. Which made Bri wonder if the sheriff hadn't hot-tailed it out of there after seeing her in the window.

Darn ornery man.

If he was playing hard to get, he was doing a good job of it. Bri walked over to the porch post and stared out at the road. Of course, a man could only run for so long. She might've giggled if a hand hadn't clamped over her mouth. A hand that smelled like fried chicken and wet cat.

"Don't scream, Little Missy. It's just ol' Olive."

Once Olive removed her hand, Bri turned and hissed at her. "Geez, Olive, you scared the crap out of me."

She sent Bri a stern look much like Bri's mother's. "You should have the crap scared out of you. After what happened tonight, you have no business outside in the dark. What are you doin' out here, anyway?"

"I could ask you the same question."

Olive shrugged. "I never have slept good. And with a criminal runnin' around, I figured I might as well keep an eye on things. Even with the sheriff parked out back." It was impossible for Bri to keep her reaction to the news from Olive's sharp eyes. "Ahh, that's what you're doin' out here, ain't it? You were hopin' to get a little cuddlin' in with the sheriff." She shook her head. "Well, I can't say as I blame you. That is one fine-lookin' man. Twice as good lookin' as that stalker boyfriend of yours."

In the excitement of the evening, Bri had almost forgotten about Jared. Now she seized on the topic and fired off questions. "So what did Jared say? What did Minnie tell him? How did she get him to leave?"

"Whoa there." Olive held up a hand. "I'm not gonna answer any questions until you get your butt back in bed where you belong. Good-lookin' sheriff or no good-lookin' sheriff, you shouldn't be galivantin' around after what you went through tonight."

Bri started to argue, but then realized that the events of the evening had finally caught up with her. The adrenaline drained out of her, and it was all she could do to walk back to her bedroom. Once Olive tucked her in bed, her eyes drooped closed.

"That's it, Little Missy." Olive sat down on the edge of the bed and smoothed back her hair. "Just close your eyes and go to sleep. I'll answer all your questions tomorrow. But for now, there's nothin' to worry about. The sheriff is right outside protecting you from ornery criminals. And ol' Olive is right here with you, protecting you from no-account boyfriends who just need a little physical persuasion to send them on their way."

Bri might've questioned what Olive meant if Jiggers hadn't jumped up on the bed and cuddled against her feet and if Starlet hadn't come in and slipped under the covers on the other side.

For a girl who had slept alone all her life, Bri had never felt so safe and content.

Chapter Seventeen

JOSIAH PULLED UP TO THE GAS PUMPS and cut the engine, then glanced into his rearview mirror to see if the sheriff would pull in behind him. He didn't. Instead, he drove right by Jones's gas station, offering nothing but a tip of his hat. Obviously, Sheriff Hicks wasn't quite as blatant about his harassment as Bramble's deputy. In the last twenty-four hours, the idiot had pulled Josiah over at least ten times, issuing him tickets for anything from failure to signal to parking too close to a driveway. If Josiah hadn't owed a good five hundred in fines, it would be almost laughable.

But Josiah was no longer in a laughing mood. Glaring after the sheriff, he opened the door and started to climb out when a skinny kid in a John Deere hat came jogging toward him.

"Don't worry, mister. I got it." The kid flipped open the fuel cover and unscrewed the gas cap. "You want me to fill her up?"

"Yes," he snapped, taking his anger out on the kid, "and don't get any gas on the paint."

The freckle-faced kid's shoulders stiffened, and for a second, Josiah thought he was going to get some punk response. Instead, the kid pressed his lips together and looked like he was fighting an inner demon. When he had it under control, he flashed a bright smile.

"No, sir. I'll sure be careful about that." He placed the nozzle in and turned on the pump. Josiah got back in the car, thinking that was the end of their conversation. Unfortunately, just like the rest of the town, the kid continued to ramble.

"Pumpin' gas ain't really my specialty." He grabbed some paper towels from the dispenser at the side of the pumps and pulled out the squeegee. "I'm more into sales, but"—he started cleaning the windshield—"makin' money is makin' money. And since the Texas Longhorns' star quarterback worked here, I figure it couldn't hurt my climb to the top. You know Austin Reeves? He used to live right here in Bramble until he moved to Austin to go to college." The kid laughed. "Austin in Austin. Now that's pretty darned funny."

A few days ago, Josiah might've laughed along with the kid and asked some questions about the star quarterback who everyone knew was headed for a Heisman Trophy and a multi-million-dollar contract with a pro football team. But a few days ago, Josiah had a plan to prove that Miss Hattie's Henhouse was a functioning whorehouse. And the people of Bramble were going to help him achieve that plan.

Now, he realized that the people of Bramble were nothing but a bunch of bumbling idiots who had only good things to say about Miss Hattie's and the Cates brothers who owned it. In fact, the only one who thought differently was Wilma Tate. And after only a few hours with the woman, Josiah understood why her husband drank.

Wilma was a ranting lunatic who believed all her neighbors were having affairs, the coffee at Josephine's Diner contained mind-altering drugs, and that aliens had once landed in her plastic flower garden. So there was no way in hell he could use Wilma as evidence that shady things were going on at Miss Hattie's.

No, he needed someone—or something—more credible.

Just then, a brand-new silver BMW sports car pulled up on the other side of the pumps. Always one who liked to mingle with money, Josiah quickly got out.

"Why, thank you, son." Josiah patted the kid on the back. "I certainly appreciate the extra dedication to your job."

The kid shot him a confused look. "You must be one of them folks that have that bi-north-polar disease."

Josiah laughed and glanced over at the man who climbed out of the car. A man who looked like he'd just lost a fistfight. "Kids," he said as he held out a hand. "Reverend Josiah Jessup."

The man ignored the hand and had just reached for the gas nozzle when the young kid raced over.

"I'll get that, mister."

The man relinquished it without a fight or thank-you. "Do you have ice?"

"Sure do, but you'll have to buy a five-pound bag. It's in the freezer in the garage." Once the man was heading toward the open door of the garage, the kid ran a greasy-nailed hand over the top of the BMW. "Some day I'm gonna have me a car just like this."

Josiah snorted. "Doubtful, kid. Haven't you ever

heard the saying, 'The rich get richer, and the poor have babies'? I'd bet money that you'll still be here in twenty years, pumping gas to feed your horde of kids." Before the boy could do more than puff up like a banty rooster, Josiah turned and followed after the man. He found him standing in front of the ice freezer, holding a few chunks of ice on his jaw.

"That's some fight you must've gotten into," Josiah said as he reached into his pocket and pulled out a monogrammed handkerchief. "Here, use this."

The man took it and put a few chunks of ice in it before placing it back on his jaw. "She said her name was Olive, but I find it hard to believe that the tattooed hulk who hit me was female."

It was hard to hide the excitement his words brought, and Josiah was forced to walk to the soda machine and pretend to study the selection. "So it sounds like you've been out to the Henhouse. I had a run-in with the same woman a few days ago. Although I wasn't beaten as much as shot at by the lunatic old woman in the wheelchair. So I assume you weren't there to enjoy the bed-and-breakfast?"

"No. Not that it's any of your business."

Josiah glanced over and smiled. "True. Very true. I was just curious as to why you haven't yet gone to the sheriff and brought the woman up on assault charges." He pulled out his cell phone. "I'd be more than happy to call him for you. The sheriff and I have become close personal friends."

For the first time, the man looked uneasy. "That won't be necessary. It was just a misunderstanding. I stopped by to see a friend of mine, and the woman got me confused with someone else."

Josiah pulled a few coins from his pocket and put them into the machine. "Don't you just hate it when that happens? So who is this friend? One of the hens?" When the man didn't answer, Josiah continued. "Of course not. A man like yourself wouldn't be calling on a bunch of old women... which means that you must've been calling on the younger woman. What did the one woman call her? Brianne?"

The man's battered face lit up. "So Brianne Cates is there?"

Having researched the Henhouse extensively, Josiah knew the name and was surprised that he hadn't put two and two together before. More than likely because of the car she'd been driving and the grandma hat disguise. And the fact that the sheriff hadn't been the least bit intimidated about handcuffing a Cates.

Unless he didn't know who he was handcuffing.

And why would Miss Cates keep her identity a secret from the law?

"Hmm, it doesn't make sense that a close friend of Brianne Cates would get beat up just for trying to visit her brother's bed-and-breakfast?" He paused for dramatic effect. "Unless he wasn't there just for a visit. Unless he was there to cause trouble."

The young man's eyes narrowed. "Who in the hell are you?"

Josiah smiled. "Your salvation, young man. Your salvation."

Chapter Eighteen

DUSTY SHOULD'VE TURNED AROUND and returned to Jones's Garage so he could hassle Reverend Jessup some more, but his heart just wasn't in it. Or maybe not his heart as much as his mind. He was still having trouble forgetting the image of Brianne standing in the foyer of Miss Hattie's. The shaft of fear that lanced through him when he noticed the blood dripping from her cheek had almost sent him to his knees. And Dusty didn't like being scared. He didn't like it at all.

He grabbed his radio and dialed to another frequency before pushing the button. "Kenny Gene."

"Yes sir, Sheriff," came the reply.

"Everything okay out at the Henhouse?"

"Yep. Right as rain. Miss Baby just brought me out some coffee and cinnamon rolls. And since Josephine's was locked up tight this mornin', they were sure appreciated."

Dusty had just passed Josephine's, and he quickly looked in his side mirror. Sure enough the parking lot was empty, and a Closed sign was hanging in the door.

"Okay then," he said. "I'll be out to relieve you in a couple hours." He started to replace the radio, then pulled it back to his mouth. "No heroics, Kenny. Anything suspicious, you call me."

"Roger that, boss."

Once Dusty finished talking with Kenny, he radioed in to Cora Lee to see if she'd heard anything from the feds. She hadn't, and he was pissed that they weren't taking what happened the night before more seriously. Agent Riley was convinced that the man wasn't Alejandro and was just some thug who got freaked when he noticed Dusty's uniform. And maybe he was right. Maybe Dusty had been staring at the wanted poster for so long that he'd conjured up Alejandro. Usually, he trusted his gut feeling, but there was no doubt he'd been distracted lately. And it was past time for him to stop thinking about Brianne Cates and start doing his job.

Dusty found Mayor Sutter bent over the drawer of his desk. When he tapped on the open door, the mayor almost jumped out of his biker shorts. The Little Debbie Swiss Roll he'd been eating slipped from his fingers and dropped to the floor. He tried to hide it by covering it with his cycling shoe, smashing the snack cake into the carpet.

"Well, good mornin', Sheriff Hicks," he said over a mouthful of chocolate and cream. He swallowed hard and then cleared his throat. "I was just enjoyin' a little whole grain muffin."

It was hard for Dusty to keep his eyes off the chocolate icing crumbs that clung to the curls of the mayor's handlebar mustache. "I assume you're stuck eating in your office because Josephine's is closed." He took off his hat and sat down in the chair. "What happened, Harley?"

"It's a sad state of affairs." Harley sat down behind the desk, leaving a squashed Swiss Roll on the floor. "It seems Josephine couldn't find anyone to work at the diner—leastways, not anyone as good as Rachel Dean. Jenna Jay is in Africa with Beau, and Hope is too busy with the kids and Bramble commerce to take on waitressin', so Josephine was forced to close the diner down until she can find someone to help her out." He shook his head. "It's a real shame." His tongue came out and collected a few crumbs. "'Course, I can't eat that fatty food anyway. Not on my gubernatorial diet."

As long as they weren't causing trouble or breaking the law, Dusty wasn't one who stuck his nose in other people's business. But as he sat there watching the man search his mustache for any remaining crumbs, he figured he couldn't let this craziness continue.

"I'm not sure running for governor is a good idea, Harley."

"What do you mean? Are you sayin' you wouldn't vote for me, Dusty?"

Dusty rolled the brim of his hat through his hands, searching for just the right words. "I'm not sayin' that at all. As far as I'm concerned, you'd make a fine governor." It was the truth. At times, Harley could be a little naïve and narrow-minded, but he had a heart of gold and a strong desire to do the right thing. Dusty simply wanted to make sure this was Harley's dream and not Reverend Jessup's idea of a joke.

He looked Harley in the eye. "Whatever happened to your plan of retiring? Of getting up early every morning and being the first one out at Sutter Springs? Just you, a fishin' pole, and a sack of Josephine's brown sugar and cinnamon donuts?"

Harley's eyes glazed over as if he was imagining doing just that. He brushed his tongue over his top lip. "I do love Josephine's sugar donuts." He blinked and straightened his shoulders. "But Texas needs me."

"Right here in Bramble," Dusty said. "Hope might be the next mayor, but she needs you to finish teaching her the ropes."

There was a long pause before Harley nodded. "Well, you do have a point. That girl can go off half-cocked if she doesn't have a firm hand to guide her. And Lord only knows that I wouldn't want Bramble suffering just because I got a bee in my bonnet to be governor."

"Exactly what I was thinking." Figuring he'd planted enough of a seed, Dusty got to his feet. "Now I better finish up my town patrol before I go see what Kenny Gene is up to."

Harley nodded as he followed him to the door. "Yesterday, on my morning bike ride, I stopped him from givin' a ticket to Moses Tate for loitering. I'll sure be glad when Sam's foot heals up."

"You and me both, Harley."

After another quick cruise up and down Main Street, Dusty decided to stop by and check on Rachel Dean to make sure she wasn't cooking up some toxic potion that would wipe out the entire town. But on the way to her house, he past Twyla's and the little blue Smart Car parked out front had him slamming on the brakes. What was Brianne doing here? She should be back at the Henhouse, not gallivanting around Bramble with a head injury. He started to back up when it dawned on him that he had no business telling Brianne Cates what to do. She wasn't his problem. He had plenty of his own already.

Unfortunately, before he could continue on his way, one of the high school football coaches came out the side door of the salon...followed by Brianne. At least, the dark, silky hair looked like Brianne's. The clothing looked more like a cocktail waitress'. The tight sweater clung to her full breasts like a second skin, the short skirt was a good six inches above her knees, and the red shoes had stiletto heels that could knife right through a man's heart.

If the dazed look on Travis's face was any indication, they already had. The assistant football coach looked at Brianne like she was one of Josephine's sugar donuts. The look got even more intense when she reached up and ran her fingers through his hair.

Well, sonofabitch.

Dusty smashed down on the accelerator and backed up next to the curb. Or more like on the curb. But he didn't care. All he cared about was making sure that Brianne didn't touch Travis again. Which was really stupid. He should be glad that her attentions were directed elsewhere. Except he wasn't glad. He was pissed. And he only got madder when he got out of the car to find Travis asking Brianne out.

"...if you don't have another appointment, we could go over to Bootlegger's. Now that Josephine's closed down, Rossie's cooking up hamburgers on his grill out back. I can't recommend Rossie's cooking, but Manuel makes a mean margarita to wash it all down with." He glanced up. "Hey, Dusty. I heard you were helping out Kenny while Sam is laid up."

Dusty ignored Travis and stopped in front of Brianne, the toes of his boots inches from the toes of her red high heels. "Just what the hell are you doing?"

A smile tipped her lips, which were painted the exact same color as her shoes. Her eyes traveled over his body like a hot summer breeze. By the time they reached his eyes, Dusty was as turned on as Travis and mad as hell that just a look could make him that way.

"Answer the question," he ground out.

Travis took a step closer. "She wasn't doing anything illegal, Dusty. She just gave me a haircut, is all. The best haircut I've ever had, by the way."

With his eyes still pinned on Brianne, Dusty spoke through his teeth. "I bet it was."

"I aim to please." Her eyes widened innocently before she turned to Travis. "So what were you saying, Travis?"

There was a slight pause as Travis looked between the two of them. "Umm, I was just saying that if you're done working for the day—"

"She's not," Dusty stated. "I'm her last appointment."

"Well, in that case…" Travis backed down the sidewalk, seeming almost relieved to be leaving. "I'll catch up with you later, Willie."

Once he was gone, Brianne turned back to Dusty. "Funny, but I didn't see your name in the appointment book."

He ignored the comment and pointed to her shoes. "Where did you get those?"

"Baby gave them to me because they pinched her toes."

"And the skirt?"

"It's mine. I just hemmed it."

"Too damned short."

She twisted around, displaying the way the black knit hugged her butt. "You think?"

"What are you doing, Brianne?" He rested his hands on his hips, his fingers curling over the metal of the hand-cuffs. Her gaze settled there. And damned if she didn't lick those scarlet lips. When she spoke, her voice was low and husky.

"I'm helping out Twyla." Her gaze lifted. "What are you doing, Dusty?" Before he could answer, she turned and went back inside, her heels clicking and butt wiggling almost as much as Baby's. Of course, Baby's wiggle never made him feel like someone had stuffed a heating pad down his pants and set it on scorch. He readjusted and stared at the screen door with the Y'ALL COME ON IN sign and tried to convince himself to turn around and get back in his car. Unfortunately, heat beat out brains, and he reached for the handle of the screen door.

He stepped inside to find Brianne sweeping hair into a dustpan. He could've continued to grump around like a bear with a thorn in his paw, but it wasn't much fun to growl at someone who wouldn't growl back. It was like Brianne knew exactly what he was pissed about and found it more amusing than annoying. Of course, any fool could see he was jealous.

Jealous of a woman he had no business with. No business whatsoever.

Without a word, he took off his hat and hung it on one of the hooks. "Where's Twyla?"

"Darla thought it would be a good idea if she got away for a little bit. So she took her to Odessa to visit Darla's sister. I told her I'd keep an eye on things until she got back."

"When's that?"

"Tomorrow."

"So I guess your head is okay."

"Nothing more than a scratch." She had moved up behind him without him knowing, and her arm brushed against his as she flipped over the sign and pulled the door closed. The lock clicked in place with the force of a sledgehammer driving home a railroad stake.

His gaze snapped over, but she merely shrugged. "Since you're my last appointment…" She let the sentence trail off as she wiggled her way to the chair and picked up the cape from the back. "You might want to take off your gun." When he just stood there, she added, "Unless you're scared of a little ol' haircut."

But it wasn't just a little ol' haircut. And they both knew it. It was something else. Something that had started the day before. Or possibly the first time he'd ever laid eyes on her. He thought that he'd avoided a head-on collision.

Obviously, he'd been wrong.

He unbuckled his belt and placed it on the hook next to his hat before he took a seat in the chair. "Just a trim."

"Just a trim," she echoed as she whipped the cape over his shoulders and snapped it, her fingers trailing a fiery path along the back of his neck. "But first I'll need to wash it." She moved over to the black sink and waited. Thinking cool water would help douse the heat that curled in his stomach, he got to his feet and followed her.

The water that she sprayed through his hair was warm and soothing, but Dusty didn't feel soothed. He felt about ready to jump clean out of his boots.

"Tough day?" she asked.

It was a simple question. A question he'd been asked before by other women. Which didn't explain why it caused a spiral of heat to tighten in his gut. Maybe because it was the first time a woman had acted like she was interested in the answer.

"Have you gotten any sleep?" She shut off the water and reached for one of the bottles that lined the shelf over the sink. The action brought her breast inches from his face...his mouth. He swallowed hard and closed his eyes.

"A little."

"Thank you for keeping a watch last night."

"It's my job."

"Is it also your job to stop by and check on me?" He opened his eyes to find her staring down at him. "Since you ran off this morning without saying good-bye, I thought you'd had enough of me." She sent him a smile as her hands cradled his head. Then her fingers started to move, and he lost track of the conversation.

Bri didn't merely wash his hair—she worshipped it. Using just her fingertips, she caressed his scalp from front to back, then pulled his soapy strands through her fingers in a slow, undulating motion. It was heaven and at the same time hell. And as much as he wanted the torture to stop, he prayed it would never end—that she would continue to adore his tresses forever.

She turned on the water and moved closer, her thigh brushing against his arm. Or *was* it her thigh? His breathing became shallow and irregular, and he struggled to hold on to his sanity as she rinsed the shampoo from his hair. The water clicked off, and her nails ran over his scalp, sending a shiver through his body.

Her hands lifted, and there was nothing but heavy silence.

He opened his eyes to find her looking down at him

with the same heat that pooled inside of him. And when she spoke, her words were barely above a whisper.

"Have you had enough of me, Dusty?"

A puff of air escaped his lips, and it took a full minute before he could speak. "Not even close." He reached up and curled his hand around her neck, pulling her down to his waiting mouth. The kiss went from zero to sixty in a second flat. Then suddenly she was straddling him and he was sitting up, water dripping down his neck and over the cape.

"Me either," she panted in between kisses. She pulled off the cape. "I can't get enough." Her hands slid up his chest, massaged his pecs, before grabbing the edges of his skirt and jerking it open in a staccato pop of snaps.

"Easy there," Dusty said against her mouth. Although he spoke more to himself than to Brianne. He was locked and loaded and felt like it would take only one more undulation of her body to send him right over the edge. Unfortunately, Brianne was not a good listener.

She shook her head as she continued to ride him like a jockey on the home stretch. "I don't want to go easy. I want it fast"—she nipped at his lip—"and hard."

It was the "hard" that did him in. All restraint dissolved beneath a wall of carnal lust, and he came to his feet. Arranging Bri's legs around him, he took control of the kiss, communicating his desire through tongue and lips. He carried her across the floor until they bumped into the counter in front of the mirror. With one swipe, he sent brushes, combs, and haircutting paraphernalia sailing to the floor. He jerked her skirt up and growled deep in his throat when he discovered that she didn't have on any panties.

He unzipped his pants and was so consumed with lust that he didn't even think about a condom until she pushed him back and pulled one out of her bra. In a flash of even teeth, she tore open the package. The first touch of her hands had him sucking wind.

"Easy there," she teased as she stroked his shaft.

The feeling that washed over him was so intense that he tipped his head back and tried not to embarrass himself. As if realizing his need, she wasted no time slipping on the condom. And with just a little adjustment, he found himself surrounded by the tight walls of her body.

The fit was so perfect that he wanted to remain sheathed inside her forever. Wanted it more than he'd ever wanted anything in his life, but his body had gone without for so long that it wasn't willing to be put off for a second more. His hips pumped forward, thrusting deep and driving Bri back against the mirror. He expected her to protest. Instead, she set her hands on the counter, tightened her legs around his waist, and boldly met his next thrust.

From there, things got completely out of hand. Without a bit of his usual finesse, he pumped into her hard and fast. He should've felt guilty; instead, he just felt wild. Like an animal that had been unleashed from its cage after a lifetime of captivity. And Bri welcomed his out-of-control lust as if it were the reason for her very existence. When Dusty thought he couldn't take a second more, she tossed back her head and moaned out her satisfaction.

The noise triggered his own release, and he was swept into an orgasm so intense he wondered if he might black out. He could have. He opened his eyes and found himself half laying on Bri, the tight hold of her legs the only thing keeping him from slipping to the floor.

He got lost in the blue of her eyes for a moment before he found his voice.

"I'm sorry."

Bri smiled. "I'm not. In fact, could we do it again?"

Chapter Nineteen

BRI FELT BUOYANT. Like she could float right up to the ceiling if Dusty's body wasn't pinning her to the counter. Too bad he looked about as buoyant as a lead balloon. With a grunt, he pulled away from her and turned to adjust his clothing.

She sat up and smoothed down her skirt. "I'll take that as a no."

He turned back around, the edges of his shirt flapping open and revealing a strip of ripped stomach that she couldn't seem to look away from.

"Good guess." He jerked the shirt together and started snapping it closed.

"My, aren't we grumpy." She got down off the counter. But since her legs were still a little wobbly, she sat down in the chair.

Once he had his shirt tucked it, he stepped closer, placing his hands on the arms of the chair so his face was inches away. "Damn straight, I'm grumpy. I don't like being manipulated. And you just manipulated the hell out of me."

Bri smiled. "Funny, but I don't think I was the one who picked you up and had my way with you against a mirror."

His eyes darkened. "No. You were just the one who planned this entire seduction. From the no panties to the condom in your bra. I wouldn't be surprised if you sent Twyla out of town and somehow lured Travis here to make me jealous."

Bri perked up. "So you were jealous."

Dusty released a growl before he turned and headed for the door.

"Fine." She got up from the chair. "I'll admit that I planned to seduce you. But Travis—" He buckled the gun belt around his waist, and there was something so masculine and sexy about it that she forgot what she was going to say.

"Was your alternate plan if I didn't show up?" He took his hat off the hook.

Desire drained right out of Bri, and she bristled. "Of course. After all, one man is as good as another." Without one more word, she turned and walked back to the station, picking up brushes and combs on her way. She had just set them on the counter when Dusty took her arm and spun her around.

"What do you want, Brianne? And don't give me any more of your lies. I want the truth." He stared back at her with eyes that were no longer angry. Just intense with a small splash of pain. It was the pain that pulled at Bri's heart. The pain that had the truth spilling from her lips.

"Maybe I just want you."

"But why—ahh, I get it. You've read that crazy *Fifty Shades* book and have a little submissive fetish going on. And you figure an officer of the law will have all the right equipment to make you his slave."

She laughed. "No. Although I do like your equipment." She glanced down at the handcuffs. "And I don't think I'd mind being your slave." She looked back up into his confused eyes and revealed more to him than she'd ever revealed to another man. "But the truth is that you're the first man who has ever made me breathless."

An awkward silence followed where Bri pretty much wanted to crawl beneath the counter and never come out. Instead, she just stood there staring into eyes that changed from confusion to something she couldn't quite read. He leaned closer and his lips parted, but before he could kiss her or tell her to take a hike, his radio crackled, and Cora Lee's voice broke the spell.

"Hey, boss, are you there?"

Dusty stared at Bri for one second more before he unclipped the radio and answered. "Yeah," he said in a voice that sounded a little strained.

"Heather called, and she sounded pretty upset. I think you better call her back ASAP."

"Thanks." Dusty wasted no time clipping his radio back on his belt and pulling his cell phone from his front pocket.

Bri could only watch and wonder who in the heck Heather was as he dialed a number and moved away to stand over by the stairs. She bent down and continued to clean up the items on the floor, but her focus was entirely on Dusty's conversation.

"What's going on, Heather?" he said in a low voice that quickly turned concerned. "Is she okay?" There was a long pause. "So why the hell didn't you let her call me?" He ran a hand through his hair. "Fine. Put her on now."

Bri had started to put the pieces together, but the puzzle became complete when Dusty spoke again.

"Hey, Nugget." There was a wealth of love in the words. So much that it brought tears to Bri's eyes. "Now what's this I hear about you refusing to eat? And don't give me any nonsense about Elsa not making anything you like. You love her cooking—much better than you like your pa's. Remember that burned pizza I made you?" He paused and cradled the phone with both hands as if he was actually cradling the person talking. "You can't not eat, Emmie, just because you want to come see me. Don't I call you every day so we can talk?"

Bri watched his shoulders tighten, and even from that distance she could feel his pain.

"Aww, baby," he said, "I miss you, too. But this is our weekend. Just a couple more days, and I'll be there. In fact, we need to start planning what we're going to do when I get to Houston. You want to spend the day at the park, or go to the zoo again, or...princesses?" Most men would've continued to toss out suggestions, anything to keep from playing princesses, but Dusty didn't hesitate to give in to his daughter. Which made Bri's heart soften into gooey marshmallow cream.

"Princesses it is," Dusty said, and a few seconds later, he laughed. "Well, I don't know if I'd call my house a castle, but it's getting there. And I promise you'll be able to come see it soon." There was another pause, but this time he slowly turned and pinned Bri with a steely glare. "My housekeeper Brianne? No, she's not a princess. In fact, she was just there for a day—yes, sort of like your mother's Mini-Maids. Now I want you to give the phone back to your mother and go eat your breakfast."

Bri knew when Emma's mother got on by the hard, cold tone in Dusty's voice. "I went along with you about not calling Emma at night, but if she wants to talk with me anytime, then she can damn well talk to me. And I don't care what the judge said." He hung up the phone, and for a minute, Bri thought he was going to toss it across the room. Instead, he gripped it tightly in his hand and turned his anger on her.

"You talked to my daughter?"

Bri shrugged. "Briefly. I answered your phone because I was worried it might be an emergency."

He continued to stand there, anger and pain radiating off of him like a furnace. She had the strong urge to walk over and wrap her arms around him. But she had been around enough stubborn, volatile men in her life to know that sympathy was never well received. So instead, she walked over and picked up the plastic cape from the floor.

"How about if I finish that haircut? Or at least blow your hair dry? You don't want to catch a cold, do you?"

It took a while for the tension to leave his shoulders. But finally he walked over and sat down, slipping the phone back into his front pocket.

"Don't scalp me."

She picked up the comb and scissors. "I wouldn't think of it."

For the next few minutes, the only sound was the snip of the shears and the squeak of the chair as Bri used her knee to turn it one way and then the other. Dusty had beautiful hair, thick with different colored strands of blond running through it. She had just turned him around to work on the front when he spoke.

"Emma lives in Houston with her mother."

Bri nodded and continued to cut.

"Her mother has full custody." He released his breath,

and his shoulders slumped. "I wanted Emmie. I wanted her so damned much that I screwed up." He swallowed hard. "I lost my temper in the courtroom and ended up adding fuel to Heather's accusations that I had anger issues and shouldn't get joint custody."

Bri hesitated with the scissors poised. "But that's crazy. Anyone can see that your bark is worse than your bite."

Dusty tipped his head up, pulling the strand of hair from her hands. "And what makes you think so? I haven't exactly been nice to you."

"I don't know about that. What just happened was kind of nice." Before he could say anything, she tipped his head down and continued to cut. "Besides, I haven't exactly been an angel to you, either."

He snorted. "Angel doesn't even come close to describing you. A little devil is much closer."

Bri laughed. "I do believe I like the sound of that. So you lost your temper in the courtroom and that's all it took for them to give your wife full custody?"

"No. Her father also has the judge in his back pocket."

She stepped back to examine her work. "Well, all I can say is that I hope you're not going to let your wife get away with it. You need to get a lawyer and fight that judgment. It sounds like Emmie wants to be with you as much as you want to be with her, and it's a shame she can't talk to you when she wants to."

She went to pick up the clippers so she could trim the back of his hair, when he grabbed her hand, turning the chair until he faced her.

"How do you know what kind of father I am?"

She smiled. "Because I happen to have the most wonderful father in the world, and he talks to me exactly like you talk to Emmie."

His hand tightened on her arm, and he pulled her closer...and closer. But before his lips touched hers, his radio crackled again.

"Sheriff." Cora's voice was filled with panic. "We got us an officer down."

Bri tried to follow Dusty out to the Henhouse, but in the Smart Car it was a losing battle. In fact, by the time she pulled into the circular drive, there was no sign of Dusty's car or an ambulance. In fact, there weren't any cars parked in front or in the parking lot.

When she got inside, the house looked completely deserted. She had to take the elevator down to the basement before she found the hens. The Jungle Room was one of the few rooms that were off limits to the guests. Bri had been in the room before but was still taken aback by the garish décor. The carpet was purple shag, the furniture animal-print, and the paintings vibrant splashes of oranges and reds.

"Don't just stand there." Minnie's voice came from somewhere in the dimly lit room. "Come on in and join us, Brianne."

She moved around a cluster of huge plastic plants to discover Minnie sitting in an orange fur chair. Sunshine sat across from her on the zebra-skin couch while Baby stood behind the bar, pouring brandy into glasses. Bri waited until she had passed the glasses out before she took the chair next to Minnie's.

"So what happened?" she asked. "How did Kenny Gene get shot?"

Minnie downed the brandy in one swallow. "We're not sure. Olive was out in the barn when she heard the shot. By the time she found the deputy in the lilac garden, whoever had shot him was long gone."

"Where are Olive and Starlet?"

"Sheriff Hicks took Olive back to Culver so she could meet with the feds for questioning. And Starlet is in the ballroom. She was pretty upset about the deputy getting shot, and playing her music seems to calm her nerves."

Bri took a sip of her drink and, wrinkling her nose, set it down on the African drum end table. "Isn't it possible that Kenny Gene shot himself? I hear that he's not exactly proficient."

"Well, you'd have to be pretty proficient to shoot yourself in the back," Minnie said.

Bri's heart sank. She had hoped that it had merely been an accident and Kenny's wound was nothing more than superficial. "Is he going to be okay?"

"The paramedics didn't say much," Minnie said, "but since Kenny Gene was still yammering when they took him away, I'd have to say yes." She shook her head. "Dusty looked worse than Kenny Gene. No doubt, he blamed himself for giving Kenny the duty of protectin' us hens from Alejandro."

"So you think it was Alejandro who shot Kenny."

"Who else could it be?"

Bri shrugged. "It just doesn't make any sense that he'd show up here for revenge and risk getting arrested again. Especially when a sheriff's car is sitting right out front."

"Maybe he came for the money," Sunshine said in her breathy voice.

"What money?" Bri asked.

"Baby," Minnie said, "why don't you and Sunshine go change the sheets on Miss Hattie's bed? I don't care if the feds are sending men to keep an eye on things. With a lunatic running around, I don't want Olive sleeping out in the barn. She can bunk with Starlet, and Brianne can sleep in Miss Hattie's room."

The two hens got up to do her bidding, but as soon as the elevator doors closed behind them, Bri repeated her question.

"What money, Minnie?"

"There's no money." Minnie maneuvered out of the chair and into her wheelchair. "Sunshine gets confused sometimes. Drug money was what Alejandro was looking for when he came the first time, so Sunshine thinks that's what he's looking for this time."

It made sense. Beau had told her all about getting his backpack confused with a drug courier's backpack that had been filled with money. But no one ever knew what had happened to that backpack. Still, there was something about the way Minnie had rushed the other hens off that didn't seem right. Before she could continue her questioning, Minnie changed the subject.

"And speaking of money, I'm not real pleased with your boyfriend evacuating all the guests out of Miss Hattie's. We had a full house through Monday. He tried to get us hens to leave, too, but I've lived here for over sixty years, and the only way I'm going out that door is feet first." She rolled toward the elevator. "I'm surprised he let you come back out here."

Bri got up and followed her. "He doesn't know."

After pushing the elevator button, Minnie glanced over. "Since you didn't deny he was your boyfriend, I'll assume that you and Dusty are an item."

"I don't know if I'd say that. Let's just say that I threw myself at him and he wasn't exactly thrilled with the gift."

Minnie chuckled. "Nothin' wrong with a woman going after what she wants. Of course, men do like to do the chasin'. So now that he's tasted what you have to offer, you need to leave it up to him on whether or not he wants seconds."

"And if he doesn't?"

"I wouldn't worry about that." Minnie smiled as the elevator doors opened. "Sheriff Hicks doesn't look like the type of man who will be satisfied with only one servin'."

Chapter Twenty

AFTER LEAVING THE JUNGLE ROOM, Bri went to her room and packed her bags. She thought about calling Twyla and breaking the news about Kenny but then decided it would be better to wait until she had more information. If Dusty didn't call within the hour, she would call him. Or Cora Lee.

While Olive had handled all her suitcases at once, it took Bri three trips to get them up to Miss Hattie's room. When both Beau and Brant were in residence, they always fought over the room. And any idiot would understand why. The room had been decorated for a man's tastes. The furniture dark and massive. The color scheme deep reds and browns. The chairs in front of the fireplace cushioned and comfortable. And the four-poster bed huge and stacked with more pillows than a sultan's tent.

On the second luggage run, it proved too much of a temptation, and Bri kicked off her heels and tested out the high mattress. She had barely stopped bouncing when she looked up and noticed the mirror on the overhead canopy. A mirror with a painting of a beautiful woman in a sexy red gown.

She laughed. No wonder her brothers fought over the room. The woman was stunning and held an expression on her face that pretty much said... "Do you want to get naughty?"

Bri wanted to get naughty. Unfortunately, the man she wanted to get naughty with was too stubborn for his own good. She knew Dusty desired her—the sex at Twyla's salon had proven that. But just because he desired her didn't mean he'd be back for seconds. And Bri was through doing all the chasing. If Dusty wanted her, he knew where to find her.

She got up from the bed and headed back down for her last suitcase. Figuring she could use the exercise, she took the stairs this time instead of the elevator. When she reached the bottom of the grand staircase, the faint sound of music had her turning toward the ballroom. The room had been turned into Starlet's music room. And when Bri opened the door, she found the young girl perched on a piano bench with her guitar. She was dressed as she always was—in an outdated formal gown that was two sizes too small for her full figure.

If there was ever any doubt in her mind about Starlet being talented enough to make it in the music business, it was dispelled by the heart-wrenchingly beautiful guitar music. Bri tried to place the song, then realized it was original when Starlet started to sing. Her voice wasn't perfect, but somehow it went perfectly with the words to the song. A song about love, betrayal, and redemption.

Unable to stop herself, Bri moved closer. Starlet didn't notice. Her eyes were closed as if the music had transported her to another place. When she was finished, her head bowed, her fingers gently resting on the strings.

Bri applauded. Although that didn't seem like enough to express how wonderful she thought the song was. Starlet lifted her head. She was crying. Tears coursed down her cheeks and dripped off her chin.

"Oh, Starlet." Bri hurried over and sat down on the bench, setting the guitar aside before drawing her into her arms. "Minnie said you were upset about Kenny Gene, but I didn't realize how much."

"It's all my fault," she sobbed.

Bri patted her back. "Of course, it's not your fault. Why would you even think that?"

"Because it is. If I hadn't taken the money, I could've given it to Alejandro, and he never would've shot Kenny Gene."

"Money?" She pulled back so she could look in Starlet's face. "What—" She paused as all the pieces came together. "Minnie lied to me about having Alejandro's drug money. It's here, isn't it?"

Starlet nodded. "I didn't know until one day when I was checking out the secret passages and came across the hidden panel in the library. I pushed it open a crack and saw Minnie opening the safe." Tears dripped down her cheeks. "I wouldn't have taken it if it had been hen money, but it was drug money. And since drugs is what screwed up my mama, I figured it was only fair that the money go to her rehabilitation." Her gaze dropped, and she studied her hands. "Except now I realize that Mama didn't spend a penny on drug rehabilitation. She lied. Just like she always has."

"So you gave all the money to your mama?"

Starlet shook her head. "There's still a little left. But not enough to appease Alejandro. When I told him the amount, I thought he was going to shoot me right then and there. He probably would've if Kenny Gene hadn't shown up."

Bri stared at her. "You saw Alejandro? You talked with him?"

Starlet nodded. "I was in the lilac garden, pruning the bushes when he came up behind me."

"Did he hurt you?"

"No. I was just scared. So scared that, when the shooting started, I ran off and hid." Her bottom lip trembled. "Leaving poor Olive to be hauled off with the sheriff when it should be me."

There was probably some truth to that. Starlet had no business taking the money. Of course, neither did Minnie. But what was Bri going to do about it? Turn in an innocent young girl who was only trying to help her mother? Or an old woman who had just undergone cancer surgery?

It took only a few seconds to decide what needed to be done.

"It's going to be all right, Starlet," Bri said. "I think I know how to fix things. Who else knows about the money?"

"Just the hens."

"What about your mother?"

Starlet shook her head. "Since I live at Miss Hattie's, she thinks I made it by prostitution."

It was hard to digest the fact that a mother would be okay with her daughter prostituting herself. But so was a mother lying to her daughter to get money. Obviously, Starlet's mother needed to get in touch with her "henness."

"So what are you going to do?" Starlet asked. "How are you going to stop Alejandro from coming back?"

Bri got up from the piano bench. "I wouldn't worry about Alejandro. He's not going to show up back here when every law enforcement officer in Texas is out to get him for shooting one of their deputies. Especially when he hears the news about the hens finding the backpack of drug money and turning it over to the FBI."

Starlet swiveled around. "But how am I going to come up with the rest of the money?"

Bri flashed her a smile. "Lucky for you, you have a wealthy friend."

Olive showed up in time for dinner. With the guests gone, the hens ate in the dining room while they listened to Olive recount what she had told the sheriff and federal agents. Some of those federal agents had followed her back to Miss Hattie's and were scattered around the property, waiting to see if Alejandro would return to the scene of the crime. Hopefully, they would keep Alejandro from returning until Bri could get the money out of her trust fund and set up her plan.

The one law officer who hadn't come back to Miss Hattie's was Dusty. He called around nine o'clock and talked with Minnie, informing her that Kenny Gene was in stable condition. After numerous attempts, Bri finally got ahold of Twyla. Bri expected hysterics, and that's just what she got. As soon as she informed Twyla that Kenny was in the hospital, the waterworks and wailing started, and Darla had to take the phone and get the rest of the information. Bri was glad she was there with Twyla.

After the exhausting day, Bri thought she'd fall asleep

easily. But once tucked into Miss Hattie's huge bed, sleep eluded her, and she found herself staring into the fire that crackled in the fireplace and thinking about Dusty and all the intense passion he brought out of her.

She had never felt this way about another man. With other boyfriends, she felt like a porcelain doll. Something to be cherished but never played with. With Dusty, she felt like a woman—an equal. She felt empowered. Like she could do anything she wanted to do. Be anything she wanted to be.

It was too bad that she didn't make Dusty feel the same way. Since he hadn't even asked Minnie about her, it was obvious that he wouldn't be back for seconds. One helping of Bri was enough.

She finally fell asleep, but awoke what seemed like only moments later to the creak of the door opening. Her first thought was of Alejandro, but before she could release a scream, a shaft of moonlight reflected off the shiny star on the man's chest.

She sat up. "Dusty?"

His hat sailed over to the chair in the corner.

"What are you doing here?" she asked. "Since the federal agents are everywhere, I'd thought you'd go back to Culver."

He removed his gun belt and tossed it to the chair before he jerked open the snaps of his shirt.

She swallowed. "Is everything okay?"

He dropped the shirt on the floor and moved closer, moonlight striping the muscles of his chest. "How breathless?"

She blinked the sleep from her eyes. "What?"

He rested a knee on the bed, his hands pressing down

the mattress on either side of her hips. "How breathless do I make you?" He brushed his lips over hers, leaving behind a heated tingle that melted everything inside her. "Do I make you as breathless as you make me?"

Bri's eyes slid closed. "More. Much more."

Chapter Twenty-one

"SO EXPLAIN THE TATTOO." Dusty leaned over and kissed the skull and crossbones, then, since he was in the vicinity, moved down and kissed the sweet spot between Brianne's legs. "Don't tell me you want to be a pirate."

"Mmm," she hummed, as his kiss grew a little deeper. "I just liked it."

He lifted his head. "You just like a lot of wicked things, don't you, Miz Cates?"

She laughed her deep, throaty laugh that always made him hard. Of course, lying naked between her legs didn't hurt.

"I guess I do." She reached out and caressed his face with the backs of her fingers. "Especially all the wicked things you did last night."

He moved up her body, enjoying the feel of her soft skin against his. "And I haven't even pulled out the handcuffs yet."

She smiled. "I'm looking forward to that." She fingered his hair, and her gaze grew intent. "I think I missed a spot. I wonder if there's a pair of scissors in Miss Hattie's bathroom."

Dusty buried his face in her neck and breathed deeply of her soft, subtle scent. "We'll worry about that later."

"It will only take a second." She pushed at his shoulders, and when he lifted his head, she scooted out from under him and got to her feet. Propping his head on his hand, he watched as she walked naked into the bathroom, her hips swaying provocatively.

"Since you seem to love messing with people's hair so much, why haven't you gotten your haircutting license?" he called into her.

She walked back out of the bathroom. "Because I'm a Cates."

Dusty might've questioned her, but it was hard to think when a naked Brianne was walking toward him. She had a perfect body. Her breasts were nice and full with just enough droop to declare their authenticity. She had a waist his hands could easily span and curvy hips that made his mouth dry. For a little bit of a thing, her legs were long and toned. But what held his attention the most was the tiny strip of dark hair between them. A strip that hid the entrance to heaven.

Unaware of the direction of his thoughts, Brianne continued to talk. "I think my parents would have a stroke if I became a beautician." She motioned at him with a tiny pair of what looked like mustache trimmers. "Sit up."

He moved over to the edge of the bed, making sure to bring the sheet with him. He didn't think she needed to know how the mere sight of her affected him.

"I guess they expect you to work for the company," he said.

She parted his knees and stepped between them. "No. They expect me to get married to some wealthy man they approve of and lead the nice, quiet life of a Southern lady."

He laughed, and when she shot him an irritated look, he held up a hand. "Sorry, but I can't see you leading a nice, quiet anything. And I didn't realize that Southern ladies have pirate tattoos and a fetish for handcuffs."

With one rather vicious snip, she cut off a piece of his hair. "I don't have a fetish for handcuffs." When he lifted his brows, she added, "I'm just curious, is all."

He took the scissors from her hand and set them down on the nightstand before he pulled her close. "And I'm more than willing to satisfy your curiosity." He nipped at her bottom lip. "But maybe we should set some ground rules. Just what do you want me to do to you once I have you handcuffed? Would you like me to do a little strip search?" He drew a line down to her belly button and dipped inside. "Or maybe you had a little corporal punishment in mind."

In the sunlight that spilled through the window, he watched her pupils dilate.

"Corporal punishment?" she squeaked.

It was hard to keep from smiling. "Nothing too harsh, mind you." His hand slid over her hip. "Just something to remind you who's in control. Who's the boss." He drew back his hand and smacked her bottom.

She flinched, and her eyes registered surprise before they filled with so much heat that Dusty sucked in his breath. He had just been teasing her, but now the joke was on him.

Her tongue came out and licked over her top lip. "I guess we could try a little corporal punishment."

Sweet Lord.

With a groan, he fell back on the bed, pulling her on top of him. But just when his lips settled over hers, she pulled away.

"What's that?"

He listened for only a second. "It's just a helicopter. They're probably switching out agents." He tried to coax her lips back to his, but she wasn't having it. She sat up and stared at the window.

"This early?"

Dusty glanced at the clock on the mantel. It was pretty early to be switching out agents. But who else could it be? Brianne answered the question only a moment later when she got up and looked out the window.

"Holy crap!" she said as she hurried back to the bed. She scrambled around in the covers until she found her nightshirt. She slipped it over her head, then scurried around collecting Dusty's clothes. "Quick." She juggled his clothes in one hand and used the other to try to pull him to his feet. "You need to hide."

"Hide?" He got to his feet and followed after her, trying to make sense out of her sudden hysteria. The only answer that came to him was one that really pissed him off.

He tugged her to a stop. "You lied about your boyfriend, didn't you? You're still together. And he isn't stalking you as much as trying to locate his runaway girlfriend. Or are you his fiancée?"

"No!" She shook her head and tried to pull him forward. "That's not it, at all. It's not a boyfriend I'm worried about as much as my big—" The doorknob twisted, and Brianne's eyes got even bigger. "You didn't lock the door?"

For a little thing, she was strong. Before he could answer her, she shoved him into the closet, tossed in his clothes, and slammed the door in his face. He stood there stunned for a few seconds, until a loud voice boomed out.

"Just what the hell is going on, Brianne? I send you here to stay out of trouble, and you bring it with you."

Another masculine voice chimed in. "Give it a rest, Brant. It's not Willie's fault that some crazy drug lord is running around."

Brianne's big brothers. That would explain her hurry to get Dusty out of sight. What brother would understand catching his little sister in bed with some stranger? Not that her brothers and Dusty were strangers. They'd talked on more than one occasion. But they still weren't close enough to keep the oldest Cates from kicking his ass.

Dusty moved farther into the closet and started getting dressed, wondering how long he'd have to hole up in there. It was one hell of a mess he found himself in. But he was no longer going to beat himself up over it. He was attracted to Brianne. What man wouldn't be? And as long as things didn't get out of control, he couldn't see where it would hurt anything. Obviously, she wanted to keep their relationship under wraps as much as he did.

He had just started to snap his shirt when he felt a cool draft. He turned to see where it was coming from and was surprised to see Starlet Brubaker step out from between a row of dresses. He recognized her immediately but couldn't figure out what she was doing in the closet.

Unaware that he was standing there, she pulled a step stool out from under the dresses and climbed up on it, carefully holding up the hem of her long dress. This one was green velvet that seemed to be busting at the seams.

"Where did I put it?" she whispered under her breath as she pushed aside the hatboxes on the top shelf.

Not sure how to alert her of his presence without startling her, he watched in silence as she started to get down. Unfortunately, the front of her gown got caught on a nail that protruded from the shelf. As she tried to get it unhooked, her eyes shifted over to him.

She released a gasp and lost her footing on the step stool. There was a loud rip as she fell backward, bumping the shelf with her flailing arms and sending hatboxes flying. Dusty made a dive for her and caught her just as the door of the closet opened.

Three sets of identical blue eyes looked back at him.

"What the hell is going on?" Brant's voice boomed. His sharp gaze took in Dusty's lack of clothing and Starlet's ripped bodice, and he didn't wait for a reply. As soon as Dusty set Starlet on her feet, a fist plowed into his jaw, sending him reeling back into the row of dresses.

"No!" Brianne yelled just as Starlet jumped in between Dusty and Brant.

"It's not like that, Uncle Brant," Starlet said. "All he did was catch me when I fell off the ladder."

Brant studied Starlet. "What were you doing in Miss Hattie's closet on a ladder?"

Her brown eyes got as big as saucers, and her face flamed a bright red. "Well...I was just..."

"I think we can figure that out." The youngest Cates brother entered the closet. Dusty had met Beckett at Jenna Jay and Beau's wedding. He was a studious-looking young man with intelligent eyes. Hopefully, he would be the voice of reason. That didn't turn out to be the case.

"There's no reason to beat him to a pulp, Brant,"

Beckett said. "It didn't look to me like the kid was fighting off his advances."

"I'm not a kid," Starlet huffed.

Beckett gave her the once-over, hesitating on the swell of her breast that pushed through the rip in her dress. "No, I guess not." He looked back at Brant. "The crazy, repressed prom queen didn't look like she was fighting him off."

Starlet released an agitated squeak. "Being a repressed prom queen is better than being a nerdy Einstein." She brushed past Beckett and out the closet door.

Once she was gone, Dusty figured it was now up to him to explain things. And the only way he could see to do it was to tell the truth.

"I wasn't here in the closet because of Starlet. I was here because of—"

"The secret passage!" Brianne cut him off. Although Dusty didn't have a clue what she was talking about. It didn't take her long to use visual aids. She hurried over and pushed some long dresses out of the way to reveal an opened door that led into a dimly lit passageway. "Obviously, Dusty stumbled on the secret passageway and followed it here." She flapped a hand at the step stool. "Where he startled Starlet while she was looking for something."

Brant's eyes narrowed, but he took a step back and crossed his arms over his chest. "And what are you doing here in the first place, Sheriff Hicks?"

Before he could answer, Brianne jumped back in. "He's protecting me and the hens, of course. Yes, I know the house is surrounded by federal agents, but everyone knows that local law enforcement has never trusted federal law enforcement."

It took only a second for Brant's shoulders to relax and a semi-smile to tip the corners of his mouth. "Then I guess I owe you an apology, Sheriff." He held out his hand. "Starlet is like a daughter to me, and I can't help but be a little overprotective."

Dusty shook his hand. "I understand completely. It was a pretty incriminating situation I found myself in."

"Crazy things happen," Brianne said with a relieved smile.

Beckett didn't say anything. He just studied Dusty with intense blue eyes.

"Well, why don't we go downstairs and have ourselves some breakfast," Brant said. "I'd like to talk to you about what's being done to apprehend Alejandro." He glanced down at Dusty's pink boxer briefs. "Although you might want to go back to your room and get dressed first."

Since there was no help for it, Dusty only nodded and turned to the door at the back of the closet. Before he ducked through, he looked back to see Brant holding out a robe for Brianne. She didn't even spare him a glance as she pulled it on and tied the sash around her waist.

Dusty didn't know why he had the sudden urge to turn right back around and kiss her senseless. Maybe because he didn't like the fact that she could dismiss him so easily. Or maybe it was because he couldn't seem to dismiss her. Everything, from her messed dark hair to the tips of her blue-painted toes, reminded him of their night of passion. And even standing in the cold draft, he felt hot and needy.

All he wanted was one look from her to say she felt the same. He didn't get it. The only one who shot him a curious look was Brant, which caused Dusty to step through the door and pull it closed behind him. He waited for what felt like forever before he reopened the door and walked into the empty closet to retrieve the rest of his clothes. He planned to update Brant on Alejandro, but he wasn't staying around for breakfast.

Lusting after Brianne in front of the hens was one thing. Lusting after her in front of her brothers was something else entirely. He had just grabbed his boots when the closet door opened, and Beckett stepped in holding his hat and holster.

The young man was so serious that it was hard to read him. Although there was a teasing note in his voice as he held out Dusty's gun.

"I figure if you're going to protect my sister, you might need this."

Chapter Twenty-two

"ARE YOU LISTENING TO ME, Bri?"

"Of course, I'm listening to you, Brant," Bri said. But she wasn't listening. She was watching Dusty, who stood in the driveway talking with some of the federal agents. His shirt was even more wrinkled than it normally was, and his jeans hugged his fine butt like melted butter on one of Baby's cinnamon rolls. One of the agents said something, and Dusty glanced back at the house. For a brief second, the mirrored lenses pinned her before he turned and headed to his car.

A part of her wanted to run after him and apologize. Except she didn't know what she wanted to apologize for. Possibly for treating him like a stranger since her brothers had arrived. But certainly he understood why. He had gotten a taste of Brant's protectiveness. Still, she couldn't help feeling guilty as she watched the cloud of dust disappear.

When she turned, Brant was still talking and Beckett was studying her with a curious look.

"What?" she mouthed, but he only shrugged and returned his gaze to Brant.

"... so I think we're in the clear as far as your picture becoming a huge media scandal." Brant glanced through a pile of mail on the desk. "So go pack your bags and you can come back with me and Beckett." When Bri didn't move, he glanced up. "What's the matter, Bri? You've been acting strange ever since I got here."

Bri looked away from her oldest brother's piercing gaze and walked over to examine the books on the shelf. "I guess I'm just worried about the hens." She ran a finger down the spine of *War and Peace*. "With Alejandro still on the loose, I don't want to leave them all alone."

"Alone?" Brant pointed at the window. "Have you looked outside? The house is surrounded by law officers. Besides, I plan on coming back after I drop you and Beckett off in Dogwood."

Bri stepped closer to the desk. "But you shouldn't have to leave Elizabeth and the kids. And I really don't mind staying here a few more days."

"And just what do you intend to do if Alejandro should make it past the federal agents?" He shook his head. "No, if the stubborn hens refuse to leave, I'll come back and stay. At least until Alejandro is apprehended."

"I'll stay."

Both Brant and Bri turned to Beckett as he rolled up from the couch. It looked as if he'd grown a good three inches in the last two months. He now was even taller than Brant. "Since I just finished setting up new computer software for the company," he said, "I don't have a lot to do right now. So why don't you let me stay and keep an eye on things."

Brant shook his head. "I don't think that's a good idea, Beckett."

Beckett's shoulders stiffened. "Why? Because you think your geeky little brother won't be able to protect the hens any better than Bri?"

Brant looked away. "Of course not. It's just…" After a few seconds, he sighed and ran a hand through his hair. "Fine. You can stay." He sent Bri a pointed look. "You go pack your bags."

"No." The word popped out of her mouth. She didn't know who was more shocked—her or Brant. She cleared her throat. "What I meant is, that if Beckett is going to stay, I'd like to stay as well. With Beckett being so busy with the company, we haven't gotten to see a lot of each other and I've missed him." She glanced over at Beckett, who seemed to find something amusing before she turned back to Brant with a pleading look. "Please, Brant."

It took him only a second of deliberation before he nodded. "Okay, but I don't want you leaving Miss Hattie's. Agreed?"

She smiled sweetly. "Of course. Where else would I go?"

Not more than two hours later, Bri was on the highway to Bramble after getting a phone call from Twyla. Twyla had given up all thoughts of breaking it off with Kenny Gene and was now at the hospital in Lubbock nursing him back to health. Which left the people of Bramble without a beautician. And Bri wasn't about to let Twyla lose business. Especially when she couldn't resist having the salon all to herself. Even if that meant breaking a promise to her big brother. Something her youngest brother had no problem pointing out.

"You do realize that you're skating on thin ice, don't

you, Sis?" Beckett tried to adjust his long legs, which were crammed against the dashboard of the Smart Car. "If Brant finds out that you ignored his orders, he'll have Mama and Daddy lock you in your room and throw away the key."

"And what will he do to you if he finds out that you allowed me to leave?"

"I didn't allow you," he corrected her. "I tried to get you to rethink leaving the Henhouse, and when you refused to listen, I had no choice but to come with you."

"You had a choice. You could've stayed there."

"No, thanks. The hens creep me out. Especially Starlet. I mean, what kind of psycho wears prom dresses every day? I'm surprised she hasn't killed us all in our sleep."

Bri laughed. "Starlet wouldn't hurt a fly. You just don't like her because she thinks you're a geek."

He reached down and tried to adjust the seat. "And I wonder where she got that? Our brothers have always thought I was a geek."

"Well, it was kinda hard not to, Beck. Especially when you carried a briefcase to school."

He stopped adjusting his seat and stared at her with confusion. "What else was I supposed to carry my laptop in? A backpack?"

Bri bit back her smile. "Of course not. What was I thinking?"

They drove in silence for a few minutes before Beckett spoke. "I could protect you, you know. Just because I'm smart doesn't mean I can't take care of myself and the people I love."

She glanced over. His expression was serious and almost hurt. She bumped his shoulder, surprised by how hard it felt. "I know that, Beck. But I have three overprotective brothers. Can't you just be my friend?"

He went back to adjusting the seat. "If that's the case, tell me about what's going on between you and the sheriff."

"What do you mean?"

Beckett rolled his eyes at her. "I'm not Brant and Billy, who believe everything you tell them, Bri. I know the guy wasn't in the closet because he was lost."

It didn't surprise her. Beckett had always been less gullible than her other brothers. He might not know about her thrill seeking and Jared stalking her, but he knew she wasn't the saint she tried so hard to portray.

"Okay," she said. "So I'm having a fling with the local sheriff—"

Beckett held up his hand. "Never mind. I suddenly realized that I'm not as immune to big brother syndrome as I thought." He squinted out the windshield. "Is that a fire?"

Bri scanned the horizon until her gaze landed on the billows of purple smoke that drifted up from the east side of Bramble. "What is that?"

"I don't know," Beckett said, "but it doesn't look good."

She followed the smoke to a small house that was on the outskirts of town. Beckett didn't even wait for her to come to a full stop before he jumped out and raced toward the house, covering his nose and mouth before entering. Seconds later, he returned with Rachel Dean in his arms.

Bri got out of the car and hurried over to them. "What happened? Do I need to call nine-one-one?"

Beckett shook his head as he set Rachel down on an

old stump. "No. There's no fire. Just this strange vapor coming from the boiling pots on the stove." He fanned the air. "But, damn, it stinks."

The air was filled with a pungent smell that was worse than any brotherly flatulence. Bri pinched her nose closed as she spoke to Rachel.

"Are you okay?"

Rachel sat for a few seconds as if she wasn't sure what had happened. "I really thought I had it right this time." She shook her head. "I guess the ammonia might've been a mistake."

Bri tried to brush the purple from Rachel Dean's hair, but it wasn't coming out. "Are you still trying to come up with a remedy for dandruff?"

"Nope. I thought I'd try somethin' a little more difficult." She felt her purple scalp. "But somehow I don't think my concoction will cure Male Pattern Baldness."

Beckett's eyes widened. "Male Pattern Baldness?"

In an attempt to keep her brother from saying something that might hurt Rachel's feelings, Bri sent him a warning look. "Rachel comes from a long line of healers, Beckett."

"It's true," Rachel said. "'Course, I never gave it much thought until Reverend Jessup showed up." Tears filled her eyes. "I was always happy just working at Josephine's. But I guess the reverend is right, a woman should do something more with her life than wait tables."

Bri had held in her anger about the good reverend for as long as she could. Enough was enough. "And I think that Reverend Josiah Jessup is full of more crap than a dog pound Dumpster!" she blurted out, causing Rachel's eyes to widen and Beckett to grin.

Bri was so wound up that she started pacing. "I mean, where does the man get off thinking that he can tell people what they should be doing? He's not God. He's just a con artist who gets his kicks out of screwing with people's lives." She stopped and pointed a finger at Rachel. "It doesn't matter what the reverend or anyone else thinks. It only matters what you think. And if you want to work as a waitress or a circus clown... or even a beautician, then I think that's exactly what you should do."

Rachel Dean cocked her head. "Whelp, I did want to be a circus clown at one time in my life. Of course, I get to do that every town parade and that seems to be more than enough—that grease paint is as itchy as a wool sweater." She tried to smooth down her frizzy purple hair. "As for being a beautician, I don't have the knack for it like you do. 'Course, I don't seem to have the knack for healin', either."

"I don't know about that," Bri said. "From what I hear, most folks counted on you to start their day out right with a smile and a cup of coffee. Isn't that a form of healing?"

Rachel's eyes narrowed in thought. But before she could answer, the entire town of Bramble converged on her house. First came an old fire truck with a crank siren blaring, then a line of American-made cars and trucks. The fire truck pulled up behind Bri's Smart Car, and Harley Sutter hopped out. Bri was surprised to see that he wasn't wearing his biker clothes. He was dressed in creased pants, pressed western shirt, and high-polished boots. He had on a beige Stetson, and his mustache was slicked and curled up on the ends.

He came chugging across the lawn and pulled Rachel right up against his big belly. "Mercy, woman. You pert near scared me to death." He released her. "Tinker spotted the smoke and rang the fire bell. We got here as soon as we could. You okay?"

The rest of the townsfolk got out of their cars and came running over to surround Rachel with love and concern. Rossie Owens picked her up off her feet and gave her a kiss right on the mouth that had her blushing a bright red. Rachel was so flustered that it took her a while to find her voice.

"Well, I sure do appreciate y'all's concern. But as you can see, I'm right as rain." She tugged on a strand of hair and chuckled. "Purple rain."

"What cure you workin' on now, Rachel?" a big-bellied cowboy in the back hollered.

"Whelp, I've been thinkin' about that," she said. "And considering my missin' eyebrows and purple hair, I'd say that there's only one thing I'm good at curin'."

"What's that?" the mayor asked.

Rachel Dean scanned the crowd with glistening eyes. "Hunger. What say we call up Josephine and get her to reopen the diner? I'm ready to serve up some grub!"

Chapter Twenty-three

THE HOTEL WAS A DIVE. There was a ring in the toilet, spots all over the puke green carpet, and something that looked a lot like blood spattered on the wall behind the headboard. The double mattress was lumpy, and the sheets were thin and smelled of mildew.

Still, it had good porn.

Josiah watched the two women on the small television as they kissed and gyrated against each other. *Stupid whores.* He rubbed a hand over his crotch. *Stupid, stupid whores.*

Of course, all women were whores. From his mother, who had left him and his father when he was only twelve, right down to the Cates bitch, who had laughed when Olive doused him with water. He smiled. Brianne Cates might've thought it was funny that he'd been doused with water, but she wouldn't be laughing for long. Not when he was in possession of Jared Avery's pictures.

Josiah had found out about the naked picture of Brianne after he'd convinced Jared to stop for a drink on his way back to Austin. Most arrogant, rich people couldn't hold their booze, and Jared was one of them. After the fourth drink, he'd been more than happy to spill his story to Josiah. The rest had been simple, especially when the arrogant bastard carried his pictures around on his phone. After Josiah got him thoroughly soused, it was easy to slip his phone from his pocket and take it to the bathroom, where Josiah e-mailed them to his own cell phone.

Not that the pictures were all that raunchy. Besides a couple of topless ones, the others were merely of Brianne skiing, skydiving, and drinking at some nightclub. Still, they were probably bad enough to get money out of the Cateses. Blackmail had always been beneath Josiah, but if his reality show didn't work out, it might be his only choice for survival.

And Josiah would always survive. No matter what it took.

A breathy moan pulled his attention back to the women on the television. He had started to reach inside his boxers, when his cell phone rang. He thought about ignoring it and calling whomever it was back, but then he glanced down at the number and the California area code had him turning down the volume to the TV and reaching for the phone.

"God be with you," he said.

"Well, he sure must be with you, Reverend," the producer's voice came through the receiver, "because I ran your idea by the big dogs and they love it."

A thrill ran through Josiah, making him even harder. He adjusted himself before asking, "So when do we get to start?"

"They want to get it on the air as soon as possible. But first they want to see the footage of this whorehouse that you were telling me about. You've been working on it, right?"

Some of the thrill and desire leaked out of him, and Josiah reached for the bottle of whiskey he'd brought back to the room and took a deep swallow.

"I've been thinking," he hedged, "maybe we shouldn't start with the Henhouse. Maybe we should start with something smaller. I discovered some pretty damaging pictures of Brianne Cates. She's the sister of the owners of C-Corp, one of the biggest gas and fuel companies in the country. So I'm thinking we could start with exposing her for the hussy she is. Then move on to bigger fish."

There was only a second's pause before Mike came back on. "No. We're not interested in the exploits of some socialite. Paris Hilton and the Kardashians are old news. The bosses are interested in Miss Hattie's. That's the premiere episode that's going to hook the viewers"—he laughed—"pardon the pun."

Josiah forced his own laugh, even though he didn't feel much like laughing. "I couldn't agree more. It's just that it might be harder to expose the evils going on out at the Henhouse than I first thought. The women that run the place are a wily lot who have the bed-and-breakfast cover down to an art form."

"Are you saying that you can't pull this off, Reverend?" Mike asked. "Because if that's what you're saying, then this conversation is over."

Josiah's shoulders stiffened, but he kept the anger out of his voice. "That's not what I'm saying at all. I'm just saying that I might need a little more time."

"Well, you don't have much. You know how this business works. A good idea today is a piece of garbage tomorrow. I'd say you've got a couple weeks tops. I'll have a camera crew waiting. All you need to do is let me know when you're ready."

The phone clicked.

Josiah set the phone back down on the nightstand and reached for the bottle. He downed the rest of it, then pulled back his arm and sent the bottle sailing at the door. Glass shattered and rained down on the carpet and the scarred table that sat in front of the window.

He fell back to the pillows and glared at the television. The two whores were still at it. Although now they had moved from foreplay to oral sex, and the blonde was nearing orgasm. It was the worst overacting Josiah had ever seen in a porno. Her face was contorted like she was in pain, and her breasts heaved with each pant. He reached for the remote and turned up the volume to her loud groans and moans. When she finally came, her facial expressions and loud scream were almost laughable.

Except Josiah wasn't laughing. He was turned on. So turned on that with only a few strokes he came along with the whore. When his breathing returned to normal, he opened his eyes to find the porno over and the movie menu back up.

He turned off the television. Obviously, it didn't matter how bad the acting was as long as the viewer was pulled into the fantasy.

Josiah's hand froze on the remote.

The viewer pulled into the fantasy.

The words had him jumping to his feet and pacing at the end of the bed.

"Of course," he said. "It doesn't matter if it's real or not as long as the viewer is pulled into the fantasy."

He didn't know why he hadn't thought of it before. Especially when his entire ministry was based on smoke and mirrors. All it took were a few tricks and people fell for his "miracles" hook, line, and sinker. Mostly because he gave them what they wanted to believe—that miracles really did happen. That cripples could walk again. And the blind could see. And the sick could be healed.

And if it worked with his ministry, and pornos, why couldn't it work for a whorehouse?

He stopped and rubbed his hands together. "Now all I need to do is get together the cast." He headed back for his phone. A shard of glass bit into the heel of his foot, but he was so intent on his plan, he barely even noticed. He found the number he wanted and pushed it.

"Hey, Frankie, it's Josiah," he said with a gleeful smile. "You still know that guy who owns that strip club in Houston? Well, I need some of his girls for a night."

Chapter Twenty-four

BRI FINISHED CLEANING OUT THE SINK and added the sponge to the pile of towels before carrying them to the washing machine that was located next to the small bathroom. It had been a long day. Not only had she given two women highlights, but she'd done two haircuts, one perm, and shaved a number 1 on the heads of the entire defensive line of Bramble High's football team.

Yes, she was tired. But it was a good kind of tired. And as she placed the towels in the washing machine, she couldn't help humming along with the country music that came from the radio. It was a Miranda Lambert song. The same song that had been playing during her car chase with Dusty. But now it didn't fill her with the desire to do something reckless. In fact, she didn't feel antsy at all. She just felt...content.

And when she glanced up and saw a handsome sheriff standing in the doorway, the feeling only intensified.

"Hi," she said, the word coming out all breathless and sappy.

Dusty didn't answer. He stood there staring at her, the lenses of his sunglasses reflecting back at her.

Suddenly feeling shy and nervous, she turned and reached for the laundry detergent. "So how was your day? My day was crazy busy. I had one customer right after the other. My last one was Cindy Lynn. It seems she's broken out in some kind of rash and wanted a facial. I was terrified to put anything on the red welts, so I just gave her a shampoo and trim. Personally, I just think the woman needed someone to talk to. Halfway through her rinse, she started babbling and didn't stop until she walked out the door. I now know all there is to know about the folks of Bramble. Some things I could've lived without knowing."

She flashed a smile toward Dusty. But when he remained standing by the door with a somber expression, her smile drooped. "So I guess you're mad about what happened this morning? But you really don't know my family. If I hadn't lied, you'd still be at the Henhouse getting interrogated. Or recovering from the injuries Brant inflicted. Believe me when I tell you that it's for the best if my family doesn't know what is going on between us."

"And what's going on between us?"

His direct question put a halt to her rambling, and she struggled to find an answer in her suddenly empty brain. She'd told Beckett that it was only a fling. But standing there looking at Dusty with her heart racing and her tummy all airy, it didn't feel like a fling. It felt like more. Much more.

She turned to the washer and fiddled with the dials. "I don't know exactly. Do you?" She had just pushed in the knob to start the machine when warm hands slipped around her waist and pulled her back against a hard body.

Dusty nosed her hair out of the way, and his lips settled on the spot behind her ear. Just that quickly, desire welled up and her knees turned to jelly. She grabbed on to the edge of the washing machine and tried to remember how to breathe as his hand slid up to cup her breast.

"No," he said against her neck as he strummed her nipple with his thumb. She whimpered with need, and he turned her around and silenced the sound with a deep kiss that took the rest of her sanity. When he finally pulled back, she felt like she was seconds from melting into a puddle at his boots. Her eyes fluttered open, and she found herself staring up into mossy amber heat.

"All I know," he said in a low whisper, "is I'm not ready for it to end."

Bri woke to brilliant morning light streaming in through the window. She blinked and focused on the most glorious of images: Dusty stretched out before her completely naked. Unfortunately, he slept on his stomach, but the view was still mighty fine. Starting at his feet, which hung over the end of the mattress, her gaze traveled up the lean muscles of his legs to his pale butt. There was a tan line that ran along his waist and high up on the back of his thighs. Since she couldn't picture Dusty walking around town in a pair of short shorts, she wondered if he ran like Beckett. That would certainly explain the running shoes and his well-developed calves and lean physique.

She reached out and ran her fingers up his back, over the bumps of his rib cage, to the thick muscles of his shoulder. He shifted in his sleep, his head turning so he now faced her. His hair was mussed, and a lock fell over his forehead. In the sunlight, it looked even blonder, like the eyelashes that rested against his cheeks. His nose was straight with a ridge at the very top that was more than likely caused by the sunglasses he always wore. In sleep, his lips were soft and much less stern. And Bri couldn't help leaning over to brush a kiss across them.

His eyes opened, and he stared at her for a moment before recognition slipped in. "What time is it?" His voice was craggy with sleep.

She outlined his bottom lip with her finger, pressing into the plumpness. "I'm not sure." She gave him another kiss. This one deeper and much wetter.

He participated for only a moment before pulling back and glancing up at the window. His eyes widened. "Shit." He rolled to his feet. "I need to get going."

Hoping to entice him back to bed, Bri pushed the sheet off and rolled to her side, striking a seductive pose. "Going? I thought you said you had Saturdays off. Or are you worried about my brothers showing up? I told you that Beckett isn't a tattletale."

Dusty barely glanced her way as he pulled underwear out of the top drawer. "He might think differently when he gets up this morning and discovers that I didn't bring you home last night. But this isn't about your brothers, Bri. I need to be in Houston by this afternoon for my visitation with Emma."

His words took all thoughts of seduction right out of her, and she sat up and covered her breasts with the sheet. "How long will you be gone?"

"I'll be back by tonight. I only get a few hours every couple weeks."

"Just a few hours? That's all you get to see your daughter?"

Dusty turned to her. "I told you. My wife's lawyers did a great job of portraying me as the bad guy."

"I just didn't realize that judge only gave you a few hours with her." Bri swung her legs over the bed. "Why, that's criminal. And your ex should be ashamed of herself for even attempting to keep your daughter away from you."

He shot her a sardonic look. "I seem to remember another woman trying to sway the decision of a judge by using her family's clout."

Bri felt her face heat up. He was right. She had been willing to use whatever it took to stay out of jail. Even when she'd deserved to be incarcerated. Which explained why Dusty had hated her so much at first. To him, she was just another little rich girl using her money and family power to get her way. And she could tell by the look in his eyes that he still thought so. And was he wrong? Wasn't she still trying to avoid taking responsibility for her own actions by hiding the truth from her brothers? Still trying to do what she wanted to do with no regard to how it would affect other people?

She looked away from his direct eyes and stared down at the blue paint on her toes. "You're right. I should've spent more than a few days in jail for my actions, instead of using my family to get out of my punishment." She blinked back the tears that formed in her eyes. "I'm so sorry, Dusty. You must really hate wealthy, spoiled women."

There was a long silence, then Dusty was there, pulling her up in his arms and covering her mouth in a heated kiss. Once her head stopped spinning, she opened her eyes to find him looking down at her with a solemn expression.

"Who said that you've gotten out of your punishment?" he said. "Just because we've started having sex doesn't mean I've forgiven and forgotten." He tapped her nose. "No, your time of punishment is coming, Miz Cates."

"It is?" she squeaked. Heat filled her entire body, her nipples stiffening against his bare chest. Her reaction set off a chain reaction in Dusty. He hardened, and his eyes turned hot and needy.

Unfortunately, he seemed to have much better control over his body's demands than Bri did. After taking a deep breath, his hands dropped and he stepped away from her. "But it will have to wait. I'm late as is and still need to drop you off at Miss Hattie's." He turned and headed for the bathroom.

It was hard to pull her gaze from his firm butt. And harder still to act as if she wasn't about to tackle him from behind and demand he give her his punishment right then and there.

Instead, she picked up his wrinkled sheriff's shirt and slipped it on before walking to the kitchen to make some coffee. By the time he was showered and dressed, she had a cup waiting for him.

"You don't need to drop me off." She handed him the travel mug, smoothing his damp hair off his forehead. "Beckett or Olive can come pick me up. You just worry about getting to Emmie."

Dusty studied the cup in his hand, and then her, and his eyes filled with something she couldn't read. "You sure?"

She nodded. "Beckett will look for any excuse to leave the Henhouse." She followed him out the door, watching as he walked to the older model truck parked next to his cruiser.

"Drive safely," she said.

His hand froze on the door handle of the truck, and he turned back. The crooked smile he sent her made her heart thwack hard against her ribs.

"I'll call you later."

Bri stood there with her arms tightly wrapped around her body until the truck disappeared. The feeling of contentment returned. Like she was exactly where she should be, doing exactly what she should be doing. Waiting for Dusty. It was an absurd thought. One she tried to push out of her mind as she walked back inside.

Her stomach growled, but while making coffee, she'd discovered that Dusty's cupboards and refrigerator were as bare as her behind. She thought about calling the Henhouse and having Beckett come get her, but instead she walked into the other bedroom. The bedroom with the cans of pink paint and the playhouse castle.

With a determination Bri didn't know she had, she picked up a paint can and gave it a good shake. She might've hated her interior design classes, but that didn't mean she hadn't learned a few things.

Enough to make a dream room for a little girl.

And her loving father.

It took most of the day to finish the room. Of course, she had some help. Beckett showed up in the Smart Car around ten and painted while Bri wallpapered. At noon, Olive stopped by. Once she discovered there was no food in the house, she left and returned with groceries and all the hens in tow—along with a couple of federal agents.

Without guests, the hens were bored silly and were just itching to have something to do. Baby cooked enchiladas for lunch and then made a variety of freezer dinners that Dusty could easily heat up in the microwave. While she cooked, Sunshine and Starlet cleaned, proving to be much better at windows than Bri had been.

Minnie had Olive lower the ironing board so she could sit in her wheelchair and iron while she directed everyone. Once she heard about Dusty's daughter, she sent Olive and one of the agents back to the house to retrieve an antique bed and dresser from the attic.

The white French provincial furniture was the perfect match for the pink-and-white-striped accent wall Bri had papered. As were the frilly curtains and bedspread Olive thought to bring along. It was well past six by the time the hens packed up and left. Beckett and Bri stayed to put on the finishing touches.

"Do you think it looks good there or over by the window?" Bri pointed to the castle dollhouse—the one thing in the room she hadn't touched. It was Dusty's gift to his daughter and something he needed to finish. Hopefully, he wouldn't feel the same way about the room.

When she didn't get a reply, Bri glanced over her shoulder. Beckett was leaning on the doorjamb with his arms crossed, and she was surprised at how much he resembled her other brothers. He had changed so much since graduating from college. Gone was the lanky boy who had trouble coordinating his feet, and in his place was a man who looked comfortable in his own skin.

A man who knew how to cut to the chase.

"So what's going on?" He pushed away from the door and stepped closer to the bed. "And don't give me that crap about it just being a fling. You don't spend an entire day painting and wallpapering just for a fling.

Especially when you're not exactly the homemaker type." She started to deny it, but he held up his hand. "I'm not saying that Mother didn't train you to be the perfect little homemaker. I'm just saying that I've spent years listening to you complain about it. And now, you look as happy as a heifer in an alfalfa field. So what gives?"

"Maybe I just wanted to do something special for someone." She left the castle where it was and brushed out a wrinkle in the bedspread. "Dusty has been so busy keeping the hens safe that he hasn't had time to decorate his daughter's room. I thought it would be the nice thing to do."

Beckett snorted. "Yeah, right. When are you going to stop playing mind games, Bri? Not only with your family, but also with yourself? I understand why you did it as a child. I grew up in the same household. I know how hard it was to have three older brothers bossing you around and telling you what to do. Four, if you include Buckley. Although he died so young that I have only a few memories of him."

Bri had no memories of her oldest brother, who had been hit by a train on prom night. She had been only five at the time of the accident and could remember nothing more than the sorrow that filled the house after his death.

"But you're a grown woman now," Beckett continued. "There's no reason you can't have an old boyfriend."

She shot a glance over at him. "Dusty is not old."

"I doubt that our parents would agree since he looks to be as old as Billy. But that's just my point, Bri. You should've listened to what you preached to Rachel Dean. It doesn't matter what Mama, Daddy, or anyone else thinks. It only matters what you think—how you feel.

And if you want to date some old sheriff"—his eyes sparkled with mischief—"then that's totally up to you. You shouldn't have to sneak around or lie about it."

"I'm not lying. Dusty isn't my boyfriend. We've never even been out on a date together." Her shoulders sagged. "I'm not even sure he likes me."

"But you like him." It was a statement more than a question. And looking around the room, Bri couldn't deny it.

"Yes."

"Then go for it." Beckett took her arms and gave her a little shake. "Decorate his house, fill his freezer with frozen dinners, clean his windows until they sparkle, and fix everyone's hair in town. And don't let our family keep you from it." A look entered his eyes, determination mixed with a huge amount of sadness. "I have something to tell you, something I should've told everyone months ago. But like you, I was worried about disappointing my family."

Bri reached up and cradled his chin. "You could never disappoint me, Beck. Don't you know that? Is this about the job you were thinking of taking with Apple?" She smiled. "Brant and Billy will hate to lose you, but if it's what you want..."

"No, that's not the job I decided to take." He released his breath in a long sigh that had fear tiptoeing down Bri's spine before he spoke again.

"I joined the Marines."

Chapter Twenty-five

DUSTY GOT OUT OF HIS CAR and looked up at the clear blue west Texas sky. It was a glorious morning. The autumn air still held a tinge of coolness, and the afternoon winds had yet to pick up. As he walked up the pathway to Sam Winslow's front door, he was surprised to find himself whistling a tune. He laughed when he realized it was the theme song to *The Andy Griffith Show*. Emmie had been humming it off and on during their visit on Saturday, and now it seemed to be stuck in his head.

Although he had to admit it was a catchy tune.

"For a man who has two counties to look after and a Mexican outlaw on the loose, you sure sound happy."

Dusty paused with one foot on the bottom porch step and glanced over to see Sam sitting on an old couch at the far end of the porch with his foot propped up. Other than the bandaged foot, Sam looked happy and healthy.

Relieved, Dusty continued up the steps. "You should know that you can't let this job get the best of you, Sam. Work is work, and your private life your private life."

Sam grinned. "Then I guess it's your private life that's worth whistlin' about."

Dusty started to deny it and then realized that he couldn't. In the last week, his private life had become something worth whistling about. And it all had to do with a little bit of a woman who had slipped under his skin without him even being aware of it.

He could argue that it was simply sexual, especially when they spent a good 70 percent of their time in bed. But no matter how good the sex was, it wasn't what he enjoyed the most about his relationship with Bri. What he enjoyed the most was the companionship. He'd gone without for so long that he'd forgotten what it was like to have someone who really listened to you. And not just listened, but cared.

Bri did both. Since coming back from Houston, he and Bri had been together every night. Sometimes, he'd stop by the Henhouse after he got off work, and sometimes, she'd meet him at the ranch. Wherever they'd decided to meet, she was always there to greet him with a kiss that knocked his socks off and four simple words that warmed his heart.

How was your day?

And then she would take his hand and lead him to the swing on Miss Hattie's porch, or the small table in his kitchen, and give him her full attention. Once they talked about his day, they would talk about hers. She was still helping out Twyla while Kenny Gene was in the hospital and always seemed to have some funny story about the townsfolk that made him laugh. After they talked about their days, they might go for a run or work on Emmie's castle or just eat dinner and continue to talk. It was those moments together that he enjoyed the most. Those moments that stayed with him during the day and had him whistling and grinning like an idiot.

Attempting to control the giddiness that had taken over his body, he sat down across from Sam and tried to change the subject. "So how's your foot?"

"Better." Sam shifted his foot on the pillow. "I guess you're more than ready to stop doing two jobs. I'm shore sorry about that, Dusty."

"No need to apologize. I know you'd do the same for me. Besides, things have been pretty quiet in Bramble since the good reverend left."

Sam shook his head. "That man sure raised a ruckus, didn't he?"

"He did that," Dusty said. "But the townsfolk figured things out before he did too much damage. Rachel Dean has gone back to work at the diner, and the mayor has given up his notion about running for governor. And as soon as you're back in uniform, Bramble will be back to normal."

Instead of agreeing with Dusty, Sam didn't say anything. He turned and looked out at the road. His reaction worried Dusty.

"What's wrong, Sam? Is it your foot? Did Doc tell you something that you're not telling me?"

It took a moment for Sam to glance back at him. "It's not my foot. Doc plans to take the bandage off tomorrow and says I'll be able to go back to work as long as I take it easy."

"Well, that's great news. So what's the problem?"

Before he could answer, the screen door squeaked and Myra came out with a tray of lemonade. "I thought I heard voices. You're just in time for a midday snack, Sheriff Hicks." She set the tray down on the table before handing a glass of lemonade to each of them.

A lot of folks in town thought that Myra was a bit of a tyrant who kept Sam on a short leash. But having spent time at their house, Dusty knew better. Sam adored his wife, and she adored him. Which was evident by the way she carefully adjusted the pillow under Sam's foot.

"Now don't overdo, Sammy," she said before she sent Dusty a smile and took the tray back inside. Even after she was gone, Sam still looked at the door with a smile on his face. The smile dropped when he turned to Dusty.

"I wasn't gonna say anything. Especially after all you've done for me." He took a deep breath and slowly released it. "But with the way Myra loves to gossip, I figure you'll find out soon enough. And I'd rather you hear it straight from the horse's mouth." He cleared his throat. "I'm retirin', Dusty."

Dusty set down his glass of lemonade. "What? But why, Sam? Don't tell me it has something to do with that fool of a reverend."

Sam took a deep swallow of his lemonade. "Actually, it does. But not how you think. The reverend never tried to get me to quit. He just pointed out that a sheriff should be proficient with a firearm. Something I'm obviously not."

Dusty was so angry he had a hard time not jumping to his feet. "A good sheriff doesn't need to be as proficient with his gun as much as with people. And you're the best people person I know. Why, you can talk a criminal straight into jail without firing a shot."

Sam smiled sadly. "And that worked pretty well when all I had to deal with were a few petty criminals who didn't carry guns. But nowadays, we're dealing with big-time criminals who don't care about killin' innocent people. And I'd never forgive myself if someone in town got hurt because I couldn't get my gun out of my holster."

When Dusty started to say something, Sam held up his hand. "I'm glad you don't want me to quit, Dusty. And I figure you want to blame the reverend for my decision. But I was thinkin' about this long before he ever arrived in town. The accident just forced me to make the decision." He took his injured foot off the table and leaned over to pat Dusty's hand. "It's time, boy. And you'll know what I'm talkin' about when you get there."

"So who's going to take your place?"

Sam just smiled. "I guess that will be up to the voters of Bramble."

Dusty didn't feel much in the whistling mood after leaving Sam's. All he needed was to have to deal with a new sheriff. He only hoped that the town didn't elect Kenny Gene. As he drove down Main Street, he couldn't help feeling more than a little relieved that things were back to normal. Josephine's Diner's parking lot was filled to capacity. Darla sat on the park bench in front of Sutter's Pharmacy, knitting and yakking away to Moses Tate, who appeared to be sound asleep. And there was no sight of bicycles or biking shorts. In fact, Harley was dressed normally and helping Rye Pickett hang a banner across the street to advertise the Fall Festival.

He waved jovially as Dusty cruised by, bumping the ladder and almost knocking Rye off.

Dusty watched in his rearview mirror to make sure Rye caught his balance before he turned off Main and headed for Twyla's salon. In the last week, he'd avoided the salon. Simply because he didn't trust himself. And the last thing he needed was someone walking in while he had Bri up on the counter. But today he couldn't help himself. He wanted to see her. Not because he wanted to make love with her—although he always wanted that— but because he wanted to talk with her about what Sam had told him.

Except when he stepped in the side door, he didn't find Bri in her cute little minishirt and red heels. He found Twyla sitting in the swivel chair and talking on the phone.

". . . well, we didn't set a date exactly. But Kenny Gene said that God had given him a vision after he got shot of me in a camouflaged huntin' outfit sittin' on a cooler of beer. And why else would I be in a camouflaged huntin' outfit unless I was married to him? It was a sign from God that we're gonna be hitched before next huntin' season—" She glanced up and a brilliant smile lit her face. "Gotta go, honey. Sheriff Hicks is here for a haircut."

Dusty waited for her to hang up the phone before he spoke. "Actually, I'm looking for—"

"Willie." Twyla's face fell. "You and everyone else. If she wasn't such a sweetie, I'd think she was out to steal my bid-ness."

He looked around. "So where is she?"

"Well, she was here, but then Bubba, I mean Billy, showed up, and she left in a hurry. I guess she doesn't realize that he's already taken."

Dusty had heard that Billy and Shirlene were back from their cruise. For a moment, he actually contemplated driving out to their mansion on some trumped-up excuse. But then he realized what a mistake it would be.

Especially when he was having the hardest time controlling his emotions where the woman was concerned. Even now, Twyla read the disappointment on his face.

"Now don't be lookin' so sad." She picked up the plastic cape. "I can give you a haircut just as good as Willie, if not better."

Luckily, before Dusty had to come up with an excuse, Cora Lee's voice came through the radio.

"Your friend Ryker called and needs you to call him."

Dusty unhooked the radio and pressed the side button. "Roger that." He hooked it back on his belt as he spoke to Twyla. "Sorry, Twyla, I'll have to take a rain check on that haircut." Pushing open the screen door, he pulled his cell phone from his pocket and dialed.

"So what's up?" he said as soon as Ryker answered.

"I just wanted you to know that I hit the jackpot."

Dusty paused halfway to his car. "You dug something up on Heather?"

Ryker laughed. "You could say that. The last time we talked, I mentioned her going to her accountant. It got me to thinking. I mean, how often does a woman need to go see her accountant? And Heather goes three times a week for over three hours a pop. So I tracked down one of the guy's secretaries and did a little sweet-talking. It turns out that the man has an apartment over his office. And when Heather shows up, they don't waste any time going upstairs. And from what this secretary told me, it's been going on for years. Long before you two ever split up."

Dusty slipped his sunglasses down and rubbed the bridge of his nose. It was funny. Here, he'd spent months and thousands of dollars hoping to dig up some dirt on

Heather, and now that he had it, he didn't feel like rejoicing. In fact, he felt sad that it had come to this.

"Dusty?" Ryker said. "You there?"

"Yeah." Dusty released his breath. "Listen, thanks for handling this. I wouldn't have trusted anyone else with it."

"No problem. I'll talk to a few more people and see if I can't get some actual pictures that will stand up in court."

Dusty slid his sunglasses back up. "Yeah, okay. I'll call you next week."

After he hung up, he got in his car and sat for a few minutes letting the news sink in. He should feel angry or hurt by Heather's betrayal. He didn't. Their marriage had ended long before the divorce. He had stayed with Heather for three years only because of Emmie.

Emmie.

The name reminded him of the reason he'd hired Ryker in the first place. And suddenly, he realized what Ryker's news meant. He would get to be with Emmie. Not full time. Even with evidence of her affair, Dusty didn't delude himself that he would get full custody. But he would be able to have her on weekends, and for holidays, and for summer vacations. He'd be able to cuddle her when she was sick and put a bandage on her scraped knees when she fell. He would be able to read her stories at night and tuck her into bed. A bed that was all ready for her thanks to Bri.

Just the thought of all the work Brianne had done on the room had Dusty starting the engine and pulling away from the curb. He didn't think. He just drove. He drove until he reached the huge, Spanish-style house that sat in the middle of acres and acres of land. He barely glanced at the half dozen SUVs and trucks that were parked out

front as he walked to the front door and rang the bell. A
young boy answered the door wearing nothing but a pair
of baggy swim trunks and a toy six-shooter strapped to
his hip. Dusty recognized him immediately.

"Hi, Brody."

The boy's eyes widened. "Hi, Sheriff Hicks. You here
to arrest Jesse for slippin' into the movie theater without
payin'?" he asked in a voice too deep for a kid so small.

Dusty smiled. "No. Actually, I'm here to talk with
your aunt Brianne."

"Oh." He stepped back and held open the door. "Okay,
but you'll have to wait in line—although Daddy ain't
talkin' as much as yellin'."

About then, a loud male voice boomed down the hallway and had Dusty's shoulders tightening.

"Don't give me that crap, Brianne! The entire town is
talking about Willie cutting hair at Twyla's. It didn't take
me long to figure out who it was. What in the world were
you thinking? You don't even have a license."

"She wasn't thinking," another voice bellowed. "Just
like she wasn't thinking when she got mixed up with that
jerk in Mexico. Do you realize the backlash that picture
could've had on the company, Brianne? You're lucky I
don't take you over my knee—"

Dusty had never been one to bust in without a warrant,
but he figured that the Cates brothers bullying Brianne
was warrant enough. He brushed past Brody without a
word and followed the loud male voices to a set of closed
doors that he didn't hesitate to fling open.

Brianne was sitting in a chair in front of a large desk
that Billy sat behind and Brant leaned against. Dusty
didn't know who looked more surprised to see him.

The Cates brothers or Brianne. Although the surprise on both men's faces quickly hardened into annoyance at having their family squabble interrupted. Dusty understood exactly how they felt. He was feeling pretty darned annoyed himself.

Striding in, he positioned himself between Brianne and her brothers. He slipped off his sunglasses and hooked them in the open neck of his pressed shirt. A shirt Brianne had washed and ironed for him just the night before. His jaw tightened.

"Is there a problem?"

Behind him, Brianne's quick inhale was followed by a masculine chuckle. When Dusty glanced over his shoulder, he found Beckett lounging in a chair in one corner with his boots propped up on an ottoman.

"Sheriff." Beckett's mischievous grin was almost as annoying as Brant and Billy's bullying. Almost. Dusty turned back around as Brant spoke.

"You seem to show up at the most unexpected times, Sheriff. And I'm starting to have my doubts that it's merely a coincidence."

"You're right," Dusty said. "This is no coincidence. I stopped by to see—"

"Sorry, Sheriff!" Brianne jumped up out of her chair, sending him a have-you-lost-your-mind look. "But I can't cut your hair. As my brothers just pointed out, I don't even have a license. So you'll have to go to Twyla."

Billy got to his feet looking thoroughly confused. "You busted into my house because you wanted a haircut?"

"He didn't bust in, Daddy." Brody strode into the room with his six-shooter swaying. "I let him in 'cause he said he wasn't gonna arrest Jesse and his friends for slippin' into the movie theater without payin'. He was just here to talk with—"

"Jesse!" Billy yelled up at the ceiling.

There was a brief moment of silence, followed by the overhead thunder of feet. And before Dusty knew it, the study was filled with a herd of women and children all wanting to know what was going on. Although Jesse wasn't anywhere to be found. In the midst of the confusion, Bri grabbed Dusty's hand and pulled him out of the room and through the foyer.

Once they were outside, she turned on him. "Just what in tarnation are you doing here, Dusty Hicks? Besides causing all kinds of commotion."

Since he didn't have an answer, Dusty did what he'd been wanting to do ever since walking into Billy's study.

He pulled her into his arms and kissed her senseless.

Chapter Twenty-six

"THERE'S NOTHIN' AS BRIGHT AS THE MORNIN'" after a good night of sex."

Startled, Bri turned away from the window to find Minnie sitting in the doorway of Miss Hattie's bedroom. She wore a knowing smile and a red negligee that showed miles of skin as wrinkled as a dried-up peach.

"It is a beautiful morning," Bri said.

Although the beautiful morning had nothing to do with a good night of sex. Dusty had spent the night before dealing with a domestic dispute, federal agents, and poachers. So the only time they'd had together was the kiss at Billy's house. And, somehow, that was enough to brighten Bri's world. There was something about Dusty's kiss that had been different. Something about the tender way he'd cradled her in his arms as his lips devoured hers that made her feel as if he cared for her. Cared more for her than just a casual fling.

"So what are you doing?" Minnie asked.

Bri turned back to her open suitcase on the bed. "I was just packing up. Since the FBI finally located Alejandro in Mexico and the Henhouse is now open for business, I figured you'd be wanting Miss Hattie's room back."

"No need for that," Minnie said. "After that federal agent stumbled upon the backpack of drug money out in the barn and the newspaper got wind of the entire story, we've had more cancellations than a hotel with bedbugs."

So as not to give anything away, Bri continued stacking the shirts in her suitcase. "That was a freak thing, wasn't it? Not to mention Kenny Gene finding out about it and coming forward to explain how, thinking it was Beau's, he'd picked up the backpack in New York and brought it to the Henhouse. Of course, I wonder how it got out in the barn?" She waited, wondering if Minnie was going to confess her part in the disappearance of the drug money. But Minnie was as good at keeping secrets as Bri.

"That is suspicious," she said with more than a trace of humor in her voice. "'Course, I've always believed that things work out if you let them."

Bri held back her own laughter. "I couldn't agree more. And now that it's all over the newspapers, there will be no need for Alejandro to come back to the Henhouse looking for the money. But I am concerned about the lack of business." She turned back around. "Maybe we should call Beau and have him come back from Africa. I'm sure he and Brant can figure out how to fill the rooms."

"No. Beau and Jenna Jay are doing good things over there. And Brant has his own life to live," Minnie said. "Besides, people will forget about it soon enough. And in the meantime, I'm thinkin' about havin' a hen party."

"A hen party?"

"A goin' away surprise party for Starlet."

It was a brilliant idea. Not that Starlet should be

rewarded for her part in taking the money. But since she had only done it to help her drugged-out mother, Bri didn't think she should be punished for it, either. Nor should she leave the Henhouse without a good send-off.

"What a great idea," Bri said. "Starlet will love that. Do you want me to start making out the invitations for the family?"

Minnie shook her head. "No, this isn't a family party. It's a hen-only party. Which means, no arrogant Cates men—although Beckett can attend. I've gotten kind of partial to that boy. Unlike some folks, he knows how to mind his own business."

It was true. Beckett did know how to mind his own business. Once Dusty had made his grand entrance, she expected Beckett to fill in all the blanks with Billy and Brant. He hadn't. In fact, he did just the opposite. He pulled their attention away from Bri by telling them about his decision to join the Marines. So instead of spending the afternoon being interrogated, she spent it defending Beckett's decision. It hadn't been easy. The thought of her brother in a war zone terrified her. But, unlike her, she knew her brother didn't make split decisions. And if this was what Beckett wanted, then she would support him.

"And speaking of mindin' their own business," Minnie continued, "Brant called and wanted me to do everything in my power to keep you away from a certain sheriff. All I can say is that I'm glad you finally owned up to it."

Bri turned back around and started unpacking. "I didn't exactly own up to it. Brant and Billy drew their own conclusions when Dusty showed up at Billy's house. But I'd still appreciate it if you didn't say anything about Dusty coming here. Not for my sake, but for his. After they almost shut down Dalton Oil and ruined Bramble, you know what my brothers are capable of. They'll do anything for their family."

There was a pause before Minnie spoke. "If he showed up at Billy's, it seems to me that Dusty is willing to take that risk. The only one who isn't is you."

"Of course I'm not," Bri said. "Why would I want to see the man I love get hurt?"

The stack of underwear she'd just lifted from the suitcase slipped through her fingers and tumbled down to the bed. Bri barely noticed. Her mind was too consumed with the word that had slipped out of her mouth without any thought whatsoever. She flopped limply down to the bed, while Minnie watched her with those piercing eyes.

"Which is exactly why you need to take the risk, Brianne." Minnie rolled closer. "Love only comes around once in a blue moon, and if you don't grab it—regardless of the risks—it might not come back around again." She reached out and patted Bri's hand. "I know you're scared. But I don't think it's just for Dusty. It's scary to leave behind your childhood and become your own woman. Not a Southern belle daughter. Or a sweet virginal little sister. Or a wealthy socialite. But a woman who is strong enough to leave behind the security of her family and stand on her own two feet."

Minnie gave Bri's hand one last squeeze before she backed up her wheelchair and headed for the door. Once she was gone, Bri didn't know how long she sat there grappling with the unanswered questions that paraded through her mind. Was Minnie right? Was she scared to become her own woman? Is that why she'd kept up the charade? She was terrified of stepping out of the security of her family? Terrified of facing life on her own?

And then there was the granddaddy question of them all—Had she really fallen in love with Dusty?

She hadn't even begun to tackle all the questions when Olive came hurrying into the room.

"We got big trouble, Little Missy. Your stalker's back. I figure you can hide out in the barn while I get rid of the rascal. It shouldn't take long. This time, I ain't gonna be so nice."

The doorbell rang out the melody to "Deep in the Heart of Texas." For a moment, Bri considered following Olive's instructions. But then something happened. A hard resolve settled inside of her as she realized that she couldn't hide anymore.

"Thank you, Olive," she said, "but I'll handle Jared."

Olive didn't argue, but she did follow Bri down the stairs and all the way to the front door. "You just holler, Little Missy," she said, "and ol' Olive will come runnin'."

Jared didn't look surprised when Bri answered the door. In fact, he sent her the same smile he'd given her the first time she met him. She didn't realize until now how arrogant and smug it was.

"Hello, Jared," she said.

After he had given her a thorough perusal, his gaze settled on her face. "You've been avoiding me."

You think?

Bri bit back the words and moved out onto the porch, closing the door behind her. "I thought I made it perfectly clear in Mexico that our relationship was over. That I thought of you as more of a friend than a boyfriend."

"And I thought I told you that you're not going to get rid of me that easily." He stepped closer and brushed a strand of hair from her face. "Not after all we've been through together."

She swatted his hand away. "All we've been through together? The only things we've been through together are some extreme sports and a Mexican vacation that was a bad idea from the start. There's nothing more between us, Jared. And you need to get that through your head."

He studied her for a moment before his expression turned mean. "So are you telling me that you used me? That I spent thousands of dollars trying to give you all your thrill-seeking excursions for a chance to get in your prissy-assed pants and you never planned on giving me more than a measly kiss or two?" He grabbed her by the arms. "Well, I don't think so. You owe me. You owe me money, and you owe me sex. And I intend to collect both."

Bri hadn't lived with four brothers and not learned how to fight. She doubled up her fist and hit him hard in the solar plexus. His breath wheezed out as he stumbled back.

Smoothing out her blouse, she kept her eyes pinned on him. "I'm not going to deny that I was wrong to lead you on. I guess I was so excited about finding someone who loved the same things I did that I didn't make our relationship perfectly clear from the beginning. But that didn't give you the right to post a picture up on the Internet. And it didn't give you the right to stalk me."

"You owe me," he snarled.

"I don't owe you anything." She turned back to the door, but he grabbed her arm and stopped her from opening it.

"That's not the only picture I have. And I don't think you want your family finding out that their perfect little angel is a thrill-seeking wild child. And I won't have any trouble spilling the beans about everything."

There was a time when his words would've struck fear in her heart. Not anymore. It seemed that Jared's arrival had helped her answer all her questions. She didn't want to be a scared little girl. Or a sweet Southern belle. Or a spoiled socialite. She was ready to be a woman. A woman who could fight her own battles. Take responsibility for her actions. And love the men she chose to love. The realization filled her with relief and a giddiness that left her light-headed and happy.

"Sorry, but that kite's not going to fly anymore." She patted Jared's cheek. "I don't care if you tell my family—or the entire world. Although I should warn you about my brothers. They might just take their anger out on the messenger."

His smirk dropped. "Why, you bitch."

Bri shrugged. "At times. But I can live with that."

Applause drifted out the open library window, and Bri glanced over to see the hens crowded in front of the glass. Baby, Sunshine, Starlet, and Olive stood circled around Minnie, who had a proud smile on her face and a derringer in her hand.

"What the fuck—" Jared started, but was cut off by the distinct click of the gun being cocked.

Bri couldn't contain her smile as she looked back at him. "I wish I could tell you that she won't shoot, but my brother Brant has the scar to prove otherwise." She lifted a hand and waggled her fingers. "Bye-bye, Jared."

Jared might be arrogant and brazen, but he wasn't stupid. With his eyes trained on the gun, he backed down the porch steps. He tripped over Jiggers, who let out a growl and chased him the rest of the way to his sports car. The dust had barely settled when Olive spoke.

"I always wondered what BMW stood for. And now I guess I figured it out. Big Male Wuss."

Chapter Twenty-seven

IT WAS WELL PAST ELEVEN BY THE TIME Dusty pulled into the parking space behind his office. The night before, he'd had to deal with some drunken poachers so he'd gotten very little sleep. Of course, it wasn't the poachers who had kept him up until well past midnight. He laid awake for hours thinking about Brianne.

Like how the very tip of her tongue slipped out of her mouth when she was concentrating on something— cutting hair, measuring ground coffee, or reaching for orgasm. And how she never held a grudge for long. And how much she enjoyed laughing. And how easily she had grown attached to the people of Bramble.

And to him.

While lying alone in bed, Dusty had realized that he'd grown attached to her as well. He also realized that he was no longer afraid of commitment. After years of guarding his heart, he was ready to follow it wherever it might lead him. At this point, it was leading him straight into Brianne Cates's arms.

Hoping to get his morning paperwork done quickly so

he could get out to Miss Hattie's, he hopped out of his car and walked inside. He stuck his head into Cora Lee's office, intending to offer her a quick good morning, when he noticed the cowboy sitting in the waiting room.

"Kenny Gene?"

Kenny jumped to his feet and tried to talk around the bite of donut he'd just stuffed in his mouth. "Yesh, shur."

Dusty moved into the room. "Aren't you supposed to be in bed?"

Kenny swallowed hard before smiling brightly. "I've had enough of Twyla's motherin' to last me a lifetime. I'm ready to go back to work." He brought his heels together and saluted. A salute that had him cringing in pain.

Before Dusty could force him to take a chair, Cora Lee came into the room with two cups of coffee.

"I tried to tell him to go home, but he wouldn't listen." She handed a cup to Kenny. The other she handed to Dusty, along with a beseeching look. "I would call that dedication, wouldn't you, Sheriff? Especially considering what he's been through. I think that someone who's been injured in the line of duty has earned the right to wear a Texas star."

As much as Dusty knew he would live to regret it, he couldn't disagree with Cora.

"All right," he said to Kenny, "you can be my deputy."

Kenny's eyes widened, and it took a moment for him to find his voice. "No kiddin', Sheriff?"

"No kiddin'." After Kenny released a hoot of celebration, Dusty held up a hand. "But not until I have a release from Doc Mathers. And not until you've graduated from the training academy."

"The academy?" Kenny looked confused. "Like them

awards on TV? I didn't know a dep-u-tee had to learn actin'."

Dusty released his breath in a long sigh as Cora Lee grinned from ear to ear.

"Go on home and rest up, Kenny," she said. "I have a feeling that you're going to need it. And be sure to tell Twyla hi for me."

"Will do." Kenny set down his cup of coffee and grabbed his hat off the coat rack. "She'll be happier than a buzzard on roadkill to hear I'm gonna be a bone-a-fide officer of the law." He paused with his hand on the door handle. "'Course, that means we'll have to postpone the weddin', seein' as how I'll be much too busy sheriffin'." A wide smile lit his face as he stepped out the door.

When he was gone, Cora turned to Dusty. "You did a good thing, Sheriff."

Dusty watched Kenny Gene almost run into a street pole as he tipped his hat at a young woman walking by.

"Yep," Dusty turned to his office. "Stupid but good."

It took him more than an hour to fill out the report on the poachers and another hour to answer e-mails. One of the e-mails was from his lawyer, and rather than e-mail him back, Dusty called him. His lawyer didn't seem that excited about the news of Heather's affair, probably because he realized that his days of fleecing Dusty were coming to an end. The lawyer did want Ryker to call him ASAP, and after Dusty got off the phone with him, he called Ryker and relayed the information.

"No problem, man," Ryker said. "I don't even think we'll need to subpoena the employee I spoke to. She's not real happy with her boss for not giving her a raise."

Dusty straightened the paperwork on his desk. "Which means she could be making the entire story up just to get even."

"I worried about the same thing," Ryker said. "So I went there this morning under the pretense of needing an accountant, and I had no problem getting proof. The dude met your ex at the door, and I clicked off a few pictures on my iPhone of them heading upstairs. You want me to send them over?"

"No, thanks. Save it for the lawyer."

There was a pause. "Look, I'm sorry, man. I didn't realize you still had a thing for your ex."

"I don't." It was surprising how easily the words came out. But no more surprising than his next words. "I have a girlfriend."

There was another pause. "I hope it's not Brianne Cates."

"Excuse me?" Dusty couldn't keep the anger out of his voice. "How did you know about Brianne?"

"Cora Lee mentioned her the other day when I called. And all I can say, man, is if you are seeing her, you need to keep it on the sly. If Heather's lawyers find out about the naked picture, they won't hesitate to use it."

Dusty's chair squeaked in protest as he sat up. "Naked picture?"

"Call me a nosy investigator, but after I talked with Cora Lee, I Googled Brianne." There was a staccato of clicks as Ryker continued. "I guess some boyfriend of hers posted a picture of her on the Internet after their hot Mexican vacation. She's not completely naked, but she's naked enough to jeopardize your case if your ex found out about it."

A ping had Dusty looking at his computer screen. Ryker's e-mail was highlighted at the very top.

"I'll talk to you later," Dusty said. Without waiting for a reply, he hung up the phone.

He didn't know how long he sat there. Seconds. Minutes. An hour. Before he reached out and clicked on the e-mail. The picture flashed up on the twenty-inch monitor like a porn screen saver. Ryker was right. The woman in the picture wasn't completely naked. A tiny triangle of turquoise covered the spot between her legs, mirroring the color of the ocean that swirled around her calves. An ocean it looked as if she'd just emerged from. Her hair hung like a dark, wet veil from her head, the droplets of water glistening like sequins on her tanned skin.

Dusty stared at the picture and tried to make sense of it all.

Maybe it wasn't her. Maybe it was another woman who looked like her. A woman with the same blue eyes. The same full lips. The same raspberry-tipped breasts. The same tattoo peeking out of her bikini bottoms.

Leaning up, he reached for the mouse and enlarged the picture, then zoomed in. Against her tanned skin, he could just make out the top of the skull and the very tips of the crossbones.

The concrete evidence had him scrolling back up to her face and the blue eyes that sparkled with emotions he remembered well from all the times she'd been in his arms after they made love.

Contentment and satisfaction.

The kind of contentment and satisfaction that Dusty had thought only he could give her. Before the pain and hurt could take hold, he tried to reason things out. But his mind kept coming back to the same heartbreaking conclusion: Brianne had played him for a fool.

As much as he wanted to deny it, all the evidence pointed to that fact. From the first time he pulled her over, he knew she was a manipulator. She had proved it by manipulating Judge Seeley into letting her off with only community service. By manipulating the folks of Bramble into believing that she was just a sweet, little ol' country gal who liked to cut hair. And by manipulating Dusty into believing that there was something more to their relationship than just good sex. That he had finally found the one woman who could love him with her entire body and soul.

But it had all been a lie. And now he needed to face the truth. He stared at the picture. This was Brianne Cates. A spoiled socialite who had nothing better to do than hang out topless on some Mexican beach with her boyfriend. A spoiled socialite who had probably just finished having sex with that boyfriend. Why else would she look so sparkly eyed and happy?

And Dusty had to wonder if the boyfriend taking the picture wasn't the same poor fool who had been at the Henhouse. Brianne had called him a stalker, but the guy was probably just some love-struck idiot trying to get closure after being broadsided by a woman who didn't know the meaning of commitment.

Well, that wouldn't be Dusty. He had learned this lesson with Heather and couldn't live with that kind of heartbreak again.

Picking up his cell phone, he pressed the contact number he'd put in not more than a week earlier. Like Heather, Brianne answered on the first ring. Unlike Heather, just her voice caused a fist to tighten around his heart.

"I was hoping you'd call." Her voice was low and sultry. "I've been thinking about the hammock in Miss Hattie's backyard. And I think if you were to meet me after midnight, we might just be able to—"

"I can't meet you." He cut her off and reached for his stress ball. "I've spent way too much time out at Miss Hattie's as is. Now that Alejandro is gone and Sam is on the mend, I need to focus my attention on Culver County."

There was a pause. "Oh. Of course, that makes sense. Well, why don't I pick up some groceries in town and meet you at the ranch? I make a mean chicken parm."

"I don't like Italian. And it's not a ranch. It's just a rundown old house that should be bulldozed. In fact, I'll probably be moving as soon as they relocate my office."

He wasn't lying. His dream of turning the house into a beautiful sanctuary was stupid. Just like his dream of living happily-ever-after with a Cates.

"What's wrong, Dusty?" Brianne asked. "Did something happen at work?"

"Nothing happened." He kept his voice devoid of the emotions that tumbled inside him. "Look, I'm not very good at this, but what I'm trying to say is that whatever we had is over." He didn't wait for her to speak before he rushed on. "Don't worry about doing any more housekeeping. Your debt is paid in full. You're free and clear to leave west Texas whenever you want to."

"And what if I don't want to leave?"

He squeezed and squeezed the rubber ball. "Then stay. Your choice."

This time, the silence that followed was deafening. And when she spoke, her voice sounded hurt and distant.

"Then I guess there's nothing left to say except I hope things work out for you, Dusty. I hope you get more time with Emmie."

Without replying, Dusty ended the call and sank back in the chair. He suddenly felt empty. Like a balloon that had been filled to capacity and then suddenly released to fly erratically around the room before landing on the floor all wrinkled, limp, and lifeless.

He glanced back at the picture, and in a surge of anger fired the ball across the room.

"Damn you!"

It ricocheted off the monitor just as Judge Seeley peeked his head in.

"I was kinda hopin' that you'd gotten over being mad at me," he said with a grin on his face.

Dusty leaned up and clicked the e-mail closed. "Just releasing a little tension, Judge. Come on in and have a chair."

"This tension wouldn't have to do with the Cates girl, would it?" The judge took a seat, the lures on his fishing vest jangling. "What did she do? Turn your underwear even pinker?"

Bri hadn't screwed up his laundry. In fact, she had bleached all the pink right out of them. Similar to what she'd done to his heart.

"No. She actually did a fine job."

The judge winked. "She's a looker, that one."

Dusty nodded before changing the subject. "So what brings you here on this fine fishing day?"

The judge's smile faded, and he got the serious look he always got when he was passing down a sentence. Dusty found himself preparing for more bad news.

"I guess Sam told you that he's thinkin' about quittin'," the judge said.

"I wouldn't say he's thinking about it. It sounded to me like he's made up his mind."

The judge nodded. "He'll be missed. He was a good man who knew how to deal with the folks of Bramble without causing a ruckus."

"I'm sure you'll be able to find someone to take his place come elections," Dusty said, trying to hurry him along. He needed to get out of there. Needed to find a way to relieve the emptiness in his soul and the tension in his chest. Unfortunately, the judge didn't seem to be in a hurry.

Leaning back in his chair, he crossed his hands over his vest and shook his head. "I don't think it will be that easy. The people of that town won't just vote for anyone. They'll have to know and trust him. And Lord help us if Kenny Gene gets it in his head to run."

"I've taken care of that," Dusty said as he got up. "Kenny Gene will be working with me once he gets his badge—if he gets his badge."

The judge's eyes lit up. "A perfect solution. With you as his mentor, Kenny Gene might actually become a good law officer. Of course, it's a shame he won't be working in his own county. And whoever does get the job of sheriff probably won't tolerate Kenny Gene. Which means that the poor boy will have to move. And once he moves, Twyla will no doubt break it off with him because there's no way she'll leave her hometown and business." He shook his head as if he were seeing Kenny's pathetic life spread out in front of him. "It's a real shame."

Dusty leaned on the edge of the desk and crossed his arms. "Okay, so what are you getting at, Doyle? You have someone in mind for Bramble's new sheriff? Someone you want me to give a shove in the right direction?"

Judge Seeley looked down at the toes of his rubber boots. "You could say that." When he looked up, he was grinning from ear to ear. "'Course, it's hard to shove yourself—"

A loud crash had them both jumping to their feet. They met Cora Lee in the hallway.

"It came from the jail," she said as she followed behind Dusty.

He opened the door to settling dust and piles of rubble.

"Good Lord," Cora Lee said. "The entire roof has caved in. What a catastrophe."

Judge Seeley peeked over Dusty's shoulder and stared up at the blue sky revealed by the huge, gaping hole. "A catastrophe? Or divine intervention?"

Chapter Twenty-eight

"NOT EXACTLY WHERE I FIGURED on finding the Southern belle of Doral County."

Bri pulled her gaze away from the sprawling vista of east Texas farmland and glanced behind her. When she saw the handsome face beneath the straw cowboy hat, she released a squeal and jumped to her bare feet.

"Beau!" She met her brother just as he finished stepping over the top rung of the ladder and flung herself into his arms. Without hesitation, he lifted her off the oak-planked floor of the hayloft and swung her around.

"If I'd known how happy you would be to see me, Cricket," he said, "I'd have come to Dogwood much sooner." He suddenly stopped when he realized she had tucked her face against his chest and was sobbing like a baby.

"Heeey." He set her on her feet and pulled back. "What's all this about?"

She sniffed and tried to get ahold of her crazy emotions. It was difficult, if not impossible. Ever since Dusty had dumped her, she'd been nothing but a weepy mess.

Which was why she had returned home. Not only did her parents' farm offer comfort and familiarity, it also was a good two hundred miles away from the last person on earth she wanted to run into.

She gave Beau a forced, quivery smile. "Maybe I'm just happy to see you."

His tone was teasing, but his eyes serious, as his thumb brushed a tear from her cheek. "I realize that I'm your favorite brother—and you no doubt missed my sparkling wit—but for some reason I don't think that's what has you crying." He tipped up her chin, forcing her to look him in the eye. "So what's going on? As Miss Minnie so aptly put it, why did you run off from Miss Hattie's like a cat with its tail on fire?"

It wasn't an exaggeration. As soon as she had hung up with Dusty, Bri had packed her bags and given Minnie and the hens nothing more than a lame excuse about being homesick before leaving.

"'Course, I wouldn't blame you if you did," Beau continued. "Not with all the craziness going on there. I arrived at the Henhouse to some wild tales of Beckett becoming a Marine, you becoming a beautician, and Minnie almost killing Elvis. I'm more than a little worried that the hens are getting senile."

Wiping her eyes, Bri shook her head. "Every speck of it is true. Besides Alejandro coming back for revenge, Beckett is set on becoming a Marine, Minnie shot at Reverend Josiah Jessup, who dresses like Elvis, and I helped out Twyla in her salon."

Beau's smile dropped. "So I guess that means the other thing they told me is true. You fell in love with Sheriff Dusty Hicks."

After a solid week of tears, Bri couldn't deny it. But she'd be damned if she'd confirm it. Pulling away from her brother, she walked back over to the hayloft door and sat down, her legs dangling over the edge. It didn't take long for Beau to join her. They sat there with their shoulders touching for a few minutes, looking out on the acres and acres of green fields and billowing trees that thrived in the thick humidity. It was beautiful. Which didn't explain why Bri missed dry wind and miles of mesquite.

"So I guess things didn't turn out so well," Beau said.

"No."

He slanted a look at her. "You want me to kick his ass?"

She released the breath that she hadn't even been aware of holding. "Brant and Billy already offered."

He nodded, and a few more seconds ticked by. "Unlike Billy and Brant, I wouldn't get carried away. Just a broken nose. Maybe a couple cracked ribs."

A smile curved her lips as she shook her head.

"Well, damn it, Bri. You can't expect me to let the guy go scot-free after hurting my baby sister."

Something about the way he said baby sister caused her to turn to him. And the words that she should've said years ago spilled out like the afternoon sunshine that spilled over the floor of the hayloft.

"I'm not a baby anymore, Beau. I stopped being a baby years ago, but everyone besides Beckett has failed to notice." He started to say something, but she stopped him. "I don't blame you. It's not your fault as much as it is mine. I should've voiced my thoughts and opinions much earlier. And who knows, maybe deep down I enjoyed being the baby. Enjoyed having four big brothers at my beck and call, fighting my battles and taking on my responsibilities."

"We enjoy taking care of you, Bri. And where's the harm in that?"

A strong breeze blew in the door, sweeping Bri's hair over her eyes. As she tipped back her head to smooth it from her face, her gaze caught on the rope tied to the rafters. She looked back at Beau, who was studying her with concern.

"Do you remember when I was six years old," she said, "and I talked you into letting me jump from the rope into the haystack beneath?"

"How could I forget?" Beau said. "You ended up breaking your arm, and I ended up getting a whipping from Daddy that I'll never forget. Which is exactly what I deserved. As your big brother, I should've talked you out of jumping instead of demonstrating how it was done."

"No." She grabbed his arm. "No, you didn't deserve a spanking, Beau. Not when I was the one who wanted to jump. You were just doing what any good brother would do, giving me the opportunity to spread my wings and have some fun. It wasn't your fault that I landed wrong. Or that you never played with me again."

Beau's eyes registered shock. "I played with you, Bri. We used to play all kinds of board and video games together."

She smiled sadly. "But I didn't want to play safe board games with you, Beau. I wanted you to teach me how to saddle-break horses, how to ride dirt bikes and jump the ravine, and how to do a donut in Mama's Grand Prix. But mostly, I wanted to play King of the Hill every night with you and my other brothers, instead of being treated like a fragile piece of glass."

He studied her. "Why didn't you say anything?"

"Because I was terrified that I was going to get hurt again. Not because I worried about the pain, but because I couldn't stand the thought of one of my brothers getting another spanking because of me. I cried myself to sleep for an entire week thinking about Daddy paddling you."

"Aww, Bri." He tucked an arm around her and pulled her close. "I had no idea. I just thought you were a girlie girl who liked playing inside more than you liked playing out. I wish you had said something."

"I wish I had, too. Then I never would've had to go to Miss Hattie's. And I never would've met..." Bri stopped, not even trusting herself to say Dusty's name without bursting into tears.

Giving her a minute to collect herself, Beau looked out on their parents' land. "Don't you think it's time to quit keeping secrets, Bri? In fact, why don't you start with telling me how you ended up half-naked in Mexico when you should've been at my wedding."

She ducked her head into his chest. "I'm so sorry, Beau. I never should've missed your wedding. Or Billy's. Or Brant's. It's just that weddings seemed to be the only time the family's attention wasn't focused on me. So it was the perfect time for me to try some of the daredevil things I never got to do as a kid."

He dropped his arm and pulled back. "You saddle-broke a horse?"

She giggled. "No, but I bungee jumped, skydived, and cliff-jumped in Mexico." She expected to see censure in his eyes. Instead, he looked almost proud.

"Well, I'll be damned," he said with a wide grin. "It looks like you took after your ol' brother more than I thought." After only a moment, his eyes squinted. "So who took the picture of you and posted it?"

"Jared. I met him the first time I went bungee jumping. He was a thrill seeker like I was so I thought we'd make a good match. When I figured out that we didn't and broke it off, he posted the picture he took after my cliff jump. I was so amped up with adrenaline, I didn't even know that my swimming suit top had come off."

Pride left Beau's eyes to be replaced with anger. "Jared who?"

"Oh, no." She shook her head. "I won't have you tossed in jail for assault. Besides, I took care of it. I'm surprised Minnie didn't tell you about Jared showing up."

"Minnie keeps more than a few secrets," he said dryly. "Including what's going to happen this weekend. Has she told you anything about Starlet's going-away party?"

"No. But from what I hear, it's hens only."

"Hens." He snorted. "The word brings to mind calm, roosting birds. Those old women are the furthest things from calm or roosting. They've cooked up something for this weekend but refuse to tell me what. And maybe it's best if I don't know." He gave her a serious look. "But I'm counting on you to call me if things get too out of hand."

"I wish I could help you out with that, but I'm not going."

"Because of Sheriff Hicks?" When she didn't say anything, he came to his own conclusions. "So what was so different about this man? I guess he didn't treat you like a fragile piece of glass."

"Not hardly. He handcuffed me, tossed me in jail, and would've thrown away the key if Judge Seeley hadn't showed up." Before the dark cloud even settled on her brother's face, she held up a hand. "I deserved it after almost running him off the road and then spraying him with the mace Billy gave me for Christmas."

Beau tipped back his head and laughed. "This sounds like the type of story I need to hear from the beginning."

It was funny how easily the words came. After spending the last week trying to forget Dusty, it felt good to finally get to talk about him. Unlike Billy and Brant, Beau was a great listener. The memories crowded in on one another, and she ended up telling much more than she had intended. She told him about being forced to become Dusty's housekeeper, about Dusty hiding her from Jared, working at Twyla's, and fixing up Emma's room. Finally, she told him about Dusty's last phone call.

When she was finished, Beau voiced her exact thoughts.

"But that doesn't make any sense. Why would he call and break it off when it sounds like things were going pretty well between the two of you?"

"Exactly," Bri said, relieved she wasn't the only confused one. "It makes no sense."

Beau squinted in thought. "The last time you talked, did you mention marriage? Babies' names? Your last boyfriend's sexual fetish?"

She sent him an exasperated look. "Of course not. I've listened to my brothers long enough to know those are no-no topics. It was something else that triggered his anger. What made you the angriest when you were dating Jenna?"

Beau didn't hesitate to answer. "Her ex-boyfriend. After we were married, I found an old picture on her phone of the two of them together, and I thought I was going to implode."

"Well, I don't have any pictures of me—" Bri stopped and stared at Beau. "That's it. He must've seen my picture on the Internet and assumed what everyone else has assumed—that I'm some partying socialite with no moral compass whatsoever." Too excited to remain sitting, she jumped to her feet. "Which means that all I need to do is explain things to him."

"Like why you didn't tell him in the first place."

"Of course I didn't tell him." she defended herself. "Why would I bring something like that up? Especially when he's so concerned about keeping a squeaky-clean reputation so he can get custody of—" All the joy drained right out of her. "Emma. Of course, he had to break it off with me. He didn't have a choice. Not when his daughter's custody case is coming back up before a judge."

Bri melted down to the floor. In the last week, she'd held on to a small spark of hope that Dusty would have second thoughts and come find her. Now she realized that he would never come looking for her. His first choice would always be Emma's welfare. Which was exactly as it should be.

Seeing her expression, Beau reached out and took her hand. "That's ridiculous. Certainly one picture of a girl-friend wouldn't change a judge's mind about custody."

"It would if the judge was already on the wife's side."

"Then you need to give Dusty that choice, Bri. Tell him about what happened in Mexico. Tell him that you love him. And then let him make the decision."

"But what if he does love me, Beau? And what if after all that he's done to get his daughter back, it's my picture that screws things up for him? How could he ever forgive me? How could I forgive myself? No, it's better to let things end like this."

"Better for who?"

"For Emma. Every daughter deserves to spend time with a great daddy, Beau."

She expected him to argue, but instead he released his breath and laid back. With all her energy drained out of her, she joined him. And for a long while, they just lay there, staring up at the bare rafters.

It was Beau who broke the silence. "Why does life have to be so danged complicated?"

"I don't know," she said. "But I'm glad we have family to help us through it."

He turned his head. "Me too, Bri, me too." He glanced up, and his smile turned impish. "What say we see if my baby sister bounces much better than she used to?"

Chapter Twenty-nine

THINGS WERE LOOKING UP FOR JOSIAH. The camera crew had arrived a day earlier and was camped out at a nearby hotel waiting for his call. And his great-aunt had fallen and hurt her hip, giving him the perfect excuse to move both the old coots out of his house in Malibu and back into the state-run care facility. Of course, he would have to fumigate his house before he moved back in. Old people had a smell about them that was hard to get rid of.

And speaking of smells...

The strong odor of onions and bacon grease hit him full in the face as soon as he stepped into Josephine's Diner. And after a night of drinking, it wasn't exactly a welcome scent. Still, he plastered on a broad smile and held out his hands to encompass the roomful of country bumpkins.

"Good morning, my God-loving brothers and sisters!"

The conversation stopped, and all eyes turned to him. Then just as quickly, they turned away and the conversation resumed. For a moment, his smile slipped as he was consumed by an overwhelming anger that such ignorant people would have the audacity to ignore him. But remembering his purpose for being there, he shoved down the anger and moved toward an empty stool at the counter. The gray-haired waitress—he'd forgotten her name—was standing behind the counter talking to the mayor.

"...Cora Lee said the sheriff is mopin' around like he's lost his best friend since she up and ran off. And I just think it's a cryin' shame."

The mayor nodded. "I couldn't agree more, Rachel. I shore wish she hadn't left. She's such a sweet little thing and gave me the best darned haircut I've ever—" He stopped and glanced over his shoulder at the woman sitting at the table behind him. "Besides you, of course, Twyla."

Twyla flapped her hand. "No need to worry about hurtin' my feelin's, Harley. I might love men, but I haven't ever liked workin' on their hair. Hair clippers remind me of that drill at the dentist office." She shivered and her breasts jiggled, causing Josiah to mentally kick himself for not making more of an effort to get the woman in bed.

"Well, I sure wish there was a way to get her back," the waitress said. She glanced over at Josiah. He thought she would continue to ignore him, but as soon as he flipped over his cup, she was there with a pot of coffee. Not that he would ever consume the thick shit she poured into his cup.

"Thank you, sister," he said. "Servitude is a true calling from God."

Her eyes narrowed for a fraction of a second before she pulled the menu out from between the sugar container and the ketchup and slapped it down in front of him. "The special is eggs and pork chops, but we ran out of pork chops so Josephine is substitutin' ground round."

Josiah replaced the menu and winked at her. "I'm sure whatever culinary delights that come from Josephine's kitchen would be worthy of a king." He paused for dramatic effect. "Or a hen." When she didn't take the bait, he was forced to be more direct. "And speaking of hens, from what I hear from Wilma, Josephine is catering quite the party out at the Henhouse." He nonchalantly reached for the cream. "What time exactly does the party start?"

Before the waitress could answer, the deputy who had given him all the tickets spoke up. "It won't do you no good to know the time. The party is for hens only."

Josiah paused in the middle of stirring cream into his coffee and felt his blood pressure shoot sky high. Hens only? How could he possibly get good footage for his teaser if there were only women at the Henhouse? He needed a bunch of horny men if he wanted to pull off his ruse. Which posed an entirely different problem. A few strippers who were willing to take off their clothes for money had been easy to come by, but men willing to take off their clothes would be much harder. Especially when he only had two days left to hire them. He had just started to panic when Sheriff Winslow joined in the conversation.

The sheriff was sitting on the other side of the mayor, looking no worse for wear after shooting off a toe. Although a pair of crutches rested against the counter next to him.

"Invitation or no invitation," he said, "I imagine every young buck in the county will be headin' out that way come eight o'clock on Saturday night to see if he can get a peek of hens partying. And poor Dusty will have his hands full corralin' the craziness."

Josiah smiled at just the thought of all those under-age boys being sucked into the evilness of Miss Hattie's. He lifted his cup in a toast to himself and took a sip, not realizing his mistake until he swallowed the foul-tasting sludge. Words spilled from his mouth before he could stop them.

"What the hell?"

Every eye turned to him, and he was forced to do some quick thinking.

"What hell destroys, heaven will resurrect," he improvised.

The waitress's eyes zeroed in on him. "And you sure caused a lot of hell, Reverend."

"She's right." A woman got up out of her booth. "It was pure hell tryin' to keep from gossipin'. And I have the hives to prove it." She pointed to the red rash on her cheeks. "And what harm was I doin' by spreadin' a little news?"

Another woman got to her feet, her knitting needles clacking. "Or spending my time craftin'?"

A large, mean-looking cowboy got up from the other side of the booth. "Or makin' money at Dalton Oil, rather than buildin' stupid birdhouses that no one wants?"

The mayor stood up. "Just what are you still doin' in Bramble, Reverend?"

Since the ignorant hicks had served their purpose, Josiah rose with every intention of spouting a few words of wisdom before heading for the door. Unfortunately, the mean-looking cowboy stepped in front of it, blocking his only exit and forcing Josiah to address the mayor and the question.

"Why, my brother, I'm here for exactly the reason I told you...to spread the word of God to my flock."

"A flock?" the woman with the teased hair and great tits said. "You got a herd of sheep, Reverend?"

Before Josiah could answer, the old man sitting on the stool behind him spoke. And since Josiah had thought he was asleep, the old guy's loud, gruff voice caused him to jump.

"I think he's referrin' to us, Twyla."

Josiah turned and found himself staring into a pair of piercing blue eyes. Eyes that held a wisdom that made Josiah instantly nervous. Or maybe what made him nervous were the people closing in on him. All the occupants of the diner had gotten out of their seats and moved closer.

"Of course, I wasn't literally referring to sheep," Josiah said. "Sheep are just a symbol that demonstrates how important a group of followers are to a man of God. A flock is a shepherd's most prized possession." Trying to calm the crowd, he reverted to the Bible. "'The Lord is my shepherd, I shall not want. He maketh me to lie down in green pastures—'"

"'He leadeth me beside still waters.'" The old man's eyes never wavered. "'He restoreth my soul.'" He looked around at the people in the diner. "How many here have felt like the reverend has restored their soul?"

Not a person raised their hand.

The old man looked back at him. "You ain't a shepherd, and we sure as heck ain't your flock. You're just some outta luck con artist who happened on our little town. And I think you've worn out your welcome, Reverend." He nodded at the mean-looking cowboy. "Rye, why don't you show Elvis here to the door."

"Now wait one minute," Josiah said as the cowboy

clamped his meat-hook hands on his shoulders. "Just who do you think you are?"

The old man pulled out a squashed Solo cup and spit into it. "The name's Moses." He winked. "And I think I've bested you before."

Chapter Thirty

"YOU ARE PRINCE ERIC." Emmie arranged the bent tiara on his head. "And I are Princess Ariel. Except I don't has flippers." She wiggled her bare toes at him. The tiny nails were painted blue. Not an electric blue like Brianne's, more of a baby blue. Still, the color caused his smile to slip, and before he could get it back, Emmie cradled his cheeks in her small hands.

"It's not sad that I don't has my flippers, Pa. 'Cause now we can dance. But 'cause I traded them to the sea witch for legs, I can't talk. Which Mommy says is sometimes a blessin'."

Unable to resist, Dusty leaned in and kissed her on the nose. "I can't imagine why."

Emmie returned the favor, kissing his cheek so hard that it caused his tiara to slip. He made a grab for it as his daughter marched over to the white wicker clothes hamper.

It was the first time that Dusty had been in Emmie's room. Usually, he took her elsewhere for his visitation. But this wasn't his usual visitation. That morning Heather had called him and invited him to Houston "to talk." Worried something had happened to Emmie, he made the trip in record time. When he got here, Emmie was fine and Heather was surprisingly nice. So nice she didn't say a word when their daughter tugged him upstairs to her room. Although he figured Heather would show up eventually to ruin the party.

But for now, he had Emmie all to himself. He smiled as he watched his daughter rifle through the hamper, flinging clothes over her shoulder until she found what she wanted: a bluish-green swimsuit with a redheaded Disney character on the front. Within seconds, Emmie had her dress slipped over her head and had pulled the swimsuit on over her Cinderella panties.

"Prince Eric found Princess Ariel on the sandy beach. But first, you need your doggie Max." She moved over to the toy box and started flipping toys out, while Dusty tried to block out the image that popped into his head of another princess on a sandy beach.

It was impossible.

While he had deleted Brianne's picture from his e-mail, he couldn't seem to delete it from his brain. It stuck there like burned cheese on a griddle. Numerous times, he'd picked up his cell phone with the intent of calling Brianne and getting answers to the questions that plagued him. Who was the guy taking the picture? Was it the same guy who showed up at the Henhouse? Did she love him? And if so, why had she started something with Dusty?

Thankfully, pride had won out and kept him from calling her. And in the last few days, he'd come to a realization. It didn't matter who the guy was who had taken the picture. Didn't matter if he was a weekend fling or a serious boyfriend. Didn't matter if Brianne loved him or hated him. Because in the end, all that mattered was that the rich, fun-loving woman in the picture would never be happy living on a rundown ranch with a small-town sheriff.

That was the cold, harsh truth. And the only thing Dusty needed to remember.

A soft thump brought him out of his thoughts, and he glanced down to see Emmie lying in front of the toy box.

"Emmie?" His heart took a dive when she didn't answer. He jumped up from the tiny chair and rushed over to kneel next to her. She was lying on her side, one arm flung over her face. When he rolled her over, she was limp and unresponsive. Quickly, he pressed two fingers to her neck. He had just located her pulse when her eyes fluttered open. His relief was so great that he had trouble finding his voice.

"Emmie, baby, are you okay?"

She sent him a weak smile before tapping her throat.

"Are you having trouble breathing?" He stroked back her hair as he pulled out his phone. "It's okay, baby. Pa's here. I'm going to get you help."

A sinister laugh had the phone slipping from his hand and bouncing out of reach. He glanced behind him to see Heather standing in the doorway with an evil smile. At least, more evil than usual.

"It's too late," she hissed in a voice similar to the one she used during their worst fights. "Her voice is mine and soon you'll be, too."

"Heather." He tried to keep his voice calm. "Emmie passed out and is having trouble breathing. We need to call an ambulance." He reached for his phone, but Heather beat him to it, kicking it away with one toe of her designer heels.

"You think you can steal the locket with the princess's voice, Prince Eric?" She winked at him before picking up the phone and hugging it to her chest. "Well, think again."

"Heather!" he snapped. "This isn't a joke—"

A Styrofoam sword whacked him in the face, and he looked down to find his daughter holding the hilt and grinning broadly.

"You gots to kill her, Prince Eric," she whispered.

For a second, he had the strong urge to paddle Emmie's butt for the scare she'd given him. But then he realized that he had only himself to blame. She had laid out the story for him. He'd just been so wrapped up in daydreaming about Brianne that he hadn't paid attention.

Emmie whacked him again with the sword and pointed at her mother, who was glaring at Dusty with renewed hatred. And he had to wonder how good her acting skills were. Probably no better than his.

Taking the sword, he jumped to his feet and pointed it at Heather. "En garde, you scallywag. I'll get the princess's voice back or die trying."

Heather snorted with disdain as she maneuvered around the little table and chairs. "As if I'm afraid of a prince. I'll just set my evil eels on you." She threw a stuffed animal at him, and he barely blocked it with the sword before another came sailing at his head. After being bombarded with all of Emmie's furry friends, Dusty shoved the table out of the way and quickly cornered Heather between the bookshelf and the bed.

"Evil eels cannot stop true love," he said as he poked

her in the stomach with the sword. "Hand over the locket, wench."

With a groan, Heather handed him the phone before dramatically slumping over to the bed. Before Dusty could even turn around, Emmie was in his arms.

"You did it, Prince! You killed the evil sea witch."

Dusty found his face covered in kisses, and when he glanced over at Heather, she was smiling.

"I hope you realize that she scared twenty years off my life." Dusty waited for Heather to be seated in one of the cushioned lawn chairs before taking a seat next to her. The back patio looked out on an infinity swimming pool, a sculptured lawn with play structure and princess castle, and the country club golf course. As much as Dusty hated to admit it, it was a dream backyard for any kid.

"I'm sorry," Heather said as she handed him the tall glass of iced tea. "But once the story starts, I've learned that it's best to let it finish. I screwed up Rapunzel once and still haven't heard the end of it."

"But how did you know she wasn't hurt?"

She shrugged. "I guess it's a mother thing."

He took a sip of his tea. As always, it was too sweet. Heather never seemed to remember that he liked his unsweetened. He set the glass down on the table. "So I guess you play princesses often."

"Every day, unless I can distract her with something else. She's quite the little actress." She glanced over at him. "Unlike her father. Scallywag? Wench?"

He laughed. "I'm not familiar with prince lingo. I figured pirate's would be close enough."

"Well, it was close enough for Emma. She was so

thrilled with your performance, I thought I was never going to get her down for a nap." She stared out at the glistening water of the swimming pool. "You surprised me. I didn't think you had that kind of playfulness in you."

"Maybe you never looked."

She shrugged. "Maybe. Or maybe the only thing I could bring out of you was anger." She glanced over at him, and he was surprised to find tears glistening in her eyes. "Did you know that you were my perfect prince? Good looks. Pure heart. Protective nature. I really believed I was going to live happily-ever-after. Then we got married, and everything seemed to change. Suddenly you seemed to hate everything I loved. Traveling. Shopping. Houston. My daddy."

Dusty didn't really want to have this conversation. To him, it was water under the bridge. But before he could point that out, he realized that she was right. He hadn't exactly been honest with her when they had first married. Or honest with himself.

He took a deep breath and slowly released it. "I wanted to be your prince, Heather. And I thought I could live in a big city in a big house with a father-in-law who wanted to 'groom me' for bigger and better things. But once Emma was born, I realized that my dreams are much smaller."

She turned away. "Did you love me?"

"Yes," Dusty said without hesitation. "And I still do. I love how you love our daughter."

She studied her hands. "But you're still going to do everything you can to take her away from me. Including exposing my affair with Darren."

He wasn't surprised that she knew. With her father's connections, she'd probably gotten it straight from Dusty's lawyer. When Dusty didn't deny it, a sad smile played on her mouth.

"Of course you will. And after the way I let Daddy's lawyers treat you, I deserve it." She looked up. "But I want you to know that I didn't start seeing Darren until I knew it was over between us. And believe it or not, he was the only one." A tear trickled down her cheek. "It turns out that an old, balding accountant who makes less a year than my massage therapist is my prince."

Dusty thought his ego would feel a little bruised. Unfortunately, Brianne had bruised it so much that it was now numb. "So why haven't you married him?" he asked.

"Because Daddy would never allow it."

"Jesus, Heather. When are you going to cut the umbilical cord with your father?"

As always, the mention of her father caused her to lose it. "That's easy for you to stay," she snapped. "You came from a poor family, so you don't know the difference. Well, I do. Which is why I couldn't live in that hovel you call a ranch and why I can't go against my father. And it's not just me. It's Emma. Do you really want her to lose all this?" She waved her hand around. "Because your child support sure isn't going to keep her in ballet lessons and Spanish classes."

Normally, he'd snap back. But this time, he pushed his anger down and spoke calmly. "To hell with ballet and Spanish. She's a kid, Heather. She'll be happy as long as you're there to play princesses with her. If you love the guy, then marry him."

She slumped back on the chair. "But what if I make the same mistake again? What if we end up hurting each other? Or worse, Emma? I just don't think I could go through it again."

Her words made him realize that she had been as hurt by their divorce as he had been. Maybe more so. If that was true, then she wasn't the self-absorbed snob he believed her to be. She was just a scared woman fighting for her child.

"Damn," he said as he stared out at the pool. "We've done quite a number on each other, haven't we?"

"It looks that way." Her voice quavered. "Too bad we can't go back."

He glanced over at her. "And change what? If we didn't get married, then we wouldn't have Emma. Yeah, we made some mistakes. We were young and horny and thought that physical attraction was enough to build a marriage on. But we're older now, and hopefully, we've learned from our mistakes." He reached over and took her hand. "Don't be afraid to take a chance, Heather. If you love this guy, go for it. To hell with what anyone else thinks. Including your father."

Instead of replying, Heather just continued to stare out at the golf course.

Although she refused to release his hand.

Dusty stayed much longer than he had intended. Once they finished their iced tea, Emmie woke up from her nap and wanted to show him how she could swim across the pool. Then Heather invited him to stay for supper. Surprisingly, it turned out to be an enjoyable meal. Or maybe what he enjoyed most was the happiness on his daughter's face. It was obvious that she loved having both of her parents together. Something she voiced when she tugged him back to her room so he could say good-bye to her stuffed animals.

"If you was nice, Pa, I bet Mommy would letted you

come back and live with us." She held out a green frog with big red lips.

Not sure what she expected him to do with the frog, he shook a webbed foot while he tried to formulate an answer that would be acceptable for a three-year-old. It wasn't easy. It took shaking the paws, hooves, and feet of Emmie's entire menagerie before he finally spoke.

"Sometimes people choose to live in different places, Em. Like Mommy lives here in Houston, and I live in Culver County." He picked her up and set her on his lap. "But just because we don't live together doesn't mean we don't love you." He smoothed the hair back that had drifted down from her side braids. "You are the most important thing in our lives."

"But I miss you, Pa." Her small arms wrapped around his waist as she buried her nose in his chest. It was impossible to keep the tears from his eyes.

"And I miss you. But hopefully, one day soon you'll get to come see me."

She pulled back. "When my princess room is ready?"

He smiled. "Yes, when your princess room is all ready." The subtle scent of expensive perfume had him glancing at the doorway. Heather stood there with a smile on her face and tears in her eyes.

"It's time for your bath, Emma," she said.

Emmie grumbled a refusal and clung to Dusty. With a heavy heart, he rose to his feet and then sniffed at her ear until she giggled. "Someone sure smells stinky, and it's not me." He tickled her sides. "Could it be the Stinky Princess of Houston?"

"I'm not a stinky princess." She giggled as he handed her off to Heather.

Heather took a sniff. "Oh, I don't know about that. I think I agree with Prince Eric. You're one stinky princess." Over Emmie's head, she mouthed two words.

Thank you.

When Dusty was back on the road to Culver, he thought about the day with Heather and Emmie. And for the first time, he thought about his marriage and the mistakes he'd made. Mistakes he couldn't take back. The only thing he could do was ensure he didn't make any more.

Pulling his cell phone out of his pocket, he retrieved Ryker's number.

"Hey, man," Ryker said. "What can I do you for?"

"I'm calling to tell you that I won't be needing your services anymore, Ryker."

Ryker laughed. "So I guess the snooty broad crumbled once she got the news that you were onto her affair."

Dusty bristled. "Her name is Heather—Mrs. Hicks to you. And she didn't crumble, Ryker, because I'm not planning on using the information against her."

"What? But I thought you wanted your kid back."

"I do," Dusty said. "Just not at the expense of her mother."

Chapter Thirty-one

"Oh, my god," Starlet said. "I look beautiful."

In the mirror over Miss Hattie's bathroom vanity, Bri looked at Starlet's awed reflection and smiled. "My thoughts exactly."

"I mean I don't even look like the same person." Starlet turned her head first one way and then the other, trying to see the waterfall of dark curls that cascaded from her crown down her neck. "I had no idea you were so good with hair." She leaned closer to the mirror and batted her eyelashes. "And makeup. Did you go to beauty school?"

Bri took out a hairpin and readjusted it. "As a matter of fact, I'm starting beauty school in just a few weeks."

"Really?" Starlet swiveled on the vanity bench, causing the glittery gold material of her dress to strain against her overflowing bosom. The gown Billy and Shirlene had bought her as a going-away gift fit to perfection, making her look twenty pounds thinner. And with her hair swept away from her beautiful features and makeup on, she didn't resemble the awkward young woman Bri had first met. Now she looked like a superstar.

A superstar with a very kind heart.

"So that means we're both starting new careers!" She flung her arms around Bri, pressing her head against the bodice of Bri's evening gown. "Maybe you could come to Nashville after you finish, and we could be roomies."

Bri hadn't given much thought to where she would live after she finished beauty school in Austin. All she knew was that it was high time she left the family farm. An image of a small adobe house flashed into her mind, but she refused to let it stay for more than a heart-piercing second before she pushed it away.

"Why not," she said as she hugged Starlet back. "Maybe I could be your hairstylist when you make it big." She smoothed out a curl. "But for now, we have a party to attend." Once the words were out, she could've kicked herself. Starlet had spent the entire day in Bramble running errands for the hens and had no idea of the surprise that awaited her.

Thankfully, she didn't read anything into Bri's words.

"I'm so glad you came back for my good-bye dinner, Bri. I love the hens, but it's nice to have someone my own age to hang out with."

"I wouldn't have missed it." Bri helped Starlet to her feet.

"Look." Starlet pointed to the mirror. "We look like sisters."

It was a bit of an exaggeration. Especially when Starlet dwarfed Bri by a good foot. Still, their dark hair and curvy bodies were similar. And right now, Bri needed all the sisterly love she could get.

She linked her arm through Starlet's. "We are sisters. Sister hens. Now let's go celebrate our new career paths. I have a feeling that tonight is going to be a night to remember."

Starlet giggled as they walked through Miss Hattie's bedroom. "Me too. Minnie got Josephine to cater so Baby wouldn't have to cook, and we're having chicken fried steak with gravy and mashed potatoes. And for dessert we're having peach cobbler and banana MoonPies because Minnie knows how much I love them."

Bri smiled. Banana MoonPies weren't the only things Starlet was going to love.

As planned, the hens were waiting at the bottom of the grand staircase. Baby in a white gown that made her look even more like Marilyn Monroe. Sunshine in a simple floral gown that made her look like a sixties' flower child. And Minnie in a bright red gown that almost matched her sky-high wig. Even Olive had dressed for the occasion in a black sleeveless dress that seemed to highlight her tattoos.

They all looked about ready to bust from the secret they'd been keeping. And Bri couldn't help getting pulled into their excitement.

"You two look as pretty as a west Texas sunset," Olive said when Bri and Starlet reached the bottom of the stairs. Compliments and hugs were circulated before Minnie broke it up.

"Enough of this cluckin'. It's time to celebrate...hen style," she said as she turned her wheelchair. Instead of heading for the dining room, she stopped at the double doors of the grand ballroom. But before she pushed the doors open, she turned to Starlet. Her eyes were filled with pride and tears as she spoke. "You came here as a young girl afraid of your own shadow, and now you'll leave as a woman who is more than ready to follow her dreams.

I can't tell you how proud I am of you, Starlet. Tonight, we aren't just celebrating your success with music, we're celebrating your womanhood and henness."

She pushed the doors open, and even Bri sucked in her breath.

The ballroom was no longer a cavernous room with only a piano and a few musical instruments. It had been transformed into a ballroom fit for a prom queen. Satin had been draped from one sparkling chandelier to another like a trail of lavender clouds. And on the other side of the high windows, the cottonwood tree had been adorned with string upon string of glittering lights that gave the illusion of looking out on a star-filled sky.

Bri's sisters-in-law stood just inside the doorway: Shirlene, Elizabeth, and Jenna Jay. They were all dressed in formals and smiling brightly, although tears glistened in their eyes as they spoke in unison.

"Welcome to the Henhouse Prom, Starlet."

Before Starlet could even utter a word of amazement, a handsome young man in a tuxedo materialized. His gaze zeroed straight in on Starlet, and he walked over and held out an arm just as the string quartet started a heart-melting waltz.

"Would you do me the honor of a dance, Miss Starlet?"

Starlet's mouth dropped open. She turned to Bri, who couldn't help the tears that flooded her eyes.

"I think the proper response in a situation like this is 'yes,'" Bri said.

Starlet turned back to the man and nodded, and within seconds, she was being swept around the floor.

Olive sighed. "Just like Cinderellie." She rubbed her hands together. "Now, bring on the grub." She headed for the long buffet table that ran along one wall, and the rest of the women followed behind her, excitedly talking about how successful the surprise had been. Only Bri and Minnie remained in the doorway.

Bri watched Starlet dance for a few minutes before looking down at Minnie. "So if Starlet is Cinderella, I guess that makes you her fairy godmother."

Minnie shook her head. "I'm just an old woman."

"So I've heard. An old woman who makes dreams come true. I'd say that qualifies you as a fairy godmother."

Minnie accepted a glass of champagne from one of the several servers who moved around the ballroom with silver trays. "And what about your dream, Brianne? Did it get fulfilled?"

Bri accepted a fluted glass. "What dream would that be, Miss Minnie?"

"With all those brothers, it isn't hard to figure out." She downed the champagne in one gulp. "They've pampered, spoiled you, and put you up on a pedestal so high you can hardly see the ground."

"And what does that have to do with my dream?"

"Just about everything. Princesses in towers only have one dream." Minnie glanced over at her. "To be rescued."

Bri shook her head. "I don't need a man to rescue me."

"Now who said anything about a man? Sometimes, it just takes the princess trying the door. And from what Beau said, I figure you already found out that it wasn't locked. Now all you need to do is climb down from the tower and grab hold of your dream."

Like Minnie, Bri drained her glass of champagne. "And what if my dream has already ridden off into the sunset without me?"

Minnie smiled. "Fortunately, you have an entire life-time of sunsets. Don't let today's sour you on tomorrow's." She handed her empty glass to a passing server and rolled into the ballroom. "Come on, Brianne, let's not keep these young men waiting."

Men?

Bri followed behind her, then stopped suddenly when she saw the cluster of tuxedoed men. She turned to Minnie. "I thought this was a hen-only party."

Minnie cackled. "It is. But it wouldn't be much of a hen party without men—preferably young, good-lookin', single men." She lifted her hand, and a burly guy separated from the group and hurried over. He didn't hesitate to lift her out of the wheelchair. From over his shoulder, Minnie winked as he carried her out to the dance floor and swirled her around.

"She's something else, isn't she?"

Bri turned to see Beckett standing behind her. Unlike the other men, his tuxedo wasn't rented and fit to perfection.

"Obviously, if she got you to attend." She reached out and adjusted his bow tie, something she had done numerous times before. But this time, she didn't hurry through the process. This time, she drew it out, terrified that it might be the last time she ever did it.

Beckett reached up and covered her hands with his. When she lifted her gaze, his familiar eyes were filled with concern. "It's going to be okay, Bri. You aren't going to get rid of me that easily."

Her hands grasped his for only a brief second before she turned the conversation to a less emotional subject. "So what are you doing here? I thought you hated the Henhouse."

He shrugged. "It's grown on me. Besides, I couldn't help being a little curious about a hen party." He glanced around. "It's not quite what I expected."

"You were thinking naked women?"

He turned to her in horror. "Not hardly. Not when most of the hens are either married or four times my age."

"Starlet's not." Bri nodded at the dance floor.

"Are you becoming a matchmaker, little sister?"

"No. I just think it would be nice if you asked her to dance."

He waved a hand at the men. "She has all these other guys to dance with."

"Guys who Minnie paid for. It would make her night if a man who wasn't getting paid made the effort."

He took her empty glass and handed it to a server. "How about if I just spend my last Saturday night as a civilian dancing with my little sister?"

And unable to speak around the tears, Bri nodded and allowed him to sweep her out to the dance floor.

The married hens left well before ten o'clock. Being pregnant, Jenna Jay wasn't much into dancing. Elizabeth was nursing and needed to get home to baby Brice. And Billy had called Shirlene saying Jesse hadn't come home after his shift at the gas station, and he needed her to watch the kids so he could go hunt him down. Bri might've been concerned if Jesse hadn't forgotten his curfew before. The teenager was a handful—much like his father.

Once the married hens were gone, the party got a little rowdier. Minnie dismissed the string quartet, and one of the men hooked his iPod up to the sound system. Tux jackets and bow ties were removed and high heels kicked

off as hens and young men boogied to Katy Perry and
Bruno Mars. Surprisingly, the older hens had no trouble
keeping up. Sunshine and Baby seemed to have twice
the energy as Bri. And Minnie hadn't left the floor once.
Although her fast dancing consisted of nothing more than
disco hand rolls as the rest of the crowd gyrated around
her wheelchair. But none of the hens compared to Starlet,
who danced like she sang, with a smooth sultriness that
had the men vying for her attention. Attention that left her
looking flushed and happy.

Or maybe that was the champagne.

The only one who wasn't dancing was Beckett. He
stood off to the side and watched while he sipped on a
glass of Minnie's brandy. For Starlet, Bri kept up her fun-
loving farce for as long as she could. But when a Miranda
Lambert song came on, she couldn't hold her depression
at bay for a moment longer and slipped out the side door
that led to the secret passages. It was a relief to step into
Miss Hattie's closet, and she didn't waste a second unzip-
ping her gown and letting it fall to the floor.

It was hard staying in Miss Hattie's room. It brought
back too many memories of the time she spent there with
Dusty. And not just the lovemaking, but also the time they
spent together afterward. The long hours of whispered
conversation and sweet caresses that finally lulled her into
a dreamless sleep.

"Minnie thought you might like some company."

Bri turned to find a young man standing in the doorway. The same young man who had asked her to dance
more than a few times that night. A practiced smile tipped
up his lips as he unbuttoned his white tuxedo shirt and
slipped it off his shoulders.

"Nice bed," he said as he moved closer, his gaze wandering up and down her body. "And really nice underwear."

Until then, Bri hadn't even realized that she was standing there in nothing but a strapless bra and panties. She went to grab the duvet, but he stepped between her and the bed.

"You want to take off the rest of my clothes? Or do you prefer a little Magic Mike?"

Bri almost laughed at the thought of him doing a Magic Mike striptease. Instead, she crossed her arms over her chest and stared him down. "I didn't particularly care for the movie. Besides, I don't think a striptease is what you were hired for."

He shrugged as he reached for the waistband of his pants. "We escorts do whatever it takes to please the clients."

Bri's arms dropped. "Minnie hired escorts?"

"All the way from Big D." He dropped his pants to reveal a pair of white thong underwear with a big blue star right over his bulge. "But if you turn out to be as good as you look, I won't charge you a dime." He glanced over her shoulder. "Not even if that guy watches."

Bri was so consumed with the fact that Minnie had hired escorts for the evening that it took her a moment to absorb what he was saying. When it finally dawned on her, she whirled around not knowing what to expect.

It certainly wasn't her nephew's face pressed against the glass of the window.

Chapter Thirty-two

MISS HATTIE'S HENHOUSE WAS THE LAST PLACE Dusty wanted to be. As soon as the well-lit farmhouse came into view, the memories became so sharp he felt like the victim of a knife fight. Thankfully, last he heard, Brianne had gone home to Dogwood. And, no doubt, her boyfriend. Which was good. If it was this painful just looking at the house, there was no telling how painful it would be to walk in and see her.

Not that he planned on going inside. He was there just to make sure that the "hen party" hadn't gotten out of control. And a quick walk around the perimeter would tell him everything he needed to know.

It turned out that he didn't have to take that walk.

When Dusty turned into the circular drive, his headlights flashed over a bunch of teenage boys standing by a ladder that had been propped against the upstairs balcony. The light had the boys scattering like a herd of frightened deer.

Having been one of those boys who had made the journey out to Miss Hattie's as a kid, Dusty couldn't help finding the humor in their antics. Of course, back then, it had only been a rundown house filled with old women and cobwebs.

Dusty climbed out of the car and walked over to the ladder. He glanced up just as a teenage kid climbed over the railing and onto the ladder.

"Holy shit!" the kid said as he climbed down. "We got to get out of here. That was my aunt—"

"Jesse Cates!"

The voice had the teenager forgoing the last rungs. He jumped to the ground and took off down the road. The voice had the opposite effect on Dusty. Instead of running, he couldn't seem to move his feet. Or any other body parts. The only thing that seemed to be moving was his heart. It raced out of control when Brianne yelled again.

"I swear when I get my hands on you, Jesse, you won't be able to sit for a week!"

There was the creak of wood, and Dusty slowly lifted his gaze. Brianne leaned over the railing, her gaze searching the area for Jesse. From his position, all Dusty could see were waves of ebony hair and two full, lacy cups that took the rest of his breath away.

It returned quickly.

Along with an entire piss pot full of anger when the naked man stepped up next to Brianne.

"No need to worry about Jesse when you have Superstar Steve."

Dusty wasn't sure if the sound that came from his nose was a derisive snort or a head of steam. Either way, it got Brianne's attention.

Her gaze snapped down to him, and those big eyes widened. "Dusty?"

He stepped out of the shadow and into the light coming from the porch. He wanted to say something clever, but at the moment, he couldn't think of one clever thing. All he could think about was climbing the ladder and punching the guy with his arm around Brianne right in the face. The guy must've read his thoughts because he held up his hands and backed toward the open balcony doors.

"Look, Officer, it was consensual," he muttered. "And no money was involved." Before Dusty could even figure out what he was talking about, he disappeared, leaving only one person for Dusty to release his anger on.

"Just what the hell do you think you're doing?" he asked. "Have you no shame, woman?"

Her nostrils flared. "Shame? Why should I feel shame?"

"How about for standing around half-naked in front of God and the world." He looked away from the tempting swell of sweet breasts. "Of course, the world has already seen twice as much, haven't they?"

"Ahh," she said, drawing his attention back up to her. "So you did see the picture online. And that's why you broke up with me." The disappointment in her voice brought a wall of guilt that had him quickly becoming defensive.

"Hell yeah, it's why I broke it off with you. You lied to me. You told me that the guy had been stalking you for months. Was this before or after you stripped naked and had sex with him?"

"I didn't strip naked and have sex with him! And if you had cared enough to talk to me about it, you might've figured that out." She leaned her hands on the railing. "But no, you had to believe the worst."

"What else was I supposed to believe when you chased after me like you did?" He jabbed a finger at her. "And when I just caught you in nothing but your underwear with some naked asshole? Do you expect me to believe that there's a reasonable explanation? Or are you planning on making up some harebrained story again? Let's see"— he stared up at the sky—"you had car trouble, and this guy stopped to help you fix it only to get grease all over his clothing—and yours—so naturally you had to come back to Miss Hattie's and strip." He looked back at her. "Is that your story? Is that what you want me to believe?"

There was a long stretch of silence where the only sound was Dusty's angry breath rushing in and out of his lungs. Finally, she lifted her hands from the railing.

"No, Dusty," she said with no emotion in her voice. "I don't expect you to believe anything." She turned and walked back inside.

Dusty didn't know what pissed him off more: the thought of her dismissing him and his accusations so easily or the thought of her going back inside with the naked dude. He was up the ladder and over the railing before he could even think about it. Unfortunately, she had locked the French doors, forcing him to stand there like an idiot and knock.

"Who is it?" she called out.

"Open the damn door."

She appeared on the other side of the glass. She smiled her wide-eyed smile before lifting one finger...the middle one. Then she whipped around and sashayed over to the bed, where she stretched out like some goddamned centerfold. Dusty scanned the room, but the guy was either hiding in the closet or gone. Since he had once been the guy hiding in the closet, he wasted no time lifting a boot and kicking open the doors.

"Talk about people losing their minds," Brianne said dryly as he stepped into the room.

"Where is he?" He moved into the bathroom.

"Who?" she asked innocently.

"You know who. Is he the same one who took the picture of you? Or is this a new lover?"

"A new lover."

He stopped in front of the bed. "You really don't care, do you? You are so spoiled that you think you can go through men like you go through shoes. And when you have them groveling for something they can't have, you label them as stalkers." He started to turn back to the window, when she grabbed his sleeve and jerked him around.

"And what about you? Do you think you're so perfect, Dusty Hicks?" She came up on her knees. "The great Sheriff Hicks who follows all the rules and never screws up. Who hides all his true feelings behind a scowl and a cold metal badge. Except I didn't let you do that, did I? I forced you to feel." She released his shirt and smoothed out the wrinkles with hands that felt as hot as branding irons. "What's the matter, Sheriff? Did I make you feel too much? Want too much?"

When he didn't say anything, she tightened her hands around his shirt and tugged him closer. "Did offering you everything make you think you'd be left with nothing?" Before he figured out her intent, she leaned in and her lips captured his.

Dusty had never taken drugs, but he had dealt with enough druggies to know an addiction. And the sensation that sizzled through his veins made him realize just how addicted he was. Beneath the drugging force of her kiss, the pain of the last few weeks melted away and only pleasure remained. All thoughts evaporated except one: *More, I must have more.*

The rational part of his brain tried to send out a warning: *She's playing you for a fool. This isn't real.* But damned if it didn't feel real. And even if it wasn't, he didn't care. He was an addict, and he needed a hit of Bri. Just one more hit.

His hands wrapped around her waist, and he pulled her up against him, consumed by the feel of her warm skin in his hands and her soft breasts against his chest. Her fingers scraped up into his hair, knocking off his hat and sending chills down his spine. And then he was falling. Falling down to the warm cradle of her body.

The snaps of his shirt were jerked open, and he reached for her panties. But before his fingers could curl around the elastic edge her lips released him, and he opened his eyes to twin pools of heartbreaking blue.

"I love you," she whispered. A puff of surprise came from his lips, and she pressed a finger to them. "I know you don't believe me. And after all the lies I've told, I can't really blame you."

While Dusty tried to swim out of the fog her words had conjured, she continued. "I know you can't love me— not now. Not when you need to get back Emma. But I've come to realize that keeping a secret from the ones you love is as bad as lying to them. And I just thought you should know before you leave."

It took him a moment to realize that Brianne was throwing him out. And not just throwing him out, but also saying good-bye ... forever. As easily as her kiss had filled him with pleasure, her words filled him with pain. Pain so intense that it was a struggle to speak.

"I can't—"

The bedroom door burst open, and Dusty turned to see Reverend Jessup striding into the room in all his Elvis glory.

"Repent, you sons and daughters of Satan!" His voice boomed off the ceiling as an entourage of half-naked women and a couple of guys with cameras hurried in after him.

Dusty quickly sprang to his feet and tossed the covers over Bri. "What in the hell is going on?"

The reverend turned to one of the cameras. "What's going on, Sheriff Hicks, is that your day of judgment is upon you." He waved a hand. "The world is going to witness firsthand the depravity and wickedness that has been going on at Miss Hattie's for over a century." As if his words were a signal, the women started dancing and gyrating for the cameras—one using the bedpost as a stripper pole.

Having reached his limit, Dusty grabbed the reverend by his silk scarf. "I'm giving you two seconds to get your ass and these people out of here before I—"

"Before you what, Sheriff?" Jessup taunted. "Hit a man of God?"

Before Dusty took him up on the offer, Beckett came charging in the room, looking like he'd just rolled out of bed. His hair was messed, and he wore a pair of wrinkled black pants with the waistband unhooked. He glanced around at all the craziness until his gaze zeroed in on Dusty. Then, in two strides he was across the room, and his fist connected with Dusty's chin.

"You sonofabitch!" he said. "You think you can just show up after what you did to my little sister."

"Beckett, no!" Brianne came up off the bed in her lacy underwear, drawing the attention of the camera before Dusty could shake off the punch and push her behind him. But being the stubborn woman she was, she ducked around and positioned herself between him and her brother.

"But he hurt you, Bri," Beckett said.

Brianne's nod hit Dusty twice as hard as Beckett's punch. "And I'm sure I'll be hurt again in my lifetime. But you can't prevent that, Beckett. Just like you need to live your life, I need to live mine." She pointed over his shoulder. "What is Starlet doing wearing your shirt?"

The camera whipped over to where Starlet stood in the open doorway of the closet. And sure enough the young woman seemed to be wearing nothing but a tuxedo shirt. Her eyes sparkled as she swayed on her bare feet.

"I didn't realize my party was going to be televised." She giggled, and before she could do more than blow a kiss at the camera, Beckett shoved her back in the closet and slammed the door behind them.

The door had barely stopped vibrating when Minnie came rolling into the room, followed by Sunshine and Baby and a bunch of men in various stages of undress, including the guy who had been on the balcony.

"Did I not tell you that Miss Hattie's was a cesspool of sin?" Reverend Jessup bellowed at the camera. "Just look at this depravity." He pointed at the man's starred thong. "Just look at this corruption." He pointed at Dusty. "Just look at these"—he pointed at the hens—"whores!"

Before Dusty could take a step to stop what he knew

was coming, the shot resounded through the room, sending cameramen, screaming strippers, and half-naked men racing for the door.

When the room had cleared, the reverend was on the floor, and Minnie was sitting in her chair holding the smoking derringer.

"I never did care for a man in a toupee."

Chapter Thirty-three

"ORDER! THERE WILL BE ORDER in my courtroom!" Judge Seeley pounded his mallet, causing the fishing lures on his hat to jangle.

The entire Bramble courtroom quieted. All except for Reverend Jessup, who hadn't stopped spouting off since regaining consciousness.

"I will not be quieted!" Reverend Jessup pointed a finger at Minnie, who, despite the commotion, had nodded off in her wheelchair. "That woman shot me, and I expect her to pay the price."

Kenny Gene piped up from the crowd of townsfolk who sat behind the railing. "I wouldn't call that little scratch on your arm bein' shot." He stood up and stripped off his shirt, pointing to the red puckered wound on his shoulder. "This here is bein' shot."

"Woo-wee." Rye Pickett leaned closer. "That's some scar you got there, Kenny."

Kenny nodded proudly. "Just your everyday, run-of-the-mill, law enforcement battle wound." He looked at Dusty, who was standing next to the judge's podium. "Ain't that right, Sheriff?"

Dusty smiled and nodded. "That's right, Kenny. All good sheriff deputies have them."

"Oh, for Christ's sakes!" Reverend Jessup snapped. "Who gives a shit about what happened to a hick deputy? I want justice, and I want it now." A muttering of disbelief and condemnation rose up from the townsfolk, but the reverend paid little attention. With his toupee hanging and his rhinestone jacket bloodied, he'd given up caring about his holier-than-thou persona. "Not only did the old broad try to kill me, but the disreputable villain you call a sheriff took the camera away from my cameraman and chucked it out the window, where some fool ran off with it."

Judge Seeley lifted a brow at Dusty, who only shrugged. "It seemed like the thing to do at the time."

The crowd laughed, and the reverend's face became so red it matched the tattered scarf wrapped around his arm. "You think this is funny, you bunch of country hicks?" he roared. "No one laughs at Josiah Jessup and gets away with it. Once my television show becomes popular, I'll have this town wiped off the map."

A loud snort came from the front row. At first, Dusty thought it was Moses Tate. But then he realized that Moses had found his way over to Minnie and was now holding her hand in his gnarled one and shooting warning looks at the reverend. Dusty glanced back at the front row in time to see Elmer Tate stand and surprise everyone by speaking—soberly.

"Bramble has survived drought, dust storms, depressions, and Dalton Oil almost closing. It sure as hell will survive some big-mouthed preacher who looks nothin' like the king of rock and roll."

"Why, you good-for-nothing drunk—" Reverend Jessup started, but Wilma Tate jumped up and cut him off.

"Just who do you think you're callin' a drunk? Elmer might make me as angry as a wet hen at times, but nobody calls him a drunk but me." She swept through the swinging gate and proceeded to whack the reverend over the head with her purse, the feathers on her hat quivering with her unleashed fury.

Dusty only stood there and smiled as the judge slammed down his mallet.

"Enough!" he boomed. The courtroom quieted, and Wilma gave the reverend one more good whack before going back to her seat. When Elmer hooked an arm around her and placed a resounding kiss on her cheek, she smiled like a shy schoolgirl.

A loud yawn pulled everyone's attention over to Minnie. "So did you get things all figured out, Doyle?"

The judge sadly shook his head. "I'm afraid it's not that simple, Min. You shot a man, and unless we have proof of malicious intent on the reverend's part, I have no choice but to have Dusty here lock you up until you can post bail."

"Now, wait one darn minute." Dusty turned to the judge. "You can't expect me to put a ninety-year-old woman in jail. Especially when it's this man"—he pointed at the reverend—"who should be behind bars."

The judge released his breath. "I couldn't agree with you more. And after huntin' with Minnie, I realize that if she wanted him dead, he would be. But that doesn't change the facts. I'm afraid breakin' the law is breakin' the law."

"But he entered Miss Hattie's without invitation," Dusty said.

"That's right," Mayor Sutter piped up. "And in the great state of Texas, we don't put up with folks bustin' into our homes uninvited." There was a mumble of agreement before the reverend spoke.

"A bed-and-breakfast is not a private home. It's a business. A business that allows the public to come and go as they please. I was merely an innocent victim looking for a room for the night."

"Who just happened to have two cameramen and a bunch of strippers with him," Dusty said dryly.

The reverend sent him a smug look. "I know nothing about strippers, Sheriff. And since they ran off without leaving their names, we can only assume that they were working at Miss Hattie's."

"We both know that Minnie didn't hire strippers."

The reverend cocked his head, the toupee drooping even more. "Then what would you call the male escorts, Sheriff?"

Dusty turned to Minnie. "You hired escorts?"

Minnie shrugged. "It wasn't the first time, and I hope it's not the last. Those boys sure can dance."

While Dusty tried to figure out a reply for that, the judge sighed and lifted his mallet. "I set the bond for..."

The loud whoosh of helicopter blades drew everyone's attention to the windows. The maple trees in the town hall courtyard blocked Dusty's view, but he had a pretty good idea of who it was in the chopper. Rachel Dean confirmed it.

"Well, I'll be. I think the cavalry has arrived."

It took only a minute for the doors of the courtroom

to be thrown open and a wall of Cates brothers to enter. Dusty had to admit the four men were an intimidating sight. Their broad shoulders, deep scowls, and low cowboy hats gave them the look of a gang of gunslingers just itching for a chance to draw. But it was their leader who held Dusty's attention.

Even in high heels, Brianne barely reached her brothers' shoulders. Yet the set of full lips and the steel in her blue eyes said that she wasn't a woman to be trifled with. Dusty wanted to do a lot more than trifle with her. He wanted to sweep her up in his arms and kiss the daylights right out of her. Instead, he watched with pride as she turned to her brothers and issued an order.

"I can handle this." Then she sashayed through the gates and straight up to the judge's desk. "I'm here to defend Minnie Ladue."

"You have evidence to prove that the shooting was justified?" the judge asked.

"No," Brianne said. "But I have evidence to prove that Reverend Josiah Jessup is a swindling con artist."

The reverend laughed. "You have nothing on me. In fact"—he pulled out his phone—"if anyone has any evidence of wrongdoing, it's me." He tapped the phone until he found a picture and then held it up. "This harlot has posed naked for—"

All the anger Dusty had kept inside since losing Emma was packed in the punch he gave the reverend. The reverend crumpled to the floor amid applause and the giggles of two old women Dusty hadn't noticed until then. More than likely because his eyes had been on Brianne, who was now looking at him as if he'd lost his mind. And he figured he had. Lost it over a petite, dark-haired woman who had a thing for pirate tattoos and handcuffs. But before he could do more than send Brianne a smile, the two old women pushed through the gates.

"Well, I can't say as I'm surprised, Josiah," the one with the walker said in a quavery voice. "You always were an obstinate child. No doubt due to your milquetoast daddy sparing the rod."

The other woman shuffled in behind her and looked down her nose at the reverend, who was still dazed from Dusty's punch. "Thought you were gonna send us back to the old folks' home, did ya?" She smiled. "Too bad for you that you left two nosy old women in your house unattended. After we gave all those accounting books we found over to that nice man with the F-B-I on his jacket, I think that the only person going somewhere is you."

Sure enough, a couple of the federal agents who had worked with Dusty on the Alejandro case pushed their way between the Cates brothers.

"You old bats!" Reverend Jessup yelled as the two agents handcuffed him. "I should've declared you mentally insane when I had the chance. But don't you worry, I'll have the chance again." As they led him out the side door, he yelled over his shoulder in his booming preacher voice. "Nothing can stop the king of kings!"

Rachel Dean shook her head. "More like the king of cuckoos."

"The charges are dismissed." The judge pounded his mallet. "And this hearing adjourned."

With the excitement now over, the townsfolk shuffled out of the courtroom. Brianne started to follow them, when Dusty stopped her. With those blue eyes pinned on him, he felt a little light-headed and...happy as hell.

"How did you know about the women?" he asked.

She shrugged. "Rachel Dean mentioned them when I was cutting her hair, and I found it odd that such a sly man would offer his home to the elderly. After you arrested the reverend and Minnie"—she sent him a very sour look—"I did a little research and came up with the reverend's telephone number in Malibu. As it turned out, his grandmother and great-aunt had already contacted the FBI about the accounting records they'd found, and there was a warrant out for the reverend's arrest. I was more than happy to give them his exact location."

"And the old gals? Why are they here?"

Brianne's gaze followed the two older ladies who her brothers were helping out the doors. "They wanted to be here for the arrest, and I didn't see the harm in sending the company jet to pick them up."

He smiled. "I guess all that money does come in handy." Dusty had been teasing, but the look that came over her face said she didn't get the joke.

"I'm not going to apologize for my family having money, Dusty." She lifted her chin. "Just like I'm not going to apologize for the picture that ended up on the Internet. Or the man that was in my bedroom. Or for falling in love with a pigheaded sheriff. I am who I am—a strong-willed woman who loves skydiving, cliff-jumping, cutting hair, and sex with men who aren't afraid to get a little rowdy. And if you can't handle that, then that's your problem."

She turned and strutted away. Dusty might've gone after her if a wrinkled hand hadn't wrapped around his wrist.

"Don't screw it up now."

Dusty looked down at Minnie. "I can't let her get away."

"Of course you can't. But now isn't the time to make your case. Not when she's all riled up and surrounded by a bunch of protective brothers. If you're gonna convince her that you love her, you'll need a grand plan that gets her full attention." She shook her head. "Especially after the dumbass way you've been actin'."

Dusty opened his mouth to deny the accusation but realized that he didn't have a leg to stand on. So he waited until Brianne and her brothers had left the courtroom before he turned to Minnie and asked.

"So what's this grand plan?"

Minnie shrugged. "You'll have to figure that out for yourself. But I recommend giving her what most women want: Chills. Thrills. And a man who will love them forever."

Chapter Thirty-four

GOOD-BYES HAD NEVER BEEN BRI'S FORTE. Which was why she'd slipped out of the Henhouse before the hens had gotten up that morning. Besides, it wasn't really good-bye. She had no intentions of staying away from Miss Hattie's, despite a certain sheriff who had broken her heart so thoroughly that she wondered if it would ever mend. And maybe it was best if it didn't mend completely. Her broken heart would serve as a reminder of her mistake: never fall for a guy with a bad attitude and commitment issues. Of course, she wasn't in the market for a boyfriend. There were too many things she wanted to accomplish first. She wanted to get her beautician's license. She wanted to get a job. And she wanted to get her own place using her own money.

And it wasn't like she was hurting for male attention.

Since her talk with Beau, all her brothers had been calling and setting up "play dates." It seemed her brothers were trying to make up for leaving her out during their childhood. Brant wanted to teach her how to fly his helicopter. Billy wanted to teach her how to hunt and fish. And Beau refused to teach her bull riding but was willing to let her try her hand at mutton busting—whatever that was. Unfortunately, Beckett wouldn't be around to teach Bri anything. He had left for boot camp the same day as Starlet had left for Nashville. And now Bri spent her nights praying for his safety.

And speaking of safety.

The vibrations of the Smart Car made Bri realize that she was going well over the speed limit. She started to lift her foot off the accelerator, when she glanced into the rearview mirror and noticed a car gaining on her. And not just any car, but a black-and-white with a row of flashing red lights.

If she had been in Culver County, she might've kept right on going. But she had planned on stopping by Bramble before she headed home to Dogwood and was right outside the city limits. And everyone knew that Sam Winslow's foot had healed and he was back to work.

Sure enough, when Bri pulled over to the shoulder, it was Sheriff Winslow who stepped out of the car. Which didn't explain the feeling of disappointment that settled in her stomach.

"Goin' a mite bit fast, weren't you, Willie?" the sheriff said as soon as Bri rolled down her window.

"It wasn't my fault, Sheriff. You see—" She stopped mid-excuse. "No, it was my fault. I wasn't paying attention."

The sheriff rested his hand on his empty holster. "Your mind on something else, was it? Or would that be someone else?"

Before Bri could figure out what he was talking about, another sheriff's car pulled in front of the Smart Car. Her heart kicked into overdrive as her worst fear got out.

"Thanks for the call, Sam," Dusty said as he strode

toward the car, not a twinge of a smile on his face. "I'll take things from here."

"Anytime, Sheriff." Sheriff Winslow winked at Bri before he turned and headed back to his car.

Finally snapping out of her daze, Bri reached for the gearshift with every intention of driving off. Unfortunately, Dusty put a stop to her escape by reaching in the window and taking the keys out of the ignition.

"Get out of the car, ma'am."

"No." Bri crossed her arms over her chest and stared out the windshield. She heard an exasperated sigh before her door was jerked open, and she found herself pressed against a tall, hard body and staring up into a pair of mirrored sunglasses.

"You just have to push the limits, don't you?" he said. And although there wasn't a lick of smile on his lips, there was definitely a smile in his voice. He turned her around and bent her over the front of the car. "Now, we can do it the easy way." He pulled her hands behind her back, and cold steel slipped around her wrists. "Or we can do it the hard way." His thighs pressed against her as he leaned over and whispered in her ear. "You want it hard, ma'am?"

Just that quickly, Bri's libido went from zero to sixty, leaving her panties moist and her brain empty. His hands curled around her hips, and she was pulled back against a hard-on that had her knees giving out.

"Hmm?" He hummed against her ear. "I'm going to take that as a yes." Then he gently lifted her up in his arms and carried her back to his squad car. It wasn't until he had her in the backseat with the door locked that she found her voice.

"What are you doing?" She searched for a door handle,

but there wasn't one. So she pounded on the Plexiglas that separated the backseat from the front. "You let me out of here! I've done nothing wrong."

"Now I wouldn't say that." Dusty started the car and pulled back onto the highway. "I have a piece of paper that says I was supposed to get a slave for two weeks. With my calculations, I figure you did about a week's worth of work—give or take. Which means you owe me at least a week more."

Bri yelled in the hole in the Plexiglas right next to his ear. "You released me from that agreement!"

"Which I had no authority to do. Only a judge can make that decision. And since Judge Seeley has gone fishin' for the weekend, I'll have to detain you until he gets back."

"Detain me? What do you mean detain me? Detain me where?"

"In jail, of course. Where else would you detain a criminal who was trying to get out of her probation?"

If Bri had been in possession of Minnie's derringer, she would've blown a hole right through the partition so she could reach through and wrap her hands around Dusty's throat. Instead, she did the next best thing. She threatened him with her brothers.

"You just wait, Dusty Hicks. As soon as my brothers find out about this ridiculous farce, there will be no place for you to hide. And this time, I won't lift a finger to stop them from whupping your butt for abusing me." She sat back against the seat with a humph.

"Abusing?" Dusty glanced over his shoulder at her. "Now, sweetheart, who said anything about abuse? I said I was planning on detaining you until you fulfilled your part of our agreement."

"We have no agreement!"

His lips curled into the biggest smile she'd ever seen on the man. "Well, we'll just have to see about that, now won't we?" Then he turned back around and started whistling.

Since her Granny Lou had the entire DVD collection of the television show, Bri recognized it immediately. She snorted. As if the ornery man sitting in front of her was even close to being as kindhearted and gentle as Sheriff Andy Taylor. Andy would never manhandle a woman. He would never "detain" her. And certainly would never break her heart.

Bri fumed all the way into Bramble. And was still fuming when Dusty opened the back door.

"Easy or hard?"

She smiled sweetly as she got out. "Hard, of course." She head-butted him in the chin.

"Dammit, woman!"

Bri would've done it again if he hadn't leaned down and flipped her over his shoulder, leaving her looking at the finest buns this side of the Pecos. He started up the path that led to the jail, when Mayor Sutter called out.

"Hey there, Sheriff! You got yourself a criminal?"

Bri tried to lift her head, but it was hard with her hands behind her. So instead she just yelled at the top of her lungs. "He's abducting me, Mayor Sutter! And someone needs to stop him."

The mayor's lizard-skin cowboy boots joined Dusty's scuffed ones.

"Is that true, Sheriff?" the mayor asked.

Dusty kept walking. "It does appear that way."

Another pair of boots joined them. "You gonna

interrogate the criminal, Sheriff?" Kenny Gene asked. "You need some help?"

"I think I can handle it, Kenny," Dusty said. "But I'd sure appreciate it if you made sure we weren't interrupted."

"Shore thang, Sheriff. No one will get past me."

Another pair of boots appeared. These female and familiar.

"Just what in tarnation is goin' on here?" Twyla asked. "Is that you underneath all that hair, Willie?"

"Yes," Bri said, hoping someone sane had finally shown up. "Could you please call my brothers and tell them that the sheriff has abducted me?"

"Now why would I call your brothers, Brianne, when there isn't a woman alive who wouldn't want to be abducted by a hot cowboy?" Twyla sighed. "It's just so romantic. Kenny Gene, how come you've never hand-cuffed and abducted me?"

While Bri rolled her eyes, Dusty kept right on walking as another pair of shoes joined the others. These were black lace-up oxfords with a spot of ketchup on one toe.

"Hush up, Twyla," Rachel Dean said. "Can't you see that the sheriff is a man on a mission? Here, let me get that for you, Sheriff." She pulled open the glass door and held it. Before the door whooshed closed, Bri heard the last of the conversation.

"I guess the sheriff didn't like the haircut Willie gave him," Twyla said.

Rachel Dean laughed. "I think he liked it just fine."

Since there would be no help from the townsfolk, Bri gave up the fight and allowed Dusty to take her where he would. He took her to a jail cell. One very different from the Culver jail. Despite the bars, this cell looked like her Granny Lou's bedroom. There was a large bed with a brass headboard and a homemade quilt. A pretty rag rug and a picture of the Texas state flag.

Bri might've commented on the décor when Dusty dumped her onto the bed if he hadn't rolled her over so her mouth was pressed into a pillow. She felt one handcuff being removed, but instead of removing the other, he rolled her back over, pulled her hands over her head, and handcuffed them to the bed. Then, with a very evil look in his eyes, he jerked open the snaps of his shirt.

Her eyes widened as the shirt dropped to the floor, followed by his gun belt. "What are planning on doing?" she croaked.

Without answering, he sat down on the edge of the bed and removed first one boot and then the other.

"Oh, no," she said. "If you think we're going to have sex, you've got another thing coming, Sheriff Dusty Hicks." She tried to make her voice stern, but it was hard when adrenaline and desire pumped through her body at just the thought of what he had planned. "I mean, I might've shown some interest in your handcuffs, but that was when I liked you."

He removed his sunglasses and set them on the sink, his eyes holding a look that had her tummy trembling. "You don't like me anymore, Brianne?" He stood up and unbuttoned his jeans. "Because I like you." His gaze swept over her. "I like everything about you. Including your need for a little danger." He unzipped his jeans with a zing that took all the moisture right out of Bri's mouth.

What it didn't do was stop her brain from working. And it only took a second to figure out why the man who had broken it off with her was now telling her how much he liked her.

"Ahh, I get it," she said. "Minnie must've explained about the picture in Mexico and the guy in my room the night of Starlet's going-away party. And now that you think I'm not a slut, you're willing to resume our relationship."

The teasing light died out of his eyes. "Is that what you think?" When she only glared at him, he released his breath and his shoulders slumped. "Of course it's what you think. Why wouldn't it be?" He snorted and turned away from the bed. "Some grand plan. I never should've let you leave the courtroom without explaining things." He turned back around. "Minnie didn't tell me anything about the picture or the escort, Brianne. And you don't need to explain, either. I won't deny that I'm jealous of any man who gets to be near you, but jealousy wasn't the reason I broke it off with you. The real reason I broke it off was because I was terrified. Terrified of falling head over heels in love with the beautiful woman in the picture. A woman who I thought could no more fall in love with a simple sheriff from west Texas than a princess could fall in love with a beggar."

He swallowed hard and looked down at his bare feet. "Of course, it was too late by then. I was already in love with you. I was just too stupid to figure it out." He hesitated for only a moment before he reached into his front pocket and pulled out a small set of keys. With sad eyes, he walked over to the bed.

"I'm sorry, Brianne." He leaned down and gave her the kind of kiss that touches a girl's soul. "Sorry I didn't figure it out sooner." He went to unlock the handcuffs, but Bri pulled her hands away.

"That's it?" she said. It was difficult to talk around the tears that had welled up in her throat. "You've gone to all this trouble to get me here and you're just going to give up that easily?" She sent him her most snooty look. "Well, I certainly expected more from the big, bad sheriff of Culver County."

Dusty looked confused for only a second before he smiled his crooked smile that always brightened her world. "You did, did ya?" He flung the keys over his shoulder and joined her on the bed. "And just what did you expect, ma'am?" He started unbuttoning her blouse, placing a kiss on each section of skin he exposed. "A little strip search, perhaps? A little corporal punishment?"

"As your prisoner, I'll leave that up to you," she whispered breathlessly. She started to close her eyes, when a thought struck her. "You locked the door, right? Because if word gets back to my brothers—"

He used his teeth to pull down the cup of her bra. "I wouldn't worry about your brothers. Not when your parents have given me their blessing." With his heated lips inching toward her nipple, it took her a moment to process his words.

"Their blessing? Their blessing for what?"

He lifted his head. "For your hand in marriage, of course. You don't think I'd ask you to marry me without first talking to your parents?"

"Marriage? You want to marry me?"

"Yes." He smiled wickedly. "And I'm prepared to torture you until I get the right answer."

"In that case"—Bri sent him her own wicked smile—"my lips are sealed."

Epilogue

"YOU LOOK A LITTLE PALE, SHERIFF," Bri said as she studied her soon-to-be husband. "Are you having second thoughts?"

"Hell, yeah, I'm having second thoughts. And third. And fourth." He looked out the window. "I should've known that marriage to you would be a dangerous undertaking."

"Now, sweetheart." Bri slid closer to him, the material of the dress that she'd had specially made for the occasion rustling. "If anyone should be nervous, it should be me. Now that Heather has agreed to joint custody, I'm going to become a stepmother. And thanks to all those fairy tales, Emmie is convinced that all stepmothers are wicked."

Just as Bri had hoped, the fear left Dusty's face to be replaced with a twinkle of humor. "And she would be right. You have a wicked streak a mile long."

She swatted at his arm. "That's not funny. I'm really worried about Emmie accepting me."

Dusty tucked a strand of hair back into her helmet. "Accepting you? After she came here for a visit, you two have become as thick as thieves. Not only did she love the room you decorated for her, but also she can't stop talking about you and her "styling" all her dolls' hair. And your bizarre choice of honeymoons clinched her devotion."

Bri smiled. "You mean, you don't want to spend the night in Cinderella's castle and have breakfast with the Disney princesses?"

A look of contentment settled over Dusty's face. "Actually, I can't think of anything I'd rather do. Having two princesses of my own, I've grown kinda partial to royalty." He leaned over and kissed her. Bri had just melted into the kiss when her big brother peeked his head in.

"It's time." Billy winked at her before he walked over and pushed open the door.

Wind whistled in, and Dusty tensed. Knowing from experience that the longer you waited the harder it became, Bri stood and tugged him to his feet.

"I love you," she said.

A look of resignation came into his eyes, and he followed her to the door and stood while Billy helped her attach the tandem harnesses. When they were secure, Dusty glanced back at her.

"I love you, too." He released his breath. "God help me."

Without further hesitation, they took the leap.

"There they go!" Rachel Dean yelled.

"Where?" Kenny Gene pushed through the crowd gathered in Miss Hattie's garden. "All I see comin' out of the plane Brant is flyin' is a spot of white and black."

"That's them," Rye Pickett said. "Ain't that right, Sheriff Winslow?"

"Just Sam, Rye." Sam Winslow adjusted the binoculars he had pointed at the sky. "Your new sheriff appears to be free-fallin' about a hundred miles an hour."

"Well, it's the craziest thing that I've ever seen," Twyla said. "Why would anyone want to fall out of the sky when they could walk down the aisle? I just hope she doesn't drop the bouquet before she gets here. If it hits the ground, there goes my chance at a summer weddin'."

"Stop worryin', Twyla," Rachel Dean said as a parachute appeared above the black-and-white speck. "You know as well as I do that any season is a good season for a weddin'."

Minnie's gaze moved over to the dark-haired maid of honor, who was the only one not looking up as the parachuting bride and groom floated through the bright blue west Texas sky. Instead, her pretty brown eyes were settled on a handsome groomsman.

Minnie smiled. "Amen to that."

When beautiful country music
sensation Star Bentley is threatened
by a crazy fan, she doesn't need just a
bodyguard. She needs a rugged cowboy
from Bramble, Texas.

Please see the next page
for a preview of

The Last Cowboy in Texas.

STARLET BRUBAKER HAD DISAPPEARED.

The only evidence of her existence was the tiny mole just above the right corner of Star Bentley's glossy, pink-painted lips. Everything else was completely different. The green eyes. The blond hair. The skinny body. And the simple, loose-fitting, flowered dress. Nothing but the mole remained of the awkward, fat girl from southeast Texas.

Starlet pulled her eyes away from the mirror and looked down at the half-eaten banana MoonPie in her hand.

Well, maybe there were a few other things that remained.

A tap on the bathroom door had her cramming the rest of the pie in her mouth.

"Star?" Kari Jennings, her manager, trainer, and general ballbuster called through the door. "You okay? Did you need something? Because we can't have the sweet-heart of country music going without."

Food. The sweetheart of country music needs food.

But instead of saying it, Starlet chewed faster and swallowed hard. "No, I'm good. I'm just touching up my lip gloss."

There was a pause. "But your lip gloss is out here in the dressing room, sugar."

Starlet rolled her eyes at her own stupidity and quickly wiped the crumbs off her mouth. A crumb slipped down the neckline of her dress, but she ignored it and opened the door, giving her manager a bright Star Bentley smile. "Silly me. I guess I'm just nervous about the concert tonight."

Even in her power heels, Kari barely came to Starlet's chin. With her petite body, short blond hair, and big, blue eyes, she looked just like Tinker Bell. Which was exactly why Starlet had hired her. Unfortunately, at the time, Starlet hadn't realized how vicious and manipulative pixies could be.

"No need to worry." Kari tugged up the neckline of Starlet's dress. "You've played much bigger venues than this." Her brow knotted as she stared at Starlet's boobs. "Speaking of bigger, I still think you should consider breast reduction. These just don't go with the new persona I've created."

"They look like they go pretty good to me."

Cousin Jed appeared in the dressing room doorway. Or more like filled it with his hulking frame, which had won him the title of "The Crusher" on the amateur wrestling tour and "The Asshole" at more than a few Texas nightclubs. While Starlet had never officially hired him, Jed had assumed the role of her personal bodyguard—something he excelled at given that he was always getting too personal with her body.

He shifted the toothpick to one corner of his wide,

bulldoggish mouth as his gaze wandered over her breasts. "There's some rodeo cowboy out there that claims you invited him backstage. Says you owe him money. You havin' to pay for it, Cuz?"

Since her manager disapproved of rodeo cowboys more than MoonPies, Starlet played dumb. "Now that's strange. When would I have had a chance to talk with a rodeo cowboy?" She fanned a hand in front of her face. "Is the air conditioner on in here?"

"Check the air conditioner!" Kari bellowed at her assistant, before turning to Jed. "Tell the cowboy he's out of luck for a backstage pass, but give him a couple tickets—not front row."

"We don't have front row, anyhow. They're filled with a bunch of hotshot military dudes. And I'm not Ticket-master. I'm the head of security and people need to show a little respect."

Kari barely gave him a glance as she fluffed Starlet's hair extensions. "You'll get respect when you've earned it. So far, all I've seen you do is stand around chatting with the t-shirt vendors."

"Nothin' wrong with bein' friendly." Uncle Bernard pushed his way past Jed. Back in Texas, Starlet's uncle had always worn overalls and a white t-shirt with ketchup stains. But since following his niece on tour, he'd taken to wearing western suits with matching boots and Stetsons. "Just a few quick signatures, Star Baby." He held out a stack of ball caps with a hideous picture of her on the front. While she gaped at the picture, he pointed a black Sharpie at her mouth. "MoonPie?"

Starlet quickly brushed at her lips, but it was too late. Kari had zeroed in.

"MoonPie?" Her voice hit a high note that had chills tiptoeing down Starlet's spine. "You know you have to watch your sugar intake, Star, especially with your metabolism. This means that you'll have to work extra hard with the ThighMaster tomorrow." She turned her evil eye on Uncle Bernie. "And didn't I talk to you about non-authorized merchandise?"

"I don't know how much more authorized you can get than family." Uncle Bernie polished the top of one cream-colored, lizard-skin boot on the back of his pant leg. "Especially when I raised Star like one of my own. It seems only right that she would want to repay me with a few signatures."

"You are so full of shit, Bernie." Starlet's mother finally roused from her pre-concert catnap and sat up on the couch, her hair wild and her eyes bloodshot. Starlet had poured out the bottle of vodka she'd found on the tour bus. Obviously, her mother had found another one. "You and that bitchy wife of yours—God rest her soul—treated my kid like crap."

Uncle Bernie's smile didn't falter. In fact, Starlet couldn't remember a time when her uncle wasn't happy and smiling. And maybe that was why it was so easy to forgive his shortcomings.

"Now, Jaydeen," Uncle Bernie said, "let's not go down that road again. I believe it was Shakespeare that said 'Thee proof is in thee puddin'.'" He reached out and pinched Starlet's cheek. "And there's no better puddin' than our little Star Baby."

Her mother groaned and flopped back on the couch. "Anyone have a hit of cocaine?"

Jed's gaze remained on Starlet. "I know what I'd like a hit of."

There was one thing Starlet had to give her family: they kept her from getting stage fright. Being stuck with them in a dressing room was much scarier than being responsible for entertaining thousands of fans.

She turned to Kari. "I'm ready."

"She's ready!" Kari called out, prompting Jed to grab his walkie-talkie and speak into it.

"The Star is walkin'."

En masse, Starlet's entire misfit posse headed for the door, even her mama, who, regardless of her hungover state, looked skinny and beautiful in her tight jeans and low-cut top. When they reached the stairs to the stage, Kari did more clothes adjusting, Jed did more gawking, her mama flirted with a security guy, and Uncle Bernie leaned in and whispered.

"Don't worry about the hats, Star Baby. I'll take care of them."

Starlet gave him a weak smile before climbing the stairs. As soon as she stepped on stage a spotlight hit her, and the entire coliseum released a deafening roar of applause and whistles. She might've panicked if a stagehand hadn't slipped her guitar over her head. The feel of the lacquered wood calmed her, and she walked to center stage and placed her mouth next to the microphone.

"Hi, y'all. You ready for a little music?"

The answering applause had barely fizzled when her band kicked in. Then there was nothing but the music. It washed over Starlet like Texas sunshine, transforming her from an awkward, insecure woman to a graceful, confident entertainer. An entertainer who could tease the crowd, flirt with her band members, and be completely comfortable sharing all the emotions she normally kept well hidden.

As usual, while performing, time flew by much too quickly. And before Starlet knew it, she had finished her last song and was headed off stage to wait for her encore.

Kari met her on the stairs. "You didn't give enough attention to the Marines in the front row."

"I thanked them for coming and dedicated 'The Price of Freedom' to them. What more did you want me to do?" Starlet took the bottle of water a security guy handed her and nodded her thanks before taking a deep drink.

"Something for a picture op," her manager said. "Call one of them up and sing to him for your encore."

Starlet shook her head. "I always do 'Good-bye Kiss' for the encore. And I'm not singing that to anyone but—" She caught herself. "I'm not singing that to some Marine."

Kari smiled the kind of smile that had always scared the crap out of Starlet. It reminded her of Meryl Streep in the movie *The Devil Wears Prada*.

"Well, of course you can do what you want," Kari said as she studied her manicured nails. "You don't have to listen to a manager with fifteen years' experience under her belt. Fifteen years of sweating it out with no-talents so that, when she finally found a person with a tiny bit of talent, she could mold and shape her into the kind of star who fills an auditorium." She waved her hand to encompass the coliseum before shrugging. "But…if you want a mediocre career that fizzles out after the first two albums, then you go right ahead and make your own decisions. I certainly won't stand in your way."

As always, Starlet conceded. "Okay, but I'll sing one of my other songs."

Kari shook her head. "'Good-bye Kiss' is your biggest hit—the one all these people have come to hear. If you leave it out, they'll charge the stage and trample you like a herd of angry elephants. So I suggest you pretend that the Marine is one of the rodeo cowboys you seem to be so enthralled with and make the best of it." She turned without another word and walked down the stairs, leaving Starlet with no choice but to do as she said.

Downing the rest of the water, she walked back on stage.

"Well, hello again," she said when she reached the microphone. "I thought I'd slow things down a bit— maybe sing a love song that you might recognize." The audience went wild. Once they'd quieted, she looked down at the front row. "But what's a love song if you don't have someone to sing it to? What say we get one of the country's finest up here?"

Starlet's gaze ran over the Marines. All were dressed in camouflaged pants and caps, green t-shirts, and lace-up desert boots. Most were standing and waving their hands to get her attention.

Except for one.

One arrogant Marine who didn't seem to be that taken with Star Bentley. In fact, with the bill of his cap pulled low over his face and his booted feet stretched out and crossed at the ankles, he looked like Moses Tate napping on a park bench. And even ninety-year-old Moses had stayed awake during the concert she had done for the small town of Bramble, Texas.

Perturbed by the Marine's audacity, Starlet had no problem pointing him out. "Now when I said I was going to slow things down a bit, I didn't mean that you could go to sleep on me." She waved her hand. "Let's get Rip Van Winkle up here and see if I can't wake him up."

The man didn't acknowledge her words, but the other Marines did. With a loud whoop, they picked him up and lifted him over their heads, passing him along until he ended up on stage. He didn't fight them, but he didn't seem too happy about it, either. Once the stagehands had him seated in a chair, he crossed his arms and stared down at his boots.

Starlet unhooked the microphone from the stand. "What do you say, soldier boy? You think you can stay awake long enough to listen to little ol' me?"

The audience laughed, but the Marine remained mute. Starlet might've continued her teasing if a wave of dizziness hadn't hit her. Not a little wave, but the kind that made your head feel like it had been flipped in a blender and set on puree. The roar of the crowd sounded muffled and distorted, and the stage seemed to rock like the deck of a ship. Not wanting to fall on her butt in front of thousands of people, she improvised and sat down on the Marine's lap.

Having dated her share of rodeo cowboys, Starlet wasn't a stranger to athletic bodies. But no cowboy she'd ever dated had a body like this one. Instead of long, lean muscles, this body had bunched, thick ones. Thighs like hard granite. A stomach like rippled steel. And arms with smooth, knotted biceps as big as grapefruit.

And Starlet loved grapefruits. In fact, they were the only things on Kari's starvation diet that she did love. Starlet had a half of one every morning—the juicy meat sectioned off and a sweet little cherry in the center.

"If you're going to sing, sing." The Marine's hissed words cut into her grapefruit daydream.

She might've been ticked at his attitude if she hadn't

been distracted by his voice. It was familiar. Too familiar. She dipped her head to peek under the cap, but before she could get a good look, another wave of dizziness hit her. She blinked it away, along with her ridiculous belief that she knew this Marine. The only Marine she knew didn't have biceps the size of grapefruits and thighs like sculptured granite. He was a skinny nerd who worked at some desk job at the Russian embassy. And even if he were in the States, he would never be caught dead at one of her concerts.

Which was just fine and dandy with Starlet.

What wasn't fine and dandy was this Marine's arrogance and nonchalance. Starlet didn't care if he liked her, but he wasn't going to ignore her. Remaining on his lap just to spite him, she lifted the microphone to her mouth and started to sing.

It wasn't easy.

"Good-bye Kiss" was the first song Starlet had ever written for the first and only love she'd ever had. It seemed wrong to sing it to someone else. So she did what Kari suggested: she imagined the love of her life and let the words of the song flow from the heart. When she finished, tears rolled down her cheeks, and you could've heard a pin drop in the coliseum. The Marine wasn't so moved. With a grumbled curse, he picked her up and set her on her feet before walking off stage.

Completely humiliated by his brush-off, she quickly lifted the microphone and ended the show.

"Thank y'all for coming. God bless!"

As always, the closing riled the crowd and had them charging the stage, yelling for autographs and tossing pink roses. Normally, she caught one and waved a good-bye. But tonight, it took all her concentration to walk. The dizziness was back and worse than ever. She stumbled over a cord and would've fallen if the security guy hadn't appeared and taken her arm.

"This way, Miss Bentley."

Struggling to put one foot in front of the other, she followed him. He released her to jump down from the stage and then reached up to lift her off. It was then that she noticed where he had taken her. They weren't in the long corridor that led to her dressing room. They were at the back of the stage, behind the curtains and lights and amid all the technical cords and wires.

Now why would he bring her back here?

"Wait—" It was the only thing she got out before a rag was stuffed in her mouth and her hands jerked behind her back and tied. Still, it wasn't until he hefted her over his shoulder and headed for a side door that she figured out what was happening.

Star Bentley, the sweetheart of country music, was being kidnapped.

And Starlet Brubaker had no choice but to go along for the ride.

**Did you miss meeting Slate Calhoun,
the sexy cowboy in Katie Lane's
first Bramble, Texas, novel?**

See the next page
for an excerpt from

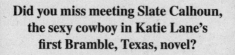

Going Cowboy Crazy.

SLATE CALHOUN SAT BACK IN THE DARK CORNER and watched the woman in the conservative pants and brown sweater take another sip of her beer as if it was teatime at Buckingham Palace. Hell, she even held her little pinkie out. If that was Hope Scroggs, then he was Prince Charles. And he was no pansy prince.

Still, the resemblance was uncanny.

The impostor swallowed and wrinkled up her cute little nose. A nose that was the exact duplicate of Hope's. And so were the brows that slanted over those big blue eyes and the high cheekbones and that damned full-lipped mouth. A mouth that had fried his brain like a slice of his aunt's green tomatoes splattering in hot bacon grease.

The kiss was the kicker. Slate never forgot a kiss. Never. And the few kisses he'd shared with Hope hadn't come close to the kiss he'd shared with this woman. Hope's kisses had always left him with a strange uncomfortable feeling; like he'd just kissed his sister. It had never left him feeling like he wanted to strip her naked and devour her petite body like a contestant in a pie-eating contest.

But if the woman wasn't Hope, then who the hell was she?

He'd heard of people having doubles—people who weren't related to you but looked a lot like you. He'd even seen a man once who could pass for George W. in just the right lighting. But this woman was way past a double. She was more like an identical twin. And since he'd known Hope's family ever since he was thirteen, he had to rule out the entire twin thing. Hope had two younger sisters and a younger brother. And not one of them was a look-alike whose kisses set your hair on fire.

The woman laughed at something Kenny said, and her head tipped back, her entire face lighting up. He'd seen that laugh before, witnessed it all through high school and off and on for years after. Hell, maybe she *was* Hope. Maybe his lips had played a trick on him. Maybe he was so upset about losing last night's game that he wasn't thinking straight. Or maybe, it being a year since her last visit, he was so happy to see her that he read something in the kiss that wasn't there.

It was possible. He'd been under a lot of stress lately. Football season could do crazy things to a man's mind. Especially football season in west Texas. Which was why he had planned a two-week Mexican vacation after the season was over. Just the thought of soft, rolling waves; warm sand; and cool ocean breezes made the tension leave his neck and shoulders.

What it didn't do was change his mind about the woman who sat on top of the bar with her legs crossed—showing off those sexy red high heels. Hope didn't cross her legs like that. And she hated high heels. She also hated going to the beauty salon, which was why her long brown hair was down to her butt. This woman's hair was styled in a short, layered cut that made her eyes look twice as big and was highlighted the color of Jack Daniel's in a fancy crystal glass.

Of course, Hope had lived in Hollywood for five long years. Maxine Truly had gone to Houston for only two years and had come back with multiple piercings and a tattoo of a butterfly on her ass. So big cities could screw you over. He just didn't believe they could change someone from an outspoken extrovert to an introvert who hadn't spoken a word, or even tried to, in the last hour.

Laryngitis, my ass.

That couldn't be Hope.

But there was only one way to find out.

Pushing up from his chair, he strolled around the tables to the spot where her adoring fan club had gathered. It didn't take much to part the sea of people. Hope might be the hometown sweetheart, but he was the hometown football hero turned high school coach. In Bramble, that was as close as a person could get to being God.

As usual, Kenny Gene was talking to beat the band. Sitting on the bar stool next to her, he was monopolizing the conversation with one of his exaggerated stories.

"...I'm not kiddin', the man blew a hole the size of a six-year-old razorback hog in the side of Deeder's double-wide, then took his time hoppin' back in his truck as if he had all day to do—hey, Slate."

Slate stopped just shy of those pointy-toed shoes and trim little ankles. Slowly, he let his gaze slide up the pressed pants, up the brown sweater that hugged the tiny waist and small breasts, over the stubborn chin and the full mouth that still held a tiny trace of pink glittery gloss, to those sky blue eyes that widened just enough to make him realize he hadn't made a mistake.

The woman before him wasn't Hope.

But he was willing to play along until he found out who she was.

"Kenny, what the heck are you doing letting Hope drink beer?" He pried the bottle from her death grip as he yelled at the bartender. "Manny, bring me a bottle of Hope's favorite and a couple of glasses." He smiled and winked at her. "If we're going to celebrate your home-comin', darlin', then we need to do it right."

"I wanted to order Cuervo, Slate," Kenny defended himself. "But she didn't want it."

"Not want your favorite tequila, Hog?" He leaned closer. "Now why would that be, I wonder?"

Before she could do more than blink, Manny slapped down the bottle of Jose Cuervo and two shot glasses, followed quickly by a salt shaker and a plastic cup of lime wedges. He started to pour the tequila but Slate shook his head.

"Thanks, Manny, but I'll get it." Slate took off his hat and tossed it down. Stepping closer, he sandwiched those prim-and-proper crossed legs between his stomach and the bar as he picked up the bottle and splashed some tequila in each glass—a very little in his and much more in the impostor's. He handed her the saltshaker. "Now you remember how this works, don't you, sweetheart?"

"'Course she knows how it works, Slate," Twyla piped in. "She's been in Hollywood, not on the moon."

Slate didn't turn to acknowledge the statement. He remained pressed against her calf, the toe of her shoe teasing the inseam of his jeans and mere inches from his man jewels. His body acknowledged her close proximity, but he ignored the tightening in his crotch and continued to watch those fearful baby blues as they looked at the saltshaker, then back at him.

"Here." He took the shaker from her. "Let me refresh your memory, Hog."

Reaching out, he captured her hand. It was soft and fragile and trembled like a tiny white rabbit caught in a snare. He flipped it over and ran his thumb across the silky satin of her wrist, testing the strum of her pulse. As he bent his head, the scent of peaches wafted up from her skin, filling his lungs with light-headed sweetness and his mind with images of juicy ripe fruit waiting to be plucked.

Easy, boy. Keep your eye on the goal line.

With his gaze pinned to hers, he kissed her wrist, his tongue sweeping along the pulse point until her skin was wet and her pupils dilated. Then he pulled back and salted the damp spot he'd left.

"Now watch, darlin'." He sipped the salt off, downed the shot, then grabbed a lime and sucked out the juice— all without releasing her hand. "Now you try. Lick, slam, suck. It's easy."

She just sat there, her eyes dazed and confused. He knew how she felt; he felt pretty confused himself. His lips still tingled from touching her skin, and his heart had picked up the erratic rhythm of hers.

"Go on, Hope," Kenny prodded. "What's the matter with you? Don't tell me you forgot how to drink in Hollywood?"

That seemed to snap her out of it, and before Slate could blink, she licked off the salt, slammed the shot, and had the lime in her mouth.

A cheer rose up, but it was nothing to what rose up beneath Slate's fly. The sight of those pink-glitter lips sucking the lime dry made his knees weak. And so did the triumphant smile that crinkled the corners of her eyes as she pulled the lime from her mouth. A mouth with full lips like Hope's but with straight, even front teeth. Not a slightly crooked incisor in sight.

Relief surged through him. The hard evidence proved he wasn't loco. It also proved his libido wasn't on the fritz. He wasn't hot after one of his closest friends; he was hot after this woman. This woman who was not Hope... unless she'd gotten some dental work done like they used to do on *Extreme Makeover*.

He mentally shook himself. No, she wasn't Hope. And if it took the entire bottle of tequila to get her to 'fess up, so be it.

He poured her another shot and had her salted and ready to go before she could blink those innocent eyes. "Bottoms up."

She complied, demonstrating the lick-slam-suck without a flaw. She grinned broadly when the crowd cheered, but she didn't utter a peep. Not even after the next shot. Damn, maybe she was Hope; she was just as mule-headed. And could hold her liquor just as well—although she did seem a little happier.

"Do a Nasty Shot," Sue Ellen hollered loud enough to rattle the glasses behind the bar.

Slate started to decline but then figured it might be just the thing to get to the truth. Besides, he'd always been a crowd-pleaser.

"You wanna do a Nasty Shot, Hog?" he asked.

She nodded, all sparkly-eyed.

For a second, he wondered if it was a good idea. She'd almost set him on fire the last time she kissed him. Of course, that was when he thought she was his close friend and her enthusiasm had taken him by surprise. Now he knew she was a fraud. A sexy fraud, but a fraud nonetheless. Knowing that, he wouldn't let things get out of control. He would get just aggressive enough to scare her into speaking up.

"Okay." Slate lifted her wrist and kissed it, this time sucking her skin into his mouth and giving it a gentle swirl with his tongue. Her eyes fluttered shut, and her breasts beneath the soft sweater rose and fell with quick little breaths.

The man muscle beneath the worn denim of his jeans flexed.

This was definitely a bad idea.

Unfortunately, with the entire town watching, he couldn't back out.

Lifting his head, Slate cleared his throat. "Remember how this works?" He covered the wet spot with salt. "Same premise, but this time we lick and shoot at the same time. Just leave the sucking part to me. Here." He uncrossed her legs and stepped between them, which prompted a few sly chuckles from the men. "For this, we need to get just a tad bit closer."

Those long, dark lashes fluttered, and her thighs tightened around him. Slate's breath lunged somewhere between heaven and hell, and his hand shook as he poured a full shot for her and a little for himself.

"Okay, darlin'." Luckily, he sounded more in control than he felt. "You ready?" He dipped his head and pressed his mouth to her skin.

She hesitated for just a second before she followed. The silky strands of her hair brushed his cheek as her lips opened and her tongue slipped out to gather the salt, only millimeters from his. Even though they didn't touch, an electric current of energy arced between them so powerfully that it caused them both to jerk back. Those big baby blues stared back at him, tiny granules of salt clinging to her bottom lip.

His mind went blank.

"Tequila, Coach," Rossie Owens, who owned the bar, yelled.

Snapping out of it, he straightened and grabbed up the full shot, then downed it in an attempt to beat back the rearing head of his libido. She followed more slowly, her wide, confused eyes pinned on him.

"The lime, Slate," Kenny laughed. "You forgot the lime."

Hell. He jerked up the lime and sucked out the tart juice, not at all sure he was ready to go through with it. But then people started cheering him on, just like they had in high school when they wanted him to throw a touchdown pass. And, just like back then, he complied and reached up to hold her chin between his thumb and forefinger as he lowered his lips to hers.

It wasn't a big deal. Slate had kissed a lot of girls in his life. Including one whose eyes were the deep blue of the ocean as it waits to wash up on a Mexican shore. Except he hadn't noticed that about Hope. Hope's eyes were always just blue. Yet this woman's eyes caused a horde of descriptive images to parade through his mind. All of them vivid...and sappy as hell.

Luckily, when he placed his lips on hers all the images

disappeared. Unluckily, now all he could do was feel. The startled intake of breath. The hesitant tremble. The sweet pillowy warmth.

"Suck!" someone yelled.

Her lips startled open, and moist heat surrounded him. Shit, he was in trouble. He parted his lips, hoping that once he did, she would pull back and start talking. But that's not what happened. Instead, she angled her head and opened her mouth wider, then proceeded to kiss him deep enough to suck every last trace of lime from his mouth, along with every thought in his mind. Except for one: how to get inside her conservative beige pants.

Slate pulled his head back. Get in her pants? Get in *whose* pants? He didn't know who the hell the woman was. And even if he did know, he sure wasn't going to get in her pants in front of the entire town. He liked to please people, but not that much.

Ignoring the moist lips and desire-filled eyes, Slate dropped his hand from her chin and lifted her down from the bar. When he turned around, the room was filled with knowing grins. He thought about explaining things. But if he'd learned anything over the years he'd lived in Bramble, it was that when small-town folks got something in their heads, it was hard to shake it. Even if it was totally wrong. Which was why he didn't even make the effort. He just grabbed his hat off the bar as he slipped a hand to the petite woman's waist and herded her toward the door.

It wasn't as difficult as he thought it would be. Which was just one more reason he knew the woman wasn't Hope. Hope was too damned controlling to let anyone herd her anywhere. Just one of the things he didn't particularly miss.

Once they were outside, Slate guided her a little ways from the door before he pulled her around to face him.

"Okay. Just who the hell are you?"

Her gaze flashed up to his just as Cindy Lynn came out the door.

"Hey, Hope. I was wonderin' if you could come to the homecomin' decoratin' committee meetin' on Monday afternoon. I know decorations aren't your thing, but everybody would love to hear about Hollywood. Have you met Matthew McConaughey yet? One of my cousins on my father's side went to college with him in Austin and—"

"Hey, Cindy." Slate pushed the annoyance down and grinned at the woman who, on more than one occasion, had trouble remembering she was married. "I know you're probably just busting at the seams to talk with Hope about all them movie stars, but I was wondering if you could do that later, seeing as how me and Hope have got some catching up to do."

"I'm sure you do." She smirked as she turned and wiggled back inside.

Realizing Cindy Lynn would be only one of many interruptions, Slate slapped his hat on his head and took the woman's hand. "Come on. We're taking a ride."

She allowed him to pull her along until they reached the truck parked by the door. "This is your truck?"

Slate whirled around and stared at the woman who sounded exactly like Hope—except with a really weird accent. He watched as those blue eyes widened right before her hand flew up to cover her mouth.

The hard evidence of her betrayal caused his temper—that he worked so hard at controlling—to rear its ugly head, and he dropped her hand and jerked open the door of the truck. "Get in."

She swallowed hard and shook her head. "I'd rather not."

"So I guess you'd rather stay here and find out how upset these folks get when I inform them that you've been playing them for fools."

She cast a fearful glance back over her shoulder. "I'm not playing anyone for a fool. I just wanted some answers."

"Good. Because that's exactly what I want." Slate pointed to the long bench seat of the truck. "Get in."

The sun had slipped close to the horizon, the last rays turning the sky—and the streaks in her hair—a deep red. She looked small standing so close to the large truck. Small and vulnerable. The image did what the Mexican daydreams couldn't.

He released his breath. "Look, I'm not going to hurt you, but I'm not going to let you leave without finding out why you're impersonating a close friend of mine. So you can either tell me or Sheriff Winslow."

It was a lame threat. The only thing Sheriff Winslow was any good at was bringing his patrol car to the games and turning on his siren and flashing lights when the Bulldogs scored a touchdown. But this woman didn't know that. Still, she didn't seem to be in any hurry to follow his orders, either.

"My car is parked over there," she said, pointing. "I'll meet you somewhere."

"Not a chance. I wouldn't trust you as far as little Dusty Ray can spit."

She crossed her arms. "Well, I'm not going anyplace with a complete stranger."

"Funny, but that didn't stop you from almost giving me a tonsillectomy," he said. A blush darkened her pale skin. The shy behavior was so unlike Hope that he almost smiled. Almost. She still needed to do some explaining. "So since we've established that we're well past the stranger stage, it shouldn't be a problem for you to take a ride with me."

"I'm sorry, but I really couldn't go—"

Kenny charged out the door with the rest of the town hot on his heels.

"Hey." He held out a purse, if that's what you could call the huge brown leather bag. "Hope forgot her purse."

Slate's gaze ran over the crowd that circled around. "And I guess everyone needed to come with you to give . . . Hope her purse."

"We just wanted to see how things were goin'." Tyler Jones, who owned the gas station, stepped up.

"And say good-bye to Hope," Miguel, the postmaster, piped in.

There was a chorus of good-byes along with a multitude of invitations to supper.

Then someone finally yelled what everyone else wanted to. "So what are you gonna do with Hope now, Coach?"

What he wanted to do was climb up in the truck and haul ass out of there. To go home and watch game film— or better yet, pop in a Kenny Chesney CD and peruse the Internet for pictures of Mexican hot spots. Anything to forget he'd ever met the woman, or tasted her skin, or kissed her soft lips, or stared into her blue eyes. Blue eyes that turned misty as she looked at the smiling faces surrounding them.

It was that watery, needy look that was the deciding factor.

"Well, I guess I'm going to do what I should've done years ago." He leaned down and hefted her over one shoulder. She squealed and struggled as the crowd swarmed around them. Then he flipped her up in the seat and climbed in after her.

"What's that?" Ms. Murphy, the librarian, asked as she handed him a red high heel through the open window.

After tossing it to the floor, Slate started the engine. It rumbled so loudly he had to yell to be heard.

"Take her to bed."

The woman next to him released a gasp while poor Ms. Murphy looked like she was about to pass out. Normally, he would've apologized for his bad behavior. But normally he didn't have a beautiful impostor sitting next to him who made him angrier than losing a football game.

He popped the truck into reverse and backed out, trying his damnedest to pull up mental pictures of waving palm trees, brown-skinned beauties, and strong tequila. But they kept being erased by soft white skin, eyes as blue as a late September sky, and the smell of sun-ripened peaches.

The town of Bramble, Texas, watched as the truck rumbled over the curb and then took off down the street with the Stars and Stripes, the Lone Star flag, and Buster's ears flapping in the wind.

"Isn't that the sweetest thang?" Twyla pressed a hand to her chest. "Slate and Hope—high school sweethearts together again."

"It sure is," Kenny Gene said. " 'Course, there's no tellin' how long Hope will stay."

"Yep." Rye Pickett spit out a long stream of tobacco juice. "That Hollywood sure has brainwashed her. Hell, she couldn't even remember how to drink."

"Poor Slate," Ms. Murphy tsked. "He'll have his hands full convincing her to stay and settle down."

There were murmurs of agreement before Harley Sutter, the mayor, spoke up. " 'Course, we could help him out with that."

Rossie Owens pushed back his cowboy hat. "Well, we sure could."

"Just a little help," Darla piped up. "Just enough to show Hope that all her dreams can be fulfilled right here in Bramble."

"Just enough to let love prevail," Sue Ellen agreed.

"Just enough for weddin' bells to ring." Twyla sighed.

"Yep." Harley nodded as he hitched up his pants. "Just enough."

THE DISH

Where Authors Give You the Inside Scoop

♥ ♥ ♥ ♥ ♥ ♥ ♥ ♥ ♥ ♥ ♥ ♥ ♥ ♥ ♥ ♥

From the desk of Vicky Dreiling

Dear Reader,

I had a lot of imaginary boyfriends when I was a kid. My friend Kim and I read *Tiger Beat* magazine and chose our loves. I "dated" David Cassidy, a yesteryear heartthrob from a TV show called *The Partridge Family*. Kim's "boyfriend" was Donny Osmond, although she might have had a brief crush on Barry Williams, better known as Greg from *The Brady Bunch*. I did a quick search online and discovered that *Tiger Beat* magazine still exists, but the stars for today's preteens are Justin Bieber, Taylor Lautner, and members of the boy band One Direction.

The idea of a big family and rock-star boyfriends really appealed to us. We traveled in imaginary tour buses to imaginary concerts. We listened to the music and sang along, pretending we were onstage, too. Of course, we invented drama, such as mean girls trying to steal our famous boyfriends backstage.

Recently, I realized that the seeds of the families I create in my novels were sown in my preteen years as Kim and I pretended to date our celebrity crushes. As I got older, imaginary boyfriends led to real-life boyfriends in high school and college. Eventually, marriage and kids led to an extended family, one that continues to grow.

In WHAT A RECKLESS ROGUE NEEDS, two close families meet once a year at a month-long house party. As in real life, much has changed for Colin and Angeline. While they were born only a week apart, they never really got along very well. An incident at Angeline's come-out ball didn't help matters, either. Many years have elapsed, and now Colin finds he needs Angeline's help to keep from losing a property that holds very deep emotional ties for him. Once they cross the threshold of Sommerall House, their lives are never the same again, but they will always have their families.

May the Magic Romance Fairies be with all of you and your families!

www.VickyDreiling.com
Twitter @VickyDreiling
Facebook.com/VickyDreilingHistoricalAuthor

♥ ♥ ♥ ♥ ♥ ♥ ♥ ♥ ♥ ♥ ♥ ♥ ♥ ♥ ♥ ♥

From the desk of Paula Quinn

Dear Reader,

As most of you know, I love dogs. I have six of them. I see your eyes bugging out. Six?? Yes, six precious tiny Chihuahuas and all together they weight approximately twenty-seven pounds. I've had dogs my whole life—big ones, little ones. So it's not surprising that I would want to write dogs into my books. This time I went big: 140 pounds of big.

In THE SEDUCTION OF MISS AMELIA BELL we meet Grendel, an Irish wolfhound mix, who along with our hero, Edmund MacGregor, wins the heart of our heroine, Amelia Bell. Grendel is the son of Aurelius, whom some of you might remember as the puppy Colin MacGregor gave to Edmund, his stepson, in *Conquered by a Highlander*. Since this series is called Highland Heirs, I figured why not include the family dog heirs as well?

I loved writing a dog as a secondary character, and Grendel is an important part of Edmund and Amelia's story. Now, really, what's better than a big, brawny, sexy Highlander? Right: a big, brawny, sexy Highlander with a dog. Or if you live in NYC, you can settle for a hunky guy playing with his dog in the park.

My six babies all have distinct personalities. For instance, Riley loves to bark and be an all-around pain in the neck. He's high-strung and loves it. Layla, my biggest girl, must "mother" all the others. She keeps them in line with a soft growl and a lick to the eyeball. Liam, my tiny three-pound boy, isn't sure if he's Don Juan or Napoleon. He'll drop and show you his package if you call him cute. They are all different and I wanted Grendel to have his own personality, too.

Much like his namesake, Grendel hates music and powdered periwigs. He's faithful and loyal, and he loves to chase smaller things...like people. Even though Edmund is his master and Grendel does, of course, love him best, it doesn't take Amelia long to win his heart, or for Grendel to win hers, and he soon finds himself following at her heels. Some of my favorite scenes involve the subtle interactions between Amelia and Grendel. This big, seemingly vicious dog is always close by when Amelia is sad or afraid. When things are going on all around them, Amelia just has to rest her hand on Grendel's head and it completely calms her. We witness a partial transformation of ownership in the small, telltale ways Grendel remains ever constant at Amelia's side.

Even when Grendel finds Gaza, his own love interest (hey, I'm a romance writer, what can I say?), he is still faithful to his human lady. We won't get into doggy love, but suffice it to say, there will be plenty of furry heirs living in Camlochlin for a long time to come. They might not be the prettiest dogs in Skye, but they are the most loyal.

This was my first foray into writing a dog as a secondary character and I must say I fell in love with a big, slobbering mutt named after a fiend who killed men for singing. I wasn't surprised that Grendel filled his place so well in Edmund and Amelia's story. Each of my dogs does the same in mine and my kids' stories. That's what dogs do. They run headlong into our lives barking, tail wagging, sharing wet, sloppy kisses. They love us with an almost supernatural, unconditional love. And we love them back.

I hope you get a chance to pick up THE SEDUCTION OF MISS AMELIA BELL and meet Edmund and Amelia and, of course, Grendel.

Happy reading!

Paula Quinn

♥ ♥ ♥ ♥ ♥ ♥ ♥ ♥ ♥ ♥ ♥ ♥ ♥ ♥

From the desk of Kristen Ashley

Dear Reader,

Years ago, I was walking to the local shops and, as usual, I had my headphones in. As I was walking, Bob Seger & The Silver Bullet Band's "You'll Accomp'ny Me" came on and somehow, even having heard this song dozens and dozens of times before, the lyrics suddenly hit me.

This isn't unusual. I have to be in a certain mood to absorb lyrics. But when I am, sometimes they'll seep into my soul, making me smile, or making me cry.

"You'll Accomp'ny Me" made me smile. It made me feel warm. And it made me feel happy because the lyrics are beautiful, the message of love and devotion is strong, the passion is palpable, and the way it's written states that Bob definitely has Kristen Ashley alpha traits.

I loved it. I've always loved that song, but then I loved it even more. It was like one of my books in song form. How could I not love that?

At the time, however, I didn't consider it for a book, not inspiring one or not to be used in a scene. For a long time, it was just mine, giving me that warm feeling and a smile on my face at the thought that there is musical proof out there that these men exist.

Better, they wield guitars.

Now, from the very moment I introduced Hop in *Motorcycle Man*, he intrigued me. And as we learned more about him in that book, my knowing why he was doing what he was doing, I knew he'd have to be redeemed in my readers' eyes by sharing his whole story. I just didn't know who was going to give him the kind of epic happy ending I felt he deserved.

Therefore, I didn't know that Lanie would be the woman of his dreams. Truth be told, I didn't even expect Lanie to have her own book. But her story as told in *Motorcycle Man* was just too heartbreaking to leave her hanging. I just had no idea what to do with her.

But I didn't think a stylish, professional, accomplished "lady" and a biker would jibe, so I never considered these two together. Or, in fact, Lanie with any of the Chaos brothers at all.

That is, until this song came up on shuffle again and I knew that was how Hop would consider his relationship with Lanie. Even as she pushed him away due to her past, he'd do what he could to convince her that, someday, she'd accompany him.

I mean, just those words—how cool are they? "You'll accompany me." Brilliant.

But Bob, his Silver Bullet Band, and their music did

quadruple duty in FIRE INSIDE. Not only did they give me "You'll Accomp'ny Me," which was the perfect way for Hop to express his feelings to Lanie; they also gave me Hop's nickname for Lanie: "lady". *And* they gave me "We've Got Tonight," yet another perfect song to fit what was happening between Lanie and Hop. And last, the way Bob sings is also the way I hear Hop in my head.

I interweave music in my books all the time and my selections are always emotional and, to me, perfect.

But I've never had a song, or artist, so beautifully help me tell my tale than when I utilized the extraordinary storytelling abilities of Bob Seger in my novel FIRE INSIDE.

It's a pleasure listening to his music.

It's a gift to be inspired by it.

Kristen Ashley

♥ ♥ ♥ ♥ ♥ ♥ ♥ ♥ ♥ ♥ ♥ ♥ ♥ ♥ ♥

From the desk of Mimi Jean Pamfiloff

Dear Reader,

When it came time to decide which god or goddess in my Accidentally Yours series would get their HEA in book four, I sat back and looked at who was most in need of salvation. Hands down, the winner was Ixtab, the Goddess of Suicide. Before you judge the title, however, I'd like to explain why this goddess is not the dreary soul you might imagine. Fact is she's more like the Goddess of Anti-Suicide, with the ability to drain dark feelings from one person and redeploy them to another. Naturally, being a deity, she tends to help those who are down on their luck and punish those who are truly deserving.

However, every now and again, someone bumps into her while she's not looking. The results are fatal. So after thousands of years and thousands of accidental deaths, she's determined to keep everyone away. Who could blame her?

But fate has other plans for this antisocial goddess with a kind streak. His name is Dr. Antonio Acero, and this sexy Spaniard has just become the lynchpin in the gods' plans for saving the planet from destruction. He's also in need of a little therapy, and Ixtab is the only one who can help him.

When these two meet, they quickly realize there are forces greater than them both, trying to pull them apart and push them together. Which force will win?

Mimi

♥ ♥ ♥ ♥ ♥ ♥ ♥ ♥ ♥ ♥ ♥ ♥ ♥ ♥ ♥ ♥

From the desk of Katie Lane

Dear Reader,

As some of you may already know, the idea for my fictional town of Bramble, Texas, came from the hours I spent watching *The Andy Griffith Show*. When Barney, Aunt Bee, and Opie were on, my mom couldn't peel me away from our console television. The townsfolk's antics held me spellbound. Which is probably why I made my characters a little crazy, too. (Okay, so I made them a lot crazy.) But while the people of Mayberry had levelheaded Sheriff Andy Taylor to keep them in line, the townsfolk of Bramble have been allowed to run wild.

Until now.

I'm pleased as punch to introduce Sheriff Dusty Hicks, the hero of my newest Deep in the Heart of Texas novel, A MATCH MADE IN TEXAS. Like Andy, he's a dedicated lawman who loves his job and the people of his community. Unlike Andy, he carries a gun, has a wee bit of a temper, and is blessed with the kind of looks and hard body that can make a good girl turn bad. And after just one glimpse of Dusty's shiny handcuffs, Brianne Cates wants to turn bad. Real bad.

But it won't be easy for Brianne to seduce a little lawman lovin' out of my hero. Dusty has his hands full trying to regain joint custody of his precocious three-year-old daughter and, at the same time, deal with a con-artist television evangelist and a vengeful cartel drug lord. Not to mention the townsfolk of Bramble, who have suddenly gone wa-a-ay off their rockers.

All I can say is, what started out as a desire to give Bramble its very own Sheriff Taylor quickly turned into a fast-paced joyride that left my hair standing on end and my heart as warm and gooey as a toaster strudel. I hope it will do the same for you. :o)

Much love,

Katie Lane

♥ ♥ ♥ ♥ ♥ ♥ ♥ ♥ ♥ ♥ ♥ ♥ ♥ ♥ ♥ ♥

From the desk of Jessica Lemmon

Dear Reader,

I love a scruffy-faced, tattooed, motorcycle-riding bad boy as much as the next girl, so when it came time to write HARD TO HANDLE, I knew what qualities I wanted Aiden Downey to possess.

For inspiration, I needed to look no further than Charlie Hunnam from the famed TV show *Sons of Anarchy*. I remember watching Season 1 on Netflix, mouth agape and eyes wide. When Charlie's character, Jax Teller, finished his first scene, I looked over at my husband and said, *"That's Aiden!"*

In HARD TO HANDLE, Aiden may have been crafted with a bad-boy starter kit: He has the scruff, the tattoo, the knee-weakening dimples that make him look like sin on a stick, and yeah, a custom Harley-Davidson to boot. But Aiden also has something extra special that derails his bad-boy image: a heart of near-solid gold.

When we first met Aiden and Sadie in *Tempting the Billionaire* (and again in the e-novella *Can't Let Go*), there wasn't much hope for these two hurting hearts to work out their differences. Aiden had been saddled with devastating news and familial responsibilities, and Sadie (poor Sadie!) had just opened up her heart to Aiden, who stomped on it, broke it into pieces, and set it on fire for good measure. How could they forgive each other after things had gone so horribly, terribly wrong?

Aiden has suffered a lot of loss, but in HARD TO HANDLE, he's on a mission to get his life *back*. A very large piece of that puzzle is winning back the woman he never meant to hurt, the woman he loved. Sadie, with her walled-up heart, smart, sassy mouth, and fiery attitude isn't going to be an easy nut to crack. Especially after she vowed to never, ever get hurt again. That goes *double* for the blond Adonis with the unforgettable mouth and ability to turn her brain into Silly Putty.

The best part about this good "bad" boy? Aiden's determination is as rock-hard as his abs. He's not going to let Sadie walk away, not now that he sees how much she still cares for him. Having been to hell and back, Aiden isn't intimidated by her. Not even a little bit. Sadie is his Achilles' heel, and Aiden accepts that it's going to take time (and plenty of seduction!) to win her over. He also knows that she's worth it.

Think you're up for a ride around the block with a bad-boy-done-good? I have to say, Aiden left a pretty deep mark on my heart and I'm still a little in love with him! He may change your mind about scruffy, motorcycle-riding hotties...He certainly managed to change Sadie's.

Happy reading!

Jessica Lemmon

www.jessicalemmon.com